Also by Stephanie Bond

BODY MOVERS: 3 MEN AND A BODY
BODY MOVERS: 2 BODIES FOR THE PRICE OF 1
BODY MOVERS

Watch for the upcoming books
in the BODY MOVERS series

5 BODIES TO DIE FOR
May 2009

SIX KILLER BODIES
June 2009

STEPHANIE BOND

4 BODIES
AND A FUNERAL

MIRA®

MIRA®

ISBN-13: 978-0-7783-2668-7
ISBN-10:   0-7783-2668-3

Recycling programs
for this product may
not exist in your area.

4 BODIES AND A FUNERAL

www.MIRABooks.com

Printed in U.S.A.

Acknowledgments

The longer my career goes on, the more I appreciate my wonderful editors, who are champions for this series. Many, many thanks to Brenda Chin, who somehow manages to read my material both as a reader and as an editor. Brenda puts a shine on everything I write. Thanks, too, to Margaret O'Neill Marbury, Dianne Moggy and Valerie Gray for your ongoing support of the series and especially for arranging the back-to-back release of books 4, 5 and 6. And to my agent Kimberly Whalen of Trident Media Group who first proposed a trilogy to help satisfy readers who were clamoring for closer release dates! Thanks to my critique partner, Rita Herron, for our weekly meetings and for not being too biased about who Carlotta will pick. Thanks to pal Blair Fisher, former soldier, trivia whiz, all-around good guy for always answering my e-mails. My undying love and thanks to my dear husband, Chris, who cheers me on with every new project and keeps me going until The End. And to all the booksellers, librarians and readers who keep the ball rolling by telling customers, patrons and friends about the BODY MOVERS series— thank you, thank you, thank you.

1

Carlotta Wren skidded onto the sales floor of the Neiman Marcus at Lenox Square in Atlanta soaked in a flop sweat. Late on her first day back—minus ten points.

"Welcome back."

Carlotta turned and manufactured a smile for Lindy Russell, her boss, who was standing with arms crossed. "Thank you. It's good to be back."

Lindy pursed her mouth. "Too bad you couldn't make this morning's staff meeting."

Carlotta's smile wavered, but she massaged the flexible cast on her arm. "Sorry. This morning was the first time I'd driven in a while, and my car battery was dead." She didn't think it would help to mention that the MARTA trains were being single-tracked for construction. Still, she decided not to dwell on transportation challenges since her recent medical leave had come on the heels of a two-week suspension to "get her personal issues worked out."

Personal issues such as her brother's gambling debts, her ruined credit, the fact that her parents were long-lost fugitives…and oh, she'd been entangled in a couple of murders as a by-product of her part-time hobby as a body mover for the morgue.

"Things happen," Lindy conceded. "Is your arm healing well?"

Carlotta flexed the fingers of the arm that had been broken when a killer had pushed her over the balcony of the Fox Theatre, where she'd dangled with her skirt around her waist for all the attendees of an Elton John concert to see. "Almost as good as new." Though, at the moment it was throbbing like a toothache.

Sympathy crossed Lindy's face. "I can't tell you how sorry I am about Michael."

Michael Lane, aka the person who'd pushed her over the balcony, had been Carlotta's former coworker and friend. He'd also turned out to have some very dark secrets.

"Me, too," Carlotta murmured, wishing her heart could be splinted like her arm had been.

"I don't suppose you've heard from him?"

She shook her head. "I was told he's in the psych ward at Northside Hospital until he's deemed competent to stand trial."

"So terrible." Lindy sighed, then checked the clipboard she held. "Well, life goes on, doesn't it?"

Carlotta blinked. It was true, but still…

"I'm glad you could come back in time for the Eva McCoy appearance." Lindy swept her arm toward the small dais that had been erected on the sales floor with several rows of cordoned-off chairs for seating.

Olympian Eva McCoy's return to her hometown had been hyped on all the media outlets for weeks. "That's today?"

Lindy arched an eyebrow.

Carlotta backpedaled. "I mean…that's today."

"Since you missed the staff meeting, here's the info." Lindy handed over a memo. "It's going to be a mob scene so I'll need all my best employees on the floor."

Pleasure suffused Carlotta's chest—her history of being a consistent top salesperson still meant something.

"And here's one now," Lindy said, looking past Carlotta's shoulder. Carlotta turned and swallowed a curse when she saw Patricia Alexander, aka Stepford Salesclerk, complete with rounded-collar suit, helmet hair and strand of pearls, walking toward them.

The blonde flashed a waxy smile. "I'd heard you were coming back, Carlotta, but when I didn't see you at this morning's staff meeting, I assumed that something else had happened. You're so…accident prone."

Carlotta's mouth tightened.

"I'll let you two catch up for a couple of minutes before the crowd arrives," Lindy said, handing them each a roll of tickets to be passed out to customers who wanted to meet the guest of honor. Then she gave Carlotta a pointed look. "I tend to agree with Patricia. There's going to be a lot of security on hand today, so try not to do anything that might draw extra attention." Lindy walked off, leaving Carlotta properly chastised—in front of her nemesis.

"Ouch," Patricia chirped.

Carlotta was able to hold her tongue because she knew she deserved far worse from her boss than a reprimand for all her…mishaps. Determined to get along with Lindy's new pet employee, she turned toward Patricia. "I suppose you took Michael's place in Shoes?"

"Yes. It's such a shame, isn't it, that he turned out to be totally insane?"

Carlotta bit her tongue.

"So, I'll bet you're happy to be back to work," Patricia offered. "You were probably bored to tears doing nothing all day."

"I didn't exactly do nothing," Carlotta muttered, although she couldn't exactly tell Patricia about the road trip she'd taken with Coop for a VIP body pickup, the unexpected appearance of her father, and the capture of a murderer while she'd been "incapacitated," on leave with a broken arm. Instead she pasted on a smile. "But I am happy to be back in my element."

Patricia made rueful noises in her throat. "I hope you had time to rest, you poor thing. The heartbreak you've been through the past decade—you must be close to the brink of insanity yourself."

Carlotta's hands fisted. Patricia moved in the Buckhead social circles, so she knew the sordid Wren family history—that ten years ago Carlotta's father had been accused of stealing from his investment clients and had skipped town rather than face a trial, with her mother in tow, abandoning Carlotta and her younger brother to fend for themselves.

At the thought of her brother, Wesley, Carlotta stole a glance at her watch. He should be arriving at the Fulton County D.A.'s office right about now, hopefully working out a plea agreement, testifying against one of his loan sharks in return for reduced charges for his part in the attempted theft of a body. His attorney, Liz, was hopeful that Wesley would get off with having his community service sentence from a prior computer hacking charge extended. But Carlotta was worried that even Liz Fuck-Me Fischer wouldn't be able to parlay enough sexual favors to make it happen. Carlotta had wanted to go with Wesley today, but he'd refused, saying it was something he needed to take care of himself. It might have been the moment she'd been most proud of him.

Except for the fact that he could be sitting in a jail cell before her shift ended.

What would she do for bail money? And what if Wesley didn't get out this time?

Patricia waved her hand in front of Carlotta's face. "Did I lose you?"

"No," she said, squaring her shoulders. "And I'm coping with everything just fine."

Patricia leaned in. "If you need something to take the edge off, I can spot you some antianxiety meds."

"No, thank you," Carlotta said through gritted teeth, although beneath the cast her arm was hot with pain. Knowing it would *really* hurt, though, if she slugged the woman, Carlotta changed the subject. "Looks like we're going to have a big crowd today for Eva McCoy."

"Yeah, speaking of crazy.... The woman wins a marathon after a bout of food poisoning, gives all the credit to a lucky charm bracelet and suddenly charm bracelets are selling like mad." Patricia shook her head, apparently bemused with the trend.

Carlotta smirked. Her coworker was only frustrated because *she* wasn't working in Jewelry, earning commissions on the trinkets that Eva would be promoting.

Customers were already gathering in the area of the dais where posters featured the smiling, fit Olympian with a gold medal around her neck and a "Lucky Charm Bracelet" on her slender wrist.

Carlotta and Patricia positioned themselves in front of the GET YOUR TICKETS TO MEET EVA McCOY HERE sign and began handing out tickets, and directing early comers where to sit or stand.

"So," Patricia asked without making eye contact. "How are you and Peter Ashford?"

Choosing her words carefully, Carlotta said, "Peter and I are old friends."

"So I've heard. Tracey Tully Lowenstein belongs to my club. She said that you and Peter used to be quite the item before…your family issues."

"That was a long time ago," Carlotta murmured.

"Tracey intimated that you two have picked up where you left off."

"Tracey talks too much," Carlotta said pointedly.

"I think it's nice that you and Peter have each other," Patricia said. "You can support each other. You know, with his wife having been murdered, and then all that you've gone through." The blonde winced. "Wait a minute. Weren't you a suspect in her murder? Gee, that has to be a little awkward."

"Not at all," Carlotta said pleasantly.

Patricia sniffed and turned her back.

Carlotta shot daggers into the woman's bony shoulder blades. In truth, Carlotta was still wrestling with her recent decision to cozy up to her former fiancé. When her father had walked up to her, unannounced and in disguise, at a rest area a few weeks ago in Florida, he'd told her to stay close to Peter—that since Peter worked for Mashburn & Tully Investments where her father had once been a partner, he was in the best position to help prove Randolph Wren's innocence. Until that moment, Carlotta would have sworn that if her long-lost father had ever approached her, she would slap him, kick his shins, spit in his face and call the police. Instead she'd been gelatinous and cooperative and…hopeful.

The fact that he made her want to believe that he'd been framed for his white collar crime made her feel used all over again.

Her father was using her—and she was using Peter. Since his wife's untimely death, Peter had made no secret that he wanted to get back with Carlotta. He'd even recovered the Cartier engagement ring that she'd pawned, *and* he'd had a diamond added on either side of the original solitaire. He was holding it for her, hoping she'd agree to pick up where they'd left off years ago. Just as if he hadn't ripped out her heart by turning his back on her when she needed him most.

But he was trying to make amends, she conceded. He'd helped Wesley out of a couple of scrapes and continued to be attentive to her. A couple of weeks ago, though, after she'd returned from Florida, his patience had worn thin. He'd been offered a position in New York and had been going to take it, unless she could make room for him in her life. She couldn't risk him leaving, on the chance that her father might call or put in another appearance soon, in need of Peter's inside access. So she'd told Peter to stay and had committed herself to making their relationship a priority.

Normally, being on the receiving end of a handsome, rich man's attentions wouldn't pose a problem, but there were…extenuating circumstances. Namely, two other men bouncing around in her head and in her heart.

"I wondered if I'd see you here."

At the sound of a familiar rumbling voice, her pulse spiked. She turned around to see one of those two men, Detective Jack Terry, standing there with a sardonic smile on his ruggedly handsome face, as if she'd conjured him up. Her entire body smiled. "Hi, Jack."

"Back to work, huh?"

She nodded. "First day."

"Are you okay? You look flushed."

She put a hand to her warm cheek. "Hectic morning. What are you doing here?"

"Extra security for Eva McCoy. It's a favor for the mayor."

Carlotta frowned. "What does the city have to do with this?"

"Apparently Eva's uncle is a state senator. He wants APD on the scene just in case. And since a uniform might send the wrong signal…" He shrugged. "Here I am."

She surveyed his gray suit and gave his red tie a tug. "You look good."

"I keep telling him that red is his color."

At the sound of a purring voice, Carlotta turned her head. A doe-eyed, exotic beauty in a dark suit stepped into Jack's personal space.

Jack gave the woman a proprietary smile. "Carlotta, I don't think you've met my new partner, Detective Maria Marquez. Maria, this is Carlotta Wren, a friend of mine."

Carlotta tried not to react. Friends? Is that what she and Jack were?

She had seen the woman once, at a distance. Up close, Maria was even more…*wow*. She was almost as tall as Jack, with killer curves, and caramel-colored hair smoothed back from her face in a clasp at the nape of her neck.

"Nice to meet you, Carlotta." Maria's English was precise, seasoned with the kind of curling accent that made words like *blitzkrieg* and *psoriasis* sound sexy.

"Same here," Carlotta murmured.

When she'd razzed Jack about getting a partner, she'd envisioned a grumpy middle-aged man with hair in his ears, not a Latina siren with perfect teeth and no wedding ring. Damn, the woman even had good taste—her suit was Ellen Tracy and the pumps were Stuart Weitzman. Carlotta knew her own Betsey Johnson tunic dress and Fendi platform sandals could hold their own, but the cast on her arm was an unsightly accessory she couldn't wait to be rid of. And she tongued the gap between her front teeth self-consciously.

"So you work at Neiman's?" Maria asked. The way she said it left the unspoken comparison of "and I carry a gun" hanging in the air.

"That's right," Carlotta said.

"Carlotta also moonlights for the morgue," Jack supplied cheerfully. "She's a body mover."

Carlotta squirmed. The gorgeous giantess packing heat made her feel like an underachiever. And short.

"A body mover? How...diverse. Is that how the two of you met?"

Carlotta exchanged a glance with Jack. He looked at Maria. "Not exactly. I'll fill you in later," he added in a low voice.

Great. He'd tell Maria all about her criminal family—her fugitive folks, her delinquent brother... Not to mention Carlotta's own scrapes with the law. And her futile—and inept—efforts to hold her life and family together.

"Speaking of your morbid hobby, how is Coop?" Jack asked her with wry amusement.

Cooper Craft—her brother's body-moving boss who had pulled her in on a couple of jobs...and who'd made it known that he wouldn't mind them being more than friends. Coop was a former medical examiner. He and Jack maintained a relationship that existed primarily of circling each other like two big-racked bucks, but collaborating when necessary.

"With this bum arm, I haven't been helping Coop lately," she said. "And after Wesley conspired with those thugs to steal the body we were hauling from Florida back to Atlanta...well, let's just say he needs to earn back Coop's trust before they work together again."

Her brother with the genius IQ somehow rationalized making the wrong choice at almost every juncture. She bit her lip and wondered how he was faring in court.

"Despite Wesley's interference, Coop received a lot of attaboys for the way he handled that VIP body pickup—and the aftermath," Jack said. "I hear that Abrams might give him more access to the active cases at the morgue."

"Good for Coop," she said, and meant it. The quiet intellectual acted as if he was content to be relegated to the job of body hauler for the morgue he used to run, but she often wondered if he missed being in the thick of things.

"I figured you'd be happy for him," Jack said in a sly reference to the road trip she'd taken with Coop to Florida for some fun in the sun before picking up the body. Their plans to get to know each other hadn't exactly panned out when Wesley had shown up as an uninvited chaperone. Still, she and Coop had had their moment…and had it snatched away.

Of course, Jack didn't have to know that.

Besides, with her promise to Peter, it was all a moot point.

"I need to get back to work," she said brightly, gesturing to the milling crowd. "Nice to see you both," she said, including the decadent Maria in her glance.

"Hey." Jack caught her good arm and leaned in, his golden-colored eyes serious. "Wes is seeing the D.A. today, isn't he?"

She lifted her chin and nodded.

"Don't worry. Liz will take care of him."

Carlotta's mouth tightened, but before she could respond, Jack picked up her left hand and rubbed his rough thumb over her bare ring finger.

"What are you doing?" she asked.

"Just checking to see if you're wearing another man's ring yet."

He winked, then walked away to join Maria. Confounded as always by Jack's behavior, Carlotta turned back to the customers to make sure everyone had a ticket before she shepherded them into line. Beneath her lashes, she stole glances at Jack and his new partner as they scouted the layout of the store event. They looked as if they belonged on TV—the great-looking partners with amazing chemistry who put away bad guys during the day…and burned up the sheets at night?

It only made sense that Jack would want to bed the beauty—he was a red-blooded man after all. And not in a hurry to put a ring on anyone's finger anytime soon.

Besides, since his sometimes-squeeze, Liz Fischer, aka The Cougar, was now banging Carlotta's little brother, the big-boobed attorney probably had less time for booty calls from Jack.

If there was a bright spot to Liz seducing nineteen-year-old Wesley, Carlotta thought wryly, it was that maybe she'd work harder to keep him out of jail. The threat of having to resort to conjugal visits in the slammer might keep her on her toes.

Carlotta fretted about Wesley between handing out tickets and informing people about the day's event, as it had been laid out in the memo that she'd memorized.

"When Ms. McCoy arrives, she'll say a few words and answer questions from the press. Then she'll step over to the jewelry section where she'll pose for pictures, sign autographs, and use an engraving tool to sign the back of any Lucky Charm Bracelet purchased. There is a limit of two bracelets per person."

It would be a sellout, Carlotta thought as she looked down the long line forming. The jewelry department, adjacent to the event area, was already selling the charm bracelets as quickly as they could ring up customers.

The novelty was that each bracelet was purportedly unique, with random charms denoting travel or hobbies or almost anything. Each bracelet was packaged in a small brown box—the recipient didn't know exactly what they were getting until they opened it after purchase. The idea was for the wearer to treat the bracelet as a suggested life list of sorts, to be inspired by the charms to try something unexpected. There were even special journals and Web sites for Charmers, as they were now being called. The craze was sweeping the nation, bolstered by Eva's appearances on national talk shows, hefting the gold medal she'd won for the marathon that had held the world captivated as she'd fought back from her illness to pass the leaders and against all odds, win the event. Hers was one of the greatest human interest stories to emerge from the most recent summer Olympics. And like many athletes, she was cashing in on her newfound celebrity.

"Are those two people over there police officers?" Patricia asked, nodding to Jack and Maria.

"Detectives," Carlotta said, trying not to let the pair's familiar body language get to her. It was none of her business where Jack holstered his gun. "Added security as a precaution."

"So it's true, then."

"What?"

Patricia covered her mouth with the back of her hand and whispered. "I read on the Internet that Eva McCoy has received death threats."

"Death threats? The woman is a world-renowned athlete. Who'd want her dead?"

Patricia shrugged. "Who knows? Sports fans can be rabid. Maybe someone doesn't like the fact that she beat their favorite runner. Or it could be one of those urban myths that start online and run wild. Regardless, I think I'll buy a charm bracelet before they're gone. Want me to pick one up for you?"

"I actually have a charm bracelet at home," Carlotta murmured. From her teenage years. A gift from her father, it was somewhere in the depths of her jewelry box. She had buried so many things from that period in her life. "Thanks anyway," she added begrudgingly. Patricia wasn't so bad, she was just…persnickety.

"Looks like we have a lull," Patricia said. "I'll be right back."

Carlotta glanced around and decided to take advantage of the break in the crowd to get a pain pill from her purse. Her arm hadn't hurt like this in a while.

She made her way to the employee break room and gave the locker of her former coworker Michael Lane a wistful glance. It had been emptied, but was still tagged with police evidence tape. No one would touch it, as if they might catch whatever it was that had taken hold of Michael. Carlotta opened her own locker to remove her purse. She checked her cell phone for messages, hoping Wesley hadn't forgotten his promise to call and let her know what happened with the D.A. But there were no messages, leaving her to fear the worst. Jack had once warned her that the D.A. despised her father so much that he might try to take it out on Wesley.

With growing apprehension, Carlotta pulled the prescription bottle of Percocet from her bag and removed the lid. When the last pill rolled out into her hand, she frowned. She'd barely touched the bottle of painkillers, and had even turned down the doctor's offer for extra refills because she hadn't wanted to become dependent on them.

She used her cell phone to dial the pharmacy and request one of the refills she had left.

"I'm sorry, ma'am, but there are no more refills on this prescription."

"But I'm looking at the pill bottle, and it says I have two more."

In the background was the sound of computer keys clicking. "According to our records, the prescription was refilled two weeks ago and again last week."

"But that's impossible—" Carlotta began to argue, then cut herself off. She suddenly felt sick to her stomach. She hadn't taken the bottle of pain pills, and she hadn't gotten the prescription refilled. Which left only one other person in the house who could have.

"Thank you," she said hastily, then disconnected the call. Her eyes pooled with sudden moisture. Had Wesley taken the painkillers recreationally? Sold them?

Or was he hooked on them?

She put a hand over her heavy heart and murmured, "Oh, Wesley. What have you gotten yourself into now?"

2

Wesley glanced all around as he hurried into the building on Pryor Street that housed, among other government agencies, the offices of the Fulton County District Attorney. He was a nervous freaking wreck after riding his bike in a circuitous route just in case anyone from The Carver's camp knew about the appointment and decided to intercept him, then *persuade* him not to agree to a plea deal in return for testifying against the brutal loan shark.

When he'd agreed to help The Carver's men swipe the body of a starlet, Wesley had told himself he was killing several birds with one stone, so to speak.

The woman was already dead, after all. It was an olive branch to offer the loan shark for an embarrassing stunt Wesley had orchestrated on him at a strip club. And The Carver had promised to erase the rest of Wesley's gambling debt in return for the favor. Besides, it wasn't as if he'd been given the option of refusing the man who had already carved the first three letters of his last name into Wesley's arm for a former offense.

At the memory, Wesley rubbed his arm through the jacket he'd worn as directed by his attorney. Underneath, the newly healed wounds itched where the skin had drawn tight.

Thinking back to the body-snatching scheme, Wesley

shook his head. Why did he think he could do it? At the last minute he'd balked and when it was over, he'd come clean with his boss, Cooper, and the police. The D.A., an asshole named Kelvin Lucas who had indicted his dad, had wanted to nail Wesley to the wall. But his attorney, Liz, had managed to persuade the D.A. that Hollis Carver was a bigger fish. Since Wesley still owed The Carver a shitload of money, it was in his best interests if The Carver went to jail for a long time.

On the other hand, The Carver could probably pull strings no matter where he was. If he found out that Wesley had turned on him, he might have the rest of his name *and* his address cut into Wesley's skinny body.

Once inside the lobby, Wesley slowed his pace so as not to attract attention from the security guards, and joined the line of bored people going through a metal detector. He jammed his hands in his pockets, trying to calm his nerves, but his brain was firing like a machine gun. Sweat trailed down his back, and behind his glasses his left eye ticked nervously. It was the OxyContin—or rather, the lack of it— kicking in.

He was really making an effort this time to stay away from the stuff. The Percocet he'd pinched from Carlotta's purse and the two refills he'd gotten had bridged the worst of his withdrawal symptoms, but he had only one pill left. He fingered the capsule in the corner of his pants pocket, yearning to swallow it, but drawing some comfort from its mere presence.

He'd hardly left the house the last couple of weeks except to go to ASS, Atlanta Security Systems, where he was poking around in his dad's trial files under the guise of doing community service for hacking into the court-house computer. So he'd definitely noticed that the house was being watched. The first appearance of the black SUV at the curb in front of the town house where he and Carlotta lived had nearly made him piss his pants. He'd gathered up anything that could be used as a weapon: a hammer, a few butcher knives, a cast-iron skillet, even a can of hairspray from Carlotta's bathroom. But when no one had emerged from the SUV with guns drawn to storm the place—the vehicle had simply left and returned at different hours of the day—he'd wondered if someone was looking out for him. Maybe Jack Terry had sent a fellow cop to patrol the house, at least until Wesley could strike his deal.

He pivoted as the line moved forward, looking for signs of trouble. When he was two people back from reaching the detector, he spotted Mouse, The Carver's head henchman, entering the front door of the building.

Wesley almost swallowed his tongue and pecked on the shoulder of the stout woman in front of him. "I'm late for a meeting. Would you mind if I go ahead of you?"

The woman frowned. "We're all in a hurry. You're gonna have to wait your turn like everybody else."

He hunched his shoulders and tried to look inconspicuous, but Mouse noticed him and came charging toward him.

The woman was chatting with the security officer, taking her sweet, fat time.

"Hey, could you put some wheels on it?" Wesley said, moving his hand in a rolling motion. His heart was galloping like a racehorse's.

She frowned, but lumbered through the metal detector. Mouse lunged for him and Wesley practically humped the woman trying to get through the narrow opening behind her. He felt a tug on his shoulders as Mouse grabbed the neck of his jacket to yank him back. Wesley held his arms behind him and walked out of the garment.

He looked back to see Mouse glaring at him, holding the jacket. Wesley gave him a little salute. No way was Mouse walking through the metal detector—the man probably had weapons stowed in his cheeks.

"You have to come out sometime," Mouse called.

Wesley swallowed and continued walking across the lobby and down a hall to the elevators. Liz Fischer, his attorney, was standing to the side, checking her watch. She was a triple threat—beautiful, blond and bossy. When she glanced up, her red mouth lifted in a chiding smile. "I was just getting ready to call you. It wouldn't look good for you to arrive late for your own plea bargain."

"It took longer to get here than I'd planned."

She frowned. "I thought I told you to wear a jacket."

"Sorry—I forgot."

She sighed. "Oh, well, at least you wore a tie. But you're sweating like a pig."

He wiped a hand across the back of his neck. "It's summer in Atlanta, and I rode my bike here."

"So why are your hands shaking?"

"I'm nervous, okay?"

She gave his shirt a little pat. "Shake it off. You need to make a good impression on the D.A. Otherwise he might worry that you'll renege on your agreement to testify against Hollis Carver." She glanced at her watch. "We should go. This will be over soon, and we can all get back to normal." Her fingers slid inside his shirt to stroke his bare skin and the tip of her tongue appeared.

Wesley swallowed. He missed banging Liz—her body was to die for—but at the moment, he'd rather have a hit of Oxy. Inside his pocket he turned the last Percocet

capsule over and over, telling himself he'd save it to celebrate after the meeting ended. Maybe he'd just chill in a
men's room and outwait Mouse.

He followed Liz onto the elevator, his pulse clicking as
they climbed floors. When the elevator doors opened, he
broke out into a fresh sweat. "Will Lucas be in the meeting?"
he asked as she led him down a carpeted hallway.

"He could send an assistant, but since it's you, he'll
probably put in an appearance."

"You mean since I'm Randolph Wren's son?"

"That's right." She stopped at a frosted glass door,
rapped sharply, then pushed it open.

Wesley followed her inside, thinking in that respect,
Liz wasn't so different from the D.A. She, too, was interested in him because of his dad. He'd recently discovered
that not only had Liz been his father's attorney, but she'd
also been his mistress.

Like father, like son.

Kelvin Lucas, an amphibious-looking man, sat at the
end of the table, his hands steepled with authority, his expression smug. At the sight of the man who had targeted
his father and reneged on a deal he'd made with Carlotta
in an attempt to lure their dad from hiding, bile backed up
in Wesley's throat. He didn't want to be in the same room
with the bastard, but he tried to keep his abject loathing of
the man from his expression.

Next to Lucas sat a petite, bookish-looking woman who
stood and introduced herself as Cheryl Meriwether, Assistant District Attorney. She seemed skittish and kept sliding
her glance toward her boss.

"Well, shall we get started?" Liz suggested, indicating
which chair Wesley should occupy.

He lowered himself into the seat unsteadily. The room

had a sterile smell and rang with the white noise of incandescent lights buzzing overhead.

Lucas narrowed his eyes at Wesley. "Well, Wren, you can't seem to stay out of trouble…just like your gutless father, wherever he is."

Wesley bit down on his tongue to keep from blurting out the fact that his father had made contact with Carlotta at a Florida rest area a few weeks ago, and was planning to resurface as soon as he could prove his innocence.

Under the table, Liz's hand closed over Wesley's knee as a warning for him to keep quiet. Liz didn't know about his father's reappearance. Carlotta had told him to keep it quiet. But he heeded Liz's advice out of necessity because his head was suddenly throbbing and he was having trouble focusing.

The lawyers opened with legal small talk to set the stage for their negotiation. Wesley zoned out, studying the books on the bookshelves, the fly trapped in the light fixture, his untied shoelace. He just wanted this meeting to be over. The Percocet capsule was burning a hole in his pocket, calling to him. He tried to concentrate on what was being discussed, catching occasional phrases.

"…deserves to go to jail…"

"…Hollis Carver is a menace…"

"…might skip town like his old man…"

"…trumped up charges…"

"…testify if case goes to trial…"

"…give a written statement…"

His mouth was cottony, and his pulse pounded in his ears. Sweat trickled down his temples.

"Wesley?"

He blinked and focused on Liz's face. "Huh?"

"District Attorney Lucas asked you to tell us what happened."

"Do we have a deal?"

"I'll decide after I hear your story," Lucas said.

"Okay," Wesley mumbled. His tongue felt thick in his mouth. "Okay."

Liz's hand was back on his jumping knee with an encouraging squeeze.

"Could I have a glass of water?" he croaked.

A.D.A. Meriwether left the room and returned a few seconds later with a bottle. He took it with one hand, then stuck his other hand in his pants pocket, wedging the Percocet between his fingers so he'd be able to slip it into his mouth unnoticed. He set the bottle between his legs to twist off the top, but his hands were shaking badly now. The white pill popped out from between his fingers and flew under the table where it bounced twice on the carpet before landing next to Lucas's ugly brown wing-tip shoe.

At least no one else had noticed. But Wesley had to exercise restraint to keep from leaping under the table and pouncing on it. He lifted the bottle to his mouth and took a drink, sloshing water down the front of his shirt. He couldn't take his eyes off that pill.

"We don't have all day," Lucas intoned.

"Wesley," Liz said, tapping the table to get his attention. He looked up.

"Tell us how you got involved in the body-snatching plan."

With great effort, Wesley brought his mind back to the matter at hand. "I was leaving a friend's house, and a guy came up to me and said he worked for The Carver, that he had a job for me. He knew I worked for Cooper Craft moving bodies for the morgue and that Coop was going to Florida to pick up that celebrity, Kiki Deerling, and bring her back to Atlanta. He wanted me to help them steal the body—to let them know where we were on the road and to keep Coop preoccupied."

"In return for what?" Lucas asked. Beneath the table, the D.A.'s foot moved, covering the capsule.

Wesley wiped his hand across his mouth. "In return for erasing my debt."

"Which is how much?"

He thought hard before telling the truth. "About twenty grand, give or take." It sounded even worse when he said it aloud.

"Why did Hollis Carver want the body?"

"His son, Dillon, sold heroin at the party where the girl died. He was afraid the drugs had killed her and that he'd be charged with murder." Ironically, as it turned out, the starlet hadn't taken any drugs, so it had all been for nothing. Coop would probably never ask Wesley to work for him again. Wesley hadn't realized how much he wanted the man's respect until it was too late.

"What were they going to do with the body?" Lucas shifted forward and his shoe pressed down where the Percocet pill had landed.

Wesley made a strangled noise in his throat. "Uh…I didn't ask."

"My client was afraid for his life," Liz interjected. "He felt as if he couldn't say no."

"Funny," Lucas said, "I heard your client say he agreed to help carry out a felony in return for twenty thousand dollars. Who is the man who approached you?"

He looked at Liz before he spoke and she nodded. "Tell him."

Wesley's throat convulsed from wanting that damn pill. "His name is Leonard."

"What's Leonard's last name?"

"We were never properly introduced," Wesley said drily. But he could ask his probation officer, E. Jones. The thug was her boyfriend, although she had no idea what kind of stuff the man was mixed up in, including moving drugs for Wesley's friend Chance.

"So how do you know this Leonard actually works for Hollis Carver?"

Wesley scratched his neck in irritation. "Because he said he did."

"He could've been lying."

"I don't think so. He knew I owed The Carver money."

"That doesn't mean anything. This Leonard character could've been using The Carver's name to pressure you into something *he* wanted done."

Wesley scoffed. "That makes no sense. The Carver and his son were the ones who didn't want the body autopsied."

Lucas spread his hands. "I'm just telling you what a defense attorney will say. From where I sit, you got nothing on Hollis Carver that can be corroborated."

Wesley looked at Liz, at a loss.

"What about calls between Hollis Carver and the celebrity's publicist?" Liz asked Lucas. "They were the masterminds of the scheme."

"We have a record of phone calls, but the content of the calls could've been about anything. For all we know, they could've been lovers." Lucas leered at Liz pointedly.

But Liz didn't shrink from the D.A.'s sly remark. "I would think that the publicist would be falling all over herself to turn on Hollis Carver."

A.D.A. Meriwether looked down and shifted in her seat.

Liz looked from Lucas to Meriwether and gave a dry laugh. "Wait a minute. The publicist has already made a deal, hasn't she?"

Lucas took his arrogant time answering. "Yes. So as it turns out, we don't need your client's testimony after all, Ms. Fischer. Although it's good to know that his story corroborates the publicist's."

Wesley heaved a huge sigh of relief and pushed to his feet. "I'm outta here." Once the room was vacated, he'd come back to rescue the flattened capsule.

But Liz stopped him with a warning glance.

"Not so fast, Wren," Lucas said, then leaned back in his seat with a satisfied smile. "You confessed to conspiring to steal a body."

Wesley sat back down, his stomach churning with dread. Something was up.

"But the body wasn't stolen," Liz protested. "And my client came clean."

"Only after the plan was foiled," Lucas returned. "And besides confessing to a felony, your client's actions revoke his previous probation. He's going to jail."

Panic skewered Wesley's chest. He'd spent a few hours in jail when he'd been arrested for hacking into the courthouse computer. He'd passed the time and kept the pervs at bay by teaching the other guys in holding how to play Texas Hold 'Em poker, but he didn't relish the thought of going back.

Liz angled her head. "Kelvin, isn't this all a moot point? We both know that Hollis Carver is an informant for the APD and will probably get a pass."

Lucas blanched. "Who told you that he was an informant?"

"I have my sources," Liz said silkily.

Wesley pressed his lips together. Liz must be back to banging Detective Jack Terry again, if they'd ever stopped.

"So why drag us in here today?" she demanded. "What do you want, Kelvin?"

The D.A. screwed up his mouth and bared his crooked teeth. "Maybe young Wren here has some information about his long-lost daddy he'd like to trade for his freedom?"

Wesley fisted his hands and started to rise. "You motherfu—"

"Wesley—" Liz cut in sharply, reaching up to place her hand on his chest. *"Sit down."*

He dropped back into the chair, but didn't bother to hide his contempt for Lucas.

"We've been over this before," Liz said calmly. "My client doesn't know anything about the whereabouts of his father. Come on, there must be something else we can do to work this out. Wesley is performing well under the terms of his probation, his supervisor in the city computer department says he's excelling at his community service."

Lucas's mouth formed a long, thin line. "If your client is so smart, he'll take what I have to offer."

Liz wet her lips. "Which is?"

"I want Hollis Carver behind bars on something that will stick. I think his son is distributing drugs for *him*."

Liz gave a dry laugh. "You want to set up your own informant?"

"We only made Carver an informant so he'd let down his guard. We thought we'd be able to get closer to him, but we need someone on the inside."

Liz's shoulders went rigid. "You want my client to go undercover in The Carver's organization?"

A smile spread over Lucas's toady face. "It's a win-win situation. He gets to work off his debt to The Carver, and work off his debt to society at the same time."

Liz shook her head. "It's too dangerous. The man is an animal."

"It'll be safer," the D.A. insisted. "Your client won't be

running from The Carver, he'll be working for him. He'll be too valuable to rough up."

"Why should I trust you?" Wesley asked. "You went back on the deal you made with my sister."

"This one will be put in writing," Lucas said.

Wesley barked out a hoarse laugh. "What am I supposed to do, just walk up to The Carver and ask him to put me on the payroll?"

Lucas nodded. "Something like that. We'll provide you with a contact in the APD who will guide you through the process."

"How long are we talking about here?" Liz asked. "A few weeks? Months?"

"That depends on your client's ability to blend in with criminals." Lucas smirked. "Something tells me he'll be good at it."

A backhanded compliment, Wesley realized, even with his mind racing in circles. "My sister will worry herself sick—"

"You can't tell your sister," the D.A. interrupted. "No one can know except the people in this room and your contact at the police department. If we discover that you've told anyone, even your damn priest, we'll find another stool pigeon, and you'll be put in a cage, got it, Wren?"

Anger was a powerful motivator, Wesley realized. His mind was misfiring and sputtering, but even through the haze, he could process pure emotion. From now on, his life's mission was to get even with Kelvin Lucas, to humiliate him the way he'd humiliated the Wren family.

The D.A. splayed his hands. "So what do you say, Wesley? Do you want to work for me or do you want to go to jail and make new friends?" Under the table, Lucas moved his foot back and forth. The capsule had burst and the precious white powder was being ground into the carpet.

Wesley gritted his teeth against the desperation swelling in his chest. God, how he'd love to spit in the man's face. But his sister would be devastated if he went to jail. And he couldn't very well help his father if he was sitting in the slammer.

"And all charges against my client regarding the body-snatching incident will be dropped?" Liz asked.

"I'll drop it to a misdemeanor and add to his community service for appearances' sake. That way no one's suspicious."

Liz turned toward Wesley. "It's a good deal," she murmured. "My advice is to take it."

"And what if The Carver finds out what I'm doing?" Wesley asked, rubbing his arm where the man had already etched part of his name.

"Make sure he doesn't find out," Lucas said flatly. "Do we have a deal?"

More than anything, Wesley just wanted to get out of the building, ride to Chance's and get a bag of Oxy. Even his eyelids were starting to sweat. "Okay," he grumbled.

"Good," Lucas said, pushing to his feet so triumphantly that Wesley immediately wanted to take it back. "We'll be in touch, Ms. Fischer."

After the pair left the room, Liz touched Wesley's shaking hand. "You made the right decision. Do this, and you'll come out debt free on the other side."

Wesley stared at the white powder stain on the carpet in despair and nodded numbly. Debt free—or dead.

3

Carlotta swallowed the last Percocet capsule from the bottle and returned her purse to her locker. She glanced in the mirror mounted on the door and smoothed her finger over the frown line between her brows that had become more pronounced recently. Leaning close, she noticed wryly that the furrow bore a distinct resemblance to the letter *W*—for Wesley.

Her brother was going to be the death of her youth.

She slammed the door closed and returned to the sales floor where the crowd waiting for the Eva McCoy appearance had swelled. Carlotta joined Patricia, who was back and passing out tickets.

"Did you get your charm bracelet?" Carlotta asked.

Patricia nodded and pulled back her jacket sleeve to display the silver bracelet and dangling charms. "But I'm confused. These charms have absolutely no correlation to anything in my life. There's a little dog charm, and I have two cats. And a baseball glove, when I've never played any sport except tennis. A lion, which might stand for Leo, but I'm an Aries. A Texas steer head, and I don't eat meat. And a broom. How weird is that?"

Carlotta pursed her mouth to keep from making a comment about the broom as a mode of transportation. "I thought the idea was that the charms are random, a way of challenging you to try something new."

Patricia frowned. "So I'm supposed to try sweeping? And baseball? Right." She sighed. "My bracelet is a bust." Then she held up a brown box. "But I bought one for you."

Carlotta gave a little gurgle of surprise. "You shouldn't have."

"I know you said you had an old one, but maybe it's time you replaced it." Patricia shrugged. "You know—start some new memories."

Carlotta sighed. She really didn't want to have to like the woman, dammit. But she accepted the box and murmured, "Thanks." She opened the box and pulled out the tray that held the silver charm bracelet.

"What did you get?"

Carlotta squinted as she fingered the tiny dangling charms. "This one looks like a puzzle piece."

"Ooh, that's intriguing—as if you need to figure out something."

Carlotta pursed her mouth again. *As if.* "And this one says *aloha*." She shrugged. "I certainly wouldn't mind visiting Hawaii someday. And this one…it's hearts."

Patricia frowned. "There's something wrong. There are three hearts instead of two."

"Uh-hmm," Carlotta murmured. "Strange, huh?" But her pulse quickened in spite of her skepticism. Three hearts, three men in her life.

"Oh, look!" Patricia said with a squeal. "It's two champagne glasses. That must mean you're going to have something to celebrate. Oh, you're so lucky!"

Carlotta scoffed. "It doesn't *mean* anything—it's just a charm. This is like opening a box of Cracker Jacks. Don't take it seriously."

"What's that one?" Patricia asked, pointing to the last charm, a long, slender piece of shaped metal.

"It looks like…a woman. Just a woman."

"Her arms are crossed over her chest—maybe she's a cheerleader."

Carlotta's eyebrows went up. "Uh, yeah."

"Were you a cheerleader?"

"A lifetime ago." Actually, high school seemed like another century. On another planet.

"Well, that must be it then," Patricia said eagerly.

Carlotta nodded and allowed Patricia to help her fasten the catch on the bracelet. She didn't want to say what the last charm looked like to her—a woman in corpse pose. And she wasn't talking yoga.

Pushing the eerie charm from her mind, she craned her neck, trying to get a three-hundred-sixty-degree glance around, wondering where the dynamic detective duo had disappeared to. Maybe they'd found an empty dressing room to inspect.

She wrestled with the unreasonable stab of jealousy. She and Jack had had a nice time in the sack when he'd stayed at her house once doing surveillance, but that episode had ended disastrously. They were on opposite sides of too many issues, including her father. Besides, since the reckless bout of bone-jarring sex with Jack, she'd flirted with a fling with Cooper Craft, and now…she'd made promises to Peter. In fact, she had a dinner date with Peter after work.

Which left no time for worrying about who—er, make that *what*—Jack was in to.

"I think that lady is trying to get your attention," Patricia said, nodding to someone in the crowd.

Carlotta turned to look and was pleased to see June

Moody, the owner of Moody's cigar lounge, waving. Carlotta threaded through the horde of bodies to clasp the woman's hands. June was dressed elegantly, as always, in a slim skirt and starched white shirt. Her hair and heels were high, and her smile, wide.

"I was hoping you'd be working today," June said, then touched the arm of a broad-shouldered man next to her. "Carlotta Wren, meet my son, Sergeant Mitchell Moody."

Remembering that June had once hinted that she and her military son weren't close, Carlotta was able to mask her surprise by the time he turned in her direction.

The first thing that struck her about Mitchell Moody was his sheer physical authority—the man was the size of a small mountain, with lots of impressive hills on the upward climb. The second thing she noticed were his eyes—they were the palest blue and laser-intense. Even in jeans, a red polo-style shirt and athletic shoes, the man screamed military. His head was shaved and tanned, his cheekbones sharp, his posture rifle straight. It wasn't hard to imagine him dressed in fatigues and combat boots, wielding a weapon and defending the American way.

A little shiver traveled up her spine. The man was rather…what was the word?

Hot.

"Hi, Carlotta," he said with a smile that seemed rusty. He swept an appreciative glance over her, and she flushed with…patriotism.

"Nice to meet you, Mitchell."

"Call me Mitch." His voice was low and clear, with the rumbling undertone of a well-tuned engine.

"Mitch is visiting for a couple of weeks," June supplied, sounding almost giddy.

"I understand you're a career army man," Carlotta said.

"That's right. Thought I'd be retiring in a few months, but with everything going on in the world, that's up in the air for the moment."

If he'd put twenty years into the army, that made him around thirty-eight years old, she estimated, although he seemed much more mature. More worldly.

"How do you two know each other?" he asked.

Carlotta met June a few months ago when she'd walked into Moody's cigar bar, asking about a stogie she'd found in the pocket of a men's jacket that Peter Ashford's wife had returned to Neiman's before she'd subsequently been murdered. But Carlotta tried to put a more philosophical spin on it. "I walked into the cigar lounge looking for answers, and your mother had them."

"I've been trying to persuade her to try a new occupation," Mitch said, glancing at June meaningfully. "Maybe she should give counseling a try."

"Now, now," June said, patting his arm. "Let's not go there."

Aware of the sudden tension, Carlotta changed the subject. "I assume you're both here to see Eva McCoy?"

June nodded to her son. "Mitch knows Eva."

"We belonged to the same running club in Hawaii where I'm based," Mitch said.

Carlotta's lips parted in surprise. "Hawaii—really?" Her hand closed over the charm bracelet that held the *aloha* charm. It was a coincidence, of course, but still…

Mitch nodded. "Fort Shafter. Eva trained there for the Olympic marathon."

"Carlotta, will you take our picture?" June asked.

"Of course."

Mitch handed her a digital camera. "Just push the silver button."

She framed them inside the small square and noticed that while June's smile was bright, Mitch's seemed a little forced. "Say 'cheese,'" she encouraged, but he still looked stiff when she took the photo. It appeared that mother and son had some fences to mend.

Carlotta handed the camera back to him just as an excited murmur swept through the crowd.

"There she is," Mitch said.

Carlotta turned as the tall, slender brunette walked in wearing a white Olympic athletic suit trimmed in red and blue. She smiled shyly as the Atlanta crowd cheered for their hometown girl. Carlotta couldn't help noticing that the woman didn't seem to enjoy being in the spotlight. Eva waved with one hand, fingering the gold medal around her neck with the other hand. Her boyfriend, fellow Olympian Ben Newsome, walked a few steps behind Eva, dressed in a dark blue Olympic athletic suit, also waving to the crowd. If Carlotta's memory served, he had medaled in a couple of track and field events as well.

A short nervous man hovered next to Eva, probably a publicist, Carlotta guessed. A beefy-looking fellow in a sport coat trailed behind, his head constantly moving, scanning the crowd. His gaze stopped on Mitchell Moody for a few seconds, sizing him up. Mitchell did stand out in a crowd, Carlotta conceded. Especially since he was taking lots of photos of Eva and waving, trying to catch her attention. At the hovering presence of the bodyguard, Carlotta wondered briefly if the Internet rumors about Eva receiving death threats were correct.

From the rear of the store, Jack and Maria came forward to speak with the bodyguard. After conferring, the three of them split up, circling the crowd, which had grown to overflow the aisles and available floor space. The detectives didn't seem concerned, only attentive, so Carlotta tried to relax. As bodies shifted, she was separated from June and Mitchell, but Carlotta managed to wave before she was swept up in the mob.

Hundreds of people had gathered to see Eva McCoy in person. Although Eva seemed a little stiff and preoccupied when she gave her talk, the crowd was rapt. She was appealing and soft-spoken—Carlotta couldn't imagine why anyone would want the woman dead unless they were a nut job.

Still, heaven knew there were plenty of those afoot.

Eva held up her wrist to display her famous gold "lucky charm" bracelet that she said had given her the strength not just to finish the marathon, but to fight back and finish first. Then she spoke fondly of the children's charity that would receive a portion of the proceeds of the Lucky Charm Bracelet sales. Afterward, she entertained questions from the members of the press in attendance.

An attractive, plump redhead stood. "Rainie Stephens, *Atlanta Journal-Constitution.* Eva, you're the most decorated women's marathoner of this decade. Are you planning to compete in the World Championships Marathon in Helsinki in a few weeks? It's the only major marathon you haven't won."

Eva smiled. "Thank you. And, yes, I am. That's one race I want to win before I retire."

"Is it true that Body League sportswear is going to pay you a million dollars if you win the World Championships?"

Eva looked uncomfortable. "That's what I've heard."

The crowd laughed.

"And what advice would you give to someone who's facing a difficult task?"

"Just keep finding ways not to quit," Eva said with a smile. "And don't try to do it alone. While I was running,

I looked at my bracelet and thought of the people who gave me the charms. I drew on their strength."

Don't try to do it alone. The words tugged on Carlotta's heart. After her parents had left, she'd felt so abandoned and overwhelmed with raising her little brother that some days she had been an automaton—numb but moving forward. Everyone she'd counted on had left her high and dry. And yet, somehow she'd found an inner strength that she hadn't known she possessed. Now that she had people in her life who wanted to help her—like Coop and Jack and even Peter again—she was having trouble letting them in. There was an upside to being lonely—at least it was safe.

"I love you, Eva!" a man shouted. The crowd tittered.

But instead of brushing off the outburst, fear flashed over Eva's face. She shrank from the podium.

"Marry me!" the dark-haired man shouted, pushing people aside to reach the front of the dais. He had a wild look in his eye, appearing to be drunk or otherwise impaired.

Eva's bodyguard stepped up next to her, poised to strike. Jack materialized in time to intercept the man who had caused the disturbance and guide him away from the crowd. The heckler didn't resist, but looked over his shoulder as he was being led away.

"Eva! Eva, I can't live without you!"

The man's words ended when Jack jammed his hand over the guy's mouth. The crowd parted to let them pass. They walked by Carlotta and she could smell alcohol rolling off the man.

The store publicist quickly took the microphone, thanked Eva, and directed the crowd to the adjacent jewelry department where Eva would be greeting the public and etching her name into charm bracelets.

Carlotta helped to facilitate the long, snaking line, unboxing charm bracelets after they'd been purchased and handing them to Eva to sign. The woman kept looking up, her gaze darting all around. Carlotta smiled and introduced herself in an attempt to put the athlete at ease. "Your own charm bracelet is beautiful."

Eva lifted her arm and studied the now-famous piece of jewelry with a fond smile. "Yes, it's very special to me. My coach tried to persuade me not to wear it during the run— every ounce of weight counts, you know. I'm glad I trusted my instincts."

"Everyone here adores you."

"I have to confess that crowds make me nervous. I started running because it's something I can do alone."

"I'm sorry about the earlier disturbance."

The woman sighed. "It's not the first time something like that has happened."

"You're very good at connecting with the public."

"No, I'm not," Eva said with a miserable smile. "I fake it."

As one hour elapsed, then two, Carlotta noticed that each encounter took its toll on Eva. She grew more skittish and pale, fidgeting in the chair that had been set up for her in front of a tall, slant-top table. Twice she slipped and cut herself with the tool she was using to etch *Eva* on the back of the charm bracelets. Carlotta kept one eye on the clock, looking for an opportunity to slip away and check her cell phone messages. Wesley should be finished by now and she needed to talk to him—about the meeting with the D.A., and about the missing prescription drugs.

"You're probably bored to death," Eva said as she handed Carlotta back yet another inscribed bracelet.

Carlotta straightened. "Not at all."

"I see you have a bracelet, too," Eva said, nodding to Carlotta's wrist. "Do you want me to sign it?"

"I wouldn't want to jump in front of all these people."

"Nonsense, I'll do it now."

Eva unfastened the bracelet from Carlotta's wrist and bent over it while Carlotta boxed the one the woman had just signed.

"These are some of my favorite charms," Eva said. "Hmm—what an interesting combination."

"Does the woman have any special significance?" Carlotta asked.

"I don't know," Eva murmured, then frowned. "In fact, I don't remember this charm." Then she shrugged. "Oh, well—there were a team of designers. I supervised, but I don't remember them all. Everything happened so fast, my head is still spinning."

Before another hour had expired, they'd run out of charm bracelets to sign, but there was still a line of people who simply wanted to speak to Eva and get an autograph. Carlotta wished she'd been more diligent about keeping up with in-store events while she'd been off work. Getting celebrity autographs was one of her favorite hobbies, and the new autograph book in her dresser drawer at home had been signed only a few times.

Carlotta glanced up to see that June and Mitchell Moody were next in line. Eva recognized Mitch and seemed genuinely pleased to see him. "What are you doing here?"

He explained he was visiting his mother and introduced June.

"My son can't say enough nice things about you," June said.

Eva blushed and glanced toward her boyfriend, Ben,

who was standing a few feet away looking bored. Suddenly, though, he was watching his girlfriend and Mitch Moody with great interest, Carlotta noticed, especially when they leaned close for June to take their picture.

"Mitch was a terrific running partner," Eva said. "He really pushed me to reach my personal best. And the fact that he's from Atlanta, too, made me feel less homesick."

"Your talk was fantastic," Mitch said, clearly taken with Eva.

The woman shook her head. "I like raising money for charity, but this is all a little too much fanfare for me."

If that was the case, then Eva wasn't going to like what was coming next, Carlotta thought as she spied a huge decorated sheet cake being wheeled toward the woman, blazing with sparklers. Carlotta frowned. Had a cake been mentioned in the staff meeting that she'd missed? The mustached man pushing the cart was dressed in white culinary garb and...roller skates? Someone started singing "For She's a Jolly Good Fellow," and the crowd joined in, parting to allow the cake through.

Just as Carlotta suspected, Eva didn't look happy with the turn of events.

Carlotta leaned close. "Are you okay?"

Eva's face reddened. "I wasn't expecting this...I hate surprises."

Alarm whipped through Carlotta. Eva didn't know about the cake? Her first instinct was to find Jack, but she didn't see him. When she spotted Maria, she waved frantically, then ran forward to block the cart.

"Take it back," Carlotta said to the man, but she could barely hear herself over the singing. At the sight of a hand tool next to the cake that didn't look like any culinary utensil she'd ever seen, she waved her arms at the man and shouted, "Stop!"

The man glared and shoved the cart forward, plowing hard into her. The edge of the cart hit Carlotta's thighs, knocking her legs out from under her. She flailed for two long seconds before falling facedown into the cake. Pain sizzled against her skin where the weight of her body extinguished the sparklers. She lay in the quiet denseness of the white cake for a few seconds, trying to digest what had happened, then lifted her head and licked sweet icing and cake crumbles off her lips. She wanted to clear her eyes, but since the cart was still moving—fast—she decided it would be better to hang on.

She felt herself being propelled like a human bowling ball in Eva's general direction. Carlotta braced for impact, and based on the force of the collision, she was pretty sure she'd taken out at least a couple of people. Then the cart tipped over, dumping her and the cake onto the floor.

Exclamations and screams sounded. Carlotta felt the crush of bodies around her and was afraid she was going to be trampled. She clawed at the gooey cake on her face and tried to blink the scene into focus, but her eyes stung and watered. Someone grabbed her by the arm and pulled her up, then shoved her against a display counter.

"Stay here," said a woman with a curling voice. Maria.

"Clear the area!" a man bellowed. "Clear the area!" A shrill noise pierced the air, which Carlotta recognized as a display-case alarm. Had someone broken into one of the jewelry cases?

When she finally blinked the surroundings into focus, she gasped. It was a mob scene. Because of Eva's white tracksuit, Carlotta was able to spot her at the bottom of a pile of people who had presumably been knocked down by the flying Carlotta-cake-cart, Patricia Alexander for one. Maria Marquez was hauling people off one at a time and finally reached the athlete, who looked dazed.

"Let's get you out of here," a man said near Carlotta's ear. She recognized the voice—and the muscular arm—as belonging to Mitchell Moody. Grateful for the assistance, she leaned on him as she slipped and slid on cake and icing that had been mashed under many feet.

He led her to the mall entrance, where clumps of customers had congregated.

"Thank you," Carlotta said, trying to catch her breath. "Did you see what happened?"

"Hard to say. It looked to me as if the guy with the cake was trying to get close to Eva."

"Did he get away?"

"I don't know. I got Mom out of there and went back to get you."

"There you are," June said, hurrying up to them. "Carlotta, are you okay?"

She nodded, then lifted her arms and stared down at her cake-matted dress. "But I can't imagine what I must look like."

Mitch gave a little laugh. "Mom said you were always into something."

Patricia Alexander emerged from the store and came stomping over, her pearls askew and her bob disheveled. "I should've known something like this would happen on your first day back."

Carlotta gaped. "Are you saying this was my fault?"

"Lindy wants all employees back in the store ASAP, and the police are asking for you. Big surprise." The woman turned and marched back into the store.

Carlotta sighed and turned to June and Mitchell. "I'm

sorry the event turned out this way. It was nice to meet you, Mitch."

"You, too," he said. "I hope I'll see you again before I leave town."

"That would be nice," she said, pulling a piece of cake out of her ear. She said goodbye to June, and retreated to the entrance of the store with as much dignity as she could muster.

This was not how her life was supposed to be. Mired in drama. Always in the wrong place at the wrong time.

Remember this when you're having dinner with Peter tonight, she told herself. If she married him, she'd never have to work another day in her life. She could spend her days having her purchases rung up at Neiman's instead of being the one doing the ringing up. She could buy a new car when her battery died. And she could make bail no matter how many times Wesley got into trouble.

The area around the event had been cleared of customers. A cleaning crew was mopping up cake that seemed to be everywhere. Carlotta realized she was tracking icing on the floor from her shoes, but it couldn't be helped. A knot of people had gathered to the side. Lindy wore a worried expression. Maria Marquez was talking to Eva McCoy, who was being comforted by her boyfriend, Ben. Eva's bodyguard and publicist were nearby, as well as the head of store security. Jack stood back a few steps, observing. When he saw Carlotta, he wiped his hand over his mouth to smother a smile.

"Didn't know you had a sweet tooth," he murmured when she walked up.

"Don't start. What happened?"

"Not sure. I'm just getting back from handing off the drunk-and-disorderly character, so I'm hearing everything secondhand. The cake was definitely some kind of ruse. No one in McCoy's camp or with Neiman's knew about it. But the guy got away. His smock was found in a trash can inside the mall."

"Did he attack Eva?"

"No. Apparently you got the worst of it."

Carlotta gave him a withering look.

Jack pulled out a handkerchief and handed it to her. "Can you describe him?"

She inhaled the scent of his aftershave on the handkerchief before she wiped her face. But the suspicion that she was only making things worse was confirmed by Jack's wince, so she gave up. "He was about five-ten. Caucasian. Wearing a fake mustache, I think."

"That's not much to go on."

"Then look for a guy wearing roller skates," she said drily. "That should be pretty easy to spot."

He pursed his mouth, then made a few notes on a little notepad. He pulled out his phone and made a call, relaying the description to someone on the other end. When he flipped the phone closed, he shook his head and muttered, "Why do I get all the crazies?" When she raised her eyebrows, he added, "I don't mean you…this time."

She frowned and crossed her arms. "Do you think he meant to hurt Eva?" Carlotta realized everyone else had stopped talking and her voice suddenly sounded very loud.

Jack gave her a look that asked her to lower her voice. "He might have meant to harm Ms. McCoy, or he might have simply wanted to give her cake," Jack said to the entire group.

"But he could've killed her," Eva's boyfriend said. His face was red, his body language vibrating with anger. "Is anyone looking for this guy?"

"Yes, Mr. Newsome. The perp's description has been

broadcast, and we have units circling the area. But let's try to keep this in perspective. As of now, the man's only crime is attempted delivery of a cake."

"I heard a case alarm go off," Carlotta said. "Was anything stolen?"

"We think it was triggered when the cart hit a glass case," Maria offered.

"Thank goodness nothing was stolen," Lindy added.

Suddenly Eva gasped and grabbed her wrist. "My charm bracelet—it's gone!"

Carlotta inhaled sharply at the loss of the iconic piece of jewelry. And from the blank expressions of the group, everyone was equally stunned.

"Did the man take it?" Maria asked.

Eva touched her forehead. "I don't know…it's possible. There were just so many people grabbing at me."

"I just remembered something," Carlotta said to Jack. "There was some kind of tool on the cart. I don't know what it was."

"Can you sketch it?" He handed her his little notebook and pen and she drew the outline as best she could remember.

"It was maybe six or eight inches long."

Jack squinted at the drawing. "Looks like tin snips, maybe. Probably to cut the charm bracelet from Ms. McCoy's wrist."

"I thought you people were here so this kind of thing wouldn't happen," Ben Newsome said, his voice accusatory.

A muscle ticked in Jack's jaw. "We can't anticipate everything, sir."

"We're pulling surveillance tapes from the store cameras," Maria added. "Hopefully those will tell us more."

"Of course the most important thing is that Eva's all

right," Ben said, squeezing her shoulders. "But that bracelet means everything to her, and it represents a lot to the American people, too."

Eva's eyes were glazed, her expression stricken. "Take me home, Ben."

"Perhaps I should stay and work with the police," he said gently.

"That's not necessary," Jack said. "Do you have a photo of the bracelet you can let me have?"

Newsome scoffed. "It's only one of the most photographed pieces of jewelry in the world, Detective."

Jack handed the man a card. "That should make it easy for you to send a close-up to this address. We'll contact you as soon as we have news."

The woman's boyfriend scowled, but he nodded curtly and led Eva away.

Carlotta noticed a redhead loitering on the periphery of the shoe department, within earshot of the group—the reporter from the *AJC*. She looked up and caught Carlotta's eye, then replaced the shoe she'd been studying, did an about-face, and headed toward the nearest exit. Carlotta frowned, wondering how long it would be before news of the stolen bracelet would be broadcast.

Lindy stepped up to Carlotta. "Are you okay?"

"Yes, but I'd like to clean up."

"Absolutely, you should go home. I'll see you tomorrow."

Carlotta nodded wordlessly. So much for not drawing attention to herself. She glanced at her watch and used her nail to scrape off the white icing dried on the face. Three o'clock. Wesley's meeting with the D.A. should be over by now—he'd probably left her a message.

Please let it be good news, she prayed. *Please let him be safe.*

"Did you drive to work?" Jack asked.

She shook her head. "I took the train."

"Get your things. We'll take you home."

4

Wesley had counted on walking out with Liz, knowing that Mouse wouldn't come near him if he was with his attorney. But as luck would have it, she had appointments in the government office building the rest of the day.

"I don't like the idea of you working for Hollis Carver," she said with a concerned frown as they rode the elevator down to the first floor. "But give Lucas what he wants and maybe he'll ease up on you."

Wesley gave a little laugh. "You know as well as I do that Lucas would be thrilled if something happened to me on the job."

"Nothing's going to happen," Liz said, but without her normal brass-tits attitude. "I'm going to request that Jack Terry be your undercover police contact."

Wesley rolled his eyes. "Anyone but him."

"I know you don't like Jack, but he's the best man for the job. I want you to be safe."

Resigned, Wesley stepped off the elevator and dragged a shaking hand through his hair. He needed a hit of something, bad.

"I'll call you," Liz said from the elevator. "Get some rest—you look like hell." The doors slid closed.

Wesley glanced in the direction of the lobby where

Mouse had probably parked his fat ass, pretending to know how to read. Which meant Wesley needed another way out of the building.

He walked up to a janitor who was pushing a dust mop. "Man, is there someplace I can step out to grab a smoke without setting off an alarm?"

The guy jerked his thumb toward a Stairs-Emergency Exit sign. "The door's left propped open for smokers and the alarm turned off. Don't tell Homeland Security."

Wesley made a zipping motion across his mouth, then headed for the stairwell. A folded empty cigarette pack was wedged between the door latch and the strike plate. He slipped outside, then carefully repositioned the cigarette pack as he closed the door behind him. A small concrete pad littered with cigarette butts was isolated by tall bushes and a whirring HVAC unit. He looked around to get his bearings, then stepped through the bushes and headed toward the parking lot where he'd left his bike, scanning for Mouse.

He merged with a group of employees who appeared to be leaving for a lunch break, then veered off when they walked past the bike racks. He stooped to spin the combination lock securing his bike, but his vision blurred and his hands fumbled. Sweat dripped off his nose. He shook his head to focus, and finally the lock sprang open. He stood too quickly and got a head rush, but stabilized himself on the bike and pushed off, feeling smug for outmaneuvering Mouse. He'd have to face the man soon enough if he infiltrated The Carver's organization, but he'd rather get the details of what was expected of him first.

As he rode out of the parking lot, he heard a car pull up behind him—close.

Too close.

Hoping it was the standard asshole Atlanta driver who had no respect for sharing the road with cyclists, he looked over his shoulder, only to confirm his worst fear.

Mouse was driving a dark Town Car with a big, impressive grill that was closing in fast on his back tire. Panicked, Wesley stood to apply extra pressure to the pedals, but his reaction time was slow. The impact of the car knocked his bike forward, his body up and back. He landed on the big hood of the Town Car with a *thunk* and slid to the windshield as Mouse brought the car to a halt.

Mouse opened the door and stepped out, then dragged Wesley off the hood by his tie and pulled his face close. "Trying to avoid me, Wren?"

"'Course not," Wesley said with a cough. "I need to get my jacket back."

Mouse shook Wesley until his glasses went askew. "What happened in there? You're not planning to rat out The Carver, are you?"

"No," Wesley said, swallowing past the pressure on his windpipe. "I told the D.A. I don't know anything. He was pissed and threatened to throw me in jail, but my lawyer's good. So all I have to do is more pain-in-the-ass community service."

Mouse looked doubtful. "You fuckin' with me?"

Wesley couldn't imagine anything on earth more unpleasant. "Nah, man. The Carver's off the hook."

Mouse released his grip. "You'd better not be lying."

"Dude, The Carver's attorney has probably already been contacted."

As the big man chewed on his lip, his phone rang. He kept one paw on Wesley while he answered the call. "Yeah…? Yeah… Yeah." He ended the call and jammed the phone in his pocket.

"Okay, you little shit, I just got verification. Now, give me a payment and we're square for a while."

Wesley lifted his hands. "I don't have any money."

"Wrong answer."

"Dude, I thought I was going to jail today. I didn't bring any cash."

Mouse frowned, then released Wesley and stepped back.

Wesley exhaled in relief, but winced as his back twinged in pain. When he looked up, Mouse was carrying his dented bike to the rear of the car.

"Hey, what are you doing?"

Mouse used a keyless remote to pop the trunk. "Making your life miserable."

Wesley could only stand and watch the man toss his bike into the cavernous trunk.

"Next time you leave the house, sport, you'd better find somewhere to stash some cash—in your wallet or up your ass, I really don't care. I'm gonna need a payment."

"Will I get my bike back?"

"Don't count on it."

Mouse slid into the car and slammed his door. Wesley jumped up on the curb to keep from being clipped by a mirror as the Town Car roared away. He swore through gritted teeth as the car disappeared—this day just kept getting better.

He pulled his cell phone from his pants pocket and brought up his buddy Chance's phone number. His hands were trembling badly and his skin felt itchy. Under the intense sun, he felt like an egg sizzling in a frying pan.

Chance's phone rang and rang, then rolled over to voice mail. Wesley cursed and disconnected the call. Chance not answering his cell phone meant one of two things—he was dick-deep in some big-butted girl, or he was dead. His guess was the former.

Wesley set off walking unsteadily toward the Five Points
MARTA station. He had enough money for train fare to get
him to midtown. From there he'd have to walk the few
blocks to Chance's place. He wiped his sleeve across his
clammy brow, then loosened the tie. His throat was parched
and every step was an effort. The one thing that kept him
going was the knowledge that a bag of sweet Oxy was
waiting for him.

He'd quit the stuff later, when his life calmed down.

A honk sounded and he jumped back, afraid that Mouse
had returned to run him over.

A silver-colored dome-shaped car pulled up next to the
curb. The passenger side window zoomed down and the
driver leaned over to shout. "Wes? Hey, do you need a ride?"

He squinted. "Meg?" Meg Vincent worked at the city
computer department where he performed his community service.

"Yeah, jump in."

The car behind her honked with impatience, spurring
him forward. He opened the door and swung inside. The
coed gave him a brief smile, then looked back to the road
and stepped on the gas.

"I thought that was you," she said. "Your bony ass
gave you away."

"Ha, ha," he said, then pursed his mouth. She'd
noticed his ass?

"You weren't at work this morning."

"That's because I was here," he said without explanation. "What about you? Do you live in this area?"

"No, I live on campus. There's a great health food store
down the street, so I came over here for lunch. Where are
you headed?"

"Midtown. But if it's out of the way—"

"It isn't."

Wesley glanced sideways at the girl who was probably his age—she was a freshman at Georgia Tech, the same as he would've been if he'd gone to college. She was whip-smart with a funky, independent style. Today she wore camouflage pants, a plain white T-shirt, and her dark blond hair was covered with a smiley-face bandana.

"What kind of car is this?" he asked, glancing around at the interior.

"It's a Prius."

"Electric?"

"That's right."

It suited her, he decided. Meg's father was a famous geneticist and apparently megawealthy, but she had a work study at the ASS office, and dressed like every other college kid who was scraping by. Plus she was living on campus in a dorm when she could easily afford her own condo in Buckhead.

"Why aren't you riding your bike?" she asked.

"Flat tire," he lied.

"Aren't you a little old to be riding a bike anyway?"

"I used to have a motorcycle."

"Used to? Is that supposed to impress me?"

He frowned. "No."

"So what happened to it?"

"My driver's license was suspended. I sold it."

"Oh, right," she said drily. "I forget that you're an ex-con."

"I'm on probation," he said irritably. "Big difference."

"Uh-huh." She glanced over at him. "Don't take this the wrong way, but you look like shit."

"Thanks a lot."

"Seriously, are you okay?"

Meg had once accused him of being hooked on something, and he'd flatly denied it. "Just hot and tired."

She reached around her seat and rummaged blindly in a container on the floorboard behind her, then came up with a Red Bull. "Knock yourself out."

He took the can and cracked it open. "Thanks." A couple of hearty drinks started to revive him. He laid his head back on the headrest.

"Are you moving bodies today?" she asked.

"Not today." And after the stunt he'd pulled, he'd be lucky if Coop ever called him again.

"Doesn't it creep you out?"

He shrugged. "It's not pleasant, but someone has to do it."

"So it's something you intend to keep doing?"

If he went to work for The Carver, there'd be no time for body moving. The realization bothered him more than he expected. "I don't know. I have a line on a new job."

"What kind of job?"

"I don't have all the details yet."

"You like being mysterious, don't you?"

"Not particularly."

"Does that mean you won't be coming back to ASS?"

"No, I'll be there for a while longer."

Something flashed across her face—relief? He must be mistaken. Meg had been apathetic toward him from day one.

"Am I taking you home?" she asked.

"Nah—to a friend's place."

She grinned. "You have a friend?"

"Ha, ha."

"Is he a dropout, too?"

"I'm not a dropout."

"Fine. Is he also too sexy for college?"

That made him smile. The only person who thought

Chance was sexy was Chance. And anyone he paid to sleep with him. "He attends Georgia State."

Her eyebrows climbed. "Really? What's he studying?"

"Business." Wesley shifted in his seat over the idea of Meg being more impressed with his buddy than with him. "Chance isn't much of a student, though."

Meg shrugged. "Most of life is about showing up."

Rankled, he took another long drink from the can. When it came to college, he'd shown up as much as Chance—to take his friend's exams when necessary.

"Where am I dropping you?" she asked.

He gave her the address of Chance's condo building a couple of blocks away.

"Nice building," she murmured when they pulled up.

"Yeah." She probably wouldn't think much of the cramped town house where Wesley and Carlotta lived. Living in a "transitional" neighborhood was fine if a person did it for philanthropic or moral grounds, like Meg. But it was a different ballgame if you were there because you couldn't afford to live somewhere else. Or if you were afraid to move because your parents wouldn't be able to find you, should they decide to come home.

Wesley realized Meg was staring at him. "Are you sure you're okay?"

"Fine," he said, opening the door to climb out. "Thanks for the ride."

"No problem. See you tomorrow morning?"

Her smile made his stomach feel funny. "Yeah, later."

The Prius rolled away, and Wesley dismissed the nausea as hunger pains.

For Oxy.

On the way inside the building, he called Chance again, and his friend answered on the third ring, panting. "Yeah?"

"It's Wes. I'm downstairs, but it sounds like you're busy."

"Uh, yeah…ah, hell, come on up." Then he disconnected the call.

Wesley waved to the concierge who knew his face, then walked to the elevator and pushed the call button. He shook his head, wondering what he'd find his friend involved in today. From the way the big guy was huffing and puffing, he might have a whole herd of prostitutes up there. His chubby buddy had a fat trust fund and made tons of money selling soft-core drugs and hard-core porn on the side. Chance worshipped vices and excess, and was fun as hell to be around.

On the ride up, Wesley mopped at his wet forehead with his sleeve. Just knowing he was close to the Oxy made him almost weak with relief. He jogged down the hall, then rapped on Chance's door.

After a few seconds, the door opened and Wesley stared.

"Are you coming in, or what?"

Chance had answered his door in just about every outfit and stage of undress imaginable, but this one topped them all.

"What?" Chance looked down at his short, red, spandex unitard. "You've never seen exercise clothes before?"

"Not on you," Wesley said. "The headband's a nice touch."

"Get in here, shithead."

Wesley walked inside and closed the door. Chance climbed on a new treadmill that took up a big portion of the living room, and increased the speed until everything on him jiggled. In the stretchy suit and black high-top tennis shoes, he looked like an overweight superhero.

Wesley pulled on his chin. "What's with the exercise kick, man?"

"Just thought I'd start taking better care of myself. This treadmill is great. I can work out and still watch TV."

The big screen TV was playing porn, as usual.

"And look—" From the tray in front of the treadmill that was meant to hold a book, Chance picked up a reefer and lit it with a lighter. "I can get high while I exercise."

"Nice," Wesley said drily. "Does this have something to do with my sister's friend Hannah calling you fat?"

"No." Chance drew on the joint until his face turned red, then exhaled a stream of smoke. "Maybe. You put in a good word for me, didn't you?"

"I will the next time I see her." Wesley shook his head. The fierce and pierced Hannah would skewer Chance's frat-boy ass and put an apple in his mouth before she ate him alive.

"Dude, I've got Grimes working on getting you into another card game. He knows he owes us since it was partly his fault we got cleaned out last time."

"Okay, sure." Wesley darted a look toward the cabinet where Chance kept his stock of pills.

Chance saw him looking. "Need some more OC?"

He tried to sound casual. "Yeah, but I don't have any cash on me."

"I'll get it out of your winnings. It's in the second drawer. Take what you want."

Wesley was at the cabinet before his friend finished talking. "I'm going to need more of that urine screen, too." To keep from testing positive when his probation officer asked for samples.

"Top drawer on the right."

He pulled out a bag of the Oxy and felt a rush just holding a pill in his fingers. He popped one in his mouth and chewed to break the time-release coating. Instantly a feeling of euphoria bled through his chest and arms. As he floated toward oblivion, the thought slid into his mind that he'd forgotten to call Carlotta to tell her he wasn't going to jail after all.

Oh, well, she was probably too busy having fun on her first day back to work to worry about him anyway.

5

Carlotta stopped by her locker for her purse and her cell phone, feeling miserable. At least the break room was empty—all employees had been dispatched in the aftermath of the disturbance.

Her dress was sticky and stiff and dotted with scorch marks from the sparklers on the cake. Cake and icing were everywhere—under her fingernails, inside her arm cast, in her bra. She winced as she turned toward the mirror, dreading the sight of herself.

She gasped in horror at her reflection. Bits of cake and icing clung to her face, eyebrows, chin and hair. She looked as if she'd been whitewashed.

The realization sent her running to the restroom to wash off what she could. She'd need mascara remover to get rid of the icing from her eyelashes, and a good exfoliant scrub to cleanse her pores. And she'd have to shampoo, rinse and repeat a couple of times to get the hardened mess out of her hair.

She dried her face and hands with paper towels, then checked her cell phone for messages. There were two messages from her friend Hannah, but nothing from Wesley. She dialed his phone but he didn't answer.

"Hey, it's me," she said into the mouthpiece, trying to

sound upbeat. "Just wondering how things went today. Call me when you can."

She disconnected the call, hoping against hope that Wesley wasn't sitting in jail. Surely he or Liz would call her if the meeting had gone south, wouldn't they? Carlotta bit her lip in frustration, tasting sugary remnants of icing. Swallowing her pride, she emerged from the break room to find the shimmering Maria Marquez waiting for her.

"Jack is pulling the car around," the detective said, gesturing to a side exit.

Carlotta nodded and fell into step next to the woman, feeling like a crusty child who was being picked up from school to be driven home.

"Are you sure you're okay?" Maria asked.

"Nothing a shower won't fix," Carlotta mumbled. "By the way, thanks for pulling me out of that mess."

"No problem."

When they got to the exit, Maria held open the door, like the parent. Carlotta walked through to see Jack's black sedan sitting at the curb. She headed for the front passenger seat, but he intercepted her by getting out and circling to the back.

"I put down something for you to sit on," he said. From his sweeping gesture, one would've thought he'd rolled out a red carpet for her instead of crinkled pages of the *Atlanta Journal-Constitution*.

"Thanks," she said as she climbed in.

"Buckle up," he said cheerfully, then closed the door.

She fastened the seat belt and watched as the two of them slid into their seats simultaneously, then checked mirrors, visors and their radios like a choreographed dance. They seemed to be perfectly in sync with each other, she noticed irritably. When the car pulled away, they conversed in low tones, as if they didn't want Carlotta to hear what they were saying.

"Is it true that Eva McCoy has received death threats?" Carlotta piped up.

Jack adjusted the rearview mirror so he could see her. "Where did you hear that?"

"It's all over the Internet."

He frowned. "I thought one of the terms of Wesley's probation is that he can't have computers at home."

Carlotta frowned back. "We don't have a computer at home. A coworker told me she saw the rumor online. Is that why you two were there?"

"No comment," Jack said.

Carlotta's mouth tightened. He would've told her if Maria hadn't been in the car. "Maria, did you notice anything special about the guy with the cake before he got away from you?"

Jack shot her a warning glance in the mirror, but Carlotta returned with an innocent eyebrow raise.

"No," Maria replied with a smile. "Except that he left tire tracks over you."

Jack pressed his lips together and turned his attention straight ahead.

Carlotta unbuckled her seat belt and stuck her head between their seats. "That reporter from the *AJC* hung around after the event. She heard Eva say that her bracelet was stolen—it'll be all over the news."

He shrugged. "That could help us. Maybe someone will see the bracelet and get in touch with the police. And a piece of jewelry known to be hot will be harder to resell."

"Maybe it was just a warning," Carlotta said. "Maybe the guy took the bracelet to let everyone know how close he could get to her. Or maybe whoever took it will ask for a ransom."

"Maybe," Jack said in a noncommittal tone. "Frankly, in the scheme of things, I don't consider this to be a high-priority crime."

"I'm with you, Jack," Maria said. "I don't understand all the hoopla around the charm bracelets in general. I see you have one, Carlotta."

Carlotta covered the bracelet with her hand. "It was a gift from a coworker," she said defensively. "Although I can see why the idea of charms appeal to women. They're mementos of special times, and they're jewelry—what's not to like?"

"It just seems silly to me," Maria said.

Carlotta frowned. "Where are you from, Maria?"

"Chicago."

"And what brings you to Atlanta?"

The woman turned her head to look out the window. "I just needed a change."

"I'm afraid you're going to find the Atlanta heat a little hard to handle," Carlotta offered.

Maria turned in her seat to smile at Carlotta. "I like the heat. In fact, I'm finding a lot of things about Atlanta that I like." Her gaze drifted to Jack's profile.

"The traffic is horrible," Carlotta muttered, sitting back in her seat. When Jack gave her a chiding look, she wanted to stick out her tongue.

"Is that why you're riding the train?" he asked.

"No." Her shoulders fell. "My car battery is dead."

"I'll give you a jump when we get you home."

His eyes met hers and she detected a flash of amusement—and desire. Her pulse betrayed her. Maria's head turned.

"Your car, I mean," he added, then turned his gaze forward as if he'd been a little boy caught with his hand in the cookie jar.

"What part of town is this?" Maria asked, looking out the window at the passing neighborhood landscape which was clearly middle to lower class.

"Lindbergh," Carlotta supplied.

"Like the cheese?"

"Something like that."

Jack spelled it for Maria and she pulled out a map. "I'm still trying to get my bearings," Maria explained.

"Me, too," Carlotta whispered to no one as they pulled into the driveway of the town house she shared with Wesley.

Jack adjusted the rearview mirror. "Carlotta, do you recognize that black SUV?"

She turned around in time to see the vehicle pull away from the curb where it had been sitting across the street. Anxiety bubbled in her stomach. "I don't think so."

Jack's mouth tightened as he put the car in Park. "Do you have your car keys with you?"

"Yes." She dug in her purse for the remote control to open the garage door.

"Please tell me that you backed into the garage when you parked."

"Only because the only thing harder than backing into the garage is backing onto the street."

She climbed out and depressed the button on the remote control.

Maria got out of the car, too. Carlotta noticed the woman taking in the shabby town house. She had done her best to weed and spruce up the landscaping as much as her bum arm allowed while she was off work, but there was still a lot of work to do. Now that her arm was almost healed, she was hoping she could get Wesley to help her with some painting and other major projects.

If they could find the money.

And if he wasn't languishing in jail.

The motor on the garage door opener made a loud, grating sound as the door raised. It was just a matter of time before it stopped altogether or, more their luck, caught on fire and burned the house down. In the car she saw Jack shake his head. He was no doubt wondering how she and Wesley had made it this long.

He pulled his sedan up to the nose of her car, the dark blue Monte Carlo Super Sport that she'd accidentally bought—yet another long story of her bad luck and ill timing—and turned off his engine.

"This is your car?" Maria asked. "I figured you'd be driving something like that little convertible sitting over there."

Carlotta gazed at her crippled white Miata longingly. "Those were the days." Coop had promised to come over and take a look under the hood of the convertible, but after Wesley's betrayal and after her and Coop's near-miss at romance, she doubted if he'd still offer free car maintenance to the Wren family.

Jack got out and removed jumper cables from the sedan's trunk. To Carlotta's chagrin, Maria opened the door to the Monte Carlo and popped the hood, then lifted it to study the offending battery. "Your battery terminals are corroded."

Carlotta peered inside and pretended she knew what the woman was talking about.

"Hang on," Maria said, then returned to the sedan and emerged with an open can of Coke.

"Hey, I was drinking that," Jack said.

Maria ignored him and emptied the can over the battery. It fizzed and bubbled and ran off the sides, leaving the battery clean enough to eat off of.

"Better," Maria said.

Carlotta stared at her in dismay. Was there anything the woman couldn't do?

Jack lifted the hood on the sedan and clamped the cable ends to his car battery. Without missing a beat, he handed the other end of the cables to Maria, who attached them to the Monte Carlo's battery, then opened the driver's side door and slid behind the wheel.

Carlotta crossed her arms, wondering if the couple would notice if she left.

Jack reached into the sedan to turn over the ignition, then Maria turned over the engine to the Monte Carlo. It caught and started, much to Carlotta's relief. The lady detective emerged from the car, then she and Jack removed the cables.

"You should pull your car outside and let it run for about twenty minutes to allow the alternator to recharge the battery," Maria said, clapping her hands to dust them off.

For some reason, getting advice from the luscious Maria almost brought tears to Carlotta's eyes. She felt so…useless.

"Why don't you go on inside and shower?" Jack suggested. "I'll babysit the car and bring you your keys."

She nodded, then looked to his tall and talented partner. "Thank you, Maria, for your help."

"No problem," Maria said, as if it were of no consequence, making Carlotta feel even smaller.

She trudged toward the house and groaned inwardly to see her neighbor, Mrs. Winningham, standing next to the fence between their houses. Not only was she the nosiest woman alive, but she was convinced that the Wrens were single-handedly eroding the property values on the street.

"Hello, Mrs. Winningham," she said cheerfully.

"What on earth happened to you?" the middle-aged woman asked, eyeing Carlotta's appearance.

"Food fight," Carlotta offered, deadpan.

The woman squinted at her, then nodded toward Jack and Maria. "Who are those people?"

"Friends of mine. My car battery is dead, so they gave me a boost."

Her neighbor's expression turned leery. "Speaking of cars, do you know anything about a black SUV parked across the street off and on the past couple of weeks? I've never seen anyone get in or out of it."

"No," Carlotta said, but her heart skipped a beat. So the vehicle that Jack had noticed wasn't simply passing by. "I'm sure it's nothing to worry about. Excuse me, but I need to go inside and get cleaned up."

"Speaking of cleaning up," the woman called behind her, "your house could use a good pressure washing!"

Carlotta bit down on the inside of her cheek. "Thank you, Mrs. Winningham."

She climbed the steps to the town house and unlocked the door. When she pushed it open, the air in the living room was stale and confining. She didn't stop to consider the room—the small television with its warped picture tube, the worn furniture, the pathetic little aluminum Christmas tree in the corner, a carryover from the short time her parents had lived there. The fact that Wesley wouldn't let her take it down after ten years spoke volumes about how much their desertion had affected him.

She turned left from the living room and walked down the hallway to her bedroom, shedding shoes and clothes as she walked across the carpet. She stepped into the bathroom and turned on the water for the shower. While it warmed, she checked her cell phone on the slim chance she'd missed Wesley's call, but there were no messages.

Mindful of the few minutes she had before Jack returned her keys, she removed the flexible arm cast and climbed in to wash away the remnants of the cake and icing. Her arm was aching again. She'd overdone it and now she was out of pain pills.

Which made her think of Wesley.

Which made her think of how messed up their lives were.

Which made her think of her absent parents.

As always, all roads led back to Randolph and Valerie Wren.

She turned off the water and toweled dry, then wrapped her hair. She pulled on her favorite full-coverage chenille robe and was walking back through the house when a rap sounded on the front door. She wasn't surprised when Jack opened the door and stuck his head inside. He was familiar enough with her home.

"Carlotta?"

"Come in," she said, walking into the living room.

He held up her keys and remote control, then looked her up and down and gave her a wicked smile. "I remember that robe—or rather, I remember what's under it."

Her bare toes curled in the pile of the carpet. Jack had that effect on her. "Gee, Jack, I thought your tastes were running toward a Spanish flavor these days."

He came over to stand in front of her and lifted her chin. "Are you jealous of Maria?"

"Of course not," she said, trying to scoff. Too bad it came out sounding like a cough.

"Oh, my good God," he said, bringing his mouth close to hers. "You *are* jealous."

"I am not," she insisted.

"It's okay," he murmured. "I think it's kind of sexy. By the way, you looked pretty tasty all covered in cake."

She let him kiss her, a hot, probing kiss that pushed all her worries from her mind…

Until her cell phone rang from her purse on the chair.

She reluctantly broke the kiss. "Sorry—I need to get it. I haven't heard from Wesley yet." She pulled the phone out of her purse, but Peter's name scrolled across the caller ID screen. "It's not him." She sent the call to voice mail and sighed in disappointment.

Jack scratched the back of his neck. "Uh, the D.A. reduced the charges to a misdemeanor and added hours to Wesley's community service."

She looked up, her mouth parting in elation. "He did? That's great! That's wonderful! That's…wait—how did you know?"

"I, um, got a call."

Her good mood dimmed. "Ah, from Liz. Of course."

Jack reached forward to stroke her cheek with his thumb. "We both have other people in our lives. It has to be that way…for now at least."

"You mean, until you arrest my father?"

"No, I mean until you make up your mind."

The charm of three hearts came to mind. The doorbell rang, startling her. She and Jack both turned and Carlotta inhaled sharply to see Peter Ashford standing on the stoop, holding his phone and peering inside. He looked every inch the successful investment broker, impeccably dressed, his blond hair cut in a sleek, precision style.

Jack looked back to her. "Perfect timing."

"Peter and I have a dinner date," she murmured, drawing the tie on her robe tighter.

"Let me guess. Ashford is taking you to eat sushi?"

She flapped her eyelashes. "Who's jealous now?"

"No comment." He started toward the door, then turned back. "If you need another jump after the Ken doll drops you off, give me a call." Jack grinned, then turned to go, leaving her shaking her head.

Carlotta uncurled her toes and went to greet Peter.

6

Carlotta manufactured a wide smile to counter the frown on Peter's face that appeared when Jack emerged from her house. The men exchanged wary looks and did an awkward dance as they passed on the narrow stoop. There wasn't room enough for both of them.

"Hi, Peter," she said. "Come in."

"I know I'm early," he said as he stepped over the threshold. "The receptionist at the firm told me about a disturbance at Neiman's. I was worried about you." He jerked his thumb over his shoulder. "The woman in the driveway said you had a dead battery?" Then he noticed what she was wearing and squinted. "What's going on?"

"Eva McCoy had a speaking event in the store today."

"The Olympic marathoner?"

"Right. Some guy used a cake as a ruse to get close to her and I…" She lifted her arms. "I wound up in the cake."

He gave a little laugh. "I'd like to have seen that."

"It wasn't pretty."

"That's impossible," he said, then sighed. "I guess superhero Jack Terry was on the scene?"

She let the jab pass. "He and his new partner were at the store for security. When they found out I'd ridden the train to work because my car battery was dead, they offered to give me a ride home."

"Ah. So that woman is Jack's new partner?"

"Yes. Detective Maria Marquez."

He pursed his mouth. "Pretty lady."

Carlotta smiled and angled her head. "Are you interested?"

"No, but I was hoping that Jack might be." He gave her a pointed look, then his expression softened. "You're rubbing your arm. Are you still up to having dinner?"

Her arm was aching, but on the heels of getting such good news about Wesley's charges being downgraded, she felt happy and expansive. "Of course. I'll pop some Advil—it'll be fine."

"You probably want time to get ready. I can come back to pick you up later."

"No—stay." She gestured to the shabby living room, suddenly noticing how yellowed the paint had become, how dingy the baseboards. She'd tried so hard to shield her dilapidated lifestyle from Peter—always meeting him at the door or in the driveway, withholding details about her and Wesley's financial and legal problems as much as possible. But if they were going to date, he needed to know how she lived. "That is, if you don't mind hanging out on the couch and watching a broken TV while I dry my hair and find something to wear."

"Sounds good to me." He seemed so pleased by the modest offer that her heart gave a squeeze.

"Give me twenty minutes," she said, then dashed back to her bedroom where she leaned against the closed door and exhaled.

She could do this. She needed to do this, to try to rekindle the feelings she once had for Peter, both to give her father a chance to prove his innocence, and to give her and Peter a chance to…test the waters. At the very least,

she owed it to herself to investigate how she felt about Peter
so she could move on.

As she dried her hair and applied her makeup, Carlotta
admitted to herself that her reluctance to get involved with
Peter again might be rooted in fear that she'd fall for him
again, and then after he'd exorcised his guilt over leaving
her, he'd break her heart…again.

Which, come to think of it, was the way she felt about
trusting her father again.

She downed a couple of Advil tablets, then dressed in
a knee-length tan skirt and white long-sleeve linen shirt,
with a triple strand of long, faux pearls and red Donald J
Pliner strappy sandals. She desperately wanted a cigarette, but knew Peter would frown on the scent that would
undoubtedly cling to her clothes. She glanced at the
charm bracelet lying on the dresser and, on impulse, decided to put it back on. Eva McCoy had said her bracelet
brought her luck, and Carlotta certainly needed all the
luck she could get.

She left her hair down and as much as she hated to, she
donned the flexible cast to support her tender arm. And
because she was working on a blister from being on her
feet all day, she tucked a pair of black Cole Haan loafers
into her shoulder bag. The bottle of over-the-counter painkillers went in, too.

After checking her appearance, she put a hand over her
racing heart and acknowledged she was nervous over their
date. Just being near Peter always left her feeling caught
between the infatuation she'd had as an eighteen-year-old
and the uncertainty of the woman she was now. She took
a deep breath, then returned to the living room where Peter
stood with his hands in his pockets, studying the tarnished
Christmas tree.

"Now that Dad has made his presence known, I was hoping that Wesley would let me take down the tree."

Peter turned. "You told Wesley that you saw your dad while you were in Florida?"

She nodded. "I decided he had a right to know. But he doesn't know that Dad called you."

"That's probably wise for now," he agreed, then reached for her hand. "You look amazing."

"Thank you."

He kissed her fingers. "I can't tell you how much I've been looking forward to tonight."

Her pulse kicked up. She hadn't considered that Peter might want to…

"Let's just take it slow and have fun," she murmured. "Ready to go?"

He nodded and they left the house. Peter's low-slung Porsche two-seater was a far cry from the beater cars in her garage. She slid into the leather seat that cradled her like a hand and allowed him to close her door. If one thing led to another, she knew Peter would buy her any car she wanted.

Any *thing* she wanted. Just for the asking. She studied him as he settled into the driver's seat.

"Everything okay?" he asked, his eyes worried as if he were expecting her to pull the plug on the date at any moment.

"Yeah," she said, smiling. "I'm hungry."

"Me, too. I thought we'd go to Ecco. Have you been?"

"No, but I've heard about their bar." Her former coworker Michael Lane had wanted her to go with him a couple of times, but it hadn't worked out with her schedule…or her finances. She hadn't known financial security since her parents had left, but after having her identity stolen and her already-compromised credit damaged further, she'd cut up her plastic and put herself on a strict budget.

"They have a great wine list, and I think you'll like the food."

"Don't we need reservations?"

He winked. "I got you covered."

"Sounds good." Good for someone else to make decisions, good to be taken care of for a change. Just…good. Carlotta closed her eyes and allowed the music on the stereo to wrap around her during the short ride to Midtown.

For a muggy Monday night, the sidewalks were busy with locals waiting out rush hour by indulging in happy hour, and visitors looking for something to do after touring the Margaret Mitchell House.

The restaurant was packed, but Peter maneuvered a place at the oversize bar where they enjoyed a leisurely glass of wine. Peter was a good conversationalist, thoughtful, yet entertaining, and startlingly handsome. She felt a rush of affection for him. Peter's rejection ten years ago had devastated her, but surely he'd suffered more than she had with his unhappy marriage, then his wife's betrayal and subsequent murder only a few months ago. Peter had even confessed to his wife's murder to protect her reputation, but in the end, her dirty laundry had been aired.

Still, Carlotta thought as she smiled up at him, his actions had been noble and selfless.

After their glasses were refilled, the hostess appeared and announced their table was ready. Their "table" was more of an open-ended booth, which allowed them to sit close and look out into the crowd, European café style. Peter's leg pressed against hers under the table while she studied the menu. Lots of variety—especially cheeses— and steep prices.

But the service was impeccable, and the menu was amazing.

When the waiter left after taking their order, Peter lifted his wineglass. "Here's hoping this meal ends better than the last one we shared together."

He was referring to the time she'd sneaked out for a smoke and had been attacked by a killer who was afraid that Carlotta was on to them. To her utter astonishment, Peter had saved her by showing up and whipping out a gun. With bullets and everything.

"Are you packing heat tonight?" she asked, clinking her glass to his.

"No. Are you packing cigarettes?"

She pouted. "I'm trying to quit." But even now she was dying for one.

He twined her fingers in his. "I'm only asking because now I have even more of a vested interest in your living a long, long time."

She pressed her lips together. Becoming part of someone else's life made even everyday choices more complicated. "So what did your company think when you turned down the position in New York?"

"The partners had encouraged me to take it, but they were fine with my decision. Everyone at the office has given me a wide berth since Angela died. And I wasn't really eager to go to Manhattan—I just needed a reason to stay." He squeezed her fingers. "I'm looking forward to us spending more time together."

She smiled. "Me, too."

He gave a little laugh. "Sometimes I think we have so much to talk about, I don't know where to start."

"How are your parents?" she ventured. When they'd reunited a few months ago, he'd admitted his parents had pressured him to end their engagement back when news of her father's scandal had broken.

"They're fine. Dad plays golf every day at the club, and mother spends hours in her rose garden."

"Sounds idyllic." Perhaps her parents would have been doing something similar had their life not taken such a felonious trajectory.

"Has your father contacted you again?"

Carlotta shook her head. "I don't suppose he's been in touch with you?"

"No. There's only been that one phone call."

"What do you think about my father's claim about there being paperwork that can prove his innocence?"

Peter took a drink from his glass. "I asked around to see what happened to Randolph's files."

"And?"

"And…I was told that everything was handed over to the D.A.'s office."

She frowned. "But surely the firm kept copies?"

"One would think, but since Walt came around wondering why I was asking questions, I decided not to push it."

Walt Tully—her father's former partner at the firm and her and Wesley's godfather. In name only, since he hadn't bothered to check on them after their parents had disappeared.

"Well, I guess we'll just wait to see what dear old Dad has in store," Carlotta said. "He certainly likes to make dramatic exits and entrances."

"So your first day back to work sounded pretty interesting."

Grateful for the subject change, she nodded. "In all the commotion, the guy with the cake stole Eva McCoy's charm bracelet."

"That's too bad. I'm sure it meant a lot to her."

"Yeah, it did. She was really upset."

"I noticed you're wearing a charm bracelet."

She stroked the links. "It's one of Eva's bracelets. All of them are supposed to be unique."

"And foretell the future, I've heard. Let's see what you got."

She put her hand over the charms. "It's silly, they don't mean anything."

He ran his thumb over her bare ring finger. "So you wear jewelry only if it doesn't mean anything?"

Carlotta felt pressure building in her chest. "Peter, let's not go there."

"You're right. I'm sorry." He smiled. "How's Wesley?"

She brightened. "The D.A. reduced the charges. He got off with having to perform more community service, which is good for him. He's so smart, you know. He really should be in college."

"He needs to follow his own path," Peter chided gently.

"I know. Still, I can't help but worry about him. It's not as if he had anyone else who cared." She sighed. "This whole thing with Mom and Dad leaving has affected him more than it affected me."

"Don't downplay what they did to you," Peter said, then grimaced. "What we all did to you, leaving like that."

"It was tough on me," she agreed. "But Wesley was young. He didn't understand what was happening, or why. He blamed himself for them leaving, and he had so many problems adjusting. No one will ever know how much he suffered." She smiled. "That's why it's so hard to be angry with him when he makes dumb decisions."

"Is he still working for Cooper Craft?"

She shook her head. "Not since the body-snatching incident. But I can't blame Coop. He gave Wesley a chance and Wesley's stupidity put Coop's reputation on the line."

Peter's eyebrows raised. "From what I heard, the doctor did himself in years ago."

Carlotta frowned. "Have you been checking up on Coop?"

"A Google search isn't exactly a background check."

She angled her head. "And what exactly did you find out?"

"That he ascended to coroner at a young age, and was considered a wunderkind...until he started drinking. There was something about him declaring a woman dead when she was still alive?"

She nodded. "Jack told me about it. He said that Coop was driving home and came upon an accident. He'd had too much to drink and declared the woman dead when she was only unconscious."

"Did she live?"

"She did, but Jack mentioned she had some lingering medical issues. He said Coop lost his job and hit rock bottom."

"And now he moves bodies for a living."

Her defenses rose on Coop's behalf. "He doesn't drink anymore, and he seems at peace with himself. And he works at his uncle's funeral home."

"I remember," Peter said, then drained his wineglass.

Carlotta closed her eyes briefly—the memorial service for Peter's wife had taken place at Motherwell Funeral Home where Coop worked. "I'm sorry, Peter. Of course you remember."

"It's okay," he said, then offered a rueful smile. "I'm looking forward to the time when we can move past all the apologies."

She nodded. "I guess that's how it is when two people have a history." But deep down she wondered if they managed to strip away the past, what would they have left?

Dinner was long and pleasurable, a feast for the senses.

When their plates were taken away, Peter leaned toward her and winked. "I hope you saved room for the burnt honey ice milk with gorgonzola. It's one of their signature desserts."

"Sounds interesting."

"I was thinking maybe we could get it to go and take it back to my place."

Her heart skipped a beat. "I don't know…" From her purse, her phone rang. She reached for her bag. "Excuse me, it's probably Wesley. I haven't talked to him since his meeting with the D.A."

"Go ahead," he said as the waiter walked up.

She removed the phone and pushed to her feet. While heading to the relative privacy of a potted tree, she glanced at the caller ID screen.

Cooper Craft.

When she and Coop had last seen each other, Peter had been carrying her away from the scene where she'd been attacked by a would-be murderer. On the heels of an interrupted trip where she and Coop were supposed to have been alone, Coop seemed to concede in a parting glance that the timing wasn't right for them.

Carlotta connected the call and covered her other ear. "Hello?"

"Hey, it's Coop."

"Hi," she said tentatively. "How are you?"

"Better than most," he said breezily. "Are you busy?"

Carlotta looked around the tree to where Peter sat, giving an order to the waiter. "I'm at Ecco, just finishing dinner. What's up with you?"

"Nothing quite so glamorous. I could use a second on a body moving job. Don't suppose you're interested?"

Her pulse leapt with excitement. Going on a pickup with Coop, working on the periphery of a crime scene, sounded more intriguing than going back to Peter's place and worrying about the outcome.

"I am interested, but in the spirit of full disclosure, I should let you know that my arm is still only about ninety percent."

"That's all right. I need your pretty brown eyes more than your muscle. Protocol requires a second person on the call in case there's a question later."

Carlotta wavered. She shouldn't leave Peter on their first official date.

On the other hand, if she turned Coop down, he might find someone else to replace Wesley. This way, she could at least try to keep the door open for Coop to someday trust her brother again.

Carlotta bit into her lip. "I could get away in, say, ten minutes?"

"Do you want me to pick you up at the restaurant?"

"Uh, no. I'll meet you at the corner of West Peachtree and Third."

He gave a little laugh. "Isn't that where the prostitutes and shemales hang out looking for customers?"

"I'll be fine. What are you driving?"

"The van. See you in a few."

7

Carlotta took a deep breath and headed back to the table where Peter sat, her mind racing.

He looked up. "Was it Wesley?"

"Uh, no. Hannah called." Her friend had called twice earlier in the day, so it wasn't a *complete* lie. "I keep missing her and she's just a few minutes away from here, so I think I'll get a ride home," she said, pointing over her shoulder to the entrance. "My arm is hurting again, and I have to get up early tomorrow."

Peter looked disappointed, but nodded. "Okay. The waiter is bringing the check with the ice cream, so we can leave in a few minutes."

He so readily accepted her lie that her conscience pinged. "Thank you for dinner, Peter. It was lovely—the food, the wine and the company."

He stood. "When can I see you again?"

She searched her mind for something they could do that was less...formal. "Why don't we go to Screen on the Green Thursday in Piedmont Park? *Breakfast at Tiffany's* is playing." A classic movie on a big screen with an enormous crowd—perfect.

"That sounds good." He looked behind her. "Here's

our gorgonzola ice cream. Why don't you take it for you and Hannah?"

She balked. "Oh, I couldn't."

He took the bag from the waiter. "I insist. She's a caterer, isn't she?"

"And culinary student."

"So she'll appreciate it," he said, pushing the bag into Carlotta's hands. "Besides, I know she doesn't like me. Maybe this will score me some points."

"Okay," she murmured to save time. "I should run."

Peter tossed an alarming amount of cash on the table. "Hold on. I'll walk you out."

"Th-that's not necessary," Carlotta said, backing away. "I'm just going to the corner."

"I'll go with you." He caught up with her and guided her toward the door.

"Really, you don't have to leave," she said nervously. Peter did not approve of her body moving escapades and would be wounded if he knew the reason she'd cut their dinner short.

"Peter!"

From the bar, a woman waved wildly, until she caught sight of Carlotta.

Tracey Tully Lowenstein, Walt Tully's daughter and Carlotta's nemesis from high school, gave them a mocking look. "Well, what a surprise to see the two of you here." The blonde hooked her hand around the arm of a dark-haired man next to her. "Meet my husband, Dr. Frederick Lowenstein. Freddy, this is Peter Ashford. He works for Daddy. And this is Carlotta Wren." She gave her husband a meaningful look. "Carlotta's father used to work at the firm, too."

Carlotta knew the second the man realized she was the

daughter of Randolph Wren. His mouth circled in an O, but he quickly recovered and extended his hand.

"Very pleased to meet you," Carlotta said.

"Same here," the man said, devouring her with his eyes and holding on to her fingers longer than necessary. She removed her hand and immediately wanted to wash it.

"Freddy's a doctor," Tracey said, her expression smug.

"Yes, I believe you've mentioned that before," Carlotta said tightly. "Congratulations."

"What kind of medicine do you practice?" Peter asked smoothly, shaking the man's hand.

Dr. Lowenstein glanced at Carlotta. "I'm an ob-gyn."

Of course he was, Carlotta thought, barely containing an eye roll.

"Join us for a drink," the doctor urged. "Peter, there's an investment idea that I've been meaning to run by Walt, but perhaps you could help me if you have a few minutes." The man's eyes strayed back to Carlotta's legs.

"I was just walking Carlotta out," Peter said. "A friend is picking her up. But I can come back."

"No, stay," Carlotta told him, happy for the diversion. "I'm sure my friend is here by now. Thank you again for dinner, Peter."

"I'll call you," he said, then kissed her briefly on the mouth.

Carlotta gave him a little smile and noticed that Tracey was taking it all in. No doubt her club friends would get a play-by-play tomorrow at their regular martini lunch. Tracey had been a close friend of Angela Ashford's before the woman had died. It was only after Angela's death that the woman's sordid secrets became public. Carlotta always wondered if Tracey knew more about her friend's extramarital activities than she'd let on.

"Good night," Carlotta said, then made her way to the

exit as quickly as she could. Out on the sidewalk she stopped long enough to switch from her high-heeled sandals to the loafers she'd stuffed into her bag. Then she pulled her hair back into a ponytail and jogged the four blocks to the corner where she'd told Coop she'd meet him.

Coop hadn't arrived yet, but Carlotta wasn't alone.

A knot of working girls—and guys dressed as girls—loitered on the sidewalk, applying lipstick and walking close to the curb when cars drove by just in case a customer was trolling. Carlotta realized that this intersection of two one-way streets was a good spot for them to work because there was plenty of room for cars to pull over and neither the prostitutes nor the johns had to worry about cops appearing from the opposite direction.

She nodded to a couple of the girls, then pulled out a cigarette and tried to light it with a sputtering lighter.

"Here you go, girl," one of the prostitutes said in a throaty voice, extending a cheap gold lighter. She was a painfully skinny fortyish white woman with dark red hair and black eyeliner that looked as if it had been applied with a Magic Marker.

Carlotta accepted the light gratefully, then took a long drag on the cigarette. She almost groaned in relief when the nicotine shot into her system.

"Are you new?" the woman asked.

Carlotta blinked. "I'm not…I mean, I'm just waiting for someone to pick me up."

"Aren't we all? I'm Pepper."

"I'm…Carlotta." It was simpler to go along, especially since she'd rather smoke than talk.

Pepper pointed to Carlotta's loafers. "No offense, honey, but men usually go for heels."

"You think?" Carlotta said, wriggling her toes.

"Oh, yeah. Men aren't hard to figure out, you know. If I could talk to the wives and the girlfriends of the guys who make time with me, I'd tell them it really only takes two things to make men happy."

Curious, Carlotta leaned in. "What are they?"

Pepper grinned. "You got a dollar? I charge for my expert advice."

Carlotta decided that was fair and scrounged a dollar from her bag.

"Thank you." Pepper stuffed the dollar bill in her bra. "The two things it takes to make men happy are chocolate cake and blow jobs."

Carlotta's eyebrows went up. "Chocolate cake and blow jobs?"

"Trust me on this. You got a man you're trying to hang on to, keep him supplied with chocolate cake and blow jobs, and you'll never have to worry about him fooling around."

Carlotta made a rueful noise. "I'm not a very good cook."

"Honey, that's why God made bakeries and Little Debbie. And as far as the blow jobs—" The woman extended a square of Bazooka bubble gum and winked. "This'll make your jaws strong. On the house."

Carlotta took the gum. "Er, thanks." At the sound of a vehicle slowing, she looked up, along with everyone else on the sidewalk, to see Coop's white van pulling up.

"Ooh, nice one," Pepper said.

"Uh, ladies, this one's mine," Carlotta said. She took a quick drag off the half-smoked cigarette, then handed it to Pepper to finish. She hurried around the front of the van and climbed up in the passenger seat, then slammed the door.

Cooper smiled in the dome light of the cab behind dark-rimmed glasses. "New friends of yours?"

"Something like that," she said, going all warm and

toasty at the sight of him. He was dressed in a sport coat and slacks, with a collarless shirt. Coop was long and lean, with broad shoulders and warm, intelligent eyes that spoke of secrets.

He raked his gaze over her and he looked as if he wanted to say something. Instead he settled for murmuring, "Hi."

She smiled. "Hi yourself."

He waited for her to buckle up before he pulled away. "Did I interrupt a romantic dinner date?"

"No. And I'm glad you called."

"Yeah?"

"Yeah." She wet her lips. "Did you call Wesley first?"

"Nope." He made a regretful noise. "And honestly, I don't know when or if I will again."

"The D.A. reduced Wesley's charges to a misdemeanor. He's getting more community service."

"I guess I'm glad for him, although it doesn't change what he did."

"No, it doesn't," Carlotta agreed. "Are you going to get someone else to help you?"

He nodded. "Dr. Abrams has a nephew who's interested." Then he smiled. "And I'll keep your number first on my list." He sighed. "If I get desperate, I'll give Hannah a call."

Carlotta laughed. Hannah had a huge crush on Coop, but she was a little, um, *aggressive*.

"What's in the bag?" Coop asked.

"Gorgonzola ice cream. Want some?"

"I'm more of a chocolate cake guy myself, but I won't turn it down."

Carlotta's head snapped around. Pepper's advice rang in her ears.

"Did I say something wrong?" he asked.

"Uh, no. It's just…I had cake earlier today." She removed the lid from one of the containers of ice cream, jabbed a plastic spoon in the softening mound, then handed it to him.

"Was the cake for a special occasion?"

She gave him a brief rundown of the incident at work.

"Sorry I missed it," he said with a grin. "Too bad about the charm bracelet being stolen, though." He spooned a bite of the exotic ice milk into his mouth. "I recorded the entire women's Olympic marathon. Eva McCoy's performance was riveting."

"June Moody was at the event today. Her son, Mitchell, is visiting."

"I'd like to meet him before he leaves. June has always spoken highly of him."

She knew that Coop didn't spend a lot of time at the cigar lounge because of the bar upstairs, but he and June were friends—the woman gave Coop cigar boxes for his hobby of creating dioramas.

Carlotta's mouth puckered at the pleasing bittersweet taste of the ice cream and pointed to it with her spoon. "What do you think?"

"It's surprisingly good."

She recalled that he'd ordered dessert after meals when they'd been in Florida. "So you have a sweet tooth."

"Eating sugar helps to fulfill the craving for alcohol," he said. "You rarely see an active alcoholic having dessert—they prefer liquid sugar."

"Now that you mention it, I don't ever remember seeing my mother eat dessert," Carlotta murmured. "I always thought she was just watching her weight." Valerie Wren had had a love affair with vodka while her husband had had a love affair with Liz Fischer. Maybe one event had triggered the other? Yet, if either one of her parents had known about the other's weakness, they hadn't discussed it in front of their children.

Carlotta cast about for a more cheerful topic. "Hey, Jack told me that Dr. Abrams is going to involve you in open cases at the morgue."

A sour expression crossed his face. "That's what I've been told, but I'm not sure it was all Abrams's idea."

"You must still have friends in high places."

He shrugged. "I like to think I did mostly a good job when I was chief M.E. before…before I did what I did."

He ate another bite of the ice cream while steering the van through the evening traffic with one hand. Carlotta could tell his thoughts had turned inward. If fact, upon closer observation, his entire demeanor had changed subtly. His brown hair and sideburns were shaggy, which wasn't like him, and he seemed more preoccupied, less quick to smile than before.

"I know what it's like to make a terrible mistake," he said quietly. "Which is why I forgive Wesley for what he did. Unfortunately, because of my own mistake, I don't have the luxury of forgiving *and* forgetting. At least not until some of the dust has settled."

"I appreciate you giving Wesley another chance when the time comes," she said, her chest expanding with affection. Coop had been such a good influence on Wesley, who hadn't had a male figure in his life for a long time…except that loathsome Chance Hollander who pretended to be a friend when all he wanted in Wesley was a toadie to make himself feel important.

Coop's phone rang. He handed his ice cream container to Carlotta, then put his phone to his ear. "This is Coop… Yes…I'm just around the corner…okay." He put down the phone. "CSI is finished processing the scene. They're ready for us."

"What happened?"

"Female found deceased in her bed. It appears to be of natural causes."

Carlotta breathed a sigh of relief that her return to body moving would be a nice, quiet call—no body snatching, no drowning, no hanging, no strangling, no gun or knife wounds. She placed their empty ice cream containers back in the bag, thinking guiltily of Peter. He would be upset if he knew she was back to body moving…with Coop… eating ice cream Peter had bought for *them* to share.

"Here's the neighborhood," Coop said. "Berkeley Heights."

Coop seemed to know the streets of what was clearly an older district of metro Atlanta. She glanced at the homes as they drove by, quaint shotgun-style houses in various states of decay and gentrification. Ahead of them on the right sat a police car, a car from the morgue, and an unmarked vehicle that she recognized as Jack's as they pulled into the driveway.

Carlotta pulled the lanyard that identified her as a courier for the county morgue from her wallet and lifted it over her head with a sigh. The cop was everywhere.

She opened the door of the van and swung down to the ground, but as she started to close the door, she spotted a flash of glass peeking out from under the seat. She reached inside to push the item back, then realized it was a full pint of vodka.

She'd seen plenty of those around the Wren house when her mother had been in residence—in the freezer, in the umbrella stand, in the couch cushions.

Her stomach bottomed out and she glanced up to see if Coop had noticed. He was preoccupied with checking the contents of a small bag of equipment he always brought on calls. She swallowed nervously and shoved the bottle of booze back under the seat, then closed the door.

Maybe Coop was the kind of recovering alcoholic who kept a bottle within reach, just to prove that he could resist it.

Then she bit her lip. Or maybe he was considering falling off the wagon?

As they walked toward the house, she mentally reviewed his mood and conversation since he'd picked her up. He had been quieter than usual…and he'd seemed distracted. Or was she simply reading too much into it?

They approached the front door of one of the nicer homes on the street where a female uniformed officer was posted. Coop flashed his credentials and Carlotta held up hers. The officer directed them inside to a rear bedroom. When they entered, a young medical examiner from the morgue, Pennyman, was leaving. He spoke to Coop and the men shook hands. From their conversation, Carlotta gathered that Pennyman had once worked for Coop.

"It looks like she died in her sleep sometime last night," the man said. "She lives alone. The police were following up on a call her employer had made when she didn't report to work. She's young, so I'm thinking maybe she had an aneurysm?"

Coop smiled and clapped him on the shoulder. "You don't answer to me anymore, Pennyman. I'm sure you're right."

But it was apparent from the man's behavior that despite Coop's lack of authority, the young M.E. wanted his approval.

The men said their goodbyes, then she and Coop proceeded through the house. In the soft-hued bedroom, a pretty dark-haired Caucasian woman looked to be sleeping peacefully in the bed. Jack stood in a corner, peeling off a pair of gloves. He nodded a greeting to Coop, but when he spotted Carlotta, he frowned.

"Are you finished, Jack?" Coop asked.

"Yeah. She's all yours."

"What's her name?"

"Shawna Whitt. Damn shame—she's young."

Coop frowned at Jack. "Why did you get called out on a natural causes death?"

"I was in the area when I heard the call on the radio."

"Since when is this side of town your area?" Coop asked conversationally as he walked over to study the woman.

"I was dropping my partner off at home."

Carlotta's ears perked up.

"You have a new partner?" Coop asked.

"Yeah." A little smile played across Jack's mouth until he looked at Carlotta.

"She's hot," Carlotta supplied drily, standing back until Coop told her what she needed to do.

Coop looked up at Jack. "Oh?"

Jack shrugged, but couldn't hold back a wolfish grin.

"Cool," Coop said, then his gaze flitted to Carlotta. "Nice scenery makes any job a little more pleasant. I'll go get the gurney."

"I'll help," she said, moving toward the door.

"No, save your arm. You can help me when I get back."

When Coop left the room, Jack raised his eyebrows. "How did you go from dinner with Peter to a body pickup with Coop?"

"I'm flexible," she said lightly.

"I remember," he said, his eyes dancing.

"Stop it," she said under her breath. "I'm filling in for Wesley until he and Coop can patch things up."

At the mention of Wesley's name, Jack's gaze dropped.

"Everything's still okay with Wesley, isn't it?" she asked, suddenly concerned. "I haven't talked to him. But you said the charges were reduced, that he's not going to have to serve jail time?"

Jack lifted his gaze. "Yeah, that's right. Everything's fine."

Relieved, she smiled. "Good."

The clattering noise of the empty gurney sounded from the hall, then Coop reappeared in the doorway.

"Need a hand?" Jack said to Coop, glancing dubiously at Carlotta.

"No, we got it," she assured him, stepping up to the bed. Shawna Whitt was slender and dressed in modest nightclothes, with no outward signs of illness or injury. Carlotta felt a pang that her life had been cut short, for no obvious reason.

"Okay, I'm going to call it a night," Jack said, heading toward the door. "It looks like you two have everything under control, and I've had a long day. The uniform will lock up behind you."

"Jack, hold on," Coop said, his voice taking on an odd tone as he bent over the woman's body.

Jack walked back. "What's up?"

"There's something in her mouth."

Jack leaned forward. "How can you tell?"

"Her lips should be more relaxed."

Carlotta stared, detecting the slightest protrusion of the woman's upper lip, unnoticeable to a layperson and perhaps unnoticed by the M.E.

Coop donned plastic gloves, then reached into the small bag he carried with him to retrieve a pair of metal tongs and a small flashlight. Very gently he pulled down on the woman's chin until her mouth opened. He snapped on the flashlight, then peered inside and slowly inserted the tongs.

"There's definitely something foreign in here," he said. Moments later, he pulled out the shiny metal object and held it up to the light.

Carlotta leaned close for a better look.

"What is it?" Jack asked.

"I'm not sure," Coop said, squinting. "But it looks like some kind of…charm."

Carlotta gasped. A charm, today of all days. What a bizarre coincidence. Of course Hannah was fond of saying there was no such thing as coincidence.

"Strange," Coop murmured, turning the silvery charm in the light. "I think it's a bird—maybe a chicken?"

"Was it there before she died?" Jack asked.

Coop hesitated. "I really shouldn't venture a guess."

"Dammit, Coop, was it in her mouth when she died?"

Coop pivoted his head to look at Jack. "Off the record, I'd say no. I think we're looking at something inserted postmortem."

Jack cursed under his breath. "Guess I'm going to be here for a while after all."

8

"A chicken?" Hannah Kizer squinted over the cream-cheese quiche she'd brought for breakfast—a leftover from some exquisite party she'd worked the night before.

From the other side of the kitchen table, Carlotta nodded at her goth-garbed friend. "I saw it. The charm Coop pulled out of her mouth was definitely a chicken."

"And the assumption is the woman *didn't* take a bottle of sleeping pills, then put a chicken charm in her mouth?"

"Coop said it was placed in her mouth after she died. Obviously whoever did it was making some kind of statement. Maybe someone was taunting her."

"You mean, saying that she was afraid of them?"

"Or afraid of a commitment—maybe she'd turned a guy down?"

"We're assuming it was a guy who killed her."

"Maria says the killer was definitely a man."

"Who's Maria?"

"Um…Jack's new partner."

Hannah's eyebrows shot up. "Jack has a female partner?"

"Women can be detectives," Carlotta said haughtily.

"Yeah, I watch TV. Is she cute?"

Carlotta lifted one shoulder. "I suppose…if you're into the leggy, busty, exotic type."

Hannah pursed her mouth. "Ouch."

"Oh, and she's some kind of a profiler. Comes up with character sketches of people who commit crimes."

"Damn, she's smart, too?"

Carlotta scowled. "That remains to be seen. She didn't seem to think it was strange that on the same day Eva McCoy's charm bracelet was stolen, a dead woman turns up with a charm in her mouth."

"Is the chicken charm from the McCoy woman's infamous bracelet?"

"I don't think so. Her bracelet and the charms were gold. This charm was silver. Besides, the timing is wrong. Coop said this woman died sometime the previous night, but Eva's bracelet wasn't stolen until yesterday afternoon."

Hannah licked her fingers. "So it could be just a coincidence."

Carlotta almost choked on her quiche. "I thought you didn't believe in coincidence."

"I'm just saying that people have gone charm crazy, in case you haven't noticed. You can even buy charms at the convenience store when you pay for gas, for God's sake. Maybe this woman was into charms, and for some reason, the person who killed her just wanted to stuff this particular piece of jewelry down her throat."

"Maria said that was a possibility. She also said that maybe the person found her already dead and wanted to put something special in her mouth as a token of love."

"Yuck."

"No kidding."

"The police discussed all of this in front of you?"

Carlotta shifted in her chair. "I sort of...eavesdropped. The whole glass against the wall thing actually works, by the way."

"I'll bet this makes Coop look pretty good for finding something the M.E. missed," Hannah said, her eyes shining.

"Jack told me that Coop had already been asked to become more involved with cases at the morgue. And, yeah, I guess this kind of catch only helps his cause."

"Do you think he'll ever be Chief M.E. again?"

Remembering the bottle of vodka she'd found under the van seat, Carlotta pressed her lips together. "I'm not sure Coop would want that, even if it were possible."

Hannah nodded, chewing. "So...how are things between you and Richie Rich?"

"*Peter* took me to dinner last night," Carlotta said in a chiding voice. "And it was very nice."

"Nice? Having hot chocolate with my dotty old uncle Harold is nice."

"We're taking things slowly."

"If you ask me, you missed a chance to get rid of him. You should've let him move to New York."

Carlotta swallowed another bite of quiche then pushed her plate away. She hadn't told Hannah about her dad approaching her at the rest area in Florida or his message to stay close to Peter. "I owe it to myself to see if things can work between us."

"Whatever. I don't know what you see in him. I've spent my life around rich bastards like Peter Ashford and they exist only for themselves."

Hannah had never discussed her family or upbringing. Carlotta had always assumed she'd grown up in a troubled home. "You spent your life around rich bastards?"

"Catering to them, I mean."

"Oh." The chip on Hannah's shoulder toward wealthy people only reinforced Carlotta's suspicions that her friend had endured an unhappy childhood.

"So...Coop is still available?" Hannah asked in sly reference to the road trip that Carlotta had taken with the man Hannah had a crush on.

"As far as I know," Carlotta returned.

Hannah smiled. "Good. How's your arm?"

"I might have overdone it yesterday at work, but today should be quieter. I just can't wait to get this cast off."

"How much longer?"

"I have to go back to the doctor Friday for another X-ray. I'm hoping he'll say I'm strong enough to stop wearing it. There are some things I want to change around the house."

"Like what?"

Carlotta gestured to the walls of the oppressive dark red kitchen with gold-tone fixtures. "Like this room. My mother hated this house, and it didn't help that she was suffering from depression when she decorated it."

"I don't know—it's got that whole nineties vibe going." Hannah drank from her coffee cup. "What does Wes think about redecorating?"

"I didn't ask him. But this whole frozen-in-time thing has got to end."

"I don't disagree. How did his meeting go with the D.A. yesterday?"

"I've been told that the charges were reduced to a misdemeanor."

"You haven't talked to him?"

"We kept missing each other on the phone yesterday, but Jack knew the outcome. And I went to bed before Wesley got home." Carlotta had waited up as long as she could to talk to her brother about the missing pain pills. But in the end, exhaustion had won out.

And some part of her really didn't want to know.

"Speak of the devil," Hannah said as Wesley ambled into

the kitchen, dressed in jeans and an untucked long-sleeve dress shirt.

To hide the ugly scars in his arm left by The Carver, Carlotta thought. Her stomach pitched when she remembered the bloody, swollen aftermath.

"Hey," he said cheerfully. "Is there enough food for me?"

"Sure," Hannah said.

"Pull up a seat," Carlotta offered. "We were just talking about your meeting with the district attorney."

He grinned. "So you heard the good news?"

"Through the grapevine," Carlotta said sourly. "Why didn't you call me? I was worried sick."

"Sorry," he mumbled, removing the orange juice from the fridge. "I lost track of time. Besides, I thought you'd be busy. How was your first day back?"

"Not great."

"There was an incident," Hannah supplied. "And your sister wound up with cake on her face."

"I think the expression is 'egg on her face,'" Wesley offered.

"No, trust me, it was cake," Carlotta said. "So, you only have to do more community service?"

He poured a glass of juice, then sat down. "Yeah."

"And how's that going?" Hannah asked. "You're working in the city computer department, right?"

"Yeah. It's okay, I guess. They're a bunch of real geeks down there."

"So you must fit right in," Hannah said.

"Ha. I'm just putting in my time." He shoveled in a mouthful of quiche.

"Any chance they'll hire you?" Carlotta asked, drumming her fingers on the table. "If you're not going to work with

Coop anymore, you need to find something that pays. You still have your court fine and, uh, *other* debts, remember."

He looked up from his plate. "You don't think Coop is going to call me?"

She shook her head. "I went on a pickup with him last night. He's not angry, but he's not ready to work with you yet."

"Did you tell him the charges were reduced?"

"Yeah."

Wesley's expression was the same as when he was ten and some bully had taken his cookie at lunch. "What kind of body pickup did you go on?"

"A young woman in her home on the west side. Seemed like natural causes at first, but Coop thinks the woman was probably murdered."

"He's good at that," Wesley said. "Even the M.E. on the scene usually defers to him."

"I noticed."

"Is he going to hire someone to replace me?"

She nodded. "He already has someone in mind."

Wesley's mouth tightened. "I can't blame him. Anyway, I have another job."

Carlotta's eyes went wide. "Doing what?"

He chewed and chewed, then said, "Courier."

"Delivering packages on your bike?"

"Yeah."

"When do you start?"

"Soon."

Carlotta grinned. "That's good. So you're going to do your community service in the mornings and work as a courier in the afternoons?"

"And probably on weekends," he said through a mouthful.

"That's...great." Carlotta tried to quell her pleasure that he would be working every day. Maybe her little brother was finally growing up. He sure had enough grown-up problems. "Wes, do you know anything about a black SUV parked across the street?"

He lifted his orange juice glass. "No, what about it?"

"Jack noticed it when he gave me a ride home yesterday. And Mrs. Winningham mentioned seeing it, too. She said it comes and goes."

He pushed to his feet. "There are other people who live on this street, you know."

"None who seem to have our issues," Carlotta said drily.

Wesley drained his glass. "I'm outta here. Hannah, my man Chance is jonesing to go out with you."

Hannah rolled her eyes to the ceiling. "You mean Fat Boy?"

"He started working out."

"Wes, do your friend a favor and tell him he can't handle me."

Wes lifted his hands. "I tried, but I think he's in love or something."

Hannah hooted. "What a loser."

"He's not such a bad guy," Wesley said. "Think about it. He'd spend a shitload of money on you."

Hannah pursed her mouth. "Would he pay to finish the tattoo on my back?"

"Probably, if you let him watch."

"I'll think about it."

Carlotta gaped at her friend. "You can't be serious."

"What? I've dated guys for worse reasons."

Carlotta sighed. Who was she to judge? She was dating Peter to help her father.

"Later," Wesley said, then scooted out of the room, grabbing his backpack on the way through the living room.

Carlotta looked at Hannah. "I'll be right back." She

wiped her mouth on a napkin and followed Wesley through the house and out the front door.

"Hey, wait a minute," she called from the stoop.

Already halfway down the driveway, Wesley stopped and looked back. "I'm kind of in a hurry."

She walked down the steps. "This won't take long." Then she frowned and gestured to the garage. "Aren't you riding your bike?"

"I, uh, left it at Chance's."

"Oh. Do you need a ride to your office?"

"No. But thanks. What's up?"

"I need to talk to you about this." From her pocket she removed the Percocet prescription bottle and held it up.

"What about it?" His voice sounded innocent enough, but his Adam's apple bobbed.

"It's empty. And when I called the pharmacy to get a refill, I was told that both refills were used up."

"So?"

"Don't play dumb with me, Wesley."

He looked contrite. "Sorry. You're right, I took them, and I got the refills. You said you didn't need them and my arm was killing me." He wrapped his hand over the site of The Carver's handiwork. "I just needed something to take the edge off."

She softened toward him. "It's okay. I just wish you would've said something."

"I didn't want you to worry." Then he suddenly looked concerned. "Is your arm still bothering you?"

"It's nothing that over-the-counter painkillers can't take care of."

"Okay. Good." Wesley shifted his backpack on his shoulder. "Uh, I don't suppose you've heard from Dad again, have you?"

She shook her head.

"So what are we supposed to do?"

Carlotta inhaled for strength. "What we've been doing for over ten years—we wait. He said he'd be in touch."

"Do you believe him?"

"I..." She swallowed a mouthful of doubt. "Yes, I do."

His shoulders fell in obvious relief. "Me, too. And you'll tell me if you hear from him again, won't you?"

"Yes, I'll tell you." Then she gave him a pointed look. "Meanwhile, in case Pops decides to pop up, let's make a pact to stay out of trouble, okay?"

9

Wesley looked into his sister's dark brown eyes and had to squash the urge to laugh. A pact to stay out of trouble?

He was on the verge of illegally accessing the records of their father's criminal case through the city computer system. Chance was trying to get him into a poker game that would, if Wesley were caught, effectively violate his probation and land his ass in jail. And before the week was over, he'd be on the payroll of one of the most dangerous loan sharks in the city.

"Sure, Sis, no problem," he said, dropping a kiss on her cheek. Carlotta was beautiful, with their mother's great bone structure, dark complexion and knockout figure. No wonder Jack, Coop and Peter all leaked brain cells when they were around her. After Peter had bailed him out of a jam, Wesley had promised to put in a good word for him whenever he could, and to play interference between Carlotta and the other two men, but there was no pinning down his sister.

He actually felt sorry for the three guys. Even the one who was lucky enough to eventually snag her was doomed to a life of trying to keep up with her.

"I think I'll crash at Chance's tonight if that's okay. I told him I'd help him get ready for a math exam." In truth, they were going to play as many practice hands of poker as they could squeeze in. "I already fed Einstein."

She hesitated, but then nodded. "Okay, but be careful?" Her smile revealed the gap between her front teeth that he—and many others—found so endearing.

"Always," he said. "See you later." He turned and jogged across the lawn, feeling like he'd dodged a bullet where the Percocet was concerned. On top of all the other grief he'd caused his sister, the last thing he needed was for her to think he had a drug problem.

Not having a bike genuinely sucked, but at least a MARTA station wasn't too far away. He put in the earbuds for his iPod and made the hike, keeping an eye out for the mysterious black SUV that had been haunting the curb. He still didn't know who was behind the tinted glass, but he figured they'd make themselves known when they were ready.

The train platform at Lindbergh was crowded with morning commuters, but at least he didn't have to worry about running into Mouse. In Atlanta, loan sharks and far-flung suburbanites had one thing in common: they both shunned public transportation.

So for him and other people living ITP (Inside The Perimeter of the I-285 beltline), MARTA was a safe zone.

A few minutes later he boarded a packed train and grabbed an overhead bar, mulling the day ahead while sleep-deprived bodies leaned into him. The Oxy made him feel tolerant of the close quarters. If he stared at a fixed point, he could achieve a dreamlike state and imagine how good things were going to be one day.

His parents would come home and Randolph would be vindicated. They'd be a family again and work through their problems together. Things would go back to the way they used to be, when his parents were always laughing, hosting parties or going out to the club. They'd been the golden couple, beautiful and successful, the envy of their friends. The Wren family had been happy. And they would be again.

He'd stolen his dad's folder from Liz's client cabinet in her home office. Among the pieces of correspondence between client and attorney, he'd found a love note his father had written to Liz. When he'd confronted Liz with proof of her affair with his father, she'd said she'd been in love with Randolph, but that she'd accepted he would never leave Wesley's mother.

And after she'd admitted to the affair with his father, she and Wesley had had sex.

If his father returned, the situation could be…sticky.

Although the inevitable question had skated through his mind: Which Wren man would Liz prefer?

Wesley shook his head free of the sordid thought. There wouldn't be a choice because he planned to stop banging Liz. He'd really only started in order to gain access to the files in her home office anyway, and he'd seen those.

Before Liz had noticed the missing file and reclaimed it, he'd gotten the dates and case numbers he needed to build keys. Once fed into a computer program, he'd be able to retrieve his father's courthouse records. But it would take time to build more keys in ranges narrow enough to include his father's data, yet broad enough to pick up sufficient extraneous data that his father's info wouldn't stand out on a report to his supervisor or to auditors. And since he was doing all of it in conjunction with his official assignment of adding encryption to the database records, he'd have to adhere to the schedule already set up to run tests against the data.

So having hours added to his community service actually worked to his advantage—it would give him more time to make sure he gathered every bit of information linked to his dad's case.

He was supposed to call Detective Terry at the Midtown police precinct to set a time to powwow on how to best worm his way into The Carver's organization. It was only a matter of time before Mouse tracked him down again, so he wanted to be able to start laying a foundation.

Of lies.

And just in case Mouse circumvented him before Jack Terry worked out a plan, Wesley had two hundred sixty-seven dollars in his wallet. Mouse wouldn't be happy with such a paltry payment, but it would be enough for the man to let Wesley live.

He got off at the Garnett Station and walked the few blocks to the city hall building on Trinity Avenue. The Oxy made him feel like a million bucks, but it slowed him down a little. Still, the trade-off was worth it.

He trudged through security with everyone else, then climbed the stairs to the seventh floor of the seventeen-story structure where Atlanta Systems Services (fondly referred to as "ASS" by most of the employees), was housed under the umbrella of the city's Department of Information Technology. His heart was racing in anticipation of accessing his father's data.

His accelerated pulse had nothing to do with the fact that he'd see Meg today.

The ASS offices were aged and crammed with cobbled-together machines and cabled networks snaking over floors and up the walls of tweed-covered cubicles. The air carried the faint smell of burnt wiring and…he winced…BO?

When he turned the corner to his shared four-plex work-station, he saw the source of the stench—one of his station mates, Jeff Spooner, was sitting in front of his laptop wearing headphones and playing a game with a homemade joystick. An open foam container of wing bones and a half-empty two-litre bottle of Mountain Dew was next to the computer. Two crumpled bags of chips lay nearby, a half-eaten burrito, and a Moon Pie wrapper. A distinct funk surrounded the guy. His hair was rumpled and his Georgia Tech T-shirt was stained. Jeff glanced up and grinned, then lowered the headphones to his neck.

"Dude, I was here all night designing a new game. I think I'm on to something. It's a card game, but the characters on the back of the cards are at war, so it's two games going on at the same time!"

"Happy for you, dude," Wes replied, waving his hand back and forth. "But I got one word for you—*deodorant.* You better go sponge off in the men's room before Meg gets here."

Across from Jeff, Ravi Chopra, the germophobe, opened a drawer at his knee, removed a can of Lysol and began spraying the air.

"Hey, watch my food," Jeff said, spreading out his arms.

Wesley dropped his backpack on his desk and flipped on the computer the foursome had jerry-rigged for him from components they'd begged, borrowed and stolen from all over the department.

"Where were you yesterday?" Ravi asked Wesley. "Moving bodies?" The guy was morbidly fascinated by Wesley's job—constantly asking for gory details, yet appalled when he got them.

"Yeah," Wesley lied. "Didn't you hear about the pileup on I-20? Bodies everywhere, man. I spent the day scraping intestines off the asphalt with a metal spatula."

Jeff stared and Ravi retched over his garbage can.

"Don't believe him. He's a pathological liar," Meg said,

sliding into her chair holding a to-go cup of coffee, giving Wesley a pointed look. She wore wide-leg jeans, platform sandals and a vintage pink Izod shirt that was snug in all the right places. Rhinestones sparkled from the corners of her cat glasses and her hair was pulled back in a messy ponytail that was somehow sexy.

Wesley scratched the back of his neck. "I was just messing with you, Ravi. No need to lose your cookies, man."

Meg tossed Ravi a pack of saltine crackers from her desk drawer. He gave her an adoring look.

"Meg," Jeff said breathlessly, "you wanna see my new game?"

"No. And you'd better not let McCormick see it, either," Meg said, referring to their boss. "We all signed papers saying anything we develop using city resources becomes the property of the city, remember?"

Jeff looked panicked. "Even on our own time?"

"Yep." She tossed him a flash drive. "Download everything and I'll look at it on my Mac during lunch."

Jeff perked up. Like Ravi, he was head-over-heels in love with the brilliant, cool Meg.

Then she wrinkled her nose. "Meanwhile, Spooner, your work area is smelling a little ripe. Try to have it tidied up by the time Wes and I get back, okay?"

Wes straightened. "Where are we going?"

"McCormick's office." Her smile was flat. "Apparently I'm going to be working with you on encrypting the mainframe databases. Fun, huh?"

Wesley had to put on his poker face to keep from reacting with utter dismay. Meg was going to be looking over his shoulder while he tried to pinch his dad's files?

He was so screwed…and not in the good way.

10

Carlotta turned over the engine to the hateful Monte Carlo, but sighed in relief when it caught. Plus ten points.

"Okay, I'm sorry for some of the bad things I said about you," she muttered to the car.

She gave Hannah the thumbs-up and waved goodbye as her friend backed her refrigerated van down the driveway. When Carlotta pulled onto the road, she looked for the mysterious black SUV, but didn't see anything out of the ordinary up and down the tree-lined street. She depressed the gas, trying to put the matter out of her mind. At least her car was running.

And really, in the scheme of things, a temperamental vehicle was the least of her problems.

She was glad that she'd talked to Wesley about the pain-killers, glad he had come clean and that the explanation had made sense. Where that madman had cut his initials into Wesley's arm must have hurt like the devil, especially after it had gotten infected. Coop had given him antibiotics, but couldn't prescribe narcotics for him. She should've offered the rest of her pills to Wesley anyway.

Remembering how Coop had helped tend to Wesley's arm brought back other memories of their weekend in

Florida, and how close she and Coop had come to consummating their…friendship.

The thought of the bottle of vodka under his van seat kept coming back to her. She wasn't conceited enough to think that their bungled attempt at a romantic weekend had driven him back to the bottle, but if he was in trouble, she'd never forgive herself for not checking up on him.

Carlotta dialed his cell number, trying to think of a breezy message to leave in case he didn't answer. He did answer, though, on the third ring.

"Hello?" His voice sounded thick and groggy.

"Coop? It's Carlotta. I'm sorry—I woke you up, didn't I?"

"It's okay," he murmured. "Although I confess this isn't the way I'd hoped you'd wake me some morning."

She smiled into the phone. "Late night?"

"Yeah."

She heard rustling in the background and imagined that he was pushing his long body out of bed. "What did you do after you dropped me off?"

"I went back to the morgue. They're way behind. I thought I'd pitch in and help with some paperwork."

She pursed her mouth. If he was covering for a binge, it was a pretty uninspired alibi. "Paperwork, huh? Did you find out anything more about Shawna Whitt?"

"Won't know anything until the autopsy. I heard Dr. Abrams assure Jack over the phone that he'd handle it himself."

"I didn't see or hear anything about the murder on the news this morning."

"I think Jack wants to keep things hush-hush for now."

In the background, Carlotta could hear the sounds of coffee-making—beeping, the scrape of stoneware, a gurgle and a trickle of liquid. Was he simply having his morning coffee, or trying to neutralize a hangover?

"Not that it isn't good to hear your voice," Coop said, "but did you call just to get an update on our body from last night? You know how Jack feels about you getting involved with cases."

"I know." She squirmed in her seat. "Actually, I called because last night you seemed…I don't know, a little out of sorts. I was just checking on you."

"Oh. Well, thanks, but I'm fine."

He sounded surprised, even perplexed. Carlotta narrowed her eyes. Or maybe evasive? "Good," she replied.

They lapsed into an awkward silence and she wondered if he, too, was thinking of bad timing and missed opportunities.

Carlotta cleared her throat. "Although…don't you find it strange that on the same day Eva McCoy's charm bracelet is stolen, a woman is found dead with a charm in her mouth?"

"Uh-oh, here we go."

"I'm just saying."

He sighed. "Could be a coincidence."

"I suppose so," she groused.

The sound of him sipping from his coffee cup filtered over the line. "Carlotta, don't go looking for trouble."

"Now you sound like Jack."

"Maybe I'm trying a new tact."

"On that note," she said brightly, "I'll let you go."

"Okay," he said, as if he didn't want to hang up.

"Sorry I woke you."

"Hey, it's our thing."

She frowned. "What do you mean?"

He laughed, his voice gravelly. "You get me up, then leave me hanging."

She sighed. "Coop—"

"I'm not complaining. Call me anytime."

"Same here," she said, then remembered her promise to Peter and added, "if you need someone to go out on a pickup with you."

He made a rueful noise. "I'd probably get in big trouble if I went out and offed somebody just to create work, but with you on standby, it's tempting."

She rolled her eyes. "I'm hanging up now."

"Me, too. Bye."

Carlotta disconnected the phone call reluctantly, thinking about her original reason for calling Coop. If he was on the verge of drinking again, would he tell someone?

She could only hope.

Her mind turned back to Shawna Whitt and what had happened to the young woman. Coop's warning not to get involved sounded in her head, but could she help it if she was curious?

Traffic was amazingly light today, she realized, glancing at her watch. In fact, she even had time to stop at the public library.

Where curiosity was encouraged.

A few minutes later she pulled into the parking lot of the strikingly modern building in Buckhead. When she walked in, a lady at the information desk looked up and smiled.

"Hi. I remember you. You came in looking for information on strangulation a few weeks ago. I'm Lorraine."

"Hi, Lorraine. You have a good memory."

"How'd that information work out for you?"

Carlotta nodded. "Pretty well for all parties concerned, I think."

"How is your arm?"

"Almost healed, thanks."

"What can I do for you today?"

"I need to look up someone on the Internet."

Lorraine smiled. "Checking out someone you're dating?"

"Uh…close."

"Smart. And relatively easy. Right this way."

Within a few minutes, Lorraine had her seated in front of a computer with a search engine on her screen.

"Just type in the name and if there's anything public about the person, it'll pop up."

"Such as?"

"Mentions in articles, Web sites, all the community social networks like Facebook. And if you want to print out anything, just hit the print button and it will go to that machine," she said, pointing toward a printer in the corner.

Carlotta thanked her, and after Lorraine walked away, Carlotta typed in "Shawna Whitt."

There were pages and pages of returned hits, but most of them were for celebrities named *Shawna* or information on family trees for *Whitt*. She remembered a tip that Wesley had given her about putting quotes around two words you were looking for to appear together, so she tried that and got a few hits, but they were on Shawna Whitts in other parts of the country, and the world. But nothing on Shawna Whitt of Atlanta or Berkeley Heights.

Then for lack of anything better to do, Carlotta typed in combinations of the words *Shawna, Whitt, charm*, and *ATL*. She got a hit on a Web site that she recognized as one of the sites set up for the group calling themselves Charmers, fans of the charm bracelets promoted by Eva McCoy. The site featured the story on Eva McCoy, and video footage of her renowned comeback. Visitors could order their own Lucky Charm Bracelet, although they were currently on back order. And under a community chat area, Charmers could post first-person accounts about their experiences with their own charm bracelets and whatever bits about their lives they wanted to share. Among them were several entries by an SWHITT in ATL.

Carlotta's pulse pounded. Was it the same woman?

She couldn't access the content of the entries unless she registered as a member of the Web site, which took a few minutes, especially since her keyboarding skills weren't stellar and her arm twinged at being held at a typing angle. By the time she'd completed the registration process, she only had time to print the entries and stuff them in her purse before waving goodbye to Lorraine and running back to her car.

When she turned the key, the engine ground, sending alarm through her, but it finally caught and turned over. She goosed the gas pedal, frowning at the *whuppa, whuppa, whuppa* sound of the muscle car's big, loud engine.

When she'd "bought" the car on a lark to take to a party she was crashing, she'd intended to return it within the twenty-four-hour period allowed for a test drive. Only, she hadn't planned to be implicated in a murder and to have the car impounded past the time limit.

Like it or not, the car was hers. And since she owed more on it than it was worth, the Monte Carlo would remain her ride into the foreseeable future.

The drive to the Lenox Square mall was uneventful, thank goodness. She parked and jogged to Neiman's, noting with relief that she was only a few minutes late. She slid toward the employee break room to stash her purse, but as luck would have it, Lindy was standing outside the door with a clump of workmen who were affixing some kind of device to the door.

Lindy saw her and glanced at her watch with a frown. "I hope this tardiness doesn't become a new habit of yours."

"It won't," Carlotta said. "What's going on?"

"I thought it best to install a card reader so that only employees have access to the break room. After yesterday's incident, I'm not confident that an Employees Only sign will keep people out. But this means that everyone will need to keep their employee ID with them at all times."

Carlotta nodded. It would be less convenient, but safer. She went inside and stowed her purse in her locker, her mind swirling over the previous day's incident, which was all over the morning news. The public reaction was an outpouring of support for Eva McCoy. The networks replayed clips from the Olympics showing Eva in her legendary run. There were rumors that Eva herself was devastated by the loss, that she had cancelled her cross-country publicity tour in order to stay in Atlanta, and that a reward would be offered for the return of the charm bracelet. The overriding question that everyone kept asking was who would be low enough to steal something with such sentimental value? Although granted, Michael Lane's empty locker was a stark reminder of just how unstable people could be.

When she emerged from the break room, her boss was talking to Ben Newsome, of all people, and it seemed as if his mood had not improved much from the previous day. It was obvious he was asking about developments in the case of his girlfriend's missing bracelet. Lindy shook her head and made comforting gestures, but he looked unappeased.

Carlotta slid past them and went to her station, then threw herself into her work. The store was crowded with customers, so she was able to rack up some impressive sales before lunch even though her mind kept wandering back to the unread pages of entries from SWHITT on the Charmers Web site.

She considered calling Jack to tip him off to the Web

site, but she decided to wait to see if the contents were relevant. Especially since Jack was so touchy about her poking her nose into police business.

Hateful man.

It was especially hard to stay focused on work because everyone was abuzz about Eva McCoy's stolen charm bracelet. The jewelry department had been besieged with customers clamoring to reserve as many of the back-ordered Lucky Charm Bracelets as they could afford.

Patricia Alexander came stamping up to Carlotta, her posture rigid. "What does it say about the police department that they still haven't found the man who stole Eva McCoy's bracelet?"

Carlotta arched her eyebrows. "Maybe that they have more important cases to solve—like armed robberies and homicides?"

"I'm just saying that people should be safe when they shop, for God's sake."

"And we are…ninety-nine-point-nine percent of the time. If this guy wanted to get close to Eva McCoy, he was going to do it somewhere, somehow. It just happened to be here."

Patricia harrumphed. "All this attention—it's ridiculous. You should see the mob in the jewelry department."

"I have." Just as she suspected, Patricia was envious of the commissions being racked up that weren't falling her way. "How's it going in Shoes?"

"Slow," Patricia said with a sigh.

"It'll pick up," Carlotta said. "It always does. Meanwhile, I'm glad you got us both bracelets." She held hers up and jingled it. "They're the hottest accessory around at the moment."

Patricia fingered hers, looking dubious. "Maybe I should put mine on eBay."

"Give it a chance," Carlotta said. "You never know what's around the corner."

"Well, everyone knows what's around *your* corner," Patricia said in a sly tone.

Carlotta frowned. "What do you mean?"

"I talked to Tracey Lowenstein last night. She said she and Freddy ran into you and Peter having a romantic dinner."

Carlotta tried to sound casual. "We were having dinner, that's true."

"So…has Peter proposed?"

A shocked laugh escaped her. "No."

"Everyone thinks he will."

Carlotta set her jaw. "It's not everyone's business."

"Maybe that's what the champagne glasses on your charm bracelet are for."

She looked down and fingered the charm absently. The detail was remarkable—two flutes touching, overflowing with bubbly, but the implication…

"I need to get back to work. See you later." Carlotta walked away, stopping at a rack to straighten clothes that didn't need to be straightened. She didn't like being grist for the Buckhead gossip mill.

Although she had to admit that it gave her a little gloating thrill knowing that Tracey Tully Lowenstein was probably losing sleep over the thought of Carlotta Wren once again moving in her social circle.

Thankfully, the next few hours were so busy, she didn't have time to think about Tracey Lowenstein. And heaven knew she needed the commissions to start paying down some of her accumulated debt. She finally managed to take a break in the early afternoon. Her heart tripped in anticipation of reading the online entries she'd found.

After downing Advil for her aching arm, she grabbed

her purse and headed to the food court on the lower level where she settled in with a Diet Coke and a Snickers bar, poring over the sheets she'd printed out. Since she didn't post on Internet bulletin boards, she had trouble following the discussions at first, but finally sorted through the "threads" to pick up the gist of what was going on.

SWHITT had made only tentative postings at first, most of them unpunctuated monosyllabic words of encouragement and praise for items other women had posted—pictures of a beloved pet, a recipe, a new hairstyle. Gradually her postings had become more frequent and friendly as she had obviously grown more comfortable with other community members.

Her most significant posting was dated six days earlier and surrounded a question that someone had posted asking if and how the charm bracelet had changed lives. SWHITT had posted that she was using her bracelet to overcome her fear of trying new things.

One of the charms on my bracelet is of two hands intertwined. I'm tired of living all alone in my house, sleeping alone. I'm going to join one of those matchmaking services—can anyone suggest a good one?

A flurry of suggestions followed, and SWHITT responding with polite thanks, but not indicating which, if any, of the services she might try. Still, Carlotta's heart pounded with excitement—it was something.

"Carlotta?"

She looked up at the tall, dark-haired man approaching her table. He was broad-shouldered, handsome, and well-dressed. Her mind raced to remember where she knew him from. That perfect smile—

"Quinten Gallagher," he supplied at her hesitation. "I'm the receptionist at Mashburn & Tully. You visited a few weeks ago to meet Peter Ashford."

"Of course. I'm sorry—my mind was a million miles away. It's good to see you again."

He gestured. "I'm sorry, I interrupted your reading."

"I was finished," she said, refolding the pages and putting them in her purse. "Would you like to join me?"

"I only have a few minutes," he said, holding up a take-out bag. "I really just wanted to say hello."

"How are things at Mashburn & Tully?"

"Unbelievably dull," he said cheerfully. "When are you coming back?"

She angled her head. "Well, if you hadn't noticed, I'm not exactly welcome around there."

"Oh, I don't know. Mr. Ashford seemed pretty happy to see you."

"Peter is a good friend."

His eyebrows climbed. "He turned down the job in New York because you're such good friends?"

"You know about the job offer?"

"I know he was getting a lot of pressure from the partners to take it, but he seems really happy to be staying."

"I'm glad," she murmured.

"Me, too. Mr. Ashford has always been good to me. So, do you work nearby?"

"I work at Neiman's."

"My favorite place," he quipped. "I'll look for you the next time I'm in there, although considering how broke I am these days, that could be a while."

She laughed.

"Meanwhile, anytime you want to come by M&T, don't let Walt Tully and Brody Jones keep you away."

She cleared her throat. "My father used to be a partner at the firm."

He nodded. "I know. I've seen his name on documents and plaques around the office. I understand he had quite a celebrity investment roster."

She nodded. "He would sometimes let me bring my autograph book to the office." Then she smiled sheepishly. "I was a teenager then. The office has changed a lot since he…left. How long have you worked there?"

"About a year. I decided to go back to school to finish a law degree. M&T pays pretty well and they let me study when the desk is slow. I can't complain."

"Ah, law school. So that's why you're broke."

He winced and nodded. "Emory University isn't cheap."

"It'll be worth it," she said, experiencing an unexpected pang for the college degree she didn't have. Coop had once suggested that she could go back to school, but it had never seemed possible. Or desirable. But maybe someday…

"I'd better run," he said, nodding toward the exit. "Nice to see you again."

"You, too."

She waved, then disposed of her trash and headed back to the store. She patted her bag, excited about finding something that might prove helpful in the Shawna Whitt case. After her shift ended, she'd take the information to Jack. The autopsy results should be in soon. If the woman was murdered, the chat information might lead to her killer.

She'd learned that the smallest detail could lead to something big.

People packed the store in the afternoon, presumably seeking shelter from the suffocating heat in the air-conditioned mall. And at this time of year, everyone seemed to have a reason to shop—summer events, vacation travel, even early school shopping, especially for the people who sent their kids to boarding schools abroad.

After several of her regular clients commented on her arm cast and her absence, Carlotta realized how many people she knew and how much she'd missed her job. Not everyone was cut out for retail, but she liked the activity, the interaction…and the clothes.

Because when it came to clothes, nobody beat Neiman's.

She stopped to finger an exquisite Zac Posen jade-colored silk blouse with bishop sleeves. Her mouth literally watered from wanting it, but even with her employee discount, she couldn't afford the twelve-hundred-dollar price tag. The sensuous gray houndstooth wide-leg pants displayed with the blouse were a cool thousand. But the fabrics, the fit and the finishing details were superb.

Her mother had taught her an appreciation for fine workmanship in clothes, that details like covered seams, quality linings and bias-cut fabrics made for a beautiful fit and a long-lasting garment.

"Remember that people who look good in this world get noticed and command respect," Valerie had told her over and over.

She often wondered how her mother had fared over the years without a fat bank account and no-limit credit cards to buy all the things she needed to satisfy her expensive taste in clothing and jewelry.

How ironic that Carlotta's knowledge of luxury goods had been her salvation when her parents had abandoned her and Wesley. Knowing the difference between satin acetate and silk charmeuse, between Jordache and J Brand jeans, had served her well. Despite having only a high school education, she'd been able to make a decent living in high-end retail.

The only problem was that it put her in direct contact with the things she couldn't afford. The buttery soft silk blouse sighed under her touch. Not long ago she would've bought it, used her tricks of the trade to wear it once to some spectacular event that she and Hannah would crash together, then return it, with tags intact and no one the wiser.

But she'd been scared straight, so to speak, after crashing an upscale pajama party only to find herself at the bottom of a pool wearing several thousand dollars' worth of silk loungewear she'd "borrowed," using her store credit card.

Carlotta shook her head in self-recrimination. The reason she couldn't be too upset with Wesley over his gambling debts to two loan sharks was because she hadn't been the best role model where money was concerned. She and Wesley had been raised with everything they'd wanted—the best of the best. Old habits had died hard and both had learned the painful lesson that a few minutes of pleasure wasn't worth the months or years it would take to pay it off.

She looked up and saw a woman in her section browsing. Carlotta automatically smiled and offered assistance. When the redhead looked up, however, she seemed familiar.

"Hi, you're Carlotta Wren, right?"

"And you are?"

"Rainie Stephens, *Atlanta Journal-Constitution*."

Carlotta's guard went up. "Yes, I remember you from yesterday's event."

"Same here," the woman said, then nodded to Carlotta's cast. "Did you injure your arm?"

"No. This was a previous injury."

"From the fall over the balcony at the Fox Theatre?"

Carlotta's cheeks warmed. "Oh. I guess you would know about that, wouldn't you?"

"Yes. And you should know that if not for me, a picture of you covered in cake and icing would've been in the paper this morning."

Carlotta winced. "Thank you."

The woman smiled. She was pretty, with bright, intelligent eyes. "I was hoping you'd be grateful enough to answer a few questions."

"About what?"

"I saw you talking to Eva, working next to her. Did she share any information with you?"

Carlotta frowned. "Like?"

"Like that she was being stalked?"

"No, nothing like that. She just said that big events made her uncomfortable."

"She didn't say why?"

"No. I sensed that she's a private person."

Rainie smiled and nodded. "Okay, fair enough. I understand that you sometimes work as a body hauler for the morgue?"

Carlotta looked all around to make sure none of her co-workers were within earshot. "Occasionally."

"Last night?"

Carlotta swallowed. "Yes."

"What can you tell me about the woman's body discovered with a charm in her mouth?"

"How do you know—" Carlotta caught herself. "I mean, I can't tell you anything about anything. You should talk to the police."

Rainie made a face. "They're not being very communicative."

"Perhaps with good reason."

"Perhaps," the woman conceded. "But if there's some kind of wacko killer on the loose, don't you think the people of Atlanta deserve to know about it?"

"Wacko killer on the loose?" Carlotta gave a little laugh. "I think you're exaggerating. If there was cause for alarm, I'm sure the police would issue a statement."

Rainie made a dubious noise and pulled a business card out of her bag. "Here's my card. Just hang on to it. If you're privy to something that you think I should know about, call me. My sources are protected."

"I don't think—"

"Just in case," Rainie said, folding the card into her hand. "As a favor to me for squashing the cake-face photo?"

Carlotta nodded uncomfortably and slid the card into her pocket. A customer walked up with a question and Carlotta gestured a goodbye to the reporter to attend to the sale. But as she assisted the customer in finding an outfit for a summer wedding, the conversation with Rainie Stephens played over in her mind. Clearly she thought there was some connection between Eva McCoy's bracelet being stolen and the charm left in the mouth of the Whitt woman.

She wondered briefly who could've told the Stephens woman about the charm, but there were lots of morgue employees who had access to forms and photos. She supposed it wasn't unusual for a reporter to have an inside source.

After she bagged the customer's items and handed them over with an appreciative smile, the phone at her counter pealed an internal ringtone. She picked up the receiver. "This is Carlotta, how may I be of service?"

"Carlotta, it's Lindy. I need for you to come to my office, please."

Carlotta frowned. "Right now?"

"Yes. I'm afraid it's rather urgent."

11

Adrenaline pumped through Carlotta's body as she hurried to Lindy's office. Obviously something was wrong. Regarding the Eva McCoy event? Concerning her own tardiness and general bad karma? Had her boss discovered Carlotta was moonlighting as a body mover? Was her car on fire in the parking lot?

Losing the Monte Carlo would be a bright spot, but the other possibilities were both varied and disturbing. And when she walked in to see Jack and Maria standing there, her heart vaulted to her throat. "Is Wesley okay?"

"He's fine," Jack said, raising his hand in assurance.

She exhaled in relief. "Is this about Eva McCoy's bracelet? Did you find out anything from the surveillance tapes?"

"No," Maria said. "They were too blurry for the level of detail we needed."

Carlotta glanced at her boss, whose expression was stark. "What's going on?"

"Michael Lane escaped from the psych ward," Lindy said.

Carlotta gasped. "When?"

Jack jammed his hands on his hips. "That's not exactly clear, but possibly as early as the day before yesterday."

"You don't know where he is?"

Jack shook his head. "Has he contacted you?"

"Of course not. I would've notified someone right away."

"The police are afraid he'll try to see you," Lindy said.

"According to Mr. Lane's psychiatrist," Maria offered, "he harbors a great deal of resentment toward you."

"He tried to kill you before," Jack said. "If he has the opportunity, he might try to finish the job."

She swallowed hard. "So what am I supposed to do?"

"The detectives are going to make sure you get home safely and check things there," Lindy said.

"What about the black SUV I saw sitting by the curb yesterday?" Jack asked. "Could it have been him?"

Carlotta shot a nervous glance toward Lindy. She didn't want the woman knowing all the sordid things going on in and around the Wren household. "I don't think so. My neighbor said she'd been seeing it for a couple of weeks."

"What about the man with the cake yesterday?" Maria asked. "Could it have been Michael Lane?"

Carlotta stopped, her mind rewinding to the man's face. She closed her eyes and put her hand to her forehead. "I don't know. The height is about right…and the build. Michael had dark hair, but the guy yesterday was wearing a fake mustache… Maybe he was wearing a wig, too, under the hat."

"You didn't mention a wig yesterday," Maria said.

Carlotta frowned. "Or maybe not, I don't remember. Perhaps someone else will."

"But it could've been Michael Lane?"

"Maybe."

"Which might explain why he mowed you over with the cart," Maria said.

Carlotta straightened. "Well, he didn't exactly mow me over—"

"Right," Jack cut in. "We were thinking the guy was

trying to get close to Eva McCoy, but maybe he was trying to get close to Carlotta."

Carlotta frowned. "If it was Michael, don't you think it was a pretty elaborate ruse just to get to me? And do what—put me in a sugar coma?"

"He had a tool of some kind," Jack reminded her.

"He could've had a knife," Maria added. "Do you remember seeing one?"

Carlotta replayed the episode in her head, but it had happened so quickly, and her memory was already getting fuzzy. "I don't remember either way."

"Do you know anywhere Lane might go?" Jack asked. "What about his apartment?"

"His landlord said it's been rented out, but no one's seen him on the property."

"Michael and I didn't hang out a lot. We mostly saw each other here at work. There's a coffee shop here in the mall he liked."

"Michael's picture has been distributed to mall security," Lindy said. "And we'll inform the other store employees in case he shows up here. I know you have some time left on your shift, but we all think it's a good idea if you go home now. I'll have Patricia work your area until closing."

Carlotta bit back a smart remark—this was no time to be worried about her sales commissions. "Can I come back to work tomorrow?"

"That's up to you," Lindy said.

"Hopefully all of this will be resolved before tomorrow," Jack said. "We have a lot of people looking for Lane."

Carlotta nodded numbly. "I need to stop by the break room to pick up my things."

The two detectives followed her out of the office, Jack walking in front and Maria behind. Being sandwiched between them as they made their way through the store made Carlotta feel conspicuous and nervous. "You're not sure when Michael escaped?"

"No," Jack said. "He was being transported to a facility in Milledgeville. It's not clear if he ever left Northside Hospital, or if he escaped once he reached Milledgeville." Jack's voice was tight and he kept turning to look her over as if he were afraid something had happened to her and she hadn't told him about it. It made her feel all warm inside.

It wasn't lost on her that she and Jack always seemed to be the most attracted to each other when danger was involved.

Then Maria strode up next to her and Carlotta pursed her mouth—except now they were a threesome.

They escorted her to the break room, where she swiped her ID card for the first time to gain access. Once inside, she pulled her purse from her locker and thought about the papers inside that she'd printed at the library, but decided it wasn't the right time to bring up the Shawna Whitt case.

Carlotta caught her reflection in the mirror and acknowledged she looked pale. And scared. The night that Michael had thrown her over the balcony at the Fox Theatre, she could've fallen to her death on the seats below. She'd uncovered Michael's scheme of plotting with members of his therapy group to steal identities—hers included. And he'd been determined she wasn't going to live to tell anyone about it.

She massaged her healing arm that suddenly thrummed with pain. When the curtain she'd grabbed on the way over the balcony had finally given way, she'd been lucky that Jack had broken her fall—her injuries might've been much worse. And Michael's betrayal had cut deep.

She chased a couple of ibuprofen gel capsules with a swallow of water from a bottle, pinched her cheeks to add a little color, then closed the locker door. She emerged from the break room and threaded through the aisles flanked by her personal security detail. The store was still thick with customers, and Carlotta found herself studying each face, expecting to see Michael Lane at every turn.

"We're parked outside this exit," Jack said, pointing. "We'll drive you to your car and follow you home."

With a sense of déjà vu, she followed them to Jack's dark sedan and slid into the backseat.

"Where are you parked?" Jack asked after he and Maria were settled in the front.

Carlotta pointed the way, then decided to take her chances with her question while Jack seemed protective toward her.

A girl had to push her advantage when she had one.

"Have you gotten the results back from the Whitt woman's autopsy?" she asked, feigning interest in her do-it-yourself manicure. Once Jack caught wind of her fascination with the case, he'd clam up.

"Not yet," he tossed over his shoulder.

"Any leads on the chicken charm?"

"We lifted a partial print from it—but it's smudged, probably unusable."

Maria shot him a questioning look. "Jack, should you really be discussing a case?"

From the backseat, Carlotta shot imaginary fireballs with her eyes into the woman's ridiculously thick, luxurious hair to give her split ends.

Jack gave a dismissive wave as he pulled up behind the Monte Carlo. "Carlotta thinks she's Nancy Drew. I've learned to humor her with a detail or two."

Carlotta glared at him. "Just for that, Ned Nickerson, I have a clue in the Shawna Whitt case and I'm not going to share it."

Jack's dark eyebrows knitted as he put the sedan in Park. "Who's Ned Nickerson?"

"He was Nancy's boyfriend," Maria offered.

Carlotta rolled her eyes. "He's wasn't really her boyfriend." She opened the door and climbed out, rummaging for her keys.

Jack got out and walked up to her car, peering inside. He waved, seemingly satisfied that Michael Lane wasn't lying in wait for her.

She slid behind the wheel and slammed the door, but when she turned the key, the only sound she heard was a clicking noise.

The battery was dead again.

Minus ten points.

She banged on the steering wheel, then rolled down her window and glanced up at Jack. "Will you give me another jump?"

One side of his mouth pulled back in a smile, then he nodded toward the sedan. "Come on, we'll take you home. You can get your car later."

Sullen, she locked her lifeless vehicle and gave the tire a kick as she walked past it. "Stupid redneck car."

"Hey, don't be abusing the Super Sport," Jack scolded. "I would've killed for that car when I was a teenager."

"Exactly," she said drily, then reclaimed her place in the backseat of Jack's life—er, car.

In the front seat Maria was on the phone, and her tone sounded official. By the time Jack fastened his seat belt and set the car in motion, she was hanging up. "That was the medical examiner," she murmured to Jack.

Carlotta's ears perked up and Jack caught her glance in the rearview mirror. "I don't suppose it'll do any good to ask you to close your ears?"

She shook her head.

He sighed, then looked back to Maria. "Was Abrams calling about the Whitt woman?"

"Yes."

"And the cause of death?"

"Natural causes. Said she had a heart attack—case closed."

Carlotta shot forward. "But what about the charm in her mouth?"

Maria lifted her shoulders in a philosophical shrug. "People have all kinds of oral fixations. Maybe she just liked to chew on things."

"That's bizarre."

"Believe me," the detective said, "I've seen more people die with strange things in their mouths than people who were murdered. I remember one lady who had change for a dollar in her mouth in quarters, dimes and nickels. And one guy who liked to suck on nine-volt batteries."

"But Coop said it was placed in her mouth postmortem," Carlotta argued.

"Guess Coop was wrong this time," Jack said. "There were no signs of forced entry, the house was locked when the uniforms arrived, and all the prints CSI lifted were the vic's. We were just waiting for confirmation from the M.E."

Carlotta slowly sat back in the seat, her mind on Coop's performance and the hidden bottle of vodka. Coop had been reserved when he'd picked her up. Something about his demeanor had seemed "off," but she'd chalked it up to the personal tension between them. He'd said he needed her as a witness for the pickup—had he been drinking and was perhaps afraid he'd do something wrong at the scene?

"Didn't mean to burst your bubble," Jack said, his tone sarcastic. "I know how much you think of the good doctor."

"Coop *is* a good doctor," she murmured, then stared out

the window while Jack and Maria talked shop—schedules, lab work…Maria's problem with her garbage disposal.

"I can take a look at it sometime," Jack offered.

"I'd appreciate it."

Carlotta bristled at their familiarity, but rather than listening to their domestic banter, she pulled the sheets of paper out of her purse and glanced over them, rereading the words that Shawna Whitt had written. It was sad to think of the young woman, not much older than herself, sitting at her computer—perhaps at work—typing in plans for jump-starting her life and meeting someone, only to die a few days later. Had Shawna known she had a heart condition? Is that what had made the woman, by her own admission, tentative?

Carlotta closed her eyes briefly. Life was so short. She was glad, of course, that the Whitt woman hadn't been done in by some random psycho, yet she suspected the reporter Rainie Stephens would be disappointed.

Although with Michael Lane escaped, she might have her wacko-killer-on-the-loose story after all. "Does the media know about Michael?" she asked.

"We didn't call them, but frankly, there were so many people involved in the transport at both facilities, I'll be surprised if we don't hear about it on the eleven o'clock news."

Jack wheeled into her driveway. "Is Wesley home?"

"No. He's spending the night with his friend Chance."

"I don't suppose you've installed an alarm in the house recently?"

"No."

He sighed. "Do you have anything to protect yourself with?"

"My wits," she said cheerfully.

"Yeah, that's comforting." He climbed out of the car,

turning to scan the area. "You two stay here. I'm going to look around."

He closed the door, effectively sealing her in the car with Maria, who was also looking all around, checking the side mirrors. Carlotta used the opportunity to study the woman from an unobtrusive vantage point. Her dark suit and pin-striped shirt were of equally good quality as yesterday's outfit. Her makeup was high-end—probably La Prairie or Dior. Her earrings were David Yurman, and the watch that peeked out from under her sleeve was a Rolex Super President, meaning the sparkly stones weren't cubic zirconia.

Hmm…this was getting curiouser and curiouser.

Carlotta felt as if she should make small talk, but she held back. A part of her didn't want to become friendly with this woman, and she could feel a similar vibe coming from the detective. The silence in the car grew oppressive.

Finally, Carlotta cleared her throat. "Do you really think Michael Lane will come after me?"

"Unfortunately, it does fit his profile."

"What do you mean?"

Maria turned in her seat to face Carlotta. "Michael Lane is a narcissist. In his mind, he's the only person who matters. Everyone around him serves a purpose, which is simply to further his interests. You can testify against him. If he gets rid of you, in his mind, his problems are solved."

"I was told there might not even be a trial."

"That's true—he was being moved to Milledgeville for evaluation to see if he's competent to stand trial. But most narcissists are obsessive-compulsive. He doesn't stop to consider what would happen to him if he actually killed you. He sees you as a loose end to tie up, nothing more."

Carlotta swallowed hard. "How can you say that? You've never even met Michael."

Maria turned back around, facing forward. "I don't have to meet him. I read his file and I've met a hundred men just like him."

"Do you think he'd hurt someone else, someone random?"

"If he thought the person was in his way, absolutely. He'd do whatever he had to do to succeed."

"Maybe he's just trying to leave town," she suggested. "People do that all the time, just disappear and are never heard from again."

"Yeah, I know." Maria made a rueful noise and turned her head back toward Carlotta. "Jack told me about your parents. I'm sorry."

She sucked in a painful breath. Most of Atlanta, as well as anyone else in the country who happened to be watching CNN at the time it had happened, knew about the Wrens taking flight. Why did it sting so much that Maria Marquez knew? Carlotta's face burned as she imagined Jack and Maria talking about her…feeling sorry for her.

"But Michael Lane isn't going to just disappear," Maria continued without missing a beat. "What the narcissist hates most is being exposed. In his mind, he can restore his reputation if he gets rid of you."

At a knock on the window, Carlotta nearly jumped off the seat, but it was only Jack. He opened the door. "All clear."

They walked her to the front door where Jack took her keys and unlocked the door. "Stay here." Then he walked into the house that he knew so well.

He'd searched it when he'd first arrested Wesley for hacking into the city's computer system. And he'd stayed with her when she'd agreed to fake her own death for the D.A. to try to lure her parents home.

She winced when she thought of the mess in her bedroom…but then Jack was better acquainted with her bedroom than any other room in the house, and he'd contributed to that mess on an occasion…or three.

Jack reappeared at the door. "All's clear. Come on in."

Carlotta turned to Maria. "Thanks for the escort."

Maria glanced at Jack pointedly.

"Uh, Carlotta," Jack said. "Maria's going to stay with you for a few hours."

Carlotta lifted her eyebrows. "Stay…here?"

"Just until we get a line on this guy," he said. "Come on, don't fight me on this. I need to go take care of a couple of things, then I'll come back and Maria and I will trade off… Okay?"

Carlotta turned back to Maria, who looked about as excited about her assignment as Carlotta felt. But they were both obligated to do what Jack said.

Resigned, Carlotta fabricated a smile. "Welcome to the Wren house, Detective Marquez, where you never know what's going to happen. By the way, how do you feel about snakes?"

12

When Carlotta realized that she and Maria were both standing in the hall watching Jack drive away, she abruptly closed the door.

To her credit, Maria didn't ask about the pitiful aluminum Christmas tree sitting in the corner of the living room—although Jack might have already informed the woman of the family, um, *quirk*.

Carlotta wondered if he'd also mentioned that when he was staying at their house, he'd unwrapped and rewrapped the gifts underneath the tree from their parents that she and Wesley had never opened. She'd discovered the betrayal when she'd noticed the brittle, yellowed tape had been replaced with new. When confronted, Jack had defended himself by saying the police should've opened the gifts when her parents' disappearance had first been investigated. But at the time, his actions had stung.

Exacerbated by the fact that he wouldn't tell her what was in the gifts.

She gave Maria the nickel tour, pointing out her room, then Wesley's directly across the hallway from hers, and referencing "an extra bedroom" at the end of the hall. She didn't find it necessary to add that it was her parents' room and had been left intact since they'd vamoosed. "The extra bedroom has a door that leads out onto the back deck, but we don't use it. It stays dead-bolted."

She led Maria to the kitchen, gesturing to another back door. "We have a small yard in the back. It's not much," she said with a sigh, "but the good news is that it'll be paid for in twenty or thirty years."

Maria smiled. "I like it. It's very homey."

"Sorry about the mess," Carlotta said, gesturing to the table. The remnants from this morning's quiche breakfast still lingered. She chastised herself for not taking fifteen minutes to clean up before she and Hannah had left. "Coffee?" she asked, crossing to the coffeemaker. "I'm afraid I don't have any cream."

"Yes, thank you. And black is fine."

She busied herself making coffee, trying not to worry about what the woman would think of the shabby town house. It gave her more incentive to get serious about doing some remodeling. She and Wesley could both use a change of scenery.

"Do you mind if I work here?" Maria asked, nodding to the breakfast bar. "I brought my laptop to catch up on paperwork."

"No, go ahead." From beneath her lashes, she watched the woman unpack her Hartmann computer bag with sure, deft movements. She was so polished, so accomplished. Smart and tough, but beautiful, too. Envy stabbed Carlotta's chest, along with dismay. Jack was bound to fall for Maria, if he hadn't already.

Carlotta was half in love with her herself, and she was straight.

She filled two mugs with coffee and carried them to the breakfast bar, setting one within Maria's reach.

"Thanks," the detective said. "And don't mind me—do whatever you need to do."

Carlotta took a drink from her cup, then opened the dishwasher and began clearing the table. Her arm twinkled with occasional pangs, but it wasn't too bad.

"I like your skirt," Maria said.

Carlotta smoothed a hand over the cream-colored jacquard fabric of the tulip-style skirt. "Thanks."

"I worked at Neiman's when I was in college," Maria offered, then grinned. "Although most of my salary went toward clothes instead of tuition."

"I know what you mean," Carlotta murmured, wondering if the woman realized how the offhand comment that she'd worked retail as a part-time job in her youth was a barb to Carlotta's ego.

"So," Maria said. "You and Jack."

Carlotta dropped a plate on the floor and winced when it broke into three neat pieces. She picked them up and carried them to the trash can. "Me and Jack what?"

Maria shrugged. "That's just it. I can't figure out your relationship."

Carlotta shook her head. "Nothing to figure out—we're friends. Maybe not even friends. More like…good acquaintance. He arrested my brother, Wesley, for computer hacking, so we didn't exactly meet under the best of circumstances."

"But he seems very protective of you."

"Jack's from Alabama—that's how boys are raised over there. And if you hadn't noticed, I seem to attract more than my fair share of trouble."

"And he's also working on your father's case?"

Carlotta nodded slowly. "When he has time, and whenever there are leads."

"That must be a bone of contention between the two of you."

"Not really," she lied. "Jack does his thing, I do mine."

"He said you have a boyfriend?"

"I wouldn't call Peter my boyfriend, but okay." Carlotta closed the dishwasher door and rolled her arm to ease the ache. "So, what's your story?"

Maria smiled. "I don't have a story."

"Really?" Carlotta nodded toward the woman's hand. "Since when can a cop afford a ten-thousand-dollar watch?"

Her smile deepened. "You have a good eye." But she didn't seem inclined to offer an explanation.

"Are you married?"

"No. But then surely you noticed that I'm not wearing a ring."

"That doesn't mean anything these days." When Maria didn't respond, Carlotta assumed the woman had run out of conversation, and turned to leave the room.

"I *was* married," Maria said in a strained voice. "But that's over."

"I'm sorry," Carlotta murmured.

The woman shook her head. "Don't be. I came here for a fresh start. Smaller city, better weather. And the APD didn't have a full-time profiler, so it was a good fit all around."

"What does a profiler do exactly?"

The tall woman picked up the coffee cup and sat back on the stool she occupied. She seemed more relaxed with the topic focused on her work. "If there's an unsolved crime and the police don't have any leads, I study the crime and the victim and come up with a general profile of the perp that might help lead the investigation in a new direction, or help the officers ask the right types of questions of witnesses and suspects. A profile also gives them a better idea of how to handle the suspect once an arrest has been made."

"Sounds complex," Carlotta offered, unabashedly in awe of the woman.

"It is. Profiling is equal parts case experience, psychology and intuition. But I enjoy the challenge."

"And you're good at it?"

Maria smiled. "Yes, I'm good at it."

Another pang of envy zigzagged through Carlotta. "I guess that means you can tell a lot about a person just from meeting them."

"Usually."

"I can't imagine what you must think of me."

"Honestly?"

"Sure—why not?"

"Okay." Maria studied Carlotta head to toe while she sipped from her cup. Just when Carlotta started to get uncomfortable, Maria leaned forward into the bar.

"You have a good work ethic, but you aren't challenged enough on your job, which is why you like to get involved in police work. You don't trust easily, you live above your means and you're impulsive. You're also loyal, kind and you have a strong sense of justice. And when you give your heart to a man, it'll be all or nothing." The woman angled her head. "You're also dying for a cigarette right now. How did I do?"

Carlotta swallowed the coffee she'd been holding in her mouth. "You're better than a *Cosmo* quiz. How did you know about the cigarette? Do I have a hand tic? Shallow breathing?"

"No." The woman laughed. "Because I'm dying for one, too."

Carlotta was already on her feet. "Is it okay if we step out on the deck? I don't like to smoke inside."

"As long as we're careful and keep an eye out."

"Menthol okay?"

"I've got my own, but thanks."

They stepped out the kitchen door that led to the small deck that squatted on their weedy little patch of backyard. Maria looked all around and positioned herself so that she was closer to the edge and Carlotta was closer to the door. As they lit their cigarettes, Carlotta felt a grudging sense of liking for the woman beginning to bloom.

Maria nodded to the colorful children's wading pool that took up most of one end of the deck.

"Do you or your brother have children?"

"No, thank God," Carlotta said with a laugh. "Wesley got the pool for me. It's kind of an inside joke." He'd said it was to make up for the pool she might have had if she hadn't been saddled with him to raise—if she'd married Peter, who had a big house, with a pool. And a pool house.

"That's nice. I'm not close to my siblings," Maria said.

Carlotta drew on her cigarette, then exhaled. "Wesley's done some stupid things, but he's basically a good guy. He's so smart, it's scary. I just hope he finds a way to channel it. I'd love to go back to school." She caught herself. "I mean, I'd love for *Wesley* to go back to school."

"How old is he?"

"Nineteen."

Maria exhaled a thin stream of white smoke. "Is there anything dumber than a nineteen-year-old man?"

"A twenty-year-old man?"

The detective laughed. "Or a forty-year-old man?"

Carlotta took another drag on her cigarette and exhaled. "So...*you* and Jack."

Maria arched beautiful eyebrows that were several shades darker than her light brown hair. "Me and Jack what?"

"Come on, you're both single and…not ugly."

The detective tapped her ash over the side into the grass. "I don't need that kind of grief. Besides…it's obvious where Jack's arrow points."

Before Carlotta could respond, Maria's phone rang. She removed it from her belt, but when she glanced at the display, her lips parted and something akin to fear crossed her face. She stabbed a button to silence the ring, then jammed the phone back into its holder.

"Your phone must ring constantly," Carlotta said breezily.

"Yes." Maria sucked on her cigarette as if it were a lifeline. When she exhaled, the smoke came out in little staccato puffs.

The phone call had obviously upset the woman. She paced back and forth, looking off into the distance. When the phone rang again, she tensed noticeably. She yanked out the phone and looked at the display. Her mouth tightened, then she murmured, "Excuse me, I need to get this."

Carlotta snubbed out her cigarette. "I should start some laundry." She walked to the door.

"I'll be right in," Maria said, turning her back. She punched a key on her phone, then brought it to her mouth and said, "How did you get this number? I told you to never call me again!"

Carlotta slid the door closed quietly, watching the detective with concern. Maria's body language was rigid and angry as she talked into the phone. The ex-husband, perhaps? Or an ex-boyfriend? Or a relative?

She knew too well how family could make you crazy.

Since she was going to be housebound for a while, she decided to tackle a few domestic chores. She put a load of towels in the washer, then went to her bedroom to change from skirt and blouse to jeans and a camisole. When she folded the skirt, the business card that Rainie Stephens had given her fell to the floor. Carlotta retrieved it and started to toss it, then changed her mind and tucked it into a corner of the mirror on her dresser.

One never knew when a contact with a reporter might come in handy.

As she unhooked the charm bracelet from her wrist, she studied each charm, marveling over the effect the bracelets had on people. She stopped on the champagne glasses charm and smiled ruefully. She knew the real power of the trinkets was the power of suggestion. But admittedly, there was something appealing about the idea of predicting one's future.

Then she gave a dry little laugh. The only thing in her immediate future was ammonia fumes. She gathered cleaning supplies, and headed to the kitchen for rubber gloves.

Maria came inside a few minutes later, her gaze averted and her mood brooding. She reclaimed the stool at the breakfast bar and worked on her laptop. Sensing the woman didn't want to talk, Carlotta tuned into a light rock music station on the television to fill the silence, then threw herself into her chores. It took her thirty minutes to clear her bed of the clothing and accessories she'd tossed there, and another thirty minutes to clean her bathroom. Feeling generous, she went into Wesley's bedroom to clean his bathroom, too.

Carlotta only glanced at the fifty-gallon aquarium in the corner that held his black-and-gray spotted axanthic ball python to make sure it was still in captivity. Who knew when Wes had begged for the reptile when he was fourteen, that it would grow to be six feet long? It had escaped from its home only once, but that in-bed encounter was burned into Carlotta's nerve endings. Just the sight of the python made her shudder.

She took in Wesley's hastily made bed as she walked into his bathroom, thinking she was lucky her brother was halfway neat and had always pitched in around the house. When he was twelve, God love him, he'd pretty much taken over all the kitchen duties, developing into a better cook than she could've ever been.

But it had been ages since they'd sat down to dinner together.

She snapped on yellow rubber gloves and raised the commode lid for a good scrubbing. She'd never once seen her mother clean a commode, and wondered wryly if Valerie had ever learned.

While she was leaned over, she spotted something on the tile floor—a pale-colored pill with a group of letters and numbers imprinted into it. She stripped her glove and picked up the tablet, frowning. It wasn't one of the Percocet pills from her prescription bottle. It could be some kind of over-the-counter medication.

She pressed her lips together. Or not.

Telling herself she wasn't being a snoop, she opened his medicine cabinet, and a package of condoms fell out onto the vanity. Carlotta shook her head—at least he was being careful.

With Liz Fischer, who was almost old enough to be his mother.

The cabinet contained typical fare: Band-Aids and alcohol, Q-tips and lotion, disposable razors and shaving cream. She smiled to see a can of one of those teen male body sprays that were touted as making women want to attack you. The seal was still on the can.

She found aspirin and a bottle of vitamins, neither of which matched the pill she'd found. She returned the condoms and closed the medicine cabinet, then tucked the tablet into her pocket. She'd decide what to do about it later.

After all, her body was growing accustomed to a baseline of stress that she felt obligated to maintain.

When she emerged from Wesley's room, she was surprised to see that it was growing dark outside. She flipped on a couple of lights as she made her way back to the kitchen where Maria was working. The detective was just closing her cell phone.

"That was Jack, he's on his way."

"Any news on Michael?"

"Afraid not." Maria wasn't making eye contact, fussing with her laptop and putting away files she had spread on the breakfast bar. She still seemed distracted, perhaps preoccupied with her previous call. Her phone sat on the counter. She kept looking at it as if she was afraid it was going to ring.

Carlotta ran her thumb over the tiny bump in her pocket and considered showing the pill to Maria to see if she could identify it.

But what if it was something illegal? She'd be forced to say where she'd gotten it, and heaven knew that Wesley didn't need any more legal problems at the moment. Besides, she really didn't want the woman to know that much about her personal business.

"Would you like something to drink?" Carlotta offered. "Iced tea?"

"No, thank you," Maria said, without looking up. "Did Michael Lane have a girlfriend?"

"Boyfriend," Carlotta corrected. "And not that I know of."

"Do you know if he was taking any kind of medication?"

"I don't."

"Any unusual hobbies?"

"Other than murder?" Carlotta asked drily. "I honestly don't know." She sighed and returned the cleaning supplies to the cabinet under the sink. "I guess one of the things that upset me the most about the whole situation was realizing how little I knew Michael. How can you work with someone so long and not know what they're capable of?"

"It happens," Maria said, then looked up, her striking eyes leveled on Carlotta. "Do you have any truly close friends?"

Carlotta straightened. "Of course I do. Hannah Kizer is my best friend."

"What's she like?"

Carlotta knew that Maria was trying to psychoanalyze her, but she was determined to demonstrate to the woman that she was normal. "Hannah is smart and eclectic. She's a culinary student. She gets me into all kinds of interesting events."

"Jack told me you were an expert party crasher."

Carlotta blushed. "It comes in handy sometimes."

"Your friend Hannah—is she married?"

"No, but she dates, um, married men."

Maria smiled. "Does she have a good family life?"

Carlotta stopped. "I...don't know. She doesn't talk about her family, and I've never met them."

"She's not from around here?"

"Um, actually I think she is."

Maria frowned. "How long have you been friends?"

"Hannah is a very private person," Carlotta said, annoyed.

"Is that why she's friends with you? Because you don't care enough to ask questions?"

Anger whipped through her. "What? Don't try to psychoanalyze me, Detective. I'm not that complicated."

"I didn't say you were complicated," Maria said lightly, closing her laptop.

Carlotta's mouth tightened, but before she could respond, the doorbell rang. She marched to the door and checked to see that it was Jack before she flung it open. When she did, she was surprised to see that he had his gun drawn.

"Is everything okay?" he asked, his expression taut. He craned to look past her into the house.

"Sure," Carlotta said, perplexed. "Why wouldn't it be?"

He sighed and reholstered his gun, then pointed to the outside doorknob.

Hanging from it was a plastic Northside Hospital bracelet bearing the name LANE, MICHAEL.

13

Carlotta sat on the couch and watched Maria and Jack square off. He'd called the precinct and arranged for a sweep of the neighborhood and the surrounding area, but frustration rolled off him in waves.

"You didn't hear or notice anything?" Jack demanded of his partner. In his hand was an evidence bag, the hospital bracelet inside.

Maria crossed her arms. "If I'd heard or seen something, don't you think I would've responded?"

"How could he get this close to the house and you not see him?"

"Jack, I didn't realize you wanted me to do surveillance. I thought you wanted me to keep Carlotta safe, which I did." She leaned in, but Carlotta could still hear her say, "You know this is already more than protocol calls for. Most people in her position would get a beeper number, not a watchdog."

His face went stony. "There are things going on here that you don't know about."

Maria laughed. "You're joking, right? I know exactly what's going on here. And don't ask me to babysit your girlfriend again."

"She's not my girlfriend," he said.

"I'm not his girlfriend," Carlotta said at the same time.

Maria held out her hand. "Give me the keys. I'll come to pick you up in the morning. Do you want me to send a CSI team to lift prints?"

"Why do we need prints?" Jack lifted the bag holding the bracelet. "The guy practically left a calling card, for God's sake."

Maria lifted her hands. "Your case, your call. I'm gone."

Jack grunted. "At least tell me what you think Lane meant by leaving the bracelet."

"It's a warning," she said over her shoulder. "He wanted to let Carlotta know he could get close to her."

The woman knew how to make an exit, Carlotta conceded. She left in a blur of nice suit, nice butt, nice perfume. She didn't touch the doorknob on the way out, yet still managed to slam the door effectively.

Jack pulled his hand down his face. "Why I thought having a female partner was a good idea, I don't know."

Carlotta stood and fingered the lapel of his jacket. "I think you like her."

He frowned. "I do like her—she's my partner."

"I have eyes, Jack."

He lifted his hands. "She's pretty, yeah, I noticed. But I don't dip my ink in the company well."

"She turned you down, didn't she?"

He frowned. "This conversation ends now."

Carlotta angled her head. "Did I hear right—are you spending the night?"

"Do you have a better idea?" he boomed. "What if this guy comes back? I swear, Carlotta, you and Wesley—" He wiped his hand over his mouth.

She narrowed her eyes. "Me and Wesley what? Is there something about Wesley that you're not telling me?" The unidentified pill came to mind, but she didn't dare show it to Jack in case it further incriminated Wes.

"No. What I was going to say is that you and your brother have both crossed paths with some pretty dangerous people, and neither one of you realize what easy targets you are for anyone who wants to retaliate."

"We can't live like prisoners, Jack."

"Fine," he said, jutting his head forward. "But install a damn burglar alarm, how about it? Or get a guard dog. And I can't believe I'm saying this, but…you need to learn how to use a gun."

Her laugh was incredulous. "Me? A gun?"

"Believe me, it's the stuff my nightmares are made of, but you should consider it."

She smiled. "Will you teach me?"

He closed his eyes briefly, then nodded. "Of course I will." He leaned over to pick up the small black duffel he'd carried inside. "Meanwhile, I picked up a couple of gadgets—some battery-operated motion detectors, and this." He held up what looked like a short black curling iron.

"A vibrator?" she asked. "Thanks, Jack, but I already—"

"It's not a vibrator," he cut in with an exasperated sigh. "It's a stun baton."

"Like a taser?"

"Yeah, except it expands," he said, demonstrating the telescoping tip. "You don't have to be as close to someone to use it as you do with a taser."

"Well…thanks," she said, taking it in her hand and hefting its weight. "What do I owe you?"

His mouth flattened and he looked away. When he looked back, he reached forward and hooked his arm around her waist, pulling her body up next to his. "You don't owe me anything. Christ, just be more careful, okay?"

She lifted her mouth and accepted his brief, hard kiss. She could tell he was holding back and she didn't press for more. Her cell phone rang, giving them a good reason to part. When she glanced at the caller ID, her heart squeezed. Peter Ashford had the most uncanny sense of timing of anyone she knew.

"I'll get these motion detectors in place," Jack said, then carried his duffel to the door.

She nodded and connected the call. "Hello?"

"Carly, it's me. I just heard on the news that Michael Lane escaped. Do you know anything about it?"

"Unfortunately, it's true. The police came to work to let me know."

"I'm coming to get you. You should stay with me tonight. Wesley, too."

"Thanks, but the police are watching the house tonight. We're fine," she said guiltily, knowing he would think she meant her and Wesley.

Instead of her and Jack.

"Okay, well, how about dinner? I can get something gourmet from Eatzi's, something to share."

"Thanks, but we're good. I really appreciate it, though. You're so thoughtful, Peter." It was true—he was considerate and generous to a fault, seemingly determined to make up for the time in her life when he hadn't been.

"If you're sure," he said, his voice sounding worried…and disappointed.

"I'm sure," she said, trying to sound upbeat. "This will probably be over tomorrow, and everything will be back to normal."

"If you say so. Call me if you need anything, okay?"

"I will." She disconnected the call, feeling small and traitorous. When she was with Peter, she always enjoyed herself…found herself slipping back into old habits, into old feelings.

But when she wasn't with Peter…

The door opened and Jack reappeared. "We're good for now." He held up a black box that looked like some kind of receiver. "If anyone comes around, we'll know about it." He closed the door and pulled at his tie. "I'm starved—how does pizza sound?"

"It sounds great," she said with a sinking feeling in her stomach precisely because it sounded so great. "Fellini's?"

"Absolutely." He pulled his phone from his belt. "I have the number stored."

And just like that, they fell into a routine, she realized, like a couple of old…friends.

The pizza arrived, which proved to be a good test for the motion detector. A red light on the black box lit up and an alarm sounded. Jack answered the door to check out the delivery guy, but all was legitimate. They found sodas in the fridge and a Braves game on the warped TV. A few minutes later, Jack took a call on his phone, and she could tell by the look on his face that the news wasn't good.

He disconnected the call. "They had to call off the search because it got too dark. They'll resume tomorrow morning."

"Are you on duty all night?"

"Officially, I'm off at midnight. But I'll be staying."

That was Jack—he didn't ask permission, just said how it was going to be. He lost his jacket and tie, and rolled up his shirtsleeves. They turned down the lights and sprawled on the couch. But as the night progressed, their legs migrated to touch, then their shoulders.

"You want another piece of pizza?" she asked.

"One more," he agreed, holding out his plate.

She picked up the wedge of pie, but instead of putting it on his plate, she brought it close to his mouth to feed it to him.

He took a bite and chewed slowly, his hungry gaze locked with hers. Then he groaned. "Don't."

"Don't what?"

"You know what." He gestured to her cleavage. "Don't be all sexy. I'm on duty."

She checked her watch. "Only for another hour."

He took the pizza from her and dropped it in his plate. "You're killing me. Let's talk about something else. Quickly."

"Okay. Any leads on Eva McCoy's stolen bracelet?"

"No. And frankly, I couldn't care less. But McCoy's uncle, the senator, is calling the mayor's office every day. Apparently, the woman's practically gone into hiding, she's so upset over losing the damn bracelet. Once Michael Lane is back in a straitjacket, we'll start canvassing pawnshops."

"Eva might have gone into hiding, but her charm bracelets are selling like hotcakes."

"What can I say? Crime pays." He took another bite of pizza and cheered when the game went into extra innings.

She bit her lip. "Have you heard anything else about my father's fingerprints being found at the hotel in Daytona?"

"No. And on closer examination, I discovered that the identification was made on only an eight-point match."

"What does that mean?"

"That the prints lifted and your father's prints were matched on eight identifying marks. The FBI uses a twelve-point standard, and our state crime lab likes at least nine. So eight is suspect, at best."

"You're saying they might not have been my father's prints after all?"

"Right. Or they could've been. Regardless, there haven't been any more leads."

Other than the fact that her father had come up to her at a rest area as she'd traveled back to Atlanta from Florida. After Jack had told her that her father's fingerprints had been lifted from the scene of a hotel robbery, she'd hitched a ride with Coop on an out-of-state body pickup as a way to get to the hotel to check it out herself. In the end, she'd had to confess to Coop that her reasons for going along hadn't been for the romantic getaway that he'd hoped for.

"Jack, about Shawna Whitt—"

"Whoa," he said, holding up his hand. "Case closed, remember?"

"I was actually going to ask if you think Coop is okay."

He frowned. "What do you mean?"

"Did you notice anything strange about his behavior last night?"

"New rule," he said, setting aside the half-eaten pizza. "No talking about other men when you're naked with me."

"But I'm not naked."

"Which I intend to remedy in the next sixty seconds. You know, since I ate dinner on the job, technically, the city owes me an hour."

"Really?"

"Uh-hmm," he said, pulling her over to straddle his lap. He looked up at her and sighed. "What am I going to do with you?"

"Last I heard, you were getting me naked," she murmured.

"We shouldn't do this," he said, lifting the hem of her camisole.

"I know." She raised her arms to be rid of the flimsy top, then unhooked her bra and let it fly, too.

He groaned and his erection surged beneath her. He leaned forward to draw a nipple into his mouth. Carlotta sighed and wrapped her arms around his neck. He stood and carried her to her bedroom, then laid her on the bed.

"This won't change anything," he said as if he were challenging her to stop while they still could.

"I know. In the morning, things will still be complicated." She unbuttoned her jeans and shed them, along with her panties, eager to have his big, warm body against hers.

Jack undressed quickly, stopping to retrieve a condom from his wallet. He crawled on top of her and smoothed her hair back from her temple.

"When I'm right here, it's the only time I know you're safe," he whispered roughly, then lifted her knee and surged forward.

But a piercing noise made them both freeze—the motion detector alarm.

"Shit," Jack muttered, and was off the bed in one movement, reaching for his pants with one hand, his gun with the other.

Carlotta scrambled off the bed and found her panties. She stepped into them, then grabbed her long chenille robe and shrugged into it as she crept down the hallway into the living room.

Jack stood next to the picture window, holding the curtain aside a few inches and peering outside.

"Is anyone out there?" she whispered.

"Uh, yeah," he said just as the doorbell rang. Jack straightened and lowered his gun. "I think you'd better get it."

Frowning, she stepped to the door and looked through the peephole, expecting to see Wesley. Instead, Coop was standing on the stoop. She gasped. "What's Coop doing here after midnight?"

"I don't know, but this should be interesting," Jack said drily.

She swung open the door and noticed instantly that Coop seemed disheveled, as if he'd been running his hands through his hair. "Coop?"

He smiled. "Hi." Then he noticed what she was wearing. "It's late. I got you up, didn't I?"

"No, I was just…getting ready for bed. Is something wrong?"

"Uh, maybe," he said. "I…didn't know where else to go."

"Come in," she said, pulling him inside. She closed the door and turned on a light.

When Coop saw Jack, he frowned, then realization dawned on his face. He strode back to the door. "I'm sorry—I shouldn't have come."

"Coop, it's fine," she said hurriedly.

"I'm here on police business," Jack said, and explained about Michael Lane.

"Oh, right," Coop said slowly. "I did hear something about that on the news. I wasn't paying much attention."

"The guy was here earlier today," Jack said. "He left a souvenir on the door. I was afraid he'd come back."

Carlotta spotted her bra on the floor and nudged it under a chair with her foot.

When Coop looked dubious, Jack nodded to the couch. "I'm sleeping out here, man. I've got motion detectors set up outside." He set his gun on a side table.

"Sit down, Coop," Carlotta urged. "What's wrong?"

When Coop didn't respond, Jack cleared his throat. "I think I'll give you two some privacy." Then he crossed to the guest bathroom.

After the door closed, she looked back to Coop. "Have you been drinking?"

He turned and walked away a couple of steps, pushing his hand into his hair. "No. But I want to."

"What happened?"

He shook his head. "No one thing. That's how it is. Little things build until one day you just want a drink." He turned back, his expression anguished. "I'm sorry. I had no right to come over here and burden you with my problems."

"Of course you had a right," she soothed. "I'm glad you came. You'll stay here tonight. Wesley's spending the night with a friend. You can sleep in his room."

"No, I couldn't impose."

"You're not imposing," she said softly, then touched his arm until he looked at her. "I don't think you should be alone tonight."

He nodded, his shoulders bowed with relief. The door opened and Jack emerged.

"Coop is going to stay in Wesley's room tonight," she said to Jack.

"If that's okay with you, Jack," Coop added warily.

Jack came to stand on the other side of Carlotta. "It's not my house, man. Carlotta decides who sleeps over...and where they sleep." He looked at Carlotta. "You were just about to get me a pillow for the couch?"

"Right," she said, tingling with embarrassment under his sardonic gaze. She went to the closet in the hall and removed two pillows and two sets of sheets. "Here you are," she said, handing one set to Jack.

"Thank you," he said, his eyes lit with amusement. She sent a warning glance to him, then turned to Coop.

"I brought a fresh pillow and linens for you, too, Coop. Wesley's pillow is so hard, no one else could possibly sleep on it."

"Thank you." His expression was grateful...and regretful.

"Well...good night," she said brightly, then walked to her room. At the door she paused and looked back to see both men standing there, holding a stack of linens, both of them watching her. She gave a little wave, then walked into her room. When she closed the door, she leaned against it and expelled a pent-up sigh.

Minus ten points for her and Jack being interrupted. But plus ten for pulling Coop back from the brink.

All in all, she guessed she was even for the night.

14

Wesley checked his watch. He had just enough time to grab a clean shirt and check on Einstein before he went to work—

He stopped short at the sight of Coop's white van in the driveway. From the dew settled on the vehicle and the driveway around it, it was clear the van had been there all night.

He hesitated before going inside—he didn't want to interrupt anything.

On the other hand, Coop finally scoring with Carlotta might mean that Coop would be more open to calling him to work with him again sometime. The man was bound to be in a good mood this morning.

Deciding the best tact would be to act as if nothing was amiss, he unlocked the door and swung it open, then walked in whistling.

"I'm home," he called loudly. Since he could hear activity in the kitchen, he headed in that direction.

He walked in to see Coop and Carlotta sitting at the breakfast table looking pretty darn comfortable with each other, both reading a different section of the newspaper. As much as he liked Coop, it was a shock to his senses to see a man at their breakfast table—Carlotta had never allowed men she dated to spend the night while he was growing up.

Carlotta looked up and smiled. "I didn't expect to see you this morning."

That much was obvious. "I came back to get a clean shirt," he said, gesturing vaguely toward his room.

Coop bent down a corner of his paper. "Hi, Wes."

"Uh, hi. How's it going?"

"Good," Coop said, biting into a piece of toast. "You?"

"Same." He cleared his throat. "Did Carlotta tell you that the D.A. reduced the charges to a misdemeanor?"

"Yeah, she mentioned it."

"So, do you think I could come back and work for you sometime? I swear, no messing around."

Coop rubbed his chin. "I'll give it some thought."

"Want some eggs?" Carlotta asked, pointing to a skillet on the stove.

"Uh, no, thanks." Wesley scratched his neck. Apparently he was the only person in the room feeling awkward. His sister was dressed in work clothes and Coop was fully dressed, too, although his hair looked damp and fresh from a shower. It was clear that interpersonal activities had taken place.

At the sound of footsteps behind him, Wesley turned to see Jack Terry emerge, his gun by his side, his dress shirt hanging open, his hair also wet from a shower.

"I heard the motion detector go off," Jack said.

"It's just Wesley," Carlotta supplied unnecessarily. "Do you want eggs, Jack?"

"Sure," he said, setting his gun on the counter. "Hey, Wes."

Wesley gaped, looking back and forth between the threesome. "Would someone please tell me what's going on here?" Then he held up his hands. "Wait—I don't want to know. I'll be out of your way in two minutes." He turned and strode toward his bedroom.

He heard Jack start to follow him, saying, "I got this," but he kept walking.

"Dude, I'm serious," he said over his shoulder. "Spare me the sordid details."

When he opened his bedroom door, he noticed his bed was neatly made, with a pile of sheets at the foot.

Jack walked in behind him and closed the door. "Don't call me dude, *dude*. And it's not what you think. Coop slept in here last night and I slept on the couch."

"Is that some kind of hinky way for both of you to keep the other one from sleeping with my sister?"

Jack jammed his hands on his hips. "No. Michael Lane escaped from the psych ward, so I came over to keep an eye on Carlotta. Coop came by after midnight—I think he was having some kind of crisis. Carlotta asked him to stay."

"Ruined your plans, huh?"

Jack straightened, but by the way he averted his gaze, Wesley knew he was right.

"Look," Jack said, "like it or not, your sister has a life."

"No, my sister *needs* a life," Wesley retorted, stepping closer. The man towered over him and outweighed him by eighty pounds, but he was past worrying about it. "You don't care about anything except getting into her pants."

"That's not true."

"Dude, I know you're banging Liz Fischer, and probably a few other broads, too. Carlotta's just another booty call to you."

A muscle worked in the detective's jaw. "I understand *you* and Liz have been getting busy."

Wesley lifted his chin. "That's right. And Liz is probably getting it from a half-dozen other guys besides us, man—that's what she's about. But my sister wants the fairy tale, and after all she's been through, she deserves it."

Jack closed his eyes briefly. "I know."

"Then step back, man. She digs your big, bad cop routine, but you can't give her what she wants. At least Coop and Peter both care about her. If you take your dick out of the equation, maybe she can settle down with someone she has a chance of being happy with." He walked over to his closet and pulled out a clean shirt.

Silence boomed in the room. Finally Jack said, "Since when did you get so smart?"

"Haven't you heard?" Wesley stripped off the old shirt and shrugged into the clean one. "I'm a genius, dude."

Jack's mouth flattened. "Well, get your genius ass to the station sometime this week. I need to talk to you and your attorney about this business with Hollis Carver."

While Wesley buttoned his shirt, he squinted, trying to recall his schedule. Lately his short-term memory was like Swiss cheese. "I have my community service this morning, then I have to meet with my P.O. How about tomorrow afternoon?"

"Won't work for me. Let's shoot for Friday afternoon. I'll give Liz a call and see if she can make it."

Wesley glanced at his watch. "I gotta get going or I'll be late."

"Your community service—how's that going?"

"It sucks a big hairy one," Wesley said. But even as he said it, he admitted he was looking forward to seeing what Meg would wear today.

"Earth to Wes."

He blinked and pushed up his glasses, then lifted his gaze from the vee of Meg's T-shirt where it gaped open just enough to reveal a pink-and-green plaid bra.

She leaned across the table where reams of paper were strewn between them. "Are you stoned?"

He scoffed. "What? Of course not."

"Your pupils look small."

"It's the glasses, man."

"I'm not a man."

"I noticed." When she raised her eyebrows, a flush crawled up his neck.

Meg was obviously unconvinced by his denial. "You're moving in slow-motion—what gives?"

"Just tired, I guess."

"You're too young to be tired. What are you going to be like when you're forty?"

"Probably dead," he said matter-of-factly. Especially considering the company he'd been keeping.

"That's not close to being funny," Meg said with a frown. She stood and started gathering her notes, her body language angry.

"What's your problem?" Wesley asked.

"You. You have everything going for you, yet you're pissing your life away."

"What does that mean?"

"You're a smart guy. Figure it out."

He lifted his hands, at a loss. "I thought we were supposed to work together on this project."

"Isn't it time for you to leave?" Meg asked, pecking on her watch.

He glanced at his watch. "Oh. Right."

"You're welcome to join me and the guys for lunch," she offered halfheartedly.

"Uh, no, thanks. I need to be somewhere." He had to meet his probation officer.

"Do you need to *be* anywhere tomorrow night?"

He frowned. "Why?"

"We're going to Screen on the Green in Piedmont Park if you want to drop by…or not, it's up to you."

He scratched his temple. "What's playing?"

"Breakfast at Tiffany's."

His back stiffened. "That's a chick flick."

"It's a classic, idget. Forget it, you wouldn't appreciate it anyway." She dismissed him with an exasperated sigh. "I'll keep working on the encryption this afternoon and we'll pick up tomorrow morning. Try to show up sober and be ready to do something besides stare at my chest for four hours, how about it? And read this." She tossed a hardcover manual at him. He tried to catch it, but his reflexes were slow. It bounced off his chest and fell on the floor with a thud. She shook her head, then turned and walked away.

Wesley watched, wondering if her panties matched the preppy, plaid bra. Then he leaned over and picked up the manual he'd already read twice. He pushed up his glasses, wondering how Meg could tell that he was on something and if she'd rat him out.

As he left the ASS offices and walked to MARTA to make the trek to his probation officer's building, he mulled over Meg's comment.

Why did women assume that if you weren't going to school to pursue some kind of corporate ball-and-chain gig, you were pissing your life away?

Although maybe he'd think about taking some college classes in the fall. A popular professional poker player had once commented that a college course in logic had given him the edge he'd needed to win some of the biggest pots in the history of the game.

He was feeling a little shaky by the time he reached the building that housed his P.O.'s office, but he decided it might not be such a good idea to pop an Oxy just before his appointment. He had the vial of neutralizer to add to the cup if E. Jones asked for a urine sample, but he didn't want to push his luck.

He walked into the waiting room and scanned the diverse collection of people slumped in chairs before walking up to the check-in window.

"Wesley Wren to see E. Jones."

"Sign in and take a seat," a woman said without looking up.

He did, easing into an empty chair and trying to relax. His neck was wet with sweat and his heart was beating a little too fast. Behind his glasses, his left eye was twitching. He passed the time by looking around the room and trying to decipher people's "tells," the mannerisms that everyone exhibited that divulged something about them to anyone interested or observant enough to study them for a while.

The prostitutes and the thugs in the room were easy to pick out from their costumes, questionable piercings and bad tattoos. The more interesting prospects were the people who looked as if they didn't belong on this end of the legal system. Take the suburban-looking woman wearing enormous sunglasses, for instance. Judging from the way she kept wetting her lips and swallowing convulsively, she'd probably gotten one too many DUIs. And the guy with grease under his nails who kept cracking his knuckles was probably a car thief. The professional-looking guy in the suit who paced near the door using his BlackBerry with an angry scowl was probably in trouble for poisoning a neighbor's barking dog. He continued around the room, making up stories that matched the tics and body language he read. People-watching kept him sharp between card games.

"Wren, you're up!" the check-in lady shouted a few minutes later.

He pushed to his feet and walked to the door that led to a hallway of offices, then headed toward the one labeled *E. Jones*. When he neared it, the door opened and his P.O.'s boyfriend, Leonard, walked out, closing the door behind him.

Wesley blinked. The big beefy guy who ran drugs for Chance had swapped his black jeans, black T-shirt and biker boots for a suit, dress shirt and…loafers?

When Leonard looked up, he did a double take, his face quickly turning from friendly to furious.

"Going to a funeral?" Wesley asked.

The big man glanced over his shoulder to the closed door, then shoved his face into Wesley's. "Yeah, yours if you say anything to Eldora about my little side business."

"Mum's the word, dude." He sniffed. "Nice cologne. Is it Celine Dion's?"

Leonard hooked his foot behind Wesley's leg and in one motion, Wesley landed on his back with an *unff*.

The door opened and E. stepped out. She wore dark slacks and a silky blouse, and her long red hair was twisted into a knot at the nape of her neck. Her lovely face was creased in concern. "Leonard? Wesley?"

"A little collision," Leonard said with a smile, then reached down to pull Wesley to his feet as easily as if he were a little girl. "You okay, man?"

He gave Wesley's shoulder a squeeze near his neck with enough precise pressure to immobilize his left side.

"Yeah," Wesley managed to say.

"You sure?" Leonard said, increasing the pressure until Wesley's eyes watered.

"Yeah, I'm sure."

Leonard released him. "Good. See you around." He turned to E. "I'll see you tonight, babe."

She nodded, casting her beautiful smile on the undeserving oaf. When he'd gone, she turned to Wesley. "Ready?"

"Sure," he said, then followed her into her office.

"Sorry about that," E. said as she walked behind her desk to sit. She gestured to a chair, so he could do the same.

"Wasn't your fault," he said, riding a line of frustration that she was oblivious that her boyfriend was such a shady character. "What does your boyfriend do for a living?"

She flipped through file folders on her desk. "Leonard is a pharmaceutical sales rep," she said absently.

Wesley almost smiled. The best lies were mostly true. "What kind of drugs?"

"Cancer drugs," she said with a proud smile.

"Really? Wow." He gave the man points for originality. Somehow he doubted the pharmaceuticals in the duffel bags Chance handed off to Leonard had anything to do with chemo.

"So, how are you?" E. asked, clasping her hands.

"Good," he said, nodding. A trickle of sweat slid over his temple and down his cheek. He caught it with a brush of his hand and hoped she didn't notice. His left eye was twitching again and his skin felt as if ants were crawling all over him. He was craving another hit of Oxy.

"I see another thousand hours was added to your community service for the body-snatching stunt."

He nodded.

"Considering how high-profile that case was, I have to confess that I'm surprised that the D.A. let you off so easily. It's no secret the man has it in for you—he could've thrown you in jail, if only for violating your probation."

So E. didn't know about his deal to work undercover for

The Carver—Lucas must have meant what he said, that only the four of them in the room and his police contact would know what was going down. "Guess I got lucky."

She looked dubious for a few seconds, then seemed to shrug off her doubts. "How's the body moving job?"

"It's on hold for a while," he said, with no explanation. "But I got a line on a job as a bike courier."

"Sounds perfect for you. Can you work around your community service?"

"I think so."

"Good. I'll need to see your W-4 form."

"My what?"

"The form for the information your employer will use to issue a paycheck and a W-2 at the end of the year."

"Uh…it pays cash," he improvised. "And tips."

"Okay, then a note from your boss will do. How's the community service going?"

"It's going."

She rolled a pen between her clasped hands. "Staying out of trouble?"

"Yeah," he said, then realized he'd answered too quickly.

"No gambling?"

"Nah." Not until Chance lined up another game for him. And his mouth watered to tell her that the last poker tournament he'd played in had grossed him twenty large, but her boyfriend and two of his friends had robbed the gaming house before anyone could collect their winnings. The men had all worn masks, but he'd recognized Leonard's big deformed arms—the man was definitely on the juice.

"How are things at home?" she asked.

He shrugged. "Fine."

"How's your sister?"

"Fine."

"I heard there was a disturbance at Neiman's the other day."

"If there was trouble, I'm sure Carlotta was in the middle of it. We Wrens seem to have a knack for finding it."

E. smiled. "That you do. Anything else you want to talk about?"

My dad's alive after all. I really don't want to work undercover for the man who sliced his name into my arm. And I'm afraid that I totally blew it with Coop. "Nah," he said. "Everything's good."

"Okay," she said with a nod. "See you next week."

"You bet," he said, then left before she changed her mind and asked him for a urine sample.

He walked to the elevator bay, then punched the button and sighed in relief. He'd dodged a bullet with E.

But when the elevator doors slid open, Tick, the collector for Father Thom, the other loan shark that Wesley owed, stood there smiling at him.

Wesley actually tried to jump back, but his muscles were slow to respond. Tick reached out, dragged him inside the elevator, and the doors closed.

15

Carlotta stood at the door and waved goodbye to Coop as he backed out of the driveway.

"Don't forget to blow him a kiss," Jack called from the kitchen.

She closed the door and walked back inside. "Be nice."

He saluted her with his coffee cup. "Sorry, I'm a little cranky from the crick in my neck I got sleeping on your couch."

"Coop needed a friend last night."

"I know," he said, taking a drink of coffee, then wincing. "I don't want to see Coop fall off the wagon any more than you do, but he has a lousy sense of timing." His gaze raked over her regretfully.

Under her olive-green Kay Unger sleeveless sheath, her body twinged with similar disappointment, but it couldn't be helped. "Did Coop tell you what was bothering him?"

"No, but…"

"But what?"

He shrugged and took another drink. "I kind of assumed that *you* were bothering him, if you know what I mean." Then he held up his hands. "But I'm not suggesting you should take ownership of his drinking problem."

She frowned. "I'm flattered that you'd think I'd have that much sway, but I'm sure something else is troubling Coop."

"Why didn't you ask him?"

"I did. He said it wasn't anything in particular."

"And why don't you believe him?"

Carlotta pursed her mouth. "Call it women's intuition."

He rolled his eyes and took another healthy drink from his mug. "Maybe being asked to consult on open cases at the morgue is too much pressure for him."

"It's probably pretty awkward, working in the morgue he used to run," she agreed.

"Yeah. As long as he's only moving bodies for them, he can stay on the periphery. But working on cases means rubbing elbows with former coworkers."

"From what I've seen, the people he used to work with respect him."

"Coop will figure it out, I'm sure." Jack glanced at his watch. "Marquez should be here soon. Are you ready to go?"

"Are you two taking me to work?"

"You don't have a car, remember?"

"I don't want to be a pain."

A dry laugh escaped him. "Darling, that ship sailed the day we met."

"Ha, ha." Carlotta studied her cuticles. "I don't think your partner likes me."

"Marquez likes you fine."

"She thinks you're giving me special treatment."

He pushed to his feet and carried his plate to the dishwasher. "No comment, on the grounds that I'll be in trouble no matter how I answer that. I wish you'd reconsider going in today. It makes me crazy that Lane is still out there somewhere."

"Jack, I don't have a lot of choice. I have bills to pay."

He nodded. "Do you have the stun baton?"

"In my bag." She walked up to him and slid her hands up the front of his shirt. "You make me feel safe, Jack."

His eyes turned smoky and he smiled. "Good."

"So what were you and Wesley talking about in his room with the door closed?"

His smile fell and he stilled her hands with his. "I just wanted to make sure he knew nothing kinky went on here last night."

"That's all you talked about? You were in there for a while." Again she thought of the pill she'd found. She'd considered showing it to Coop when Jack was in the shower, but since Coop and Wes's relationship was on such thin ice at the moment, she didn't want to give Coop more reason to think ill of her brother.

Jack looked away, then back. "If you want to know the truth, your brother told me to leave you alone."

She gave a little laugh. "You're joking."

"No. He said I couldn't give you what you need." He locked gazes with her, then made a rueful noise. "And although I think Wes generally exhibits exceptionally bad judgment, in this case, I tend to agree with him."

Carlotta pulled back and crossed her arms. "So the two of you know what I need, do you?"

Jack squirmed. "Carlotta, I'm not exactly the settling down type."

"If I wanted to settle down, I could marry Peter tomorrow."

"Maybe you should," he murmured.

She blinked. "You think I should marry Peter?"

He reached up to stroke her cheek with a callused thumb. "I think it's the life you were meant for."

The piercing sound of the motion detector alarm knifed

into the air. Jack dropped his hand and strode to the front window. "There's Marquez. Let's go."

"Talk about timing," Carlotta muttered.

Feeling blindsided by Jack's assessment, she grabbed her purse and sunglasses and followed him outside into the morning sunshine. The black sedan sat on the driveway, engine humming. After Carlotta locked the front door, Jack shepherded her into the backseat and he slid into the front passenger seat. Carlotta was surprised his macho ego would allow him to let a woman drive. It actually elevated him in her eyes.

But it didn't make up for the abrupt kiss-off, which hurt more than she cared to admit.

And quite possibly changed everything.

Meanwhile, Maria looked like a million dollars in a wine-colored pantsuit, her lush, bronze-colored hair coiled into a chic chignon that brought her amazing bone structure into finer focus.

"Good morning," she said to Carlotta in the rearview mirror. "Did you two sleep well?"

Carlotta didn't miss the sly intonation.

"One of us did," Jack muttered.

Carlotta bit her lip. Was it her imagination, or had Maria's shoulders relaxed at the subtle assurance that she and Jack had slept apart?

"No incidents?" Maria asked.

"No. Any updates on Lane?"

"No. But every available uniform is out looking for him."

The two of them talked about work on the drive to Lenox Square. Carlotta sat back and looked at the sky through the window, wondering where Michael Lane was, and what frame of mind he was in. He'd had everything going for him, but he'd gotten greedy, and people had died because of it.

The ugly memory of what he'd done, in juxtaposition to a beautiful, sunny day like this one, made Carlotta philosophical. The women he'd killed would never enjoy another day like this one…and neither would Shawna Whitt. The sad truth was no matter the cause, each of the women was just as dead as the others. And none of them had seen it coming—the randomness of death was positively breathtaking.

She wondered idly if anyone would know to take down Shawna's profile from the online dating service. She supposed that it would expire eventually, but how many men had looked at her bio in the past few days, had sent a note hoping to meet with her soon? If she had lived, would Shawna have married one of the men? Had children? The woman's headstone should read "What Could Have Been."

Most disconcerting, though, was why Shawna Whitt had had that charm in her mouth when she'd died. Maria's explanation of an oral fixation sounded bizarre…but then again, Maria was the expert.

"Carlotta?"

Jack's voice jarred her out of her thoughts.

"I need your car keys."

She glanced around and realized they were pulling into the mall parking lot.

"Are you going to boost my car battery again?" she asked as they pulled up to the Monte Carlo.

"No, I got you a new battery yesterday."

Her eyes widened. "You did? Thank you…I'll pay you back, of course."

"Forget about it," he said, then turned to Maria. "Pop the trunk, will you?"

He climbed out and Carlotta noticed Maria's gaze linger on Jack. "I'll give you a hand," the woman said to him as she got out.

Carlotta pressed her lips together. So Maria was interested in Jack after all, but—at least for now—she wouldn't cross the professional boundary. If the two of them would let themselves go for it, they'd probably be the perfect match, Carlotta conceded miserably.

Maybe Jack was right. Maybe there *was* something to be said about fitting into the other person's world.

As a token gesture of support, she opened the door and slid out to watch the dynamic duo swap her old battery for a spanking brand-new one. As they loosened bolts and re-fastened cables, she felt totally inept. It was moments like this that she wondered how she'd managed to raise Wesley in one piece.

Not that she'd done such a bang-up job, considering all the trouble he'd been in. In hindsight, it was a good thing her little brother hadn't run on batteries.

When Jack started her car, Maria went back to the sedan to answer a radio call. After a few seconds, she stood and waved to get Jack's attention. "Lane was spotted leaving the North Springs MARTA station. He's on the run, but there's a traffic chopper in the area on its way."

Jack sprang into motion, turning off Carlotta's car and locking it. "Come on, Carlotta, we'll drop you off at the door. I'll drive," he said to Maria.

Carlotta jumped in and held on as Jack raced to the Neiman's entrance. "Michael is a long-distance runner," she offered as she opened the car door to get out.

"Good to know," Jack said, picking up the radio. "I'll call you as soon as I have news."

She stepped out and closed the door. "Be—"

But the car was already speeding away, siren flashing from the dashboard. "Careful," she whispered.

Carlotta walked into Neiman's, her mind clicking with worry. She hoped that Michael was apprehended without anyone else getting hurt. In the employee break room, a group of people were gathered around the TV in the dining area.

Patricia saw her and waved. "Michael Lane's on the news! The police are tracking him. There's a helicopter and everything."

She walked over, hugging herself. On the screen was an aerial view of a man wearing what appeared to be scrubs sprinting through a neighborhood. Occasionally he would disappear beneath the leafy branches of trees, only to reappear a few seconds later, having zigzagged.

"Where is that?" Carlotta managed to ask.

"Near Johnson Ferry Road," someone said.

Not too far away, she realized. Jack should be there any second.

"Do you think they'll shoot him?" someone near her asked.

"Not unless he tries to hurt someone," she murmured.

"Well, I for one, hope they catch him and strap him down this time," Patricia said. "I've been a nervous wreck thinking he'd come back for me." She fanned herself. "When I think how close I was to a murderer at that concert, I can barely sleep."

Carlotta glanced at her sideways, wondering what the woman would think if she knew that Carlotta had first suspected Patricia as the person who had masterminded the identity theft ring.

When she'd first met Jack, he'd told her that anyone was capable of murder. Since that time, she had come to believe that it was probably true.

The aerial camera jerked, then zoomed in on the man's panicked face. Carlotta's heart jumped and the room erupted in gasps and exclamations.

"It's really him!"

"He looks like a wild animal!"

Carlotta had to agree. Michael's chiseled features were sharp, the skin drawn tight over his cheekbones, his eyes sunken. His dark hair was shaggy and his jaw was covered with a few days' worth of ragged beard growth. He did indeed look wild and unstable as he ran doggedly away from the pursuing helicopter.

The camera zoomed out, showing police cars approaching from both directions on Johnson Ferry Road, stopping behind traffic, angling their vehicles to create barriers and waving civilians out of the way.

"If you're just joining us," the announcer said, "fugitive Michael Lane, who escaped from the psychiatric unit of Northside Hospital yesterday, where he was being held to determine if he was mentally fit to stand trial for murder and attempted murder in connection with an identity theft ring, is on the run. He was reportedly spotted at the North Springs MARTA station about thirty minutes ago and has since eluded authorities on foot. Soon, however, the fugitive will have no place to go. Atlanta PD is closing in on both ends of Johnson Ferry Bridge. Hopefully we'll have a nonviolent resolution soon."

Carlotta chewed on her thumbnail as her heart thumped against her breastbone. Michael ran to a car and pounded on the driver side window, but the driver refused to open the door. Michael pulled out what looked like a surgical knife and banged on the hood, his face contorted with rage.

Exclaims sounded around the room.

"He's going to kill somebody!"

"The police are going to shoot him for sure."

Michael ran to another car, wielding the knife. The driver shrank away, but refused to open the door. Horns sounded from the cars all around, which were sitting haphazardly on the bridge. Police officers poured from their vehicles, many with their weapons drawn. Carlotta saw Jack striding forward, a bullhorn to his mouth. Her breath caught in her lungs.

"The police are instructing people to lock their doors and stay put," the announcer said. "And apparently, they're trying to appeal to the fugitive."

Michael jerked his head up and looked at Jack, who was still several yards away. Then he glanced at the wall of police cars at either end of the bridge. Michael's face crumbled, obviously realizing he had nowhere to go. Suddenly, he bolted for the side of the bridge and swung his legs over the concrete railing.

"He's going to jump!" Carlotta said. She couldn't believe the scene unfolding on the television. It was surreal.

"This isn't good," the announcer said. "It looks like Lane is threatening to jump into the Chattahoochee River, a drop equivalent to a three-story fall. And the waters of the river are running rough from the recent heavy rains north of the city. One plainclothes officer is trying to talk to him."

Jack had halted a few feet away, still speaking through the bullhorn. He held up his free hand in a stop signal, obviously asking Michael to reconsider what he was about to do.

Michael looked over his shoulder, then gracefully slid over the edge, disappearing from view.

Everyone in the room gasped. Carlotta covered her mouth with her hand.

"He jumped!" the announcer said. "Lane jumped!" The helicopter zoomed to the other side of the bridge to catch the action that their unfortunate position had caused them to miss. But the shot showed only the thick brown waters of the Hooch, ugly and choppy with more volume than usual. The camera scanned the spot where Michael would've entered the river, then the columns of the bridge, the banks, and even a long shot downstream.

But Michael was nowhere to be seen.

The jerky camera shots captured Jack leaning over the edge, scanning the water and the surrounding area with binoculars. Then he jogged to the other side of the bridge and looked downstream, his body language rigid.

"Oh, my goodness, what a nasty fall," the announcer said. "Assuming Lane wasn't injured in the drop, it would still take a strong swimmer to fight the swift current of the river. And Lane would have had to be tired after traveling on foot almost four miles from the MARTA station."

Carlotta closed her eyes. Michael was gone, but at least it was by his own choice. She reached into her purse and removed her cell phone. Walking away a few steps for privacy, she punched in Jack's number. After several rings, he answered. "Goddammit, he got away."

"I know. I watched everything on TV. But, Jack, it would be a miracle if Michael survived that fall. He can't swim."

"Are you sure?"

"Yes. When he told me he was a long-distance runner, I asked him if he competed in triathlons. He said no because of the swimming segment. He told me he could barely tread water."

Jack heaved a sigh. "Okay, thanks for the info. We'll keep looking for a body. Are you okay?"

"Yeah," she said shakily. "Just glad it's over."

"Me, too," he said. "I'll check in later."

She disconnected the call and expelled a pent-up breath.

"Do you think he's dead?" Patricia asked, her eyes wide.

Carlotta nodded.

"Leave it to Michael to go out in dramatic fashion."

Carlotta managed a bittersweet smile and left the melee in the dining area to walk to her locker, glancing at Michael's, with anguish. Why did people have to be so complicated?

Trying to push the matter from her aching head, she left the break room, tears pressing behind her eyes. She made her feet move, and with every step, she felt a tiny bit better. On the way to her station on the second floor, she met Lindy, whose expression was grim.

"I just heard about Michael," her boss said. "It doesn't sound good."

"No, it doesn't," Carlotta agreed, inhaling to compose herself. Michael had done terrible things, but she'd known him longer as a friend than as a murderer. She wondered if he'd had some kind of psychotic break while in the hospital. His behavior seemed to have stretched way beyond narcissism into criminally insane.

"It's hard to grasp that Michael's gone," Lindy said, "but I'm glad that you're safe. I understand he was at your house yesterday?"

Carlotta frowned. "How did you know?"

"Detective Marquez called me this morning so we could arrange extra security for you today."

Carlotta tried to mask her surprise. "That was…nice of her."

Lindy made a rueful noise. "I'm truly sorry about Michael, but at least you won't be dragged through a lengthy trial."

"There's that," Carlotta conceded with a nod. "I am ready for things to get back to normal."

"Me, too. I miss seeing your name at the top of the sales sheet. Try to have a good day. If you need to take some time, Patricia can cover for you." Her boss walked off.

Carlotta closed her eyes to gather her reserves. Of course Patricia would cover for her—she'd be happy to take Carlotta's job altogether. When she opened her eyes, the woman was standing in front of her, holding a box of tissues. Speak of the devil.

"I thought you might need these," Patricia said, extending the box.

"Thanks." Carlotta snatched the tissues and strode toward her station. She wished she could put her finger on why the woman annoyed her so much.

Patricia fell into step beside her. "I see you're wearing your charm bracelet. Me, too," she said, shaking her arm for a jingle. "I decided to give it a chance, to see what happens. Who knows? Maybe something exciting is just around the corner for me."

"Good for you," Carlotta said sarcastically.

At the wounded look on Patricia's face, though, remorse washed over her.

Carlotta stopped and put her hand to her forehead. "I'm sorry. I really just need to be busy right now. Do you mind if we talk later?"

"No problem," Patricia murmured.

She watched the prim woman walk away stiffly and Carlotta chastised herself. Minus ten points. Patricia wasn't so bad, she was just so…inconvenient.

"Carlotta."

At the sound of Peter's voice, frustration billowed in her chest. Speaking of inconvenient. But by the time she'd swung around, she'd manufactured a smile. "Hi."

He looked handsome and polished in a black suit, snowy

shirt, and silver-gray tie. Concern furrowed his brow. "Hi, yourself. I've been calling to check on you."

"Oh." She gestured vaguely. "We're not supposed to have our phones on the sales floor. I guess you heard about Michael Lane?"

"That's why I came. I'm sorry for him, but I'm also glad."

She nodded. "Thanks. I know what you mean."

"So," he said, pushing his hands into his pockets, "I drove by your place late last night."

Carlotta flinched because she had a feeling she knew where the conversation was going. "Why didn't you stop in?"

"Because I wasn't invited…and because Cooper Craft's van was sitting in your driveway."

She looked at her feet, then back up to meet his gaze. "Coop spent the night, but it's not what you think, Peter."

Hurt reflected in his cornflower-blue eyes. "Oh?"

"Jack was there, too."

His expression went from hurt to confused to shocked. *"What?"*

She held up her hands. "Let me explain." She told him about Michael Lane leaving the hospital bracelet on the doorknob.

"That maniac was at your *house?*"

"Apparently. That's why Jack stayed overnight—he set up motion detectors outside in case Michael came back. Coop stopped by unannounced around midnight." She squirmed, reluctant to share Coop's secrets. "He was having…personal problems and needed someone to talk to, so I offered him a place to stay."

"Did Lane come back?"

"No. Jack and his partner brought me to work this morning. They got the call about him just as they dropped me off."

Peter looked contrite. "I jumped to conclusions. I'm sorry for saying anything."

Any guilt she might have felt over her near-lapse with Jack was mitigated by her irritation over Peter spying on her house. And Jack's pronouncement that perhaps she should marry Peter made her feel inexplicably antsy around her former fiancé. "I really appreciate you coming by, Peter, but I have to get back to work."

He nodded. "We're still on tomorrow night for Screen on the Green?"

She smiled, warming toward his eagerness. "Absolutely. I'll bring the picnic dinner."

"And I'll bring the wine. Pick you up at seven?"

"Sounds perfect."

He reached forward to squeeze her hand. "Get some rest tonight."

She nodded. "I'm sure a lot of people will be sleeping easier."

He strode away and she gave herself a stern lecture. She had to declutter her mind and focus on her future before her future got tired of her dragging her feet and went on without her.

Certain that the day could only get better, she switched into sales mode. She desperately needed strong commissions this first pay period back after her medical leave. Thankfully, the store was still buzzing with customers who'd heard that Eva McCoy's famous charm bracelet had been stolen and wanted to visit the scene of the crime. The waiting list for the charm bracelets was rumored to be several hundred names long now. Business in her own department was steady and strong. Some of her best customers who knew of her relationship with Michael Lane came in, offering words of sympathy while furtively trolling for details. She obliged them with as few facts as possible while processing high-dollar purchases. Controversy was good for business.

For lunch, she headed to the mall food court for half a sandwich and an iced coffee. While she sipped, she fingered the charm bracelet she wore and reflected on her earlier conversation with Patricia about the trinkets. Carlotta conceded that even as she told herself that the idea of the charms having meaning was utterly ridiculous, she nonetheless had reached for the bracelet again when she'd gotten dressed that morning.

Deep down, she guessed she, too, was hoping for a little magic… Admittedly, though, the "dead woman" charm on her bracelet didn't hold much appeal.

Then the ribbon of a thought slipped into her head. Maybe the dead woman represented by the charm was Shawna Whitt…maybe it was fate that Carlotta had been on her body pickup. Maybe she should poke around a little, ask a few questions.

Okay, maybe Michael's death was affecting her more than she cared to admit, but doing something for Shawna Whitt gave her something solid to hold on to.

She fished out her cell phone and punched in Coop's number. He might know about a memorial service for the woman. His uncle's funeral home sometimes benefited from Coop moving bodies for the morgue. If a family didn't have any particular religious or traditional ties, they sometimes chose Motherwell out of convenience.

After five rings, Coop's voice mail kicked on. "Hi, it's Coop," his voice said, but it was so slurred, it was almost unrecognizable. "And here's the beep."

The sharp beep mirrored the alarm going off in her head. "Hi, Coop. It's Carlotta. Call me as soon as you get this message." She disconnected the call as worry squeezed her lungs.

This couldn't be good.

16

Tick, Father Thom's henchman, had the front of Wesley's shirt fisted in his big paw. They were alone on the elevator.

Wesley swallowed. "Going down, man? What a coincidence."

The big guy gave him a teeth-rattling shake. "Shut up and pay me before we get to the ground floor."

"Okay, okay. Let me go and I'll get my wallet."

Instead Tick used his free hand to remove Wesley's wallet from his back pocket, then released him with a shove. Wesley watched helplessly while the man removed the two hundred sixty-some dollars.

"Is this all you got?"

"Yeah."

Tick threw the empty wallet back at him. "You can't be serious."

"I'm starting a new job soon," Wesley said in a rush. "Tell Father Thom I'll be able to start making regular payments again."

"Next Wednesday I'll need a grand." Tick smacked him hard, then the elevator dinged and the doors opened.

Wesley waited until the stars subsided before he shuffled out among the people trying to enter. Tick was long gone, thank God.

He stopped at a water fountain, then reached into his backpack to root for the bag of Oxy. But Meg's taunting words came back to him and he resisted. He didn't need the OxyContin—he could quit any time. He leaned over to allow the cold water to splash on his face. It revived him somewhat. He looked for a vending machine, then realized he didn't even have enough change to get a Coke.

Damn, he needed a card game.

Pondering how he might get home, he left the building.

Only to find Mouse waiting for him in the front of the parking lot, leaning on his Town Car, filing his nails.

"Shit," Wesley muttered under his breath.

"Nice to see you, too," Mouse said. The man wore a decent suit and could've passed for an attorney…except for the jagged facial scars and the shapeless nose that had been broken a few times.

With nothing to lose, Wes gave honesty a try. "I don't have any money, man. Father Thom's guy just jumped me in the elevator and took everything I had."

Mouse made a rueful noise. "Then I'm gonna have to beat you."

Wesley winced. "Come on, man, don't do that."

"I don't want to. Every time I get my nails looking good, I have to mess them up again. The ladies like nice nails." Mouse flexed his huge hands.

Wesley sighed. "I don't suppose you could cut me some slack this one time?"

"Nope. Maybe you should call that preppy dude who bailed you out before."

Peter Ashford had bought Wesley's way out of The Carver's warehouse where the man himself had held Wesley and mutilated his arm, but Wesley didn't want to keep involving Peter in his problems. For a few crazy seconds, Wesley considered making a run for it, but rationalized it would only postpone the inevitable.

Then a thought fell into his brain—*duh*. He was looking for an opportunity to go undercover in The Carver's organization, and here it was, towering over him. "I'll collect for you."

Mouse laughed. "What? You're crazy."

"Nah, I'm serious. There must be someone on your list that I can get to easier than you can. I'll work to help pay down what I owe The Carver."

Mouse looked away and dragged his hand over his mouth.

"I know how to get into places," Wesley said. "Just give me a chance, I'll show you."

"I don't know, I could get into big trouble."

"How? I help you collect money and you put in a good word for me with The Carver. We could be partners."

Mouse glared at him.

"Just a suggestion."

Mouse hesitated, then narrowed his eyes. "Okay, there's a college kid who owes me two grand, but he never leaves his dorm and I can't get in."

Wesley grinned. "I'm your man for the job."

Mouse lifted a fat finger. "Fuck this up and I'll have to break something. Get in the car."

Wesley climbed into the front seat, praying he hadn't bitten off more than he could chew. "Who is this guy and where does he live?"

"Name is Brent Crandall. He lives in Caldwell Residence Hall at Georgia Tech. But there's a sign-in desk with a security guard, and I can't pass myself off as a student."

Wesley scanned Mouse's hefty frame. "No kidding. Pull in to that pizza place."

"You can eat lunch on your own time, shithead."

"Dude, it's part of the plan. Pull in."

Mouse sighed, but steered the Town Car into the parking lot.

"What do you like on your pizza?" Wesley asked.

"Anything but mushrooms."

Wes held out his hand. "I need a twenty."

The big man looked murderous, then pulled out his wallet. "If you don't come back, you're a dead man."

Wesley took the cash and went into the pizza joint. He placed an order and while he waited, he walked around the restaurant picking up napkins, a to-go menu and anything else with the company logo on it. When his order number was called, he paid for it, then held up the five-dollar bill he had left over.

"Five bucks for your hat," he said to the guy at the counter.

The guy rolled his eyes upward, as if he could see the pizza logo on the front. "This hat?"

"Yeah."

"Deal."

They traded, and Wes walked out with his bounty, then climbed into the car. "Brent Crandall just ordered a pizza."

Mouse pursed his mouth. "Not bad. Let's see if it works."

It worked. With a hat, a fragrant pizza, and a, "Dude, my car's running and I got to deliver this pie" story, he was given Crandall's room number and breezed past the sign-in desk.

He rode up the elevator, found the room and knocked. "Pizza." When no one answered, he pounded harder. "Pizza!"

He heard movement behind the door, then it opened a crack to reveal a bleary-eyed guy. "I didn't order a pizza."

Wesley scratched his head. "Are you Brent Crandall?"

"Yeah, but I didn't order a pizza."

"Maybe one of your roommates did."

"Nobody's here, dude. And I'm trying to sleep."

Wesley pushed hard on the door, knocking the guy back. He walked into the room and closed the door behind him.

From the floor, the guy gaped. "What the hell?"

"I'm not here to hurt you," Wesley said, suddenly realizing he was sweating profusely. "I'm here to collect for The Carver. Just give me the cash, and I'm on my way."

"I don't have any cash," the guy said, pushing to his feet. He was bigger than Wesley and could probably pummel him.

Wesley kept one hand behind him, hoping the guy would think he had a weapon. "Dude, that's not what I want to hear. That stereo is top-of-the-line, and so is the gaming system. Just give me the cash, and I'm outta here." He swallowed. "Otherwise, your roommates are going to have a mess to clean up when they get back."

The guy hesitated and Wesley was on the verge of retreat when Crandall held up his hands. "Okay, okay." He went over to one of the two bunks, lifted the corner of a mattress, and pulled out a plastic baggie. "Two grand, right?"

Wesley's brain churned. "Yesterday it was two grand, today it's twenty-two hundred."

The guy counted out twenty-two one-hundred-dollar bills and handed them over.

Wesley folded the bills and stuffed them in his pocket. "Thanks. Have a nice day."

"Don't I at least get to keep the pizza?"

Wesley lifted the lid and handed over a slice, then left. He took the stairs down to the lobby.

"He wasn't there?" the security guard asked, nodding to the pizza.

"We screwed up the order," Wes said. "Want it?"

"Sure."

He removed a slice for himself, then left the pizza box with the guard. "Cheers."

After discreetly removing two of the hundreds from the wad and sticking them in another pocket, he walked out to the parking lot and climbed into the waiting Town Car.

"How did it go?" Mouse asked.

Wes reached into his pocket and removed the wad of hundreds. "Two grand."

Mouse grinned and took the cash. "Well done."

"Told you."

Mouse counted the money and stowed it, then nodded to the slice of pizza. "You didn't save a piece for me?"

"I will next time."

"Who says there'll be a next time?"

"Come on, Mouse. Let me work off my debt. It's a win-win situation for The Carver. Will you talk to him for me?"

Mouse eyed the slice of pizza. Wesley sighed and handed it over. "Now will you talk to him?"

Mouse took a bite. "I'll think about it."

"Okay. Can I at least get a ride home?"

Still chewing, the big man leaned over and popped the back. "Your bike's in the trunk. Get the hell out of here."

Wesley jumped out and walked around the car, then lifted the trunk lid, happy to see his bike. He pulled it out, feeling pretty good about the way things were unfolding. The collection job hadn't been so hard, and he had two hundred bucks in his pocket. Maybe working for The Carver wouldn't be so bad after all.

He removed his bike and started to close the trunk lid when he noticed his jacket wadded up in the corner, the one Mouse had stripped from him as he'd walked through the metal detector the day he'd met with the D.A. Wes grabbed it, but frowned when he realized the fabric was sticky and wet. When he unfolded it, he nearly swallowed his tongue.

Wrapped inside was a bloody finger.

He jerked his head up, but since the trunk lid was raised, Mouse hadn't seen a thing. Wesley almost dropped the finger, then frantically rewrapped it and shoved the jacket back into the corner of the trunk. He slammed the lid and backed away, almost falling over his bike in his rush to put distance between himself and the severed digit.

Obviously a souvenir from a past-due customer.

Mouse turned the car around and saluted with the half-eaten slice of pizza as he pulled out of the parking lot. "I'll be in touch."

Wesley lifted his hand, feeling sick.

17

Despite the humid temperatures, Thursday evening's Screen on the Green event at Piedmont Park had drawn thousands of people to the rolling lawn for a sunset viewing of *Breakfast at Tiffany's* on a giant screen. While it was still daylight, everyone enjoyed picnic meals and the preshow entertainment of a cover band and crowd sing-alongs.

Sitting on a checkered blanket, her stomach full of shrimp salad and chive butter crackers, Carlotta lifted her glass of chardonnay to Peter's and smiled. It was exactly the kind of date they needed—casual and fun, with no pressure and no interruptions.

Peter leaned forward to kiss her, but stopped and looked past her. "You didn't mention that Wesley was going to be here."

"Wesley, *here?* You must be mistaken."

"It's him," Peter said, pointing. "With a pretty girl."

She swung her head around. "No way. Did you bring binoculars?"

"No. But you could just go over and embarrass him."

"I think I might."

"I was kidding—"

But Carlotta was already making her way to the spot where her brother sat on a *flowered* blanket, no less, with two geeky-looking guys, but leaning toward a seriously cute girl with a sassy ponytail and funky clothes.

"Hel-lo," Carlotta said.

They all looked up and Wesley sprang to his feet. "Hey." His face flamed red and he was perspiring—more than was warranted by the heat.

"What a surprise running into you," she said brightly, sweeping a curious glance over his companions. "And your friends."

His expression reminded her of the time she'd found out he'd asked Britney Jansen to the eighth-grade dance. "That's Jeff and Ravi and Meg. Yo, everyone, this is my sister, Carlotta."

They all chorused hello, and Meg pushed to her feet. "Nice to meet you," she said, sounding more mature than her probable age.

"Same here," Carlotta said, sizing her up as a rich kid. If she wasn't, she'd be better dressed. Her mismatched vintage-grunge look was carefully constructed to appear nonconformist and under-the-radar. But the girl's teeth were an orthodontic masterpiece and her glasses were pure Prada.

"Would you like to join us?" Meg asked.

Carlotta glanced at Wesley simply to torment him. His eyes bulged and he shook his head in an almost imperceptible "no."

Carlotta turned back to Meg. "Thanks, anyway, but I'm with a friend over there." She pointed and Peter lifted his hand.

She looked back to Wesley and smiled. "I just wanted to say hi. Enjoy the movie."

He gave an eye roll. She turned and picked her way back across the lawn between blankets and low-slung chairs to lower herself next to Peter, who was smirking as he popped a strawberry into his mouth. "Did you humiliate him sufficiently?"

"I think so," she said with a grin.

"Is that his girlfriend?"

"I noticed something between them, but I think he's still proving himself to her."

Peter's mouth curved into a rueful smile. "I know that feeling." He lifted a deep-red strawberry to her mouth and she bit into it, but was disappointed that it wasn't quite as sweet as it appeared. Then she reminded herself that what mattered most was they were here together, their own little oasis in the middle of a big, anonymous crowd as the sun slipped below the horizon on a gorgeous summer day. Peter leaned forward to kiss her and she pushed everything else out of her mind. The evening stretched before them, with no intrusions—

"Well, isn't this cozy?"

Carlotta pulled back from Peter and looked up to see Tracey Tully Lowenstein and her smarmy doctor husband, Frederick, standing there, holding a blanket and take-out bags from Star Provisions, an exclusive deli.

"Hi…Tracey," Carlotta said, managing a smile. "And Frederick."

The way he raked his gaze over her made her glad she wasn't a patient of his—*ew*.

"We can't find a place to spread our blanket," Tracey said. "Do you mind if we share yours?"

Carlotta and Peter exchanged a regretful glance, then Peter moved his long legs to make room for them. "Please, sit down. The movie should be starting soon."

Carlotta felt a rush of affection toward Peter. He didn't want them around any more than she did, but he was too well-bred to be impolite. He probably also suspected that Tracey's gossip about them would be even more malicious if they turned her away.

"We're running a little late," Tracey said, setting their food everywhere and nearly pushing Carlotta and Peter off the blanket in the process. "Freddy had an emergency C-section to perform." Then the horsey woman poked Carlotta hard with her elbow. "But don't worry—he washed his hands." She and Freddy laughed uproariously while Carlotta and Peter forced smiles.

Tracey leaned closer to Carlotta as she pulled food containers out of the bags. "We didn't interrupt anything, did we? I mean, Patricia said you told her that you and Peter are just friends."

"That's right," Carlotta said.

"So that was a friendly kiss you were sharing when we walked up?"

She gritted her teeth. "Something like that."

Tracey returned a sly smile and extended a thin cracker topped with a glistening black blob. "Russian caviar?"

Her mother's favorite, Carlotta recalled with a start. She'd found two tins of it after her parents had left, when she'd been forced to go through the kitchen and use everything on hand to feed herself and Wesley. They had spread it on toast for breakfast, and Wesley had gagged.

"No, thank you," she said. "We've already eaten."

"I'll bet Peter won't pass this up." Tracey leaned toward him. "Caviar, Peter?"

"Don't mind if I do," he said, accepting the delicacy.

Carlotta wet her lips. The shrimp salad she'd picked up at a chain grocery deli paled a little in comparison. Her palate was more sophisticated now, but the only caviar she'd had recently were the bits of garnish she'd scooped off the edge of a plate at events she'd crashed with Hannah. And after all, Tracey owed them for barging in.

"Maybe I'll have just a taste," she said.

Tracey smiled, heaped a spoonful from a small tin onto another cracker and passed it to Carlotta.

A pungent, salty aroma tickled her nostrils just as she bit into the dollop of dark fish eggs. The texture was firmer than she'd remembered, almost crunchy, releasing a fresh burst of tangy flavor on her tongue. Her eyes closed involuntarily as a moan of pleasure erupted in her throat.

"Divine, isn't it?" Tracey asked with a giggle.

Carlotta nodded, still savoring the morsel.

"Two hundred sixty dollars an ounce," Tracey sang, "and worth every penny."

At the realization of how much money she had in her mouth, Carlotta was hesitant to swallow. She overchewed the food until it practically disintegrated, and refused another bite, even though her mouth watered for more. Paying that kind of money for shoes or clothes was one thing—you could wear them again, stroke them while they hung in your closet…even spread them on the bed and roll around on top of them if the mood struck. But paying that much for something that lasted thirty seconds, tops, was a little scary. When she and Wesley had forced themselves to eat it, the luxury of the dark roe had escaped her. In hindsight, she probably could've returned the caviar to the store and fed them for a month.

"Good, huh?" Peter said, brushing crumbs off his neat navy chino shorts.

"Delicious."

"I'll feed you caviar every meal if you'll let me," he murmured out of Tracey's earshot.

Jack's words came back to her—that she was better

suited to Peter's world, a world she had been born into, only to have it yanked away when her parents had fled. She knew that Peter couldn't possibly know how much his teasing comment affected her, but it drove home the point that he would lavish her with everything—including love— when she was ready. His patience was endearing. He made her feel safe, but in a different way than Jack made her feel. Jack would pluck her out of danger in an instant, but Peter would leverage his connections and his wealth to make sure she had everything she needed every day to be happy and to feel secure. It was a promise she could build a life on.

She smiled, but was saved from answering by the booming start of the soundtrack and the flicker of frames on the gigantic screen that had been set up for the weekly summer event. It was almost completely dark now, but the light from the projector reflected on the crowd, who turned excited faces toward the opening credits.

Carlotta sighed, instantly transported to New York in the early sixties, where the men and women dressed in chic clothes, and an entire generation seemed to be caught between a proper upbringing and improper urges. She'd seen *Breakfast at Tiffany's* a half-dozen times and never tired of it. Audrey Hepburn was luminous as Holly Go-lightly, a charming gamine who allowed men to shower her with gifts and attention in return for the pleasure of her company. She was the life of every party, managing to slip in and out with a drink in one hand and a long cigarette holder in the other, quipping one-liners and leaving admirers in her wake.

Including George Peppard's Paul, who was mesmerized by Holly, convinced that she'd cured his writer's block. But both Holly and Paul were constrained by their desire for a lifestyle they couldn't afford on their own. She had a stream of sugar daddies, and he had one loyal "pa-troness," who was more interested in his manhood than his manuscripts.

Meanwhile, Tracey and Frederick talked nonstop during the movie. "Did you see the spread in the *AJC* this morning about the Michael Lane police chase?" Tracey asked.

"Yes. It was…thorough."

"And the local stations keep playing the footage of him jumping off the bridge over and over. You must be relieved that he's dead."

Carlotta squirmed, then nodded.

"They haven't found his body yet?" Freddy asked.

"No."

"After this amount of time, it's not going to be pretty when they do."

"It's such a nice night," Peter cut in with an easy smile. "Why don't we talk about something more pleasant?"

She gave his hand a grateful squeeze, and he squeezed back.

"So, Carlotta," Tracey said, licking her fingers, "Patricia said you went face-first into a sheet cake the day Eva McCoy's charm bracelet was stolen. Too bad the *AJC* didn't have a picture of *that*." She laughed.

Carlotta made herself smile and silently thanked Rainie Stephens for arranging to squash the photo. She owed the woman.

"Have the police recovered the charm bracelet?" Freddy asked.

"Not yet," Carlotta said, deciding not to mention that the lead detective didn't consider it to be a priority crime.

"Has there been a ransom request?" he pressed.

"Not that I know of, but I suppose it's not out of the question. I've heard that Eva is devastated over the loss."

"Why doesn't she just buy a new bracelet with all her Olympic money?" Tracey asked.

"I believe it's sentimental to her," Carlotta offered, then turned her attention back to the movie, mentally shaking her head. Thankfully the Lowensteins had lapsed into a discussion between themselves about their gardener. Carlotta immersed herself in the romance building on-screen between Holly and Paul.

"What's your favorite part?" Peter whispered.

"Where they steal the cat and dog masks. Do you have a favorite part?"

"The end, of course," he said with a wink. "Where they both realize that even though they'll face obstacles if they're together, they know it'll be worth it."

Peter had always been a romantic, even when they were young. He'd had the physique of a graceful athlete, had played quarterback for his high school team and had been an accomplished rower, too. She had been dazzled by his golden good looks and tall, muscular build, but it was his romantic side that had won her over. He'd always known her favorite color, favorite flower, favorite song.

When he looked back to the screen, she studied the chiseled profile that was so familiar to her. Peter had been her first lover, and they had been good together. She bit her lip and entertained the thought of going back to his place tonight. Maybe this was why the timing had been off for her and Coop, and why things continued to be rocky between her and Jack. Because deep down, she knew she would have to reconcile her feelings for Peter before she could commit to anyone else.

Maybe Jack was right. Maybe she should turn her mind toward the thought of marrying Peter. She wasn't getting any younger.

Tracey leaned toward Carlotta. "It's a good thing the two of you are just friends," she whispered. "Because you'd have a lot of competition from women in my and Peter's circle. I'd hate to see you get hurt…again."

Carlotta shrank back, stunned by the woman's blatant attempt to put Carlotta in her place. Tracey was determined to keep reminding her that the Wren family's fall from grace had been neither forgiven nor forgotten.

The weight of a hand fell on Carlotta's shoulder, startling her. "Sis?" Wesley crouched next to her, his face near her ear. "Coop just called me. He needs our help."

Her pulse rocketed. "What's wrong?"

"He needs us to make a pickup for him. It's not too far, so it shouldn't take long."

"We don't have a vehicle," she whispered.

"I called Hannah and she said she'd pick us up. Hannah and I could handle it, but Coop said you had to be there."

Because he still didn't completely trust Wesley. And because Hannah was a loose cannon, with an exuberance for body moving that bordered on Hitchcockian.

"Can you leave?" Wesley asked, his eyes pleading.

He wanted so much to get back into Coop's good graces. She hesitated, torn.

Peter leaned forward. "Is something wrong?"

"Um…Wesley needs my help with something. I have to leave."

Peter's face creased in disappointment. "Now?"

"I should be back before the movie ends," she said, then gave him a quick kiss.

She pushed to her feet and left without saying goodbye to Tracey and Freddy, following Wesley carefully through the seated crowd, trying to avoid stepping on anyone. When they finally broke free, he pointed toward the Park

Tavern. "Hannah's going to pick us up on Monroe. She's stopping at Motherwell's on the way to get a gurney and a body bag from Coop's uncle."

Carlotta pressed her lips together—Hannah would be in her element. She only hoped her friend's tattooed and pierced appearance didn't frighten the older Mr. Craft. "Did Coop say why he couldn't make the pickup himself?" She'd left him several messages since yesterday, but he hadn't called her back.

"No…he just said he was busy and it would be better if we did it."

Worry ate at her stomach. Was Coop at a bar getting hammered?

"Is Peter mad?" Wes asked.

"Probably," she said, chewing on her thumbnail. "Did Coop give you any details on the pickup?"

He turned over his hand and read off the notes he'd scribbled there with a pen. "Woman fell and bled out in a house on Argonne, near Ponce de Leon."

"Wow, that is close."

"Do you have your morgue ID with you?"

She nodded. "I keep it in my wallet." She removed the lanyard identifying her as a body hauler and looped it over her neck.

Wesley pulled out his own ID and lifted it over his neck. She noticed his hand was shaking, but reasoned he had to be nervous going on a body pickup without Coop. Her little brother would be the senior body mover on the scene.

A few minutes later, a horn sounded and Hannah pulled up, her eyes wide with excitement. "Get in! This is great! Who died?" She had replaced the magnetic catering sign on her van with one she'd had made up herself that read "Body Movers—You're Going to Need Us Eventually."

"Nice sign," Carlotta said drily. "Better not let Coop see it. Did you have room in the back for the gurney?"

"I had to offload a few frozen pies at the funeral home, but Mr. Craft seemed happy to get them."

"Please tell me there's no food back there right now."

"It's all in coolers and happily contained, don't worry."

"I'm not worried, but the health department might have a bone to pick with you."

Carlotta spent the short drive stressing to Hannah how important it was to be professional, for Coop's sake. Hannah nodded, but as they parked on the street behind a squad car and an unmarked car, she accidentally leaned on the horn and loudly announced their arrival.

"That's one way to let them know we're here," Carlotta muttered.

When they climbed out, Wesley handed them both gloves matter-of-factly. Carlotta noticed he was sweating bullets again.

"Nice house," Carlotta observed as they walked up the front steps illuminated by the porch light. Even in the darkness it was obvious that the bungalow and yard were well cared for. Wesley rang the doorbell. A uniformed officer answered and when Wesley flashed his ID, he told them to go back to the kitchen. The officer returned to the living room where a baseball game was playing on the set.

They quietly traipsed through the house in the direction the man had indicated. The scent of burnt popcorn assailed Carlotta as she walked into the room. A thirty-something Hispanic woman lay on the floor, dressed in jeans and a striped top. One flip-flop lay near her body, the other a few feet away, near a step stool. Blood was pooled around her head and shoulders. A willowy black woman with cropped hair and a badge hooked to her belt looked up as they walked in. "Who are you?"

Wesley showed her his ID. "We're here to transport the body to the morgue. I'm Wes—this is Carlotta and Hannah."

"I'm Detective Salyers." The woman looked at the trio dubiously. "You've done this before?"

"Yes, ma'am, all of us," Wesley said. "I've been working with Cooper Craft for a while. He sent us."

The detective smiled. "I know Coop—great guy."

"Are you ready for us to take the body?"

"Yeah, the M.E. already left, and I'm just finishing up my report. Her name is Alicia Sills, thirty-four years old."

"Anything we need to know about the body?" Wesley asked, impressing Carlotta with his mature demeanor.

"Just that there's a lot of blood, as you see, all coming from a wound on the back of the vic's head." The detective made a thoughtful noise in her throat. "Looks like she climbed onto the step stool, lost her balance and hit hard. You want my opinion, those flip-flops probably tripped her up. Those shoes cause all kinds of accidents."

"That's why I prefer these," Hannah piped up, sticking out her foot to show off the heavy tread lace-up boots she always wore. "Talk about traction."

The detective squinted at her.

Carlotta elbowed her friend. "Be. Quiet," she said out of the corner of her mouth.

"How long has she been lying here?" Wesley asked, surveying the scene.

"The M.E. said maybe a couple of hours," Salyers said. "She was supposed to meet a friend. When she didn't show up, the woman came by to check on her."

Carlotta winced, feeling sorry for the friend who'd come upon the bloody scene.

"Would it be all right if I look for a sheet to wrap the body?" Wes asked.

"Try the hall closet."

"We'll get the gurney," Carlotta offered. They left and Hannah was practically skipping on the way back to the van.

"This is so exciting!"

"Hannah, take it down a notch," Carlotta chastised. "Someone died. That poor lady climbed up on a stool to get something stupid like a casserole dish she never uses, and next thing she knows, she's lying on the floor, mortally wounded."

Hannah blanched. "Do you think she suffered before she died?"

"I don't know, but either way it's terrible, so lose the cheerfulness, okay?"

"Okay, you're right. Sorry."

They removed the gurney from the refrigerated compartment. Carlotta was relieved to see three sets of scrubs folded on top, because all that blood was going to be a mess. They pulled on the loose garments over their clothing and headed back to the house, bumping the rolling gurney along the sidewalk.

"Get the door," Hannah said.

Carlotta opened the storm door, but Hannah was over-eager and slammed the edge of the gurney into the glass, breaking out a little chunk and sending a cobweb of fractures through the entire panel.

"Fuck!" Hannah shouted.

"Shh!" Carlotta hissed. "Slow down. And good grief, try not to break anything else."

They made their way back to the kitchen, where Wesley stood holding a sheet and talking with the detective. Carlotta handed him a set of scrubs, which he pulled on, then he lowered the gurney to the floor. When he snapped on latex gloves, she and Hannah followed suit.

"Carlotta, help me wrap the body," Wesley said. "Hannah, spread the body bag on the gurney and unzip it."

They followed Wesley's orders and Carlotta was amazed at how competent her brother could be when it mattered. He took the lower body, where most of the weight was concentrated. She took the top, positioning her pale Fendi loafers at the edge of the blood pool and leaning down to clasp the woman's arm. They rolled her onto her side to put one edge of the sheet underneath her. Carlotta tried not to look at Alicia Sills's face, but she couldn't help it. Later, she would be thankful for her morbid curiosity. Because if she hadn't been looking down, she might have missed the silver charm that rolled out of the woman's mouth.

Carlotta gasped and dropped the woman's shoulder. The body fell back with a thud, splattering thick blood over her loafers and everywhere else.

"What's wrong?" Detective Salyers asked. She had finished her paperwork and was putting the pen back into her jacket pocket.

Carlotta's mouth opened and closed as she backed away, gesturing frantically for Wesley to do the same. "Call Detective Jack Terry. Tell him to get here right away. There's a double-murderer on the loose."

18

"The *AJC* is calling him The Charmed Killer," Hannah announced from the breakfast table where she pored over the Friday morning newspaper. All three of them had had a late night. Jack and Maria had arrived at Alicia Sills's home, M.E. Pennyman had returned, and the scene had to be rephotographed and reprocessed by the CSI unit before the body could be removed.

"The Charmed Killer, huh?" Carlotta said from the refrigerator, where she rooted for the milk jug.

"They all have to have a name, you know, for posterity."

"And for sensationalizing."

"Leaving a charm in the mouth is his signature," Wesley offered from the stove where he flipped pancakes. He pushed up his glasses. "I heard Detective Marquez say that last night. Jack's new partner is smoking hot."

Carlotta slammed the refrigerator door. "Go ahead, Hannah. I'm listening."

"The APD," Hannah read, "is downplaying the similarities between the two women's deaths. Shawna Whitt was found deceased in her west Atlanta home Monday night, presumably of natural causes, and Alicia Sills was found dead in her Midtown home Thursday evening, presumably from an accidental fall. There is no obvious connection between the victims. But a source in the county morgue admitted that in the mouths of both women was a charm, the kind that one might find on a bracelet."

"Do they identify the charms as a chicken and a cigar?"

"No."

"Are you sure the charm you saw last night was a cigar?" Wesley asked.

"I'm sure," Carlotta said. "When Jack picked it up with tweezers, it was coated with blood, but I saw it for a few seconds when it first fell out of her mouth. I wonder if the chicken and the cigar *mean* something."

"They both start with the letter *C*," Hannah offered.

"Or a smoking bird?" Carlotta asked with a frown.

"The cigar could be sexual," Wesley said.

Both girls stared at him.

"What? There was that little incident between an intern and the leader of the free world, remember?"

"Do you want to hear the rest of the article?" Hannah asked.

"Go ahead," Carlotta said.

"In a bizarre coincidence, Atlanta native and Olympian Eva McCoy, who almost single-handedly triggered a nationwide craze for charm bracelets after attributing her miracle marathon run to the charm bracelet she wore during the grueling foot race, was involved in an incident at Lenox Square mall earlier this week during which her infamous lucky charm bracelet was stolen."

"At least the store wasn't mentioned," Carlotta muttered.

Hannah looked up. "There's a picture."

"Crap."

"What? It's good advertising!"

"Maybe, although I don't think Lindy would mind if

things calmed down a little. What's the name of the reporter who wrote the article?"

"Rainie Stephens."

Carlotta's thoughts went to the woman's business card on her dresser. "So she does have a source in the morgue."

Wesley turned. "You think there's a leak in the morgue?"

"It's probably a quid pro quo arrangement," Hannah offered. "Off the record, but a way to make sure that what's reported is accurate."

Carlotta's eyebrows rose. "You seem to know a lot about it."

Hannah squirmed, which was unusual for her. "I read the paper, I watch the news...and courtroom TV. By the way, there's an update on Michael Lane on page three. They've dragged the river, but still zip."

"At least the story moved off the front page." Carlotta nudged Wesley from behind. "You're awfully quiet—thinking of Meg?"

"Who's Meg?" Hannah asked.

"Nobody," Wesley said with a frown.

Hannah gave a little laugh. "Wesley, do you have a girlfriend?"

"No, I do not have a girlfriend."

Carlotta poured three glasses of milk and carried them to the table. "He was at Screen on the Green watching *Breakfast at Tiffany's,* just for the hell of it."

"Breakfast at Tiffany's?" Hannah said. "Boy, you got it bad."

"Meg's just someone I work with," Wesley said. But his face was so scarlet, affection rushed Carlotta's chest.

"I thought she was cute. And she seemed very mature."

"She's smart, too," he added eagerly, as if he was trying to sell his sister on a puppy.

Hannah scoffed. "So what's she doing with you, shit-head?"

"Very funny. It's not wise to insult the chef."

"You're a cook," Hannah corrected, and extended her plate. He deposited a pancake onto it with a slap, but she suddenly looked concerned. "Dude, your hand is shaking—what's up?"

Carlotta peered under her lashes to observe his response.

He shrugged, then turned back to pour batter into the nonstick pan. "Too much coffee, I guess."

"You *could* be a chef, you know," Hannah offered. "If you wanted to apply yourself."

"He's a courier now," Carlotta said, still watching her brother. "Delivering packages on his bike."

"Cool," Hannah said. "When did that happen?"

"It hasn't started yet," he said. "Hey, Sis, this is the big day, right?"

"Did I miss something?" Hannah asked.

Hmm, clever subject change, she noted. "I'm going for my last X-ray today I hope." She flicked the soft cast on her arm. "I can't wait to stop wearing this ugly thing."

"It is starting to look pretty gnarly," Hannah agreed. "Do you need a ride?"

"No, thanks. I have a new battery in the Monte Carlo."

"When did that happen?" Wesley dropped a pancake onto Carlotta's plate.

"Jack put it in the day before yesterday."

"Jack, huh?" Wesley scraped more batter from the bowl into the pan. "So was Peter pissed about you leaving the park last night?"

Carlotta's chest squeezed with remorse. "He was nice when I called, but disappointed. He's not too crazy about me doing this body moving thing."

"Why not?" Hannah asked. "I think it'd make a great conversation starter at the country club."

"I think he's worried about my safety," Carlotta chided.

The piercing sound of the motion detector alarm suddenly filled the room. Carlotta went to the front room window and glanced outside to see Jack standing on the stoop, jacketless and rumpled. A quick check of the curb revealed that the black SUV that had been sitting there when she'd retrieved the newspaper this morning was gone.

"It's Jack," she called back to the kitchen, then opened the front door. The detective's broad shoulders were rounded and his face was lined with fatigue.

"You look like hell," she said, leaning on the doorknob.

"Good morning to you, too. Can I come in?"

"Sure." She stepped aside, then closed the door behind him. "Wesley's making pancakes."

"Got any coffee?"

"Straight ahead. Have you been to bed?"

"Not yet."

He seemed to take it in stride—the long hours and the unpredictable cases. Jack was well-suited to his demanding job, but it underlined his previous comment that he wasn't the settling-down type. He was the quintessential cop, she thought as she followed him into the kitchen.

Jack greeted Hannah and Wesley and leaned against the breakfast bar while Carlotta poured him a cup of coffee.

"We're reading about The Charmed Killer," Hannah said.

He frowned. "What?"

She handed him the newspaper. He scanned it for a few seconds, then tossed it down with a curse. "This is all we need, a nosy reporter vying for a Pulitzer. Did any of you talk to this woman about the case?"

"No," they chorused.

He looked at Carlotta pointedly. "Are you sure?"

She frowned. "I said no, Jack."

"Well, don't. Did any of you notice anyone else on the scene last night, other than the uniform and Detective Salyers?"

"No," they chorused.

"Think hard. Anyone loitering on the street? A curious neighbor? Someone walking a dog?"

"No."

"Nope."

"Uh-uh."

His jaw hardened. "Were any of you ever alone with the body?"

Carlotta jammed her hands on her hips. "What are you getting at, Jack?"

"We have to rule out that someone on the crime scene put those charms in the victims' mouths."

Her eyes widened. "You think we would do something like that?"

A muscle in his jaw jumped. "Carlotta, it's been noted that you were at both crime scenes."

She gave a little laugh. "Jack, you can't be serious."

"I have to ask because—"

"Because why?"

He sighed. "Because you…fit a profile."

Her head jutted forward. "A profile that Maria came up with? For a serial killer?"

"No, not for a killer. For someone who likes to…involve herself in solving crimes."

"That's bullshit," Wesley said, his face contorted. "How dare you say that about my sister?"

Jack lifted his hand. "Relax. The reason I'm here instead

of someone else is because I know how far-fetched that scenario is."

She recalled Maria's personality "profile" of her. *You aren't challenged enough on your job, which is why you like to get involved in police work.* "So your partner thinks that I want so badly to *involve* myself in cases, that I would plant evidence to create the illusion of a serial killer?"

"It's been known to happen," he said quietly.

She gasped. "Jack, you were at Shawna Whitt's house when I got there. When Coop left to get the gurney, you were with me the entire time. I didn't even touch the body before he found the charm."

"I know," he said, then averted his gaze. "If it comes down to it, would you be willing to take a polygraph exam?"

She knew her mouth was open—she could feel air on her tongue.

"Don't be offended," he said.

"How can I *not* be offended?"

"Because this is what happens when you—all of you," he said, including Wesley and Hannah, "are on crime scenes—even if it's after the fact. You become part of the process. If you can't handle the pressure, then you need to get out of the body moving business." He straightened. "By the way, do you know how hard it's going to be to prove that someone did or didn't break in through the front door of Alicia Sills's house after you three managed to break the glass?"

Hannah lifted her hand sheepishly. "Uh, I own that one."

Carlotta exchanged glances with Hannah and Wesley, then looked back to Jack, contrite. "You're right. Do whatever you have to do to eliminate any of us as suspects, so you can move forward with the investigation."

He gave a curt nod, then pushed off the counter. "I came by to take down the motion detectors. I'm assuming you haven't seen anything suspicious."

"No, nothing." She hesitated, then added. "Except the black SUV that keeps showing up on the curb."

"But you said your neighbor spotted it a couple of weeks ago, right?"

"Right. So it couldn't have been Michael—he was still in the hospital."

Jack looked at Wesley. "Do you know anything about it?"

Wesley shook his head. "No, nothing."

Carlotta studied Wesley. When he was little, she could always tell when he was lying, but now she didn't have a clue. The realization scared her.

"If either of you see it again," Jack said, "call me. No confrontations, okay? If I'm busy, I'll have a uniform drive over to get a plate number. Hopefully, it's nothing." He drained his coffee cup, then jerked his head toward the living room. "Carlotta, why don't you keep me company while I dismantle the system?"

So the police believed Michael was dead. She followed Jack outside where he began removing the motion detectors that he'd installed a few days ago, assuming he wanted to talk to her about something.

"One of Lane's shoes washed up on the bank a couple miles down from where he went in," he said as he pulled out hand tools from a duffel bag.

"You're sure it's his shoe?"

"We matched it to the film of the foot chase."

"But no body?"

"No." Jack stowed the motion detector he'd removed and moved on to the next. "At this point, he's presumed dead."

"What happens if they don't find his body?"

"We'll work with the family to have Lane declared deceased."

She pressed her lips together and nodded. "Keep me posted?"

"Of course." He made short work of removing the second detector, then removed a handkerchief to wipe his forehead. "The day Marquez and I drove you home after the cake incident, you said you had a clue about the Shawna Whitt case. What did you mean?"

Carlotta crossed her arms. "Oh, so now you want my help?"

He sighed. "Work with me, Carlotta. I've been up all night."

She tried to hold out, but the man was impossible to resist. "Come back inside. I'll show you what I found.

"I did some searching on the Internet," she said as they backtracked into the house. "An S-W-H-I-T-T from Atlanta was a member of a Web site for fans of Eva McCoy's charm bracelets. In the community chat section, she posted that she was using her bracelet as an incentive to change her life. In her last post, she said that she was looking into a match-making service—it was dated only a few days before Shawna Whitt was found dead. If it's the same woman, you might look for the charm bracelet in her home. Maybe the charm that was placed in her mouth was from her bracelet. Maybe the second victim is a member of the site, too."

Jack chewed on his lip. "Do you remember the name of the Web site?"

She had to fight not to feel too smug as they went down the hall to her bedroom. "I kept all the printouts. Do you want them?"

He shook his head in obvious consternation. "Yeah, I'll take them."

She pushed open the door and Jack looked at her bed longingly, but she suspected it had more to do with the allure of her mattress after his sleepless night than with her. She picked up her purse and delved into an inside pocket for the sheaf of papers she'd printed and folded. "There. Read the last post."

He scanned the page. "'I'm tired of living all alone in my house, sleeping alone. I'm going to join one of those matchmaking services—can anyone suggest a good one?'"

"What do you think?" Carlotta asked eagerly.

Jack frowned. "I think this woman announced on the damned Internet that she lives and sleeps alone. Do you know how many perverts would see that as an invitation?"

"You have to be a member of the Web site to read the forums."

"I'm assuming you have to fill out some kind of profile to join? With personal info, like your address?"

She nodded.

"Great—so we just narrowed our suspect pool down to any psycho with access to a computer."

"I can help," Carlotta offered. "What can I do?"

He held up a hand. "Oh, no. You will not be *helping* on this investigation."

"But I already have," she insisted, gesturing to the papers he held.

"Maybe. We'll see."

"Do you think this has anything to do with Eva McCoy's charm bracelet being stolen?"

"I don't see how except that everyone seems to have gone berserk over charms."

"Any leads on Eva's bracelet?"

"No, and now that these murders have fallen into our laps, we don't have the time or resources to worry about it. Meanwhile, McCoy's senator uncle is leaning on us to find the damn thing, saying it's a matter of national pride." Jack rubbed his eyes. "I really don't give a shit whether we find the bracelet or not, but apparently the woman's being hounded—by the media…and everyone else. We have a car nearby to watch her place, but right now, we need all our guys in the field, not babysitting."

Carlotta pressed her lips together. "So what do you think, Jack? Does Atlanta have a serial killer?"

She could tell he didn't want to answer, that even from his jaded perspective the prospect was almost too daunting to say aloud. "I'm afraid it's looking that way."

She released a pent-up breath. "Do you think he'll kill again?"

"He might've killed before. In hindsight, the discovery of the charms in these two cases was accidental. He could've killed before and nobody noticed the charms."

"How's that possible?"

He shrugged. "If foul play wasn't suspected and if the charm was small, it simply could've been overlooked. Or if it showed up on an X-ray it might've been mistaken for dental work. If the body had been cremated, like Shawna Whitt's, the charm would ultimately be melted down."

"Shawna Whitt was cremated? That's unusual in the South." Baptists needed a body to bury.

His frown deepened. "Yeah, and it's unfortunate, too, in this case. Because without the body, it's going to be hard to prove she didn't die of natural causes. But Coop's going to do what he can."

"Coop's working on the case?"

"At least the lab work."

Carlotta's shoulders fell in relief to know that he hadn't returned her calls because he'd been busy.

Jack checked his watch. "I'd better be going, let you get to work—" He stopped and his eyes narrowed.

Too late, Carlotta realized he'd zoned in on the business card of Rainie Stephens, staff reporter, *Atlanta Journal-Constitution*, stuck in the mirror of her dresser. His face hardened. "I thought you said you didn't talk to the reporter."

She plucked at her cast guiltily, looking for something to do with her hands. "I didn't, not about the murders. She gave me her card at the store. She was asking questions about Eva McCoy, but I didn't tell her anything…not really."

Jack frowned and snatched the card from the mirror. "I'll take this off your hands." He pointed his finger at her. "Behave, Carlotta. I mean it."

19

Carlotta was still steamed at Jack as she drove to her doctor's office. Admittedly, she had *involved*—borrowing Maria's wording—herself in a police case or three. But adding up all the pluses of her contributions and the minuses of the problems she'd inadvertently caused, she'd like to think that overall, she was still in the positive range.

In the waiting room, she simmered to a slow boil and sat glued to the news to see if the networks had jumped onto the serial killer story bandwagon. They had, with both feet. The two known murders at the hands of The Charmed Killer were relayed by the newscaster with a sinister silhouette of a man's head in the background overlaid with a generic charm bracelet. She wondered how long the graphics department had worked to come up with just the right mix of ominous titillation.

"Atlanta authorities are calling him The Charmed Killer because he leaves a charm in the mouths of his victims," the female anchor delivered in an apprehensive tone. "The murders may be related to the charm culture that has erupted around Olympian Eva McCoy, who famously credited a charm bracelet for her comeback win in the women's marathon competition last summer. Coincidentally, McCoy's charm bracelet was stolen earlier this week during a disturbance at a public appearance in Atlanta."

At least they didn't show the store, Carlotta thought in abject relief.

"Officials will not confirm if the charms found in the mouths of the victims are from the missing bracelet. Meanwhile, in the aftermath of the incidents, Eva McCoy has reportedly decided not to compete in the upcoming World Championships Marathon competition in Helsinki, Finland, a much-anticipated event that would have secured her title as the reigning women's long-distance runner and earned McCoy a million-dollar bonus from one of her sponsors, Body League. McCoy allegedly has received anonymous death threats to dissuade her from competing, proof that the sport has high stakes. We will keep you updated as this intriguing story develops."

Aerial photos of Eva's house on the affluent stretch of West Paces Ferry showed photographers and fans lined up along the security fence, holding signs of support, hoping to get a glimpse of their hero. Carlotta suspected that all the attention was suffocating Eva, who was already gun-shy around the public and understandably scared over the death threats that Jack had as good as confirmed by his silence on the subject.

The news camera panned over the crowd and at the sight of a familiar figure, Carlotta lurched forward on her chair.

Mitchell Moody?

He glanced over his shoulder, then turned his face away from the camera and walked out of the frame.

The sequence passed so quickly, she wondered if she'd imagined it. Why would June's son be holding vigil outside Eva McCoy's house?

The sound of her name being called interrupted her

thoughts. She shouldered her purse and followed the doctor's assistant into an exam room. From there she was shuffled into X-ray, quizzed about her chance of being pregnant, then had her arm thoroughly radiated. Afterward she sat and waited for Dr. Eames, her orthopaedist who, fifty minutes later, walked in with assistant in tow, holding what was presumably her X-ray film up to the light.

"Now that's a beautiful bone if ever I've seen one," he quipped, turning to her with a smile. "How are you, Ms. Wren?"

"I'm fine, thank you."

"Good. Any pain?" he asked, palpating her arm where the break had occurred.

"Only when I overdo it."

"Are you taking the pain meds I prescribed?"

"No, ibuprofen does the job." The unidentified pill she'd found in Wesley's bathroom was in her purse. She'd brought it to show the doctor, even though her mind still whirled for a plausible explanation of where she'd found it and why she'd care what it was. If only his assistant would leave...

"It looks as if this will be the last time we'll see each other," the doctor said.

She smiled in relief. "No offense, but that's very good news."

"None taken."

"So I can ditch the cast?"

"We'll dispose of it for you." He picked it up from a table, holding the soiled soft cast by a corner. Weeks of adventures and incidents stained the neoprene surface, including cake and icing. The doctor gave her a wan smile, then handed off the cast to the assistant, who left the room carrying it as if it were roadkill.

But at least they were alone. Carlotta reached for her purse, eager to find out how much she should be worried about Wesley's new habit.

"Ms. Wren, I know this isn't any of my business, but are you Randolph Wren's daughter?"

Surprised, she nodded. "Yes, I am."

"It occurred to me after your last visit that you might be."

"Did you know my father?"

"We were doubles partners at the tennis club." He smiled. "Your dad was a great guy."

Carlotta blinked. No one had ever told her that before.

"I never believed what they said about him. In fact—" Dr. Eames scratched his head "—the last time I saw Randolph, he was worried. He said that someone in his firm was trying to frame him. He wanted to bring me something to hold for him in case he ever needed it."

Carlotta's heart thudded in her chest. "What was it?"

Dr. Eames shrugged. "Randolph was arrested before our next game, so he never got the chance to hand off whatever it was. Papers of some kind, I think. After he was released on bail, I wondered if he might show up and ask for my help. But then…he simply left town." The doctor lifted his hands. "Like I said, it's really none of my business…"

"That's okay," she murmured. "Did he mention the name of the person he thought was trying to frame him?"

"No. I understand that no one has seen him since he disappeared?"

She nodded.

"What's it been now, about ten years?"

"That's right."

"Well, if you ever speak to him, tell him that Marty Eames says hello."

"I will," she promised, squashing her question about the

pill in her purse. On the heels of their conversation, it now seemed inappropriate.

She left the doctor's office with Eames's words about her father dancing in her brain. The story gelled with what her father had told Peter about papers that could exonerate him.

On the other hand, maybe Randolph had simply stuck with the same lie from the beginning.

On the way to the mall, Carlotta had an inspiration concerning the pill and pulled over at her new favorite place, the public library. Lorraine was working and quickly got her settled at a computer for more "research." When the woman turned her back, Carlotta pulled out the pill and typed the letters and numbers imprinted on the surface into the search box. Within five seconds, she had her answer.

Generic OxyContin. She knew a little about the drug. She'd heard that it was called "Hillbilly Heroin" because of its popularity in rural areas, and that it had become a fashionable prescription drug for recreational use. But the more she read, the more the information terrified her—how readily available it was, and how addictive, especially if rid of its time-release coating, effectively turning it into oxycodone. OxyContin was an effective pain reliever—oxycodone produced uncontained euphoria, ergo the rampant addiction.

It wasn't a stretch to figure out Wesley's source. She knew that Chance Hollander was into all kinds of vile businesses.

But was Wesley using, or dealing? Or both?

As she scrolled through a list of symptoms of OxyContin abuse, she began ticking off behaviors she'd first noticed in Wes when they'd gone on the road trip with Coop: irritability, mood swings. And more recently, sweats and tremors.

Panic bled through her chest, leaving her cold and laboring to breathe. The two prescriptions of Percocet that he'd stolen from her—had they been to prop up a habit he was trying to conceal?

She left the library with a heavy heart. If she had felt incompetent before about mothering Wesley, she now felt completely out of her league. She picked up her cell phone to call him, then put it away. She needed to think through things, then talk to him face-to-face. If she reacted in anger, it would be too easy for him to shut her out.

She drove to the mall teary and tense, but pulled herself together enough to clock in for her afternoon shift. Friday afternoon was always busy, and she was glad to have something to keep her mind off her problems. And when she did remember, she reminded herself that those problems were still relatively small compared to the two women across town who were dead at the hands of a madman.

In the scheme of things, it wasn't such a bad day. Whatever was wrong, she and Wesley would get through it somehow. What didn't kill her would only make her stronger…provided it didn't kill her.

She'd seen on *Oprah* that it *was* possible to worry oneself to death.

Near the end of her shift, she spotted a woman wearing a scarf and big sunglasses loitering in her department. The disguise wasn't so unusual—lots of women in Buckhead stopped for a healing bout of shopping therapy after a visit to their dermatologist or plastic surgeon. But there was something familiar about this woman.

When she looked up and saw Carlotta watching her, the woman started to leave, then apparently changed her mind and walked up to the counter. "Carlotta, right?"

Carlotta's mind raced to place the voice. "That's right."

"It's Eva. Eva McCoy."

She tried to hide her surprise. "Hello. Can I help you with something?"

"I think I'm being followed," Eva said, her voice low.

Sensing the woman was nearing some kind of breaking point, Carlotta tempered her response. "What makes you think so?"

"I can feel it."

"Okay." Carlotta glanced around surreptitiously. "Are you alone?"

"Yes."

"What about your bodyguard?"

"I can't trust anyone," Eva whispered.

"Why? What do you mean?"

"They're trying to get rid of me."

"Do you mean the death threats?"

Eva nodded.

"Has something else happened since your charm bracelet was stolen?"

"No…not really. But it's made me see things in a different light. Things I dismissed before."

"Like what?"

The woman hesitated. "Like the food poisoning incident at the Olympics. I'd suffered from food poisoning before, but that time seemed different, somehow. More…toxic."

"Are you saying that someone might have spiked your food?"

"Maybe," Eva said, her voice breaking.

Carlotta had encountered more than her fair share of certifiably crazy people in her life, and recognized the signs of paranoia. "Ms. McCoy, would you like for me to call someone?"

She shook her head. "No."

"What about Mr. Newsome?"

"No. Ben's in Chicago, standing in for an appearance I had to cancel. I don't want to worry him."

"If you're scared, let me call the police."

"No! That's worse. They're watching my house, you know."

"I understood that was to make sure that none of your fans bothered you," she said gently. The image of Mitchell Moody outside the woman's gate flashed into her head. "Did you drive yourself here?"

Eva shook her head. "I sneaked out of the house and called a taxi to pick me up a few blocks away. I didn't plan to come here, but I didn't know where else to go. I felt like a sitting duck in that house."

"It's okay," Carlotta soothed. "What about your uncle? Surely he can help you?"

Eva chewed on her nails, as if she was considering the idea.

"Why don't you call him?" Carlotta encouraged. "You shouldn't be alone. I'm getting ready to leave, so maybe I can take you to his office?"

The woman nodded nervously and pulled out her phone. "I'll do that." She punched in a number, then asked for Senator Porter McCoy. From what Carlotta could hear of the one-sided conversation, he managed to persuade Eva to come to his office.

Eva closed her cell. "I would very much appreciate that ride you offered. Uncle Porter's office is in the Washington Street state building downtown." Her hand was shaking. "Is there a water fountain close by?"

"This way." Carlotta led the woman to the employee break room where she swiped her ID to get in and retrieved her purse while Eva tossed back a couple of capsules and washed them down with water. As they left the store, Eva's head moved continually, scanning for whomever she thought was pursuing her. Carlotta felt sorry for the woman—she was obviously spooked.

"It's not a limo," Carlotta apologized when she unlocked the Monte Carlo. "But it has a new battery."

"It's great," Eva said as she slid into the passenger seat. She checked the side mirror and seemed antsy until they were underway. But once on the road, she removed the scarf and the sunglasses and seemed more like herself. "You must think I'm crazy," she murmured.

Carlotta glanced over at the slight brunette. "No. I think you're under a lot of stress. And I can't imagine what it must be like to be in the spotlight like you've been."

A sad little laugh escaped Eva. "I trained my entire adult life for the Olympics, yet sometimes I'd give anything to go back to the way things were before, when I was anonymous."

"But your charm bracelets are raising a lot of money for charity."

"I suppose you're right." She wrapped her fingers around her bare wrist, obviously pining for the piece of jewelry that had meant so much to her. "Still, no good deed goes unpunished."

"You haven't heard any news about your bracelet?"

"No, and I really don't expect to."

Eva's sadness sent another pang through Carlotta as she headed south on Peachtree toward downtown. The young woman had accomplished a feat few individuals could boast, and she'd done it in heroic fashion while the world had cheered her on. She should be on top of the world, enjoying the accolades and the benefits of being a gold-medalist. Instead, she was a victim of her own celebrity.

"Eva, the death threats you've received—how were they communicated?"

"Always anonymously, via e-mail from Internet cafés or a scribbled note in the mail."

"Do you think they're from fans or competitors?"

She shrugged. "Maybe. Or someone I inadvertently dissed at an appearance. We turned everything over to the FBI, but nothing was ever substantiated. They told me to get on with my life." The woman touched her head. "I'm trying, but it's wearing on me. Sometimes I have anxiety attacks."

"Is that what the pills were for?"

"Yes, and they help." She gave a little laugh. "I wish I could've taken them during the Olympics, but unfortunately, I couldn't have anything like that in my system, because of the doping blood tests, you know."

"It must have been an ordeal. I heard on the news that you've decided not to compete in the World Championships?"

Eva nodded. "Now they're saying there's some guy out there killing women and stuffing charms in their mouths— maybe because of me?"

"There's no reason to think those deaths have anything to do with you," Carlotta soothed.

"I just want all of this charm insanity to stop. I never meant for any of this to happen. I only wanted to raise money for charity." Eva inhaled deeply, then released the breath. "I have one more contracted appearance on Monday at Atlantic Station, then I'm finished."

"I'm sure no one will blame you." Carlotta tried to inject a casual note into her voice as she flipped on her left signal to turn onto Ralph McGill Boulevard. "Eva, how well do you know Mitchell Moody?"

"Mitch?" She squirmed in her seat. "Not very well, really. He ran with a small group of us for the three months I was in Hawaii training."

Carlotta decided not to alarm the woman by telling her

that Mitch had been outside her home with other fans. Instead she manufactured a smile. "I got the impression at the Neiman's event that Mitch had a crush on you."

Eva looked away and laughed nervously. "Um, maybe. But please don't ever say that when Ben's around."

"Is Ben the jealous type?"

Eva smiled. "It's his competitive nature."

Carlotta steered the car right onto Courtland, which turned into Washington, and soon the Coverdell Legislative Office Building came into view on the tree-lined street. "Do you want me to go in with you?"

"Thank you, but I've inconvenienced you enough."

"It wasn't any trouble," Carlotta assured her as she pulled to a stop in front of the building.

"Still, I'm very grateful. Thank you." Eva reached over and squeezed Carlotta's hand. "I've been feeling out of sorts since my charm bracelet was stolen," she said, her voice trailing off. "I never realized how much I'd miss it."

"I'm sure your bracelet will turn up soon."

Eva nodded, but Carlotta could see in the woman's eyes that she didn't believe her. Eva climbed out of the car and waved, then hurried toward the building, her head pivoting as she scanned the area that bustled with people ending their workday. Carlotta's heart went out to the woman who seemed caught in a no-win situation, and whose mental toughness hadn't prepared her for such an emotional blow.

Carlotta bit her lip. Jack had admitted that Eva's missing charm bracelet wasn't high on his or the department's priority list. And he'd been clear that he didn't want Carlotta poking around in The Charmed Killer case.

But he hadn't said anything about her poking around in the missing bracelet case.

In fact, Jack might actually be grateful if she did some

legwork for him. Or better yet—if she helped him clear the case from his backlog altogether. The thought of helping return something so special to Eva excited her.

Meanwhile, she didn't relish the thought of heading back north with a hundred thousand other commuters at this time of day. She wished she was close to the library so she could do some research on Eva McCoy that might help her figure out where to start. Then she realized she was only about a mile away from the building that housed the offices of the *Atlanta Journal-Constitution*, possibly the single largest repository of information in the city.

Carlotta wondered if Rainie Stephens worked late.

"I always work late," the redhead said with a wry grin. "Have a seat, Ms. Wren."

"Carlotta," she corrected as she lowered herself into the guest chair in Rainie's messy cubicle.

"Okay, Carlotta." Rainie's eyes sparkled with interest. "Did you come here to talk about The Charmed Killer?"

"Uh, no. Actually, I came to ask you what you remember about the incident at Neiman's where Eva McCoy's bracelet was stolen."

"I think you had a better point of view than I did."

"Until I fell into the cake. Can you pick up the story from there?"

Rainie sat back in her chair. "Can't you get that from the surveillance tapes?"

"This is sort of on the Q.T."

"Ah. Well, I'm afraid I can't add much except that the man went for Eva, then a few seconds later, he bolted for the mall entrance and disappeared."

"Did your photographer get anything?"

The reporter rummaged for a file, then handed it over.

"Lots of pictures of you and the cake, but nothing useful of the guy or his getaway. This was only the photographer's second assignment. When things blew up, he freaked."

Carlotta opened the folder and winced at the sheet of black-and-white photos. Her face and fall were captured in embarrassing detail, but only the back of the perp was visible. She looked up. "Have I thanked you for keeping these photos out of the paper?"

"You're welcome. You can keep those." Rainie clasped her hands. "So, what's the personal interest in Eva McCoy's bracelet? Has some kind of reward been offered?"

"No. It's just that Eva's so upset and the police are swamped with crowd control around her estate—"

"And The Charmed Killer?"

"Uh…I really couldn't say."

"But you were there—at both scenes, in fact."

Jack's warning not to talk to the woman about the murders rang in her ears. "That was…inadvertent."

"Can you confirm that the charm in the Whitt woman's mouth was a bird of some kind?"

"I…can't. Sorry."

"How about the charm in the Sills woman's mouth?"

"I've been asked not to talk about the cases."

"By your boyfriend, Jack Terry?"

Carlotta frowned. "Jack's not my boyfriend."

"Right." Rainie nodded, seemingly unconvinced. "I'm a reporter, Carlotta. I have sources everywhere."

"Do your sources know anything about the death threats that Eva McCoy has received?"

The redhead hesitated. "Just that she has, which, frankly, isn't so strange for someone with such a high profile. There are a lot of crazies out there who think women shouldn't be elite athletes. And the competition is stiff—there are fewer sponsors in women's sports. There was a case a couple of years ago where a death threat was sent to a female golfer. Come to find out, the coach of a rival golfer was behind it."

"Do you think that Eva's food poisoning at the Olympics could have been an attempt to sabotage her?"

Rainie looked dubious. "I guess it's possible. But since many of the athletes ate the same thing as Eva, some theorized that she'd simply allowed her meal to sit out too long." Rainie shrugged. "Or maybe it was just a viral bug. Regardless, the experience seems to have made her paranoid."

"Just because she's paranoid doesn't mean someone isn't out to get her."

"True. Or at least get her bracelet. By the way, if you get a line on it, I'd love an exclusive."

Carlotta stood. "You got it."

"And that goes for anything related to The Charmed Killer, too."

Carlotta gave her a flat smile, but didn't respond as she turned to go.

"One last thing?"

Carlotta turned back. "Yes?"

"While I have you here, you wouldn't want to speculate on your father's whereabouts, would you?"

Carlotta swallowed hard. What was it about the reporter that made Carlotta feel as if she could see directly into a person's head? "No, I wouldn't." She turned and walked out of Rainie Stephens's office, unsure if she'd just made a friend…or an enemy.

20

"It was good of you to stay late today," Meg offered as she and Wesley left McCormick's office and headed back to their workstation.

Wes lifted his hand to push up his glasses, but when he noticed the way it trembled, he quickly shoved it into his pocket. "No problem." He was eager to get the project rolling…and Meg had worn a skirt today.

"I was sorry you had to leave last night," she said.

"Yeah, well, duty called." He longed to tell her that he'd been picking up the latest victim of The Charmed Killer, but Jack had warned them not to talk about the case. And he didn't want to foul up the first call that Coop had trusted him with.

"You missed the best part of the evening."

"The end of the movie?"

"No, silly, taking me home."

A flush climbed his neck. He didn't know what to say, so he decided to keep his mouth shut and keep walking.

Meg sighed and stopped. "You're totally blowing it, you know."

He stopped, too, utterly confused. "Blowing what?"

"You could be my boyfriend if you'd straighten up."

He raised his eyebrows. "Huh?"

She snapped her fingers in front of his nose. "Hello? Dude, you're not fooling anybody, especially me. You're baked."

"No, I'm not." In fact, his head ached from lack of Oxy. He'd had a hit last night after returning home from the body moving gig just to relax after all the commotion, but he had resisted all day—for her, dammit.

"If you're not, then you're worse off than I thought," she said, shaking her head. "What are you doing, meth or Oxy?"

"Not that meth shit," he said, then bit his tongue.

"Ah, you're on the cotton. Figured." She turned to walk away.

"Hey, it's just a baby habit," he said after her. "I can quit anytime."

She turned around, walking backward. "Sure you can. See you later, loser."

Her smug remark sent anger whipping through him. Who did she think she was, judging him? He didn't want to be her damn boyfriend anyway. Prim little princess was just a cock tease. He'd been sporting wood all day, and for nothing.

He checked his watch and muttered a curse. Because he'd wanted to stare at Meg's bare, tanned legs all afternoon, he was going to be late for his meeting with Jack Terry and Liz to discuss his working for The Carver. He turned and stomped away, eager to put distance between himself and the girl who lived to mess with his head.

At least he had his bike back. He pumped the pedals hard toward the midtown precinct to work off his bad mood, but Meg's words ate at him like acid. When he got to the precinct and locked up his bike, he was craving a hit, bad. From his backpack his phone rang. He pulled it out to see Liz's number come up on the screen. Connecting the call, he answered, "Yeah."

"You're late," Liz chided.

"I just got here."

"I'm in Jack's office, come on back."

He walked into the building, went through a metal detector and down the hall to enter the lobby of the precinct. When he walked in, the lady behind the Plexiglas window looked up. Her name tag read "Brooklyn" and her body language read "don't eff with me."

"Well, aren't you just as cute as a June bug?" she said, looking him up and down. "What can I do for you, sugar?"

"Uh, Wesley Wren to see Detective Jack Terry."

"Wren? You any kin to Carlotta Wren?"

"She's my sister."

"Good girl, that one. Go on over to that door and I'll buzz you in. Somebody on the other side will tell you how to find Detective Terry."

He went through the door and ran a shaky hand through his hair. He needed a haircut and a breath mint and he probably looked like crap. The OxyContin in his backpack was calling to him. It would calm his jumpy nerves and get rid of the headache hammering at his skull. But Meg's smug expression kept him from giving in.

Loser…loser…loser.

Once inside, he stopped at a vending machine and bought a can of Diet Coke because it packed a bigger caffeine punch than regular Coke. He cracked it open and sucked it down in three gulps, then asked for directions to Jack's office.

As it turned out, Jack and Liz were waiting for him in an interview room, along with the mousy Assistant District Attorney, Cheryl Meriwether. Jack looked like he'd been run over by a truck and Liz looked sexy as hell in a snug skirt and a blouse with a deep V that showed off her great knockers.

"Glad you could make it," Jack said, his voice thick with sarcasm.

"We could've talked about this over breakfast this morning at my house and saved us both some time," Wesley offered. Predictably, Liz shot Jack a look, assuming he'd spent the night there.

Jack glowered. "Sit down."

Wes sat and clasped his knees under the table, trying to look like a good boy.

"A.D.A. Meriwether and your attorney filled me in on the expectations that were discussed in your meeting with the D.A. Basically, you're to infiltrate Hollis Carver's organization in an effort to find out if and how deeply he might be involved in drug distribution, especially heroin. I'll be your contact for any information you hear. And I'll pass along things you should be looking out for."

Wesley nodded.

"The key to all this, of course, is getting you into the organization in the first place."

"I got that covered," Wes said.

Jack's eyes went wide. "What do you mean?"

"Well, it's no secret that I owe the man money. So when one of his collection agents came calling a couple of days ago, I convinced him to let me help him collect from another client to help pay down my debt." He shrugged. "Things went well, and he said he'd put in a good word for me with The Carver."

Jack nodded, seemingly impressed. "Okay. Good. Who's the guy you worked with?"

"I only know the big fathead as Mouse."

"Yeah, I know who he is," Jack said.

"Jack," Liz said, "I'm concerned about Wesley working with these thugs. That animal already carved his name into Wesley's arm."

"Not his entire name," Wesley offered.

Jack frowned. "Is that what happened when you disappeared a few weeks ago?"

Wes nodded.

"Show him," Liz said.

He unbuttoned his shirt and took his arm out of his sleeve to show the red, taut crisscrosses of scars. Jack grimaced. "Damn."

"See what I'm saying?" Liz said. "I don't want him in there any longer than necessary."

"I hear you," Jack said. "But from where I'm sitting, this is a good deal for everybody." He looked at Wesley. "Be smart about this and you just might be able to walk away with a clean slate."

Wes thought about the severed finger wrapped in his jacket in Mouse's trunk. "What if they ask me to do something…bad?"

"They'll probably give you a phone so they can call you whenever they need you. We'll have a GPS chip installed inside it. If you find yourself in a situation you can't get out of, all you have to do is call me and we'll come to you."

Wesley nodded. "Sounds simple enough." Assuming he had time to get a call off before the bullets started flying.

"When do you expect to hear back from this Mouse character?" Cheryl Meriwether asked Wesley.

"He'll turn up in a couple of days."

"I'll wait to hear from you," Jack said. "Are we done here?"

Everyone nodded and pushed to their feet. As the two women made their way to the door, Jack leaned into Wes and murmured, "It goes without saying that Carlotta can't know anything about this."

Wes looked up. *"Duh."*

"You don't have to be a smart-ass."

"Right back at you, Detective. See you at breakfast?"

Jack scowled. "Get the hell out of here."

Wes walked out of the building with Liz and the A.D.A. The women talked about shoes and complimented each other's perfume. Liz sent her best wishes to Kelvin Lucas, but even the A.D.A. looked pained at the mention of her boss. After Cheryl Meriwether split off toward her car, Liz turned and smiled at him.

"Where are you headed?"

He shrugged. "Nowhere."

"Come home with me."

Liz rarely asked, just commanded. But after Meg's snub earlier today, Wesley's ego needed a stroke. His gaze dropped to Liz's cleavage and his cock started climbing. "Will my bike fit in your trunk?"

"We'll make it work."

His bike was too big, but he used his tie to secure the trunk lid, then jumped into the passenger seat of Liz's red convertible Jag. She didn't have the top down, but it was still a sweet ride. Liz was on the phone the entire drive back to her place, tying up loose ends for the week. Wesley's dick was hard in anticipation, but his stomach was in knots, his mind rewinding to Meg's snarky comment.

You could be my boyfriend if you'd straighten up.

What would that be like? He'd never had a steady girlfriend. Would that mean screwing whenever they wanted, or would she make him wait? Would he have to meet her parents? Would she give him grief about playing cards and hanging out with Chance? And what if his working for The Carver put her in danger?

"We're here," Liz announced, pulling into the driveway of her posh home. Not that he'd seen anything other than the guesthouse. "Go ahead and get your bike out of the trunk before I pull into the garage."

So he could leave afterward without disturbing her—that was cool.

When they walked into the shady guesthouse, his head was still pounding and his shirt stuck to his sweaty back. His mind was full of Meg, his thoughts bouncing around like a pinball. He wouldn't take the Oxy…he wouldn't… he'd show her…

"I'll pour us a drink if you want to shower," Liz said, pulling her blouse from her skirt.

"Sure," he said. He hadn't had anything to drink for a while because Chance had warned him about taking Oxy with alcohol. He walked into the bathroom and set his backpack on a fussy chair. The Oxy was in there, waiting for him.

Sudden anger billowed in his chest toward the holier-than-thou Meg Vincent. Who did she think she was, announcing that she would *let* him be her boyfriend if only he did what she said? He reached in his backpack for a tablet. Adrenaline flooded his body at the mere feel of the pill between his fingers.

"I changed my mind about the drink," he called out the door. "Can I have iced tea instead?"

"No problem."

He tossed the pill into his mouth, then chewed, breaking the bitter time-release coating that guaranteed the full effect of the drug would be dumped into his system all at once. He sighed as sweet ecstasy seeped through his body. His headache vanished, his hands stopped shaking, and the fussy chair suddenly looked beautiful. He climbed into the shower and was aware of every exquisite drop of water falling over him like magic fingers.

When he stepped out, he felt invincible, not even taking the time to dry off before rolling on a condom and crawling on top of Liz in her bed. Her protests were fleeting, ending when he drove his dick into her, hard and fast, just the way she liked it.

She played with herself, then guided his hand down to her crotch to take over. All that work on a pencil eraser computer mouse came in handy as he finessed her clit like a little joystick. With the other hand he tweaked her nipples.

"Easy," she murmured. "They're tender today."

She had big, firm boobs, and fantastic, long legs. He wanted to stay between her thighs forever. Every thrust was a jab at Meg…he'd show her…

His balls tightened with an impending climax. "Come on," he urged, and put some extra effort into it so they'd finish together. Liz bucked beneath him and screamed like he was murdering her. He took that as a good sign and blew his load like a water pump—feeling vindicated with every stroke. Triumphant, he rolled to her side and lay there, allowing the Oxy to carry him along on a euphoric recovery. Everything in the world was right and good…and fuchsia.

Liz propped herself up on her elbow and ran a long fingernail over his chest. "I've missed you."

He grunted in response, wanting to enjoy his high by expending as little effort as possible.

"Wesley, I've been thinking a lot about Randolph lately. Have you and Carlotta considered having your parents declared legally dead?"

His eyes popped open. "What?"

"I'm only thinking of you. It might be nice to have some closure."

Laughter bubbled in his chest, the good feeling amplified by the Oxy. "Liz, if I tell you something, you can't tell anyone."

"I won't," she murmured.

"Dad's alive. He talked to Carlotta in person only a few weeks ago."

Her jaw dropped. "You're kidding. When?"

"Remember when you and Jack came tearing into the rest area in Florida? A few minutes before then, Carlotta was at the vending machines and Dad walked up to her in disguise."

She sat up and covered her mouth. "Oh, Wesley, that's…that's wonderful news! Where has he been? Is he okay?"

"He didn't say where he'd been, but Carlotta said he seemed okay. He told her that he'd been keeping tabs on us. He also said he was gathering evidence to prove he'd been framed and that he'd be in touch soon." Wesley smiled, happy to be talking about happy things and feeling so…happy.

"I can't believe it," she murmured. "I always thought he'd come back someday."

"Won't that be great? You can't say anything, though."

"Don't worry. But you'll keep me posted?"

"Sure." He closed his eyes…life was good.

"So, cowboy…who's Meg?"

His eyes flew open again. "What?"

"Meg. You said her name when we were having sex."

"No, I didn't."

"Yes, you did." She gave a little laugh. "Relax. I don't mind, I'm just curious, that's all."

"I don't know a Meg," he lied.

"Okay, sweetie, whatever you say." She lay back down with a sigh and a few minutes later, she was asleep, probably fueled by the empty martini glass sitting on the nightstand.

Wesley sat up and cursed under his breath. He'd said Meg's name while he was drilling Liz? Damn, what a buzz killer. He reached for the glass of iced tea that Liz had poured for him and downed it.

You missed the best part of the evening...taking me home...you could be my boyfriend...you could be my boyfriend...you could be my boyfriend...

Annoyed at Meg for intruding on his thoughts and at himself for giving in and taking the Oxy, he pushed to his feet and backtracked to the bathroom to dress. Liz didn't stir as he let himself out through the French doors. Walking to his bike, he pulled out his phone and dialed Chance.

"Yo," his friend answered. The guy was breathing hard and in the background, Wesley could hear the droning noise of the treadmill.

"It's Wes, what are you doing?"

"Working out and getting high," Chance said, his voice tight from holding his breath. Then he exhaled noisily. "And I just got off the phone with Grimes. He's supposed to call me back with details of a card game tomorrow night. Can you do it?"

"Sure," Wes said, not sure at all with everything he had going on.

"Good. Are you coming over?"

"Yeah, I'll be there in a few minutes."

"Wait until you see me, dude—I've lost two pounds. You can tell Hannah that I'm looking *good.*"

"Uh, about that. She might be interested in going out with you if you'd be willing to pay for finishing the tattoo on her back."

"I'm in if I can watch."

Wes smiled at his friend's predictability. "I'll let her know. Anything you need that I can pick up on the way over there?"

"Yeah. Get me a Coronary Bypass Burger from The Vortex."

Wesley winced. The Bypass Burger was a cardiologist's nightmare: a gi-normous hamburger topped with a fried egg, three slices of American cheese, four slices of bacon and served with a bowl of mayo. For those who were skinny, brave, or terminally ill, the *Double* Bypass Burger offered an extra jolt of cholesterol by exchanging the buns for grilled cheese sandwiches.

"Whatever you say, Richard Simmons."

"Who?"

"Later, man." Wesley ended the call and pedaled to The Vortex in Midtown, weaving through waning rush hour traffic that was giving way to people coming in from the 'burbs to go to the Fox Theatre or just to cruise Peachtree Street between the blocks of Twelfth and North Avenue. He locked up his bike next to a line of motorcycles in front of the restaurant that had a reputation for great grill food and leather-bound servers. He felt a pang for the motorcycle he'd had to sell, but consoled himself with the promise that he'd have another one someday.

Wes walked inside, assailed by the sounds and scents of fun times and good food, then went to the bar to place a to-go order of two Double Bypass Burgers with Tater Tots on the side. He wasn't hungry now, but he knew he would be when the Oxy wore off. While he waited, he nursed a Coke and caught some footage from a World Series of Poker tournament that was playing on a TV over the bar, mentally calculating the best hand possible for each player and the odds of getting the "nuts." During a commercial he glanced around, then his stomach dropped.

Across the bar, Meg Vincent sat at a table with a preppy-looking older guy, sharing a plate of nachos. Their heads were close and they seemed deep in conversation. Unreasonable jealousy whipped through him, fueled by anger over her earlier dismissal. She'd told him he could be her boyfriend, but she obviously already had one—what a poseur. He set his Coke on the bar and walked over, gratified when she looked up and did a double take.

"Wesley…hi."

"Hi."

"Um…Mark, this is Wesley, a coworker of mine. And Wesley, this is Mark—a friend."

Wes nodded at the guy, taking in his sissy plaid shorts and sandals with a smile. "How's it hanging, dude?"

"Er…fine," her companion said. He looked to be in his mid to late twenties.

Meg fidgeted in her seat. "What are you doing here?"

"Getting something to eat, same as you." Jesus, she was wearing lipstick for this goober.

"Would you like to join us?" she asked reluctantly.

"Nah, I'm getting takeout. I'm going to a friend's place to get ready for a big game tomorrow."

"What sport do you play?" Mark asked.

"Cards," Wes said, pushing up his glasses. "I'm going to be in the World Series of Poker."

"Someday," Meg added wryly.

"I see," Mark said. "Are you a Tech student?"

Wesley deflated a little. "No."

"Someday," Meg said, giving Wesley a pointed look.

Her attitude made him want to shout that he'd just left the bed of a gorgeous older woman who thought he totally rocked between the sheets, but at the last second, his verbal filter kicked on. Plus the newly formed pussy-whipped area of his brain reminded him that when he'd been rocking between the sheets with Liz, he'd been thinking about Meg.

"Order for Wesley!" someone shouted from the bar.

He jerked his thumb over his shoulder. "That's me. You kids have fun."

"See you Monday," Meg said.

He walked back to the bar, gritting his teeth. Dammit, why were women such a conundrum? He picked up his order and sauntered outside, knowing the couple could see him through the window and wishing he had a Harley to mount versus a Schwinn. A horn sounded and he looked up to see a familiar Town Car in the mix of the vehicles that were cruising by. Mouse's fat face appeared through the lowered window.

"Get in," he called.

Wesley sighed and jogged across a lane of traffic to the car, then slid into the passenger seat. "You following me?"

"Yeah." The car moved forward. "Got a problem with that?"

"Uh, no. What's up?"

"You're in," the big man said. "The boss said I could bring you on board."

Wes didn't know whether to be relieved or horrified. "Okay…what now?"

Mouse flipped on his left blinker and edged the giant car out far enough to cut someone off and make the turn he wanted to make. "There's a phone in the glove box. Take it and keep it juiced up. Don't turn it off."

Wesley opened the big glove box and removed a box that contained a prepaid cell phone and battery charger. "Listen, I have to do community service in the mornings or I go to jail. So I'm only available in the afternoons."

"What about evenings?" Mouse asked.

"I'm on call for the morgue to move bodies."

"We can work around it," Mouse said in a congenial voice. "It might come in handy having someone on the payroll who knows how to move a body."

Wesley swallowed hard. "So, how do I get paid? Is it a percentage of my collections?"

"It's kind of like real estate," Mouse said, turning left on a side street. "The fee changes depending on the transaction."

"I need to know that I'm working toward clearing my debt, man."

"Don't worry, I'll personally oversee your account." Mouse turned left again to circle back to The Vortex, then nodded to the bag. "What'cha got in there?"

"Burgers."

"Smells good. I haven't had dinner yet."

Wesley pulled out one of the Double Bypass Burgers and set it on the console. "Knock yourself out, dude." Maybe he could slowly murder the man with trans fats.

"Thanks." Mouse pulled to a stop in front of the restaurant. "I'll call you."

Wesley stepped out of the Town Car and jogged back to the curb just as Meg and Mark were walking out. Meg looked back and forth between him and the Town Car that was pulling away. Wesley rushed to unlock his bike, stuff the remaining food in his backpack, and took off without looking back, not caring that she probably thought the worst of him.

Yeah, right.

21

Dusk was falling when Carlotta left the *Atlanta Journal-Constitution* building. With everything going through her mind regarding Wesley, her dad, Eva McCoy and The Charmed Killer, one more thing niggled at her: Coop. He hadn't returned any of her calls, and she hadn't spoken to him since he'd left her house after spending the night. She was worried about him.

She used her cell phone to call him again, but it went to voice mail and she didn't want to leave yet another message. On a whim, she called Moody's Cigar Bar, and June answered.

"Moody's." From the noise in the background, happy hour was in full swing.

"June? It's Carlotta Wren."

"Hello, dear. I have some pictures for you when you have a chance to stop by. I got an extra set printed of the photos Mitchell took at Neiman's, and there are some rather good ones of you."

"That's nice of you. June, I'm actually looking for Coop and I wondered if, by chance, he was there."

"As a matter of fact, he is."

Carlotta wet her lips. "Is he drinking?"

"No, dear. But he's upstairs in the lounge with Mitchell. And I'm worried about him—he seems troubled."

Carlotta's phone beeped to indicate she had another call coming in. "I'll stop by there in a few minutes. See you then." She ended the first call and glanced at the screen to see that Peter was calling. After running out on him last night, she owed him some makeup time. She connected the call. "Hello?"

"Hi, Carly. Is this a bad time?"

"No, it's a good time. Do you have plans tonight?"

"No. I was hoping we could get together."

"Meet me for a drink? I have a bit of news to share."

"Sure, where?"

Carlotta gave him directions to Moody's and slowly disconnected the call. She had mixed feelings about introducing Peter to Moody's because it was a place where Coop hung out sometimes, a place where she and Hannah had gone on more than one occasion to relax or to meet someone they were trying to shake down for information. But if she and Peter were going to date, she needed to make an effort to fold him into her life. And other people in her life needed to get used to seeing them together.

She arrived first, noting Coop's vintage white convertible Corvette in the parking lot. She smiled when she walked through the entrance to the main level of the cigar shop—the atmosphere never failed to warm her. A black horseshoe-shaped counter dominated the room that was lined with glass cases full of cigars and smoking accessories. An original tin ceiling and black-and-red checkerboard linoleum tile floor framed the Art Deco fixtures and swept customers back in time. The bar attracted a mix of people and she wondered idly if Alicia Sills could've been a patron—ergo the cigar charm found in her mouth. She made a mental note to check with June.

At this hour, the shop was full of suited executives who were looking for a stogie to take upstairs to the martini lounge to enjoy with a sipping drink. Sinatra played overhead. The scents of tobacco and cherry and wood filled the air. Carlotta inhaled to draw the aromas into her lungs, her tongue dry and her fingers itching for a dose of nicotine.

Clerks manned the counter, helping customers choose a cigar to suit their smoking level and their mood. Carlotta spotted June tending to a customer in the rear of the shop, past the set of stairs that led to the second-level lounge. Carlotta waved, then asked one of the clerks for an Amelia—the mild cigar that June had turned her on to when she'd first come into Moody's.

On the counter near her elbow sat the diorama that Coop had made for June in a cigar box. Inside was a miniature duplicate of the first floor of the cigar shop, down to exacting detail of tiny cigars in the tiny boxes in the tiny cabinets. The exquisite workmanship told her how many hours Coop spent alone on his precise hobby. He'd once told Carlotta that it kept him focused and his hands busy, which had, in turn, helped him to stay sober.

She hoped that was still the case.

Carlotta paid for the cigar, then walked upstairs to the packed martini lounge. The bar sat immediately to the right, with stools and comfortable upholstered chairs opposite, then the room opened up to larger rooms with tall ceilings furnished with mismatched couches and enormous ottomans that patrons could sit on in groups. Overhead fans kept the cigar smoke from being too oppressive, and the eclectic decor kept the ambiance from being too stiff.

She spotted Coop and Mitchell Moody at the far end of

the bar. Her gut told her the men didn't have much in common, but Coop was probably extending himself because he was so fond of June. Coop glanced up and waved, his face splitting into a smile that made her heart squeeze. Mitchell turned around and beckoned for her to join them. She made her way over to them and said hello.

"Hey, no cast," Coop said, gesturing to her arm.

She flexed her atrophied muscle. "I got rid of it today."

"So you're back to one hundred percent if I need you," Coop said, then added, "On a job, I mean."

"All you have to do is call," she said lightly, then turned to Mitchell. "I see the two of you have met."

"Yeah, getting to know each other," Coop said. He wore black jeans and a T-shirt, with faded Chuck Taylor Converse tennis shoes. His hair had gotten long enough to pull back into a low ponytail. She tried to maintain eye contact with him, but he wouldn't cooperate, puffing on the smoldering cigar he held. So…he *was* avoiding her.

"You look a lot better than you did the last time I saw you," Mitch said with a grin. He wore jeans, a short-sleeve shirt and athletic sandals. He also appeared to be a little tipsy. In front of the two men sat a couple of glasses, half-full with clear, fizzy liquid.

She laughed. "No doubt. Are you enjoying your time off?"

"Oh, sure. Mom took me to the Aquarium and the New World of Coke. And I've been catching up with old friends."

She seized the opening. "Have you seen the crowds staking out Eva McCoy's house?"

Mitch blanched, then laughed and picked up his drink. "No, can't say that I have." He swirled the liquid in his glass, then took a drink.

He was lying, but why? "I heard she's decided not to compete in the World Championships after all."

"Um, I heard that, too," he said, nodding. "Damn shame."

"So what brings you here?" Coop asked Carlotta.

"June has some pictures for me, and I was in the area," she said, improvising. "And I'm meeting Peter Ashford for a drink."

"Ah," he said, then pulled on his cigar.

Nathan, the bartender, came over. "Hi, Carlotta. What can I get you?"

She looked at the guys. "What are you having?"

"Gin and tonic," said Mitch.

"Just tonic," Coop said, but his eyes said that he wished it was something much stronger.

"Tonic water for me, too," Carlotta said to Nathan.

"Put that on my tab," Coop said. "And I'll have a beer."

Alarm bolted through her. "Coop," she whispered, "what are you doing?"

"Having a beer," he murmured, his brown eyes defiant. "A man should be able to have a damn beer."

She set her jaw and with her eyes she pleaded with him to reconsider.

"Are you a smoker?" Mitch asked, gesturing to the unlit cigar she held. Fortunately, he was oblivious to their quiet exchange.

"Sometimes," she said, nodding. "Your mom converted me. She has a great place here."

He gave a dry laugh. "Yeah, except that she's selling cancer to everyone who walks through the door."

Carlotta blinked, surprised at his animosity. "That's a little harsh, don't you think? Everyone is here because they want to be."

He shrugged his big shoulders. "Yeah, it's a free country and all that. I just don't think it's the kind of place my mother should be spending all of her time."

Once again, Carlotta recognized that there were issues between Mitch and June. She swallowed the words she wanted to say—that he didn't know how lucky he was to have such a great mom who actually gave a damn about him. Instead Carlotta said, "I think your mother is delightful, and she seems very happy."

Mitch gave her a sweeping glance. "I bet *your* mother isn't running a smoky bar in a seedy part of town."

"Hey, man," Coop cut in, saving her from having to respond, "your drink is turning to water."

She gave Coop a grateful glance, and he nodded to indicate that someone was behind her.

She turned to see Peter standing there, dressed in a flawless black pin-striped suit, scanning the crowd. She waved to get his attention. He smiled and moved toward her, but his smile dimmed when he caught sight of Coop.

"Look who I ran into," she said brightly. Peter and Coop shook hands, albeit woodenly, then she introduced Mitchell to Peter and picked up her drink. "Why don't I find someplace for us to sit while you get something from the bar?"

He nodded, then signaled Nathan. "I'll have Crown and Coke, and put the lady's drink on my tab."

"I already got it," Coop said.

"No, I'll get it," Peter said, his tone harsher than necessary.

Coop lifted his hand in concession and reached for the beer that Nathan set in front of him. He wrapped his hand around it and looked up at Carlotta.

"Don't," she mouthed.

He looked away. She turned and wove her way through the crowd, keeping an eye out for open seating. Jack had warned her not to take ownership of Coop's drinking problem—it predated their relationship, after all. Still, she couldn't help worrying about him. She regretted that Jack had been at her house the night Coop had stopped by. He'd seemed keen to share something with her, and once again, their timing had been off.

She spotted someone leaving a couch and moved to claim it. Unfortunately, the seat gave her a clear view of Cooper at the bar, who sat staring into the beer in front of him. "Don't do it," she whispered. "Be strong, Coop."

She was distracted by Peter walking up, cradling a caramel-colored drink in his hands. "Nice place," he said, settling down next to her and glancing all around.

"I like it," she said, reaching for the cutter on the table in front of them to snip the end of her cigar. She removed the mother-of-pearl lighter from her purse and lit the cigar the way that June had tutored her. Soon an ember glowed at the tip and a ribbon of fragrant smoke floated toward the ceiling. She sat back, expecting Peter to scold her for smoking. Instead, he smiled and removed a cigar from his inside jacket pocket and proceeded to do the same.

Carlotta gave a little laugh. "I thought you didn't smoke."

"If you can't beat 'em," he said, puffing, "then join 'em."

She scoffed. "This isn't your first cigar."

He exhaled into the air. "Okay, you're right, but I don't indulge often. And while I hate to see your pretty lungs polluted, I have to say that you look very sexy with that cigar between your lips."

She smiled at the erotic allusion and remembered what her friend Pepper, the hooker, had told her about keeping a man happy. *Chocolate cake and blow jobs.* She laughed to herself—except for the odd diabetic priest, there wasn't a man alive who'd turn down both. And it reminded her of the months of delicious heavy petting that she and Peter used to engage in, in the spacious backseat of the Caddy he drove in high school that led up to her losing her virginity. Teenagers today who skipped the foreplay and rushed headlong into sex were missing out.

"On the phone you said there was something you wanted to tell me," Peter prompted.

"I'm sorry again for bailing on you last night. I truly thought I'd be back before the movie ended."

"That's all right—the Lowensteins kept me company." He rolled his eyes and they both laughed. "I heard about this guy on the news they're calling The Charmed Killer— was that what you were doing with Wesley, picking up one of the victims?"

"Um…I'm not really supposed to talk about it."

He seemed to measure his words. "I don't like the idea of you working around crime scenes. It puts you in too much danger."

"I understand how you feel, but by the time I get to the scene, the danger is past."

He drew on his cigar, then exhaled. "So you say."

She drew on her cigar, then exhaled, too. "Yes, I do."

"You could've said you were sorry on the phone," he said, picking up her hand. "Not that I'm complaining about seeing you two nights in a row." He leaned in and kissed her. She returned the kiss, but wondered, in the back of her mind, if Coop was watching. She hadn't meant to bring Peter there to flaunt their relationship.

Carlotta pulled back and smiled. "I wanted to tell you that I went to the doctor today for one last X-ray and guess what? He knew Randolph."

"Sweetie, lots of people knew Randolph."

"But they were tennis partners. Dr. Eames said that just before my dad was arrested, he told him that someone in his firm was trying to frame him. Randolph asked him if he'd hang on to something for him."

"What was it?"

"That's just it—they never had the chance to talk again. But Dr. Eames said it was some kind of papers."

Peter wiped his hand over his mouth and nodded. "Okay, well, that's something, I guess. Did he say who Randolph suspected of framing him?"

"No."

Peter sighed. "But it corresponds with what your father told me when he called."

"So why didn't he just come out and tell you who it was? And why didn't he tell the D.A. when it first happened?"

"I wish I knew."

"I wish he'd stop being a coward and come back to defend himself." She drew on the cigar too deeply and her lungs rebelled in a coughing spasm.

Peter rubbed small circles on her lower back until she caught her breath. "I could start by getting a list of everyone who worked for the firm during that time period," he said, "and start eliminating people. Maybe if we do some detective work on this end, we'll have something figured out before your dad gets back in touch with us."

"But why work blindly when he doesn't seem so eager to help himself?"

Peter took a hearty drink from his glass.

"Wait a minute," she said. "If we start poking around on our own, we can be more objective."

"Right," he said slowly. "Meaning…this could go either way."

"We might find something to further incriminate Randolph."

"Or we might find nothing," Peter said. "But if we do this, you have to be prepared for whatever happens."

She shook her head. "I don't think this is a good idea. You could lose your job, Peter."

"And I'd get another one."

But she wasn't so blasé when it came to his career. "Mashburn & Tully is the only place you've ever worked— it's your home."

"Let me worry about that. Don't you want to know the truth?"

She nodded.

"Then let me help you do this. Please?"

She looked into his eyes and was swept back to a time when the two of them had planned their future. Together they had been optimistic and unstoppable. She sighed and nodded. "Okay. Let's do this."

He folded her hand in his. "Are you going to include Wesley?"

She bit her lip, thinking of the OxyContin pill in her purse. "Eventually. Right now Wesley has a lot on his plate."

"Okay." Peter took another drink from his glass. "I might have to find someone at the office to help, someone I can trust."

"What do you know about Quinten Gallagher?"

"The receptionist? Seems like a decent guy." He nodded thoughtfully. "He's a possibility."

"I don't want him to get in trouble."

"I'll make sure that doesn't happen," Peter said. "I'll talk to him when the time's right."

"Okay," she said, happy to turn it all over to someone else for the time being.

"Peter, fancy meeting you here."

They looked up to see Brody Jones, chief legal counsel for Mashburn & Tully.

"Hello, Brody," Peter said. "I think you know Carlotta Wren."

"I do indeed." The man spoke with a thick Southern accent that she supposed some people found pleasing.

"Hello, Mr. Jones."

"Carlotta, you look astonishingly like your mother. I don't suppose you've heard from Valerie lately?"

"Not since she left town with my father," Carlotta said stiffly. From her purse, her phone rang and she gladly murmured, "Excuse me," to remove herself from the conversation. Peter stood to talk with Brody, ill at ease himself, if the way he jingled change in his pocket was any indication. No doubt because they'd been discussing snooping through the company's records just before the man appeared.

Carlotta pulled out her phone to see Jack's name on the screen. He could be calling about so many things—Wesley, Michael, her father. She put her hand over one ear and answered. "Hi, Jack. What's up?"

"Where are you?"

"I'm at Moody's. Why?"

"Stay there. I need to talk to you."

"Okay, I'll meet you downstairs." She ended the call and glanced up at Peter, who was still talking to Brody. She touched Peter's arm. "I have to go."

"I'll walk you out," he said.

"No, stay and enjoy your cigar. I'll call you tomorrow." Her glance told him that it was probably a good idea if Brody saw them leaving separately, and he conceded with a nod.

She left her drink, but took her cigar. Sneaking a peek at the bar as she passed by, she noticed that Coop and Mitchell both were gone…and that the beer sitting at Coop's place appeared to be untouched.

Plus ten points.

Coop had resisted, and that was enough for today. Carlotta smiled in relief as she descended to the first floor. June was stacking cigar boxes in Coop's arms. Carlotta climbed on a stool nearby and relit the cigar that she'd allowed to go out, enjoying their interplay. June and Coop behaved more like mother and son than June and Mitchell did. She glanced around, but didn't see him.

"Did Mitchell leave?" she asked when they came closer.

Coop shot her a warning look and nodded. When she noticed the pinched expression on June's face, Carlotta abruptly changed the subject.

"You said you had some pictures for me?"

June smiled and reached under the counter, then handed over a photo-processing envelope.

"What are these from?" Coop asked, craning to see.

"Eva McCoy's appearance at Neiman's earlier this week," Carlotta said, hurrying to shove the envelope in her purse.

"Mitch took some great photos of Carlotta," June said.

"Let's see," Coop encouraged.

She sighed, wondering if "great" was code for "plastered with cake." She handed over the pictures and looked over Coop's shoulder as he flipped through them. There were photos of the crowd, of the empty dais, of Eva McCoy arriving and talking, and several of the line of people waiting to have a charm bracelet signed. While they waited, Mitchell had snapped a couple of candids of Carlotta as she worked with Eva. In one, she was laughing at something, and although she'd never considered herself particularly photogenic, she was surprised that it was a decent photo—flattering even.

Coop smiled and picked it up. "Can I have this?"

She shrugged. "Sure."

He lifted the lid of one of the empty cigar boxes and dropped the photo inside. "Did Peter leave?"

"No, he's upstairs with a colleague." She put the rest of the photos back in the envelope and shoved them into her purse, talking around her cigar. "Jack called and said he needed to talk to me about something, that he'd meet me here."

"Maybe they've found Michael Lane's body," Coop said.

"Maybe," she agreed, then looked at June. "Does the name 'Alicia Sills' mean anything to you?"

She noticed Coop stiffen.

June frowned. "The name sounds vaguely familiar."

"Could she be a customer?"

"Carlotta," Coop said, his tone a warning.

"Wait a minute," June said. "Isn't she the woman I read about in the paper—the one they think is a victim of The Charmed Killer?"

Coop looked away as if to say he wanted no part of the discussion.

"Uh…is she?" Carlotta said.

June frowned. "Why would you think she might be a customer of mine?"

Carlotta bit her lip.

"Never mind," June said, lifting her hand. "I don't need to know why. Let me check."

When June walked away, Coop gave Carlotta a pointed look. "Jack would crucify you if he knew you were asking questions about his case."

"What Jack doesn't know won't hurt him."

Coop's expression suddenly changed and he turned in the opposite direction.

"What don't I know?"

She whirled around to see Jack standing there. And

even though he was wearing a different shirt, from the haggard lines on his face, it was clear he still hadn't been to bed. "Uh, nothing."

"I know nothing?"

"No—you know everything, Jack," she said breezily.

June came back and leaned over the counter. "Carlotta, I didn't find Alicia Sills's name in my customer database."

Next to her, Carlotta could almost hear the blood vessels bursting in Jack's head. "Thanks for checking, June." She turned and flashed her brightest smile at Jack.

His face was nearly purple. "I *told* you not to talk about the case!"

"Relax. June doesn't know why I was asking. And now you can cross a possible connection to Moody's off the list."

His mouth tightened. "No one confirmed that the second charm is what you think it is."

"It was a cigar, Jack. I saw it with my own eyes. And you're welcome." She crossed her arms. "Now, what did you want to talk about?"

He pulled his hand down his face and appeared to be counting to himself. When he looked around, apparently to make sure no one was within earshot, she started to worry. "What is it, Jack?"

"Your father's name came up as a possible suspect for our serial killer."

Her mouth opened. "What? How?"

"His name was spit out of the system. He fits a profile."

"Maria's profile?" she asked drily. "The same one that *I* fit?"

He glared. "The one you fit wasn't for a murderer, just a meddler. Which you are."

"Why would my father be flagged as a possible suspect?"

"Because he has a record…"

"And?"

"And he was known as a bit of a…womanizer."

She set her jaw. "I know. What else?"

"He might have known Alicia Sills."

Her eyes went wide. "How?"

"She used to work in the same building where your father worked."

"Jack, there are thousands of people working in that building on any given day."

"I know, but there are also the charms."

She frowned. "What about them?"

A muscle worked in his jaw. "You have to promise me not to repeat any of this to anyone."

She swallowed hard under his piercing gaze. "Okay."

"Goddammit, I mean it, Carlotta."

"I said okay."

He looked dubious, then sighed. "There's a theory that the charms might have something to do with the identity of the murderer."

"I'm confused. What does that have to do with my father?"

"When your father disappeared, he got the name 'The Bird' from his last name."

"And for flying the coop," she added. "I know—I heard it all. So they think the bird charm has something to do with my dad?" She made a face. "That's a stretch."

"Carlotta, two women are dead. The department is pulling out all the stops here. Do you remember if your dad was a cigar smoker?"

Her thoughts went to the box of cigars still sitting on his nightstand in the bedroom at the end of the hall. They'd dried out long ago, but she still smelled the scent of tobacco the few times she'd gone in to dust or run the vacuum. "Yes, he was."

"And what about the charms themselves?" he asked. "Does that mean anything to you? Did your dad ever buy them or did your mother have a bracelet?"

"No, Mother didn't have a charm bracelet," she said. "But I do."

"Where did you get it?"

She hesitated, then said, "Dad bought it for me."

"Do you still have it?"

"It's buried in my jewelry box somewhere."

"Find it. I'm going to need to see it."

She nodded. "Of course." Unbidden tears filled her eyes.

"Hey, hey," he said gently, leaning in. "I've told you before that I can't take the tears. This is just a theory. Don't get worked up about it."

Carlotta sniffed and blinked rapidly. She looked up to find Coop watching her from a few feet away. He looked concerned and walked toward them.

"Is everything okay?"

She nodded.

"What's going on here?"

At the sound of Peter's voice, she turned around to see him flanking her as well. "Nothing, Peter…I'm fine. I was just leaving."

"I'll drive you home," the three men said in unison, then exchanged frowns.

"No," she said loudly, chopping the air with her hand. "I'll drive myself home. Good night."

Carlotta left, suddenly nursing a headache, her throat aching from unshed tears. In the space of one day she'd gone from having someone tell her that Randolph was a great guy to hearing that he might be a serial killer.

She couldn't bring herself to think of her father as a murderer, someone who killed for kicks…but then again, how well did she really know Randolph? Who knew what crimes he might have committed in the ten years he'd been gone? Jack was willing to dismiss the idea of her father committing the armed robbery at the hotel in Florida based on the fingerprint match algorithm. But she had the benefit of knowing that Randolph actually had been in the area.

Which greatly improved the odds that he was the culprit.

Even though it was relatively early when she arrived home, Wesley was already in his room, the door closed and the fan running. With the pill in her purse still weighing on her mind, she lifted her hand to knock, but changed her mind. She couldn't take any more confrontations today, and she needed to talk to him when he wasn't half-asleep. She opened the door just enough to make sure he was in bed and okay.

Wesley looked much like he had when he was little, sleeping on his back, with his arms thrown wide, his chest moving up and down. It was hard sometimes to believe that he was nineteen, a full-grown man as everyone liked to remind her. And she had to admit that even if she couldn't share all her worries with her brother, having him in the house was a comfort to her.

She closed the door and traipsed to the kitchen to grab a carton of yogurt from the fridge, then crawled into bed and went to sleep watching celebrity news. Idle entertainment was a welcome escape from the drama of her life. She dozed and slept fitfully, dodging nightmares about her father. In her dreams she searched for him, but he was always out of reach. Yet somehow he always hovered over her, God-like, pressuring her.

Carlotta awoke with a start to a dark room. Her pillow was wet from tears and she had an eerie feeling lingering from her dreams that she was being watched. She longed for a warm body next to her, someone to reassure her, and she reminded herself that any one of her three men would've been willing to oblige tonight.

Yet as long as she put off making a decision, she was destined to wake up alone…and lonely.

22

When Carlotta rolled out of bed the next morning, her arm twinged with pain and her head still throbbed. She downed a couple of Advils and took a quick shower, hoping to catch Wesley before he left the house so she could talk to him about the OxyContin tablet. But when she emerged from her bedroom, he was already gone. He had, however, made coffee, as well as washed, dried and folded a load of laundry. The simple domestic chores demonstrated the paradox of her brother's personality—he could be so reckless one minute, so thoughtful the next.

Then again, one of the symptoms of oxycodone addiction was mood swings. How long had this been going on under her nose? All the trouble he'd gotten into over the past couple of years—the gambling debts, the arrest for hacking into the city computer system, even conspiring to have a body stolen during transport—paled in comparison to the danger of this new threat. Something was definitely up because he was avoiding her. She felt sick to her stomach just thinking about the confrontation, but it had to happen. Carlotta picked up the phone and dialed Wesley's cell phone number. When he didn't answer, she hung up, frowning in puzzlement. Where could he be?

Then she smiled in realization—of course! He'd probably started his courier job today.

Feeling much relieved, she walked to the table where the clothes had been neatly stacked. She lifted a snowy-white handkerchief from the pile and pressed her face into it. It was Jack's. Like every good Southern boy, he always had one in his back pocket to attend to whatever emergency presented itself, be it a bloody nose or a crying woman. Single-handedly, she'd probably depleted most of his inventory—she had a laundered stack of them in her dresser drawer. She'd have to make a point to give them back to him sometime.

Now that Jack had decided that she should marry Peter, she could clean up her messes with *his* handkerchiefs… which were probably monogrammed.

The image of Peter's face tugged on her heart. He'd been so kind last night—his offer to help her figure out whether or not her father had been framed went beyond generous. The fact that he was willing to put his career on the line to help her find answers to the questions that had plagued her all her adult life meant more than she could express.

Something had changed between them last night. She had felt herself warming toward Peter, could feel it even now. It was as if they were drifting back together…or rather, she was drifting and he was calmly moored, waiting for her. It made her feel…hopeful.

On impulse, she called Peter, and soon his muffled voice came over the line. "Hello?"

"It's Carly. I'm sorry I'd forgotten it's Saturday. Were you sleeping in?"

"No, I'm up," he said sleepily. "How are you today?"

"Good. Better. I'm sorry I left the cigar bar so abruptly last night. Jack had some upsetting news and I needed to be alone."

"I asked him what you'd talked about, but he wouldn't tell me."

"You're not going to believe this. My dad's name came up as a possible suspect in The Charmed Killer case."

"What? That's ridiculous."

"I thought so, too, but Jack's new partner is a profiler, so I guess they're tackling this one by the book. I know Jack's just doing his job."

Peter made a sound that implied he didn't give the man that much credit. "Are you working today?"

"No, it's my day off. But I have errands to run and there's plenty to be done around here."

"Can I see you tonight?"

She smiled into the phone. "That sounds good. Dinner?"

"Great. Pick you up at seven?"

"It's a date," she said, realizing she was truly looking forward to spending time with him. "See you then."

She hung up the phone and carried Wesley's folded clothes to his room, setting them on the foot of his bed. All the while, she kept one eye on the thick python coiled up in the aquarium. The reptile was motionless as a little white mouse crawled all over it, cavorting and twitching, oblivious to the fact that as soon as the snake either got hungry or annoyed, it was lights out. Carlotta shuddered, left the room and closed the door behind her.

She glanced at the door to her parents' bedroom at the end of the hall, then carried her folded clothes to her own room to put away. While stowing bras and panties, she removed the stack of Jack's handkerchiefs she'd accumulated and set them on top of her dresser. When she started to close the drawer, her gaze landed on a white leather box she hadn't opened in a long time. Remembering her promise to Jack from the night before, she removed the box and carried it to her bed. She sat cross-legged on the bedspread and lifted the lid.

A hundred memories suddenly assailed her. There was the Cinderella watch that she'd begged for at Walt Disney World when she was ten years old. And strands of colored glass beads that her mother had bought for her at a roadside stand when they'd vacationed in Jamaica. The purple wampum shell was from Martha's Vineyard, and her diaries for each year of high school still sat in the corner, each with a padlocked flap. One of them still contained the tiny tasseled skeleton key that would open any of the locks. She set them aside to read later.

She picked up a pink satin box and opened the lid to reveal a gold charm bracelet that her father had bought for her when she was fourteen. Dangling from the links were charms of teen girl things: purses and shoes, puppies and kittens, flowers and pink lips. Her father had given her additional charms for special occasions—cheerleading pom-poms, a *Sweet 16* charm, a little convertible for the precious Miata he'd bought for her first car.

When her parents had left, she'd stopped wearing the bracelet. For someone who'd had to grow up fast, it had suddenly seemed childish. And she'd been so bitter toward her father, she hadn't wanted to wear anything that once represented such a bond between them.

She snapped the box closed, reminding herself that Randolph had broken that bond. He'd left her to cover for him every time his name came up in police matters, like now. The stink that he'd caused lingered still, cloaking her and Wesley. Frustration and anger plowed through her— why didn't her father just come home and face his problems like a man? She didn't think Randolph was capable of murder, but if the accusation brought him out of hiding, she wouldn't mind. Maybe she and Wesley could finally get some answers.

Her thoughts turned to Jack and she wondered if he'd made it to bed yet. He and Maria were no doubt putting in long hours over this serial killer business. Carlotta supposed all that togetherness would naturally make them closer. She tried not to let it bother her. Jack had made it clear that he wasn't interested in more than an occasional hook-up, and now she had Peter. In light of the phone call Maria had taken the day she'd been at the town house, it sounded as if the woman could use a strong shoulder to lean on. It appeared that she'd left a bad situation in Chicago.

Carlotta frowned when she recalled the woman detective "profiling" her—accusing Carlotta of dabbling in police work because she was bored. Had it not occurred to the woman that Carlotta helped out when she saw an opportunity because she was *good* at it?

In a huff, Carlotta shoved the handkerchiefs and the bracelet into a side compartment of her purse. In the process, her hand brushed the file of photos that Rainie Stephens had given her. She pulled out the sheet of black-and-white pictures, along with the photos that June had given her and carried them to the kitchen to spread out on the breakfast bar. Over a cup of coffee she looked for inspiration on how to begin searching for the man who'd stolen Eva McCoy's bracelet.

And as she stared at the images, a forehead-thumping idea occurred to her. She picked up the phone and dialed Hannah's number.

"I was fucking asleep," Hannah answered.

"Wake up and focus. Can you tell where a local cake came from just by looking at a picture?"

"I could probably narrow it down to a manageable number of places. Why?"

"I need your help."

Hannah sighed. "Okay, give me a few minutes to get the cobwebs out of my eyes."

Remembering what Maria had said about her not knowing much about Hannah, Carlotta said, "I can come pick you up—just give me the address."

"Uh…no, that's okay. I'm with a guy. See you in a few."

"I'll have coffee."

"I'll bring donuts."

Carlotta ended the call and smiled. Hannah was always up for a challenge, a no-nonsense, low-maintenance friend.

She poured coffee into two travel mugs and gathered up the pictures, then stood by the living room window waiting for Hannah to pull up. The mysterious black SUV was nowhere to be seen this morning, thank goodness. Carlotta wondered who else she could wake up to kill some time. As she ticked through a mental to-do list, her thoughts turned to someone she definitely *wanted* to disturb.

She pulled up the number on her phone and punched a button to connect.

"Liz Fischer," the woman said, her voice a croak.

"Liz—Carlotta Wren. I didn't wake you, did I?"

"Uh, no. I think I'm coming down with some kind of bug. What's up, Carlotta?"

Besides your skirt? Swallowing her ire, she said, "I've been thinking about my father a lot lately, and I was wondering if you could send me a copy of his case file."

Silence vibrated on the other end. "Can I ask why the sudden interest?"

"No reason," Carlotta lied. "It's really just to satisfy my curiosity."

"Carlotta, my client files are confidential. You and Wesley should both know that."

Carlotta frowned. "Wesley asked for the files?"

"Actually, no. He stole them and I had to threaten him to get them back. I understand that the two of you have a lot of questions about your dad's case, but I'm telling you this for your own good, Carlotta—let it go."

"You make it sound as if there's something you don't want us to find out, Liz."

"That's not true. It's just better for everyone involved." The woman made a retching sound. "I have to go. Bye, Carlotta."

"Feel better," she sang, then disconnected the call, her mind racing. Why had Wesley stolen their father's file?

Probably for the same reason she wanted it. But why hadn't he told her about it?

Probably for the same reason she hadn't told him about *her* snooping.

A horn sounded as Hannah pulled her van into the driveway. Carlotta waved, then walked outside, locking the door to the town house behind her. She bounded down the steps and across to the van, then climbed up into the passenger seat, handing Hannah a mug of coffee.

"Cream filled," Hannah said, pointing to a box of donuts on the dashboard. She was dressed Goth Lite this morning, having skimped on the black lipstick and going without her usual dog collar. "Let me see this cake."

Carlotta passed her the pictures, then helped herself to a donut. "The guy who crashed the event at Neiman's with this cake stole Eva McCoy's charm bracelet. I'm thinking if we can find out where the cake came from, maybe we can find him."

Hannah took a swig of coffee and studied the photos for

a few seconds. "The bad news is this is your chain grocery variety cake."

"Oh."

"The good news is I know which grocery chain uses this god-awful color of blue icing."

"Great!"

"The bad news is I drove past at least four locations on the way here. It could be one of forty or so locations in the metro area."

"So we'll start with the ones closest to the Lenox Square mall and work our way out."

Hannah made a face. "You're assuming I had nothing else to do today."

"Do you?"

"Sadly, nothing more interesting. We're going to need a map of store locations." Hannah leaned over, pulled a laptop from behind her seat and handed it to Carlotta. "I know where we can get drive-by wi-fi not too far from here."

A few minutes later, armed with locations of the groceries, they began to canvass each one, approaching the bakery manager with a picture of the blue and yellow "Let's Celebrate!" cake and asking if it came from their bakery.

The employees were helpful, no doubt responding to the culinary smock that Hannah had donned, but none of the first dozen or so recognized the cake from their stock designs. Road traffic was terrible and before they knew it, they'd eaten up the morning with nothing to show for it but an empty box of cream-filled donuts. They stopped for lunch at a Chick-fil-A and Carlotta filled Hannah in on what she'd learned about the Eva McCoy situation.

"Do you know anything about food poisoning?" she asked her friend.

Hannah gave a dry laugh and stuffed a waffle fry into

her mouth. "Food safety is drilled into us at culinary school. Small amounts of bacteria are introduced to most foods either in the production process or in handling, but it usually gets washed away or destroyed during heat preparation. Either that, or it's present in such tiny amounts that it doesn't affect the digestive system."

"But?"

"*But* if the bacteria isn't washed or cooked away, it can multiply in warm temperatures, to the point that the digestive system can't fight it off."

"So if foods are left out?"

"Right—or aren't cooked to the right temperature in the first place."

"So uncooked foods are the most susceptible?"

"Right. That's why you occasionally hear about E. coli contamination in produce. E. coli is found in animal intestines, so if produce is fertilized with manure…well, you get the gist."

"Apparently Eva ate at the Olympic Village cafeteria, along with other athletes, but no one else got ill."

"That happens. Some people are simply more susceptible. And even prepared 'healthy' foods have a higher incidence of contamination because they contain fewer preservatives, which can inhibit bacteria growth."

"But is it possible to spike someone else's food with bacteria and make them sick?"

Hannah shrugged. "I guess so, but you'd need a petri dish, and still, it wouldn't be an exact science. The better choice would be to use some kind of poison that mimics food poisoning."

"Such as?"

"Lots of things. But if she was at the Olympics, her blood was being tested for chemicals, right?"

"I think so, yes."

"So, chances are, it would be something organic—like, I don't know—apple seeds."

"Apple seeds are poisonous?"

"Not one or two, but in enough quantity. So are peach and apricot and cherry pits. And lots of plants."

"If you were going to poison someone with a food or plant, what would you use?"

An employee of the fast-food place who was cleaning the table next to them stopped and stared.

Hannah arched her eyebrows at the guy. "Do you mind? This is a private murder conversation."

He scurried off and Hannah considered the question. "To kill the person, or just make them sick?"

"Just to make them sick—too sick to compete."

"Ah, then I'd definitely go with an azalea. Every part of the plant is poisonous to some degree, but it's not fatal."

"But wouldn't carrying around an azalea plant draw attention?"

"Yep. And it would have to be local because you can't get anything fresh like that past Customs." Hannah chewed on the straw in her fountain drink. "But really, would someone have gone to that much trouble? Maybe the woman just had a flu bug. It's really hard to tell the difference."

"I know," Carlotta said. "Besides, how would you ever be able to prove someone sabotaged her food?"

"You wouldn't…unless you had a witness."

Carlotta checked her watch. "We're close to the Midtown police precinct. Would you mind if I dropped something off with Jack before we hit the rest of the bakeries?"

"Knock yourself out."

At the precinct, Hannah parked the van and waited for

Carlotta. Once in the lobby, Carlotta made small talk with her buddy Brooklyn.

"I met your brother yesterday," Brooklyn said. "Cute little thing."

Carlotta frowned. "My brother, Wesley, was here yesterday?"

"Yeah. He met with Detective Terry."

"Oh…right," Carlotta said, pretending she'd only forgotten. "Is Detective Terry around? He asked me to drop off something."

"Yeah, go on back."

Carlotta walked through the door the woman buzzed open for her and followed a familiar trail to Jack's office. Inside he was sitting shoulder to shoulder with Maria Marquez, poring over reports that were spread out in front of them, their voices low and comfortable, the desk littered with coffee cups. Carlotta squashed the tiny bubble of jealousy bouncing around in her chest. A blind person could see where the relationship between the two of them was headed. Not only were they physically matched to each other, but she could tell from the expression on Jack's face that he was truly listening to what Maria was saying. They were intellectual equals, with a shared passion.

It was the way it should be.

She lifted her hand and rapped on the outside of the wall. Both of them turned in her direction. Jack's expression opened, while Maria's closed. Carlotta ignored the snub.

"Hi, Jack. I found the, um, *article* we talked about last night." She reached into her purse and pulled out the bracelet box, then handed it to him.

He stood and opened the box. "When did your father give this to you?"

"When I was fourteen."

Maria took the box from him and Carlotta stiffened.

"Did he give you all these charms?" the woman asked.

"Most of them, yes. It was our father-daughter 'thing,' I guess."

"Are any of the charms missing?" Maria asked.

"No."

"Are you sure?"

She gritted her teeth. "That's what I said."

"Thanks for bringing it in," Jack said, breaking through the tension.

"No problem." Carlotta crossed her arms. "Jack, why was Wesley here yesterday?"

"Hmm? Oh…he just needed to sign some paperwork having to do with the recent charges."

"Good. Because I was beginning to wonder if you and your partner were systematically accusing every member of the Wren family of being The Charmed Killer." She smiled sweetly at Maria. "Did you want me to take that polygraph exam while I'm here?"

"We'll let you know," Jack intervened.

Carlotta reached into her purse. "I brought these, too," she said, placing the stack of folded handkerchiefs in his hand. Maria saw the exchange and turned back to the reports. Something fell on Carlotta's shoe and she looked down to see the piece of Bazooka bubblegum the prostitute Pepper had given her.

Jack leaned over to pick it up and handed it back to her with a smile. "Bubblegum?"

She flushed at the memory of the woman's promise that it would make her jaws strong and for what purpose. "I…am trying to quit smoking." She unwrapped it and popped it into her mouth.

"Has the black SUV been back?" Jack asked.

"Not that I've noticed," she said around the stiff gum.

"You'll call if you see it again?"

She nodded because her mouth was so full, then gestured to the exit. "Hannah's waiting, so I should go."

"Is that your best friend, Hannah, the one you know nothing about?" Maria asked, her eyebrows raised.

With great effort, Carlotta maneuvered all the bubblegum to one side of her mouth, then looked back to Jack. "I'm leaving now."

He shifted his feet. "We'll get the bracelet back to you as soon as possible."

Carlotta turned and walked away, chewing like a cow. Jack and Maria were now a "we."

23

Carlotta walked out of the police precinct telling herself that Detective Marquez was trained to get under people's skin—it was undoubtedly how she gleaned information from people to "profile" them.

Still, when Carlotta climbed back into Hannah's van, she studied her friend's profile, which was actually very pretty, and conceded that while Hannah seemed to happily blend into the Wren family—she was like a surrogate aunt to Wesley—Carlotta knew next to nothing about Hannah's background.

"Hannah, where are your parents?"

"Hmm?" Hannah pivoted her head, then looked back to the road. "They're in the area."

"What do they do?"

Hannah frowned. "What's with the questions?"

"Just making conversation. You never talk about them."

"Oh…they're in business."

"What kind of business?"

"This and that—property, mostly."

"Do you have any siblings?"

"Yeah."

"Well—sisters? Brothers?"

"Yeah."

Carlotta lifted her hands. "And?"

Hannah's face darkened. "And we don't get along. End of story. Change channels."

"Okay," Carlotta murmured, sorry that she'd pushed her friend, and angry with Maria Marquez for making her feel as if she should.

They spent the afternoon driving in an ever-widening circle, visiting more grocery store bakeries and coming up empty until they were as far east as Decatur. Carlotta was losing hope that they'd find what they were looking for. She glanced at her watch.

"You got a date?" Hannah asked.

"Peter is picking me up for dinner in an hour."

Her friend made a face.

"He's trying to suck up to you," Carlotta said. "He sent you gorgonzola ice cream the other night."

"When?"

"When Coop called about a body run Monday evening. I was having dinner with Peter and I, um, sort of fibbed and told him you were picking me up. He sent you ice cream from the restaurant."

"What happened to it?"

"Coop ate it."

Hannah sighed. "I would've wanted him to have it."

"I'm worried about Coop. I'm afraid he's on the verge of falling off the wagon."

"All recovering alcoholics are on the verge of falling off the wagon," Hannah replied as she parked the van in yet another grocery store parking lot.

"I guess you're right," Carlotta murmured, then opened the door to climb down.

A few minutes later they were standing in front of the bakery manager, showing him the now-curled picture of the cake. When he scratched his head, Carlotta's shoulders fell, but then he nodded and tapped the photograph. "Yep, that's one of Tina's designs—she's our main cake decorator."

Carlotta's heart raced. "Is Tina working today?"

The man checked the clock on the wall. "She just took a break—she should be back in forty-five minutes."

Carlotta turned to a rack of clearance summer items in front of the bakery counter and picked up a pack of sparklers. This was definitely looking like the place. "We'll come back."

She and Hannah went back to the van to wait, but Carlotta was too anxious to sit still. "Pray that this Tina knows who bought the cake. If we need to come up with a receipt, we're screwed."

"I take it Jack doesn't know anything about this little information-gathering exercise."

"Uh, no. Wait—look!" Carlotta pointed. "By the Dumpster."

Hannah squinted. "All I see is a guy on roller skates."

"The guy with the cake *was* on roller skates. It has to be him!" The man wore the dark utility jumpsuit of a handyman. He was using the roller skates to transport a stack of broken pallets to the Dumpster, a few pieces at a time.

"Do you recognize him?" Hannah asked, handing her a pair of binoculars.

Carlotta adjusted the focus. "Same height, same build." Then she looked at his feet. "Same skates. It's him, I'm sure of it."

"Do you want to call Jack?"

Carlotta lowered the binoculars. "No, let me see if he'll talk to me." She opened the glove compartment and removed a map. After opening the van door and jumping to the ground, she set off toward the guy.

"Excuse me," she said, waving the map—the international damsel-in-distress signal. "Can you help me?"

He stopped and looked her up and down. "Sure."

"I'm lost." The closer she walked to him, the more sure she was that he was the man who'd mown her down with the cake cart. "I'm looking for the Lenox Square mall," she said.

"Honey, you're way off. You need to get back on that road and head toward I-285—" He stopped and narrowed his eyes. "Do I know you?"

"I might look more familiar if I were facedown in a sheet cake," Carlotta said wryly.

His eyes widened and he turned to flee.

She grabbed his arm. "What did you do with Eva McCoy's charm bracelet?"

"I don't know what you're talking about." He shoved her to the ground and lunged toward the street, swinging his arms to gain momentum on his skates.

"Stop!" she shouted, stumbling to her feet. "Come back, I just want to talk to you!"

A few strides later something struck him in the head and he dropped to the ground, his legs tangled. Carlotta ran up to him, and Hannah was right behind her. A lumpy broken brown-and-white crumbly mess lay all around the groaning man, who had a bloody gash on the back of his head.

"What did you do?" Carlotta asked Hannah.

"Nailed him with a frozen chocolate cream pie. It works the same as a Frisbee." Her friend pointed to the tin pan rolling away. "It's all in the wrist."

"You could've killed him."

"But I didn't." Hannah bent down and pulled the guy up by the collar. "Tell my friend what she wants to know, or else I got a frozen layer cake with your name on it, too."

"I don't know anything," he said with a moan, holding his head.

"What's your name?" Carlotta demanded.

"Give me a break here—I'm on parole."

Hannah shook him. "What's your name, dammit."

"James Canary."

"Why did you steal Eva McCoy's charm bracelet?" Carlotta asked.

He didn't respond, so Hannah pinched him on the back of the arm.

He howled. "All right, all right! Somebody hired me to roll in a cake cart and steal the charm bracelet. I cut it off the woman's wrist, but I dropped it. When all hell broke loose, I got outta there."

"Who hired you?"

"I…can't say."

Hannah twisted his ear. "Start singing, Canary."

"I don't know! Everything was coordinated over the phone. I picked up five hundred bucks cash at a drop-off point. I was supposed to handle getting the cake and swiping the bracelet. She told me to toss it in the river when I was through."

"She?" Carlotta said.

"Yeah…it was a chick. But I don't know her name and I never saw her, I swear."

Carlotta gave Hannah a curt nod and she let the man fall back to the ground.

"Did that tell you what you needed to know?" Hannah asked as they walked back to the van.

"I'm not sure," Carlotta said, her mind racing, tossing around bits of dialogue in her conversation with Eva.

You haven't heard any news about your bracelet?

No, and I really don't expect to…I just want all of this

charm insanity to stop…I never realized how much I'd miss it…

When she opened the van door, Carlotta's phone was ringing from her purse. She thought it might be Peter, but instead Coop's name was on the caller ID.

"Hello?" she answered.

"Hey—we've got a third body."

She gripped the phone. "With a charm?"

"Yeah. I called Wesley, but he isn't answering. And I can't get hold of the new guy who's supposed to be helping me."

"Where are you?"

He gave her the address. "It's a motel, a little run-down."

Carlotta glanced around to get her bearings. "Hannah and I aren't too far away. We'll meet you there." She ended the call and swung into her seat, reciting the address to Hannah.

"The Charmed Killer strikes again?"

"Looks that way." Carlotta tightened her seat belt as Hannah screeched out of the parking lot.

She dialed Peter's number and he answered on the second ring.

"Uh-oh. I'm supposed to pick you up in twenty minutes—this can't be good."

"A last-minute situation," she said. "I'm so sorry."

"Tell me this doesn't have anything to do with that serial killer."

"Okay," she said, wincing.

He sighed. "You're scaring me to death."

"I'm with Hannah, and there are police on the scene. I'm just filling in for Wesley. Can I get a rain check on dinner?"

"Always," he said. "Call me."

"I will." She disconnected the call, then tried to reach Wesley, but he didn't answer. She left a voice message for him to call her and cursed under her breath.

"Where's Wes?" Hannah asked.

"I think he started his courier job today." Carlotta pointed. "Turn here. The High Crest Motel should be up ahead. See Coop's van?"

Hannah peeled into the parking lot on two wheels, attracting the attention of everyone on the scene and sending a couple of locals scrambling for cover. The person wearing the biggest frown when they alighted was Jack. He was standing next to his sedan, talking on his radio. Maria stood in the open door of a motel room talking to an M.E. Yellow police tape cordoned off the area. Coop stood nearby with an empty gurney, wearing scrubs. Carlotta hung back and yanked on one of Hannah's chains to keep her at bay until Coop signaled them over a few minutes later.

"Carlotta," Maria said drily when they walked up. "What a surprise to see you here."

Carlotta swallowed a tart comment. "Detective Maria Marquez, this is my friend Hannah Kizer."

The women traded hellos, but she could tell from her friend's body language that she didn't like the way Maria was sizing her up.

"I think they're ready for us," Coop said, handing them scrubs.

Carlotta looked up sharply because she smelled something that brought back a long-lost memory—antiseptic mouthwash. Her mother used to swish it constantly, even though it was difficult to smell vodka on someone's breath. "You doing okay?" she asked him.

He hesitated, then nodded, pushing his hand into his hair.

"What do we have in there?" she asked, nodding to the open door.

"Unidentified Caucasian female, forties, stabbed to death."

She pulled on the scrubs and snapped on the latex gloves just as Jack walked up. "What kind of charm this time?" she whispered.

Jack frowned. "You know I can't tell you that."

"I'm going to find out anyway. You might as well tell me and save yourself a lot of grief."

His mouth tightened. "It's a car."

"What kind?"

"Generic."

"So your killer drives a car?"

"Or my victim," Jack groused. "Along with four million other people in this city."

"Not always. Some of them drive trucks, motorcycles and vans."

"Sorry if I can't get excited about this clue—if it even *is* a clue."

She gave him a tight smile. "Well, at least I have witnesses that I had nothing to do with this crime scene. I've been with Hannah all afternoon."

"Do I want to know what doing?"

"Uh…in due time."

She followed Coop into the motel room and winced at the partially nude woman on the bed who still had a knife in her chest. Blood pooled around her on the bed in the shape of wings. But when Carlotta looked at the woman's face, she gasped.

"I know her."

Jack's eyes flew wide and Maria stepped into the room. "You know the victim?"

"I met her once," Carlotta said, taking in the dark red hair and the harsh eyeliner. "Her name is Pepper. She's a prostitute who hangs out on Third and West Peachtree."

Jack gaped. "How do you know a prostitute?" Then he

raised his hands. "Never mind. But you can't work the scene if you know the victim, not in this case anyway."

Carlotta swallowed nervously. Not in a case where she'd been on the crime scene of two of the victims of The Charmed Killer, and was acquainted with the third.

Minus ten points.

24

Wesley climbed into the Town Car and closed the door with a thunk.

"Took you long enough," Mouse grumbled.

Wesley handed over a fat roll of cash. "Happy?"

"How much did you get?"

"Twelve hundred from Jennings, eight hundred from Greene, a thousand from Rivera." Plus the hundred he'd crammed into his shoe.

Mouse gestured to the Georgia State residence hall. "Was it hard to get in?"

"Not for me."

Mouse was counting the money. "You keep this up and you're going to make a career for yourself."

Wesley thought not. "Listen, Mouse, I know you said I could pay down what I owe The Carver this way, but I need some cash, too. Father Thom's leaning on me. He wants a grand by Wednesday, and I'm not going to have it."

"Why am I supposed to care?"

"Because if I'm in a body cast, it's going to be hard for me to collect for you, man."

Mouse considered his request. "I'll take care of Father Thom's guy."

Wesley's throat convulsed. "What do you mean, you'll take care of him?"

"I mean I'll pay him off. It's better if you owe just The Carver anyway."

"Oh." Wesley's shoulders fell in relief. "I guess that's okay. Are we through? I need to be somewhere the rest of this evening."

"Yeah, just keep your phone on, Little Man."

Mouse dropped him off at Chance's building and Wes got his bike out of the trunk, relieved to see that his jacket, covered in the blood of the severed finger, was gone, replaced by a cardboard evergreen air freshener. He slammed the trunk closed and after the car drove away, he locked his bike on a rack, then called his friend.

"Dude, you're late," Chance said, breathless.

"I'm downstairs. Come on, we'll make the game in plenty of time."

While he waited for Chance, Wesley popped an Oxy pill and soon was feeling as if he could take on the world. He high-fived Chance when he emerged.

"Ready to win, dude?" his friend asked.

"Feeling good," Wesley replied, cracking his knuckles. "And feeling lucky."

It was a magical night of poker-playing—he'd never felt more relaxed or more happy. And it was as if he willed the cards to fall his way. Out of twenty-five players in the tournament, he beat everyone playing at his five-top table in record fashion to win a place at the final table to compete for the winning pot of twenty grand. Since Chance always footed the entry fee, they would split the winnings down the middle.

When play kicked off at the final table, Wes sat back and let the cards come to him. He was dealt two superb facedown pocket cards at the beginning of every hand, then watched as the five face-up community cards, divided into three reveals of the flop, the turn and the river, all conspired to give him some of the most gorgeous hands he'd ever played. They were so good that the five table bosses gathered around to make sure he wasn't cheating. But Wesley didn't mind—it only added to the drama. After promptly losing early in the tournament, Chance stood near his table and cheered him on with lots of fist-pumping and primal screams.

Wesley didn't have to bluff, didn't have to decipher tells—he merely consistently had the best hands. It was as if the cards were alive in his grasp. He could sense the colors bleeding into his fingertips, could feel the curves and the points of the four suits, noticed the winks and smiles of the face cards. The Oxy helped him to stay relaxed and focused, and he parlayed it into a spectacular finish with a straight heart flush, queen high.

He thought Chance was going to have a stroke. His friend dry-humped him in jubilation, then poured a beer over Wesley's head. He didn't care—it felt so damn good to win without the panic attacks of previous tournaments.

The Oxy, as it turned out, was his good luck charm. And he never intended to play without her again.

25

Carlotta woke up suddenly, sitting straight up in bed, her heart pounding. From the moment she closed her eyes, nightmares had chased her nonstop—the sheets tangled in her legs were proof of that. She lay back down on her pillow but the sense of being pursued, of being watched, clung to her until her breathing slowed. Her clock read 8:15 a.m., but she didn't feel rested. Coming home last night to a dark, empty house after seeing Pepper, who had been so alive only a few days ago, murdered, with a knife stuck in her thin body, had saddened and disturbed her.

Wesley hadn't been home and Hannah couldn't spend the night because of something she had to get up early for. So Carlotta had huddled in bed with her lamp light on, telling herself there was no reason to be scared. The doors and windows were locked. She was simply letting her imagination run away with her. But she couldn't get the image of that knife out of her head, wondering when Pepper had realized she might be in danger, and how much pain the woman had endured before she'd died.

Three bodies in one week—The Charmed Killer was wasting no time in racking up impressive numbers. He was out to get everyone's attention, and it appeared that the violence of his methods was escalating.

She shuddered in the warm air and laid there, her mind whirling, folding in new thoughts with every revolution. For example, who had hired James Canary to steal Eva McCoy's bracelet. Was it Eva herself, who was tired of the publicity and the danger? Or was someone else involved?

When it was clear she wouldn't be going back to sleep, Carlotta swung her feet over the edge of the bed, found her slippers and put on her robe. She was relieved to hear the drone of the fan behind Wesley's closed door, but after last night's ghastly experience, she felt compelled to look in on him, just to reassure herself that he was okay.

She turned the doorknob and eased open the door. Then squinted. And gasped.

Wesley lay in his bed in a pool of money.

She blinked to make sure that all the green papers around him being ruffled by the air of the fan were indeed dollar bills. While she watched, a twenty was dislodged and floated to the floor. There must be thousands of dollars. Her heart lodged in her throat. Where would her brother get that kind of money? Drugs?

Wesley must have heard her or sensed she was in the room because he stirred and rubbed his eyes. When he moved on the money, it crackled, which seemed to further rouse him. He looked around and blinked her into focus. "What time is it?"

She opened the door wider and crossed her arms. "Time for you to tell me where you got all this money."

He lifted his head and looked all around him. When he raised his arms, dollar bills stuck to them. Then he propped himself up on his elbow and grinned. "I won it."

"In a bet?" she asked. "Because you promised me you wouldn't play cards."

He blanched. "But I *won*. For you...for us. We can do

some of the things around the house you've been wanting to do."

Carlotta bit her lip. "How much is it?"

"Ten grand, give or take."

She inhaled sharply. "Ten thousand dollars?"

"Yeah."

Carlotta clasped her hands in front of her face like a child.

"Cool, huh?" he said.

"I'm not condoning how you got it, but I admit that, yes, it'll be nice to have some extra cash to fix things up around here." Then she remembered the pill she'd found in his room and sobered. "Get dressed, okay? I need to talk to you about something else."

She collected the Sunday paper from the stoop and glanced around for the mysterious SUV, but didn't see anything amiss.

Predictably, The Charmed Killer was front-page news. Rainie Stephens's source in the morgue was thorough— she knew the victim's name and presumed occupation, as well as the fact that there was no question that the victim had been murdered this time, and violently.

The reporter also described the charm as a "miniature car," and added that police were still perplexed about the actual meaning of the charms. Finally, she took advantage of the Eva McCoy missing charm bracelet connection, leaving the reader to believe that the charms found in the mouths of the victims might be from the McCoy charm bracelet.

Carlotta carried the paper to the kitchen and made coffee, peering through the window over the sink up into an overcast sky. She had to work this afternoon, and tell Jack about James Canary…and confess what she and Hannah had done…and hope the perp hadn't left town.

And all the while, thoughts of Coop kept popping into her mind. He'd looked so haggard last night, as if he hadn't been sleeping…or had been drinking.

"Hey." Wesley walked into the kitchen and poured himself a cup of coffee. "What's up?"

She walked over to her purse that she'd left on the breakfast bar, reached in, and removed the little baggie holding the OxyContin pill she'd found. "This is what's up."

He picked up the baggie and scratched his head. "What is it?"

"Don't play dumb with me. I found it on your bathroom floor."

He shrugged. "Okay."

"I looked it up. It's generic OxyContin."

He still looked perplexed. "Okay."

"I read up on it. It's highly addictive. What are you doing with it?"

He put his hand on his scarred arm. "Chance gave it to me when my arm was hurting."

"I thought you took my Percocet refills for your pain."

"This was before the Percocet." He frowned. "What were you doing in my bathroom?"

"Cleaning it."

"Well, don't."

She held up her hands. "So you're telling me that you're not taking this OxyContin stuff?"

"Right. I have to give urine samples when I meet with my probation officer. Why would I risk it?"

Carlotta's shoulders fell in relief. She hadn't thought about the drug screening. All this time, she'd been worried for nothing…fretting, doubting her brother, thinking the worst. "I'm sorry, I should've known you wouldn't get mixed up in something like that."

He nodded. "Is that all you wanted to talk about?"

"There is one more thing. I called Liz Fischer to ask about Randolph's case file, and she said that you'd stolen it?"

"Yeah," he said sheepishly.

"Cool. Did you photocopy everything?"

"The things that looked important."

Carlotta's eyes widened in understanding. "That's why you were seeing Liz? So you could steal Dad's file?"

He squirmed. "You know about me and Liz?"

"I figured it out. Can I see the file?"

"Why do you want it? Has Dad contacted you again?"

"No. But Peter and I have decided to start looking into things in the interim. I'm going to review the external paperwork, and Peter's going to poke around inside Mashburn & Tully."

"Won't that get Peter in trouble at the firm?"

"If they find out, yes. I was hoping I could count on you to help me."

He nodded eagerly, pushing at his glasses. "Let me get the file." He disappeared into his room and came back carrying a folder. "This is what I have so far."

"There's more?"

He nodded. "I'm getting all the police reports and courthouse records for the case."

"I thought those were available only to Dad or his attorney."

He lifted his coffee cup for a deep drink.

"Wesley, what are you up to?"

"Remember when I broke into the courthouse database?"

"To fix your traffic tickets, yeah."

"I didn't hack into the computer to fix my traffic tickets." He took another gulp of coffee.

She gaped. "You broke in to get Dad's records?"

"More specifically, I broke in to leave a backdoor so I could get back in later."

"Later?" She covered her mouth with her hand. "Your community service—"

"Is pretty convenient."

She crossed her arms and tried to look harsh. "Almost as if you planned it."

He pursed his mouth and nodded. "Almost."

Carlotta shook her head in wonder. "Why didn't you tell me?"

"I thought it was better if you didn't know. Besides, at the time, I didn't think you'd be so keen on trying to help Dad."

She held up her finger. "I didn't say I was going to *help* Randolph. I'm going to follow the truth and see where it leads me."

"Sounds good," Wesley said happily. He was so certain that their father would be exonerated, he couldn't imagine another outcome.

For his sake, she hoped that was the case.

From his pocket a cell phone rang, and Wesley seemed slow to answer it.

"Is that a new phone?"

"For my courier job," he said, then flipped up the cover. "This is Wes…hey… Yeah… Yeah…okay." He closed the phone. "Gotta go."

She frowned. "You're making a delivery on Sunday morning?"

"Uh…some of our clients are in church."

"You mean some of your clients are churches?"

"Right. If it's late and I'm on the other side of town when I'm finished, I might crash at Chance's for the rest of the weekend."

She bit her tongue to keep from saying anything bad about Chance. "Wesley?"

He turned back.

"Where are you going to put the money?"

"In my sock drawer for now."

"I'm just throwing this out there—how about the bank?"

He looked appalled. "Records? Taxes? No, thanks."

"It was only a suggestion," she called. "Wesley?"

He turned back.

"I'm proud of you. Your methods may be questionable, but your heart is in the right place."

He smiled and flushed scarlet, then left the kitchen. A few minutes later, he shouted goodbye before he banged through the front door.

She smiled into her coffee, then went to the breakfast bar to study the pictures from the Eva McCoy event with fresh eyes. Now that she knew James Canary had cut off the bracelet and dropped it, perhaps she would see who'd taken it. Unfortunately, none of the pictures revealed anything new.

Knowing that Eva herself might have funded the bracelet robbery made her think about the food poisoning incident at the Olympics. Had the woman spiked her own food, or was her life truly in danger? Maybe she'd even faked the illness? Carlotta's conversation with Hannah floated back to her.

How would you ever be able to prove someone sabotaged her food?

You wouldn't…unless you had a witness.

A witness…footage of the venue…of the event itself?

She picked up the phone and dialed Coop's number. After several rings, he answered, his voice gluey. "Hello?"

"Coop…it's Carlotta. Is this too early?"

"Not at all," he said, over a yawn. "Is this going to become a habit of yours?"

She laughed. "No, I'm sorry. You mentioned once that you recorded the women's Olympic marathon event. Do you still have it?"

"Yeah, somewhere."

"Can I borrow it?"

"To watch on your TV?"

"Good point. Can I watch it on yours?"

"Sure. When do you want to come over?"

"Now?"

"Okay." Coop's laugh rumbled over the phone, then he gave her directions. "See you in a few."

26

Carlotta had never seen Coop's place before, but when she pulled up to the two-story concrete building with a red door, she immediately liked it. He lived in the eclectic neighborhood of Castleberry Hill, known for its art galleries, novel restaurants and offbeat hair salons. Instead of condos, many early residents had bought entire commercial buildings and converted them into residences. Coop's home looked like it had once been some kind of business with a sidewalk storefront and garage, maybe an auto parts or repair shop, with a storeroom on top. The exterior had been stripped of all ornament, leaving it sleek and minimal, masculine and appealing.

The tall midcentury garage door was raised and Coop emerged to guide her inside. He looked lanky and handsome in old jeans, a white button-down shirt and tennis shoes. The first floor, she realized as she was steered inside, was actually an open-plan story and a half that housed his white Corvette convertible, his white van, a piano, home theater and kitchen on a shiny sealed concrete floor. A row of tall orange cabinets lined the wall opposite the cars, flanked by a drafting table. A set of stairs led to another floor, and an old-fashioned freight elevator sat in the corner.

She climbed out of her car and turned to greet him after he lowered the door. "Coop, this is amazing."

He grinned. "I like it. I'm glad you do, too. Coffee?"

"Do you have decaf? I've already hit my limit of caffeine for the day."

"Up bright and early, huh?"

"Hardly. I didn't sleep well."

He made a rueful noise. "No wonder, after last night's incident."

"Coop, have you ever seen anything like this serial killer before?"

"No."

"What's happening? Why would someone do this?"

He pulled his hand down his face. "I don't know. Jack said his partner would have a full profile soon. Fortunately and unfortunately, the more murders, the more information they have to go on."

"And they're sure the first two deaths were murders?"

"No, not yet."

"If they'd listened to you on Shawna Whitt, she could've been autopsied properly."

"Water under the bridge. They have their hands full now."

"I hear you're helping on the cases?"

He shrugged as he loaded the coffeemaker and started the drip. "I help when I can, where I can."

"How's Abrams?" she asked, glancing around the kitchen. The photograph of her that he'd lifted from the envelope of extras at Moody's was attached to the side of the stainless steel refrigerator with a magnet.

"Abrams is the same. We try to stay out of each other's way."

"So who hired you back?"

"I'm not really an employee…more like an advisor."

"It must have been someone over Abrams's head?"

"The state M.E. suggested it, and Abrams went along."

So someone at the top was looking out for Coop.

"If you don't mind me asking," he said, "why are you so interested in the footage of the Olympic marathon?"

"I'm hoping it'll tell me something—about Eva McCoy, about her competitors, about the venue. She thinks someone sabotaged her."

"Do you believe her?"

"I don't know. She could be paranoid…or maybe she likes the limelight more than I think she does."

He set a mug under the drip spout until it was full, then handed it to her. "Well, let's see, shall we?"

The boxy sofa was surprisingly comfortable. Coop loaded the DVD he'd burned and sat down in front of the screen beside her to watch. "Let me know if you want to skim, skip, rewind, whatever."

"Okay. Tell me anything you think seems pertinent."

"This is a shot of the Olympic Village."

Carlotta nodded at the elaborate sign and landscaping that marked the entrance. "This is familiar."

"Yeah, they showed it a lot during the Games. And there are the announcers talking about the possibility that Eva McCoy won't run in the marathon."

He allowed it to play and she studied the pictures of the two female athletes who, according to the statistics, had the most to gain from Eva dropping out: a runner from Great Britain named Bianca Thaler and a Venezuelan, Ruda Napor. The announcers indicated there was no love lost between the three women, either. Thaler and Napor were very competitive and had been accused of unethical behavior in the past, such as tossing spent water bottles in the path of other runners, and bumping against competitors when it got down to the sprint at the end.

"So chances are," Carlotta said, "if they didn't get along, those two women wouldn't have had access to Eva's food."

"I don't see how," Coop agreed. "Okay, here are the racers at the start, and there comes Eva in the back."

"Pause it, and go back a few frames. Can we watch Thaler and Napor take their places at the line?"

He found the spot and forwarded the frames slowly. "There's Thaler…and there's Napor."

Carlotta frowned at the screen. "Thaler keeps scanning the crowd as if she's trying to find someone. Let's see if the camera catches who she's looking for."

Coop slowly advanced the screen. "There—her hand doesn't go up, but her head does."

"And there," Carlotta said, pointing. "Someone nods in response. Can we get a closer view?"

Coop took it out of view mode and into edit, where he cut and pasted, zooming in on the person in question—or rather, the *man* in question.

Carlotta gasped. "It's Ben Newsome, Eva's boyfriend."

"Maybe he and Thaler just know each other from having competed at all the meets," Coop suggested.

But as the race got underway and Eva's miracle run unfolded, her face pale and her skin waxy, it seemed that when the camera panned the crowd, Ben Newsome was always looking someplace else. Not once did he give Eva a thumbs-up or a big smile.

"What's that in his shirt pocket?" Carlotta asked. "It's some kind of flower—a buttercup?"

"Maybe a daffodil," Coop said. "If I remember correctly, they were all over the Olympic Village. Remember the flowers in the opening shot?"

Her conversation with Hannah about organic plants came back to her. "Are daffodils, by chance, poisonous?"

Coop pursed his mouth. "Yes, the bulbs are. They contain narcitine and narcicysteine."

"What are the symptoms of daffodil poisoning?"

"Nausea and cramping."

"Like food poisoning?"

Coop nodded. "And it can be fatal."

"Maybe that's how Ben did it," she said excitedly.

Coop looked dubious. "It fits, but narcitine poisoning seems a little extreme."

"Not if Ben Newsome is in love with Bianca Thaler and was trying to knock Eva out of the running so Bianca had a better chance of winning."

"Still, unless someone saw him spike Eva's food, it would be impossible to prove."

Carlotta pressed her lips together in thought. "Wait a minute. Don't the athletes have their blood drawn regularly for doping testing?"

"Yes."

"Would the poisons you mentioned show up during toxicology screening?"

"Sure…if you were looking for it. But it's not likely the testers would be watching for that."

"It would still be in her blood sample that's been stored, though. Right?"

He smiled. "Yes, it would."

"Well, at least that gives Eva recourse. Can you make me a copy of this DVD, Coop?"

"Sure, give me a few minutes."

While he was setting up the machine to tape, she wandered over to the drafting table sitting next to the row of orange cabinets. On the table was a ruler, mechanical pencils and a finely detailed drawing on thin paper. "Is this your work area?"

"My hobby area," he said, walking over to join her. He opened various cabinets to reveal stacks of cigar boxes, and trays of tiny supplies. "It's where I build the dioramas."

"Do you have any finished ones?"

"Just a work in progress," he said, then carefully pulled out a cigar box and opened the lid.

She looked inside and smiled. "It's a library—how wonderful."

"It's far from finished," he said, then removed one tiny book with a spine that read *POE*. He opened it and she was astonished to see that it had writing on the pages.

"The amount of detail is simply incredible," she breathed.

"That's the point," he said with a little smile. "It'll probably take me another couple of years to finish it."

The DVD recorder beeped. Coop set down the box to retrieve her disc. "Eva's going to be so grateful to you."

"I'm not so sure about that," Carlotta said. "But thank you for everything. I have to get going, but I love your place, Coop. It's so…you."

"Maybe next time your schedule will allow for a full tour."

She lifted her gaze to the stairs, which undoubtedly led to his bedroom.

"There's a rooftop garden," he said with a twinkle in his eye.

She laughed. "I'd like to see it sometime." Then they lapsed into an awkward silence.

"Coop—" she said

"Carlotta—" he said at the same time.

They laughed.

"Me first," he said, then wet his lips. "I know that our chance to be together might have passed me by, but I just want to tell you that no matter what happens to me, no matter what I might do or say, I don't regret a minute I've spent with you."

Carlotta frowned. "Coop…what's wrong? Something, I can tell." She hadn't seen any liquor bottles, or smelled booze on his breath, but for all she knew, the upstairs could be littered with empties. "Are you drinking?"

"No. I've been able to hold off."

"Please tell me what's making you so sad."

"Nothing you've done," he said. "And there's nothing you can do. Don't worry about me." He nodded to the DVD she held. "You're really good at this stuff, helping people."

She scoffed. "I'm just putting puzzle pieces together, that's all." As soon as the words left her mouth, she glanced down at the charm bracelet she'd worn and fingered the tiny puzzle charm.

"It's a gift," he murmured. "Don't stop."

Confidence swelled in her chest. Maybe she and Peter and Wesley could figure out her father's case after all. "Thank you, Coop, for always listening to me."

His brown eyes crinkled. "That's no chore."

She reached up and kissed him on the cheek. "I have to get to work. Talk soon?"

He looked as if he wanted to say something else, but just nodded. "I'll get the garage door for you."

She climbed into her car, then backed out onto the street carefully and waved goodbye. He waved back until she could no longer see him in her rearview mirror. She replayed their conversation in her head. She had the strangest feeling that Coop was trying to warn her about something…something that was going to happen to him…or something he was going to do.

On the drive to the store, she called Jack. She wanted

to ask him to keep an eye on Coop and to talk through some things in the Eva McCoy case, but he didn't answer. While his voice message played, she made a snap decision. When the beep sounded, she asked him to come by the store in the morning at ten and bring the security surveillance tapes with him from the day of the cake incident.

Next she called the grocery where she and Hannah had located James Canary and asked for him.

"He didn't come in today," she was told.

"Do you have a home phone number for him?"

"Ma'am, we can't give out that information even if we had it."

She grimaced. "May I speak with Tina in the bakery, please?"

"Hold one moment."

After a few seconds of commercials, the line rang and a woman's voice said, "Bakery, this is Tina."

"Tina, I'm trying to reach James Canary. Can you help me?"

"Who is this?" She sounded suspicious…and nervous.

"Just tell James the lady from the parking lot called. Tell him to get his butt to the office of the general manager of Neiman Marcus at Lenox Square tomorrow morning at ten o'clock, without the roller skates. If he shows up ready to tell the truth, I have a cop friend who might put in a good word with his parole officer. If he doesn't show up, he's rolling back to the joint."

"Okay," the girl croaked. "He'll be there."

Reaching Eva McCoy was a little more tricky. Carlotta wound up leaving a message with Eva's publicist's answering service asking Eva and her boyfriend, Ben, to meet at the store the next morning for an update on the case.

Then she made one last phone call—to Rainie Stephens,

offering an exclusive on a story in return for running a piece of information that could help break a case.

Meanwhile, she kept sorting through the details and fragments of the day of the event, trying to remember something that would make everything fall into place. Lost in thought, she didn't remember parking her car or walking inside Neiman's, but she must have because her next conscious movement was swiping her employee ID to get into the break room. She gave herself a mental shake and stowed her purse in her locker. She needed to get her mind on the workday ahead.

The door beeped and Patricia Alexander walked in. When she saw Carlotta, her face lit up. "You're not going to believe this!"

"What?"

"Guess!"

"I can't imagine. Just tell me."

"It has something to do with my charm bracelet." Patricia held up her arm and shook it vigorously. "I met a baseball player," she said, holding up the little baseball glove. "And his name is Leo." She held up the little lion's head charm. "Baseball—Leo. Ha! This thing really works!"

"That's great, Patricia, really."

The blonde frowned. "Have you been reading about The Charmed Killer? They found his third victim last night."

"I saw that. Very sad."

"I hope they catch the guy before this goes any further."

"Me, too." She fingered the corpse charm and wondered if she'd unleash some kind of cosmic chaos if she simply removed the corpse and tossed it away.

On the other hand, she didn't want the charm winding up in someone's throat…especially hers.

She immersed herself in work and at the end of the day,

felt positive about her slow ascent back to the top of the sales reports. After she retrieved her purse, she walked toward the entrance, entertaining the thought of calling Peter to make up for their missed dinner tonight. Suddenly a long arm came out of nowhere and pulled her into a dressing room.

Her mind went to the stun baton in her purse, but then some part of her realized that her "assailant" was holding her loosely, his hand barely covering her mouth.

Jack.

She bit down on a finger.

"Ow!" he said, yanking away his hand.

"What's wrong with you, scaring me like that?"

He glared. "Is that how you put up a fight? You didn't even scream. Where's the stun baton I gave you?"

"In my bag."

"So get used to walking with your hand inside your bag. Once upon a time I gave a little speech in this very store on self-defense, remember that?"

"Yes, but forgive me if I assumed I was safe walking through the accessories department."

He lifted his finger. "Don't get complacent."

"So you'd rather I be paranoid instead?"

"No, I want you to be aware of your surroundings."

She sighed. "You came here to lecture me on safety?"

"No. I got your voice message." He scowled. "You're summoning me to come down here in the morning to talk with Eva McCoy and her boyfriend about an update? What update?"

"I…think I know who's behind the death threats. And the stolen bracelet."

His eyebrows flew up. "You *think* you know?"

"I don't have it all figured out yet, but almost."

His eyeballs bulged out of his head. "You can't be serious."

"I am. Walk out to my car with me."

He followed her, but he looked as if the top of his head was going to blow off.

"By the way, Jack, you need to call Coop. Something's wrong. I think you should keep an eye on him."

"I've got a hundred things on my plate right now that are more important than Coop's broken heart. And don't change the subject. I won't be party to a damn game of *Clue* that you're orchestrating in your general manager's office with *hors d'oeuvres!*"

"Good idea. I didn't think of that."

"Count me out."

She allowed him to hold open the exit door while she passed through under his arm. "Jack, I think it's important that you be there in case someone needs to be arrested."

He massaged the bridge of his nose and sighed. "You told that *AJC* reporter about the charm in the third victim's mouth, didn't you?"

"Now look who's changing the subject."

"Answer me!"

"No, I didn't."

"Then how did it get in this morning's paper?"

Anger spurred Carlotta to walk faster. "Rainie Stephens told me she has a source in the morgue. Am I the first person you think of when somebody has loose lips?"

His gaze darted to her mouth. "Well…yeah. Because you're kind of famous for not minding your own business—*and* not keeping your mouth shut." He gestured to her arm. "You're walking outside and your hand isn't in your purse."

She looked out to the settling dusk, uncharacteristically early tonight because of the overcast skies. They were practically alone in the parking lot. Her car resembled a big blue walrus, beached on concrete. "That's because I'm with you, Jack. You'll protect me."

"You didn't even park under a light. Goddammit, Carlotta, there's a serial killer out there."

"Sorry. I'll park under a light next time, I promise."

"Where's your keyless remote?"

She dug it out of her purse.

He took it from her and pointed it at the car that was still twenty yards away. "Use it as far away as you can. When the headlights flash, you'll at least be able to see all around the car."

He hit the button...and an explosion rent the air, knocking them off their feet. Jack rolled to cover her body with his as they were pelted with raining debris. The heat was intense. When things stopped falling, he helped her to sit up. "Are you okay?"

She tested all her limbs. "Yeah. My ears are ringing, but that's all."

They turned to stare at what was left of the Monte Carlo, as flames shot high in the air.

Carlotta swallowed hard. "You're right, Jack. That trick really improves visibility."

27

"And it had a new battery," Carlotta lamented as Jack drove her home.

"Enough about the battery," he said, jamming soot-covered hands into his hair. "You could've been killed."

"I've been dead before," she reminded him.

"Not funny. Why don't I take you to the emergency room, just to have you checked out?"

"I'm fine, Jack, really." She reached up to touch one of several small abrasions on his forehead. "You took the brunt of it…as usual."

His jaw hardened. "When I think of losing you like that—"

She put a finger on his lips. "We're both fine."

He reached over and clasped her hand. "I'm staying tonight."

"That's not necessary. You don't know that someone rigged the car to blow. I've put that car through hell. It was stolen and *that* person put it through hell, too. It's been in and out of body shops—who knows what could've gone wrong with it?"

"CSI will let me know what they find. But cars with electrical problems and engine problems catch on fire and burn—they don't explode and incinerate. Couple that with the fact that you've meddled—"

"Excuse me?"

"*Been involved in* some pretty serious murder cases over the past few months." He wet his lips. "When did you leave that message for Eva McCoy and Ben Newsome about getting together tomorrow?"

"I left it on their publicist's messaging service right after I left the message for you. I was on my way to work."

"And what did you say, exactly?"

"Just that we wanted to update them on the case."

"Who else did you call?"

"Uh, the cake guy."

"You found the cake guy?"

"Yeah, Hannah and I found him. He said he'd only talked on the phone to the person who hired him. He was supposed to snatch the bracelet and get rid of it."

"My, what a chatty fellow," Jack said drily. "He just volunteered all this information?"

"Well, Hannah sort of roughed him up with a frozen pie first. You know how intimidating she can be."

His hands tightened on the steering wheel. "Did you ever consider that this guy might be dangerous?"

"Oh, he is. He's on parole."

He wiped his hand over his mouth. "And does this felon have a name?"

"James Canary."

"Well, there's that, at least. Assuming it's a real name that I can put through the system." A muscle in his jaw worked. "Did you call anyone else?"

"Uh…"

"Don't lie to me, Carlotta. If I have to, I'll get your cell phone records."

She frowned. He would do it. "I called Rainie Stephens."

"I *knew* you were talking to her!"

"For a favor. I didn't tell her anything about The Charmed Killer case, I swear."

He expelled a noisy sigh. "Well, since I doubt our intrepid local reporter is a cold-blooded murderer who wants you dead, that leaves us with Eva McCoy, Ben Newsome, someone on their support team, or the felon on roller skates who might've wired your car. Where has your car been today?"

"Locked in the garage at home, then I went to see Coop."

"Oh?"

"He had a DVD I needed."

"That excuse never works for me," he said with a sardonic smile.

"Very funny."

"How long were you there?"

"I don't know—maybe thirty minutes." She punched him. "Stop smiling like that. Coop and I aren't…we never…and it's none of your business anyway."

"You're right," he said, then smiled a little smile.

"And then, the car was parked in his place," she continued.

"You mean the garage?"

"It's all sort of together. You've never been to Coop's house?"

"No, why would I?"

"I don't know. I thought you two were pals."

"Yeah, but we don't have sleepovers."

"So what's your place like, Jack?"

"Hmm?"

"Where do you live?"

"Nowhere special."

"Is it a house, an apartment?"

He shrugged.

"Okay, never mind. What, are you afraid I'm going to stalk you?"

"Yeah. So your car was nowhere else?"

"That's it—home, Coop's and the mall."

"We can't count out the guys that Wesley's messed up with as possible suspects."

"Oh, I keep forgetting to tell you. Wesley has a new job."

He frowned. "Really. Doing what?"

"He's a courier…on his bike. They gave him a cell phone and everything. And he must be doing great because they've been keeping him busy."

"You don't say? Will he be home tonight?"

"He told me he might crash with a friend."

"Good." He nodded. "Because I want to sleep in your bed."

Her thighs tingled. "You must really like my mattress."

He grinned. "I never heard it called that, but yeah."

It was dark when they got to the town house. Jack parked the sedan in the garage, then they took the world's longest shower together. He was such a beautiful man, all hard and craggy and proud.

"We shouldn't do this," she whispered against his neck.

"Last time, I promise," he murmured in return.

"In that case…" She pushed him back against the tiled wall and devoured him, putting those new and improved jaw muscles to good use.

He drove his hands into her hair and made happy caveman noises until he exploded in her mouth. Later, he sat her on the sink and returned the favor. She pressed her heels into his shoulders and rode his tongue like a roller coaster. They fell into bed, exhausted…almost. Jack kissed her until her lips were swollen, then he rolled on a condom and covered her body with his, burying his cock inside her warmth, his face in her hair.

He breathed her name, catching her up in a gliding rhythm, a slow dance after their shower disco. She let the waves of molten pleasure course through her until they found their shared release, a shot of pleasure-pain that whipped through her like an electric charge. In those minutes she clung to him. "*Jack…Jack…Jack…*"

"Did you bring the surveillance tapes?" she asked.

"Yes, but you already watched them twice this morning." Jack's head moved side to side as they walked across the parking lot toward the store. "There's not much on them."

True, but she'd hoped they would give her some clue as to who had actually stolen the charm bracelet. The most obvious choice was Ben Newsome, but if he'd taken the bracelet, what had he done with it? The item was too bulky to hide easily, and Ben had been wearing a close-fitting athletic suit. He could've handed it off to the bodyguard or the publicist, but she didn't see them interact on the tapes.

"Are you sure James Canary will show?" Carlotta asked.

"His parole officer said she'd bring him herself," Jack reassured her.

If her hunch was right, this little pointing-the-finger party could be revealing, even though she didn't have every piece in place yet. But if she was wrong, she'd go down in flames in front of Jack and her boss, possibly fueled by a couple of counts of slander and assault. Lindy had been dubious about the meeting when Carlotta had talked to her, but in the end she just wanted to put an end to the bad publicity.

And Jack was so sure the CSI was going to call him and tell him not only was her car rigged with a bomb, but there was some speck of evidence to tie it to someone in the room. He was going to be mighty disappointed if they told him it was caused by a battery that had been recalled. His car bomb theory was the only reason he was here.

She rubbed the little puzzle piece charm on her bracelet for good luck. Coop had told her she had a gift. Now was the time to put it to the test.

"I'm sore," she whispered as they rode up the escalator.

One side of his mouth lifted. "From me or the bomb?"

"From you, big boy. Forget the bomb. You blew me away."

He winced. "I was fishing for that one, wasn't I?"

"Uh-huh." Then she smiled. "But it's sort of true."

"The bedroom is the one place where we agree," Jack said, warming her with a wink. "It was a nice way to go out, darling."

It was. She'd slept like a baby last night for the first time in ages—no tossing and turning, no jarring nightmares. Just lots of firm, warm skin to curl up to, and a natural wake-up call.

In the surveillance tapes, Ben had disappeared off camera for a few seconds…which meant he'd gone into a part of the store that didn't have cameras—the restrooms, the dressing rooms. But they'd all been searched methodically by security, including the trash, toilet tanks and ceiling tiles.

If Ben *had* stolen that bracelet, he would have had to either put it in a place where it would be disposed of unnoticed, or somewhere he could come back to get it.

Carlotta lifted her head. "Jack, I think I know where the charm bracelet is!" She stepped off the "up" escalator and walked across to get on the "down" one, taking the steps two at a time. She jogged to the employee break room and carded in. Jack was a few steps behind her. She walked in and looked around for hiding places. There were no surveillance cameras in the break room. On the other hand, it would be tough to hide something here because the room was so well-used. Then her gaze landed on Michael Lane's old locker.

Well, there was *one* area that no one seemed to want to touch.

She walked over and fought a shudder. Michael's locker had been cleared out by the cops, but since the police tape was still on it, everyone was half afraid to touch it. Frankly, no one wanted the bad karma of taking over Michael's space.

She lifted the slide handle and swung open the door. In the corner of the locker, Eva McCoy's charm bracelet sparkled back.

"What do you know," Jack said. "I assume you also know how it got there?"

She nodded. "Got an evidence bag?"

He pulled out a small plastic bag, then used a pencil to pick up the bracelet and drop it inside.

"Do you think James Canary would be willing to work with us on something?"

"His parole officer said he'd give us whatever we needed."

Carlotta told him her plan on the way back upstairs. When they stepped off the escalator, Jack nodded to a suited woman holding a briefcase and a rough-looking young man standing near a customer-service counter. "That looks like our guy."

"Yeah, that's him," Carlotta confirmed. "Can you explain what we talked about? I'll get the ball rolling."

"I'm right behind you."

When she walked into Lindy's office, she saw that Eva McCoy and Ben Newsome were already there. Eva sat in a chair, looking tired and nervous. Ben was standing, his body vibrating with irritation. After abrupt greetings, he lifted his hands. "So what is this update that you wanted to share?"

Carlotta smiled. "Eva, before we get started, I want to say how pleased I was to see in the *AJC* this morning that you've reconsidered running in the World Championships. I'm sure that's wonderful news for all your fans."

Eva looked confused. Ben turned toward Eva. "What? You changed your mind and didn't tell me?"

"No, I—"

Carlotta unrolled the newspaper she had under her arm and handed it to Ben, letting him see the announcement in print. "Eva told me the other day that she wanted it to be a surprise for you, since you're her biggest supporter."

Eva touched her forehead, and Carlotta hoped the woman's general state of fatigue would prevent her from refuting the bogus report.

Ben stopped behind Eva and put his hands on her shoulders. "Eva is much too stressed over losing her bracelet to keep competing."

Carlotta clapped her hands together. "Oh, then I have good news. The man who came in with the cake and cut off your bracelet was found and your bracelet has been recovered. Isn't that wonderful?"

Eva brightened, but now Ben looked confused. "Are you sure it's Eva's bracelet?"

"Let's see. The man who stole it wanted to give it back to you himself and apologize."

Ben stepped up. "Wait just a minute. This guy is a criminal. I don't want him anywhere near Eva."

Carlotta made a rueful noise. "How do you feel about it, Eva? A police officer is with him."

"I…guess it would be okay."

"Good." Carlotta went to the door and signaled for Jack to bring in James.

When the men walked in, James was nervous, which played well. "I'm James Canary. I'm sorry I took your bracelet," he mumbled to Eva. "Here it is back." He clumsily handed her the bag that held the jewelry.

Ben Newsome jabbed a finger in the air. "That could be a cheap copy, for all we know."

Eva shook her head. "No, Ben, it's my bracelet." She looked up at James. "Thank you. This means so much to me."

Jack cleared his throat. "I'm sorry, ma'am, but please don't take it out of the bag just yet. We still have to lift fingerprints from it for formal paperwork."

Ben stood stock-still. "Fingerprints? Well, that's just silly. There are probably all kinds of prints on that bracelet."

"Not really," Jack said. "Just a couple of clear ones that we're pretty sure will belong to Mr. Canary, but you never know."

"I'm curious, why did you take it?" Eva asked the man.

"That's a good question," Carlotta cut in. "Mr. Newsome, perhaps you'd like to answer."

"How should I know why this thug would do something so cruel?"

"Because you hired him."

Ben gave a little laugh. "What? That's ridiculous. Before he attacked my fiancée, I'd never seen this man before in my life."

"The woman who hired me handled everything over the phone," James said. "She gave me five hundred dollars cash to create a diversion, cut off the bracelet and get rid of it."

Ben lifted a hand. "See? A woman hired him."

Eva stood, as if she suspected something was about to implode. "What woman?"

"She never told me her name," James said.

"This is an exercise in futility," Ben said. "Eva has her bracelet back, and that's what matters. We're leaving."

But Jack stepped up to block his way. "Let's hear what else Carlotta has to say."

Carlotta turned to James. "Please turn around, James. I'm going to play several female voices and I want you to tell me if any of them belong to the woman you talked to on the phone."

"Okay." He turned his back and Carlotta turned on the TV across from Lindy's desk, cuing up the DVD interviews of the women who were considered to be the top five women's marathon contenders.

"I insist that you stop this nonsense," Ben cried.

Jack pointed to a chair. "Sit down, Mr. Newsome. I'm not going to tell you again."

"Be quiet, Ben," Eva chided. "I want to understand where this is going."

Carlotta hit a button and everyone but James saw that a New Zealand runner identified as Lenore Willa was speaking. Carlotta let several seconds of the interview play before going on to Ruda Napor from Venezuela, then on to Bianca Thaler.

"Wait—that's her," James said, turning around. "That's the woman I talked to on the phone."

Eva shook her head. "I don't understand."

"Eva," Carlotta said gently, "Mr. Newsome and Bianca Thaler have been plotting against you. They conspired to hire Mr. Canary here to steal your bracelet in order to shake your confidence, so you wouldn't compete in the World Championships."

The woman looked shell-shocked. "Ben, is that true?"

"No, all of this is total fabrication," Ben said, clasping

her hands. "They've caught the man who stole your bracelet. Obviously, he's trying to get out of being punished by making up all these stories."

Eva looked to Carlotta who shook her head slowly. "You know in your heart that he's not making sense. It's only a matter of time before the police have phone records and bank withdrawals to back this up."

"That man is lying!" Ben shouted. "He didn't even steal that bracelet!" Ben stopped and wiped his hand over his mouth.

"Why not, Mr. Newsome?"

He didn't respond.

"Because *you* stole it, didn't you?"

Eva turned to stare at Ben. "You? How? Why?"

Carlotta gestured to James. "Mr. Canary told me and the detective that while he did intend to steal the bracelet, he dropped it after he cut it off. And when things started getting crazy, he ran away. I suspect that Mr. Newsome saw the bracelet on the floor and knew he had to get rid of it for his plan to work, but he didn't have anywhere to hide it. So he ran into the employee break room and put it in an empty locker, intending to come back and retrieve it later. But when he came back the next day, our manager had added employee ID security—he couldn't get into the room."

Eva was shaking her head at Ben. "Why would you do something like that?"

He reached for her, his expression contrite. "Because you were just so stressed out. I thought if we got rid of the bracelet, it would give you a legitimate reason to drop out, and you wouldn't have to feel so bad about it." He gestured around the room. "I'm only guilty of doing something to protect my fiancée. No one was seriously injured and Eva has her bracelet back. I think Eva and I need to be left alone to sort things out."

Carlotta angled her head. "Nice try, Mr. Newsome, but there's more." She softened her expression. "Eva, I want to show you some clips. Remember when you told me that you felt as if the food poisoning incident at the Olympics was something more?"

Eva nodded.

"Watch." Carlotta picked up the remote control so she could stop at different points in the Olympics DVD. "Here is the Olympic Village. Note the abundance of daffodils, the yellow flowers. The bulbs are poisonous, by the way. If ground up and added to someone's food, it would cause nausea, vomiting—all the symptoms of food poisoning. Here are the announcers declaring that you might have to drop out of the race and then the camera moves to the two women who were most likely to benefit—Ruda Napor and again, Bianca Thaler. Fast-forward to the beginning of the race. I'd like to draw your attention to Bianca Thaler, trying to make eye contact with someone in the audience. And lo and behold, it's you, Mr. Newsome."

He scoffed. "That's a blob—it could be anybody."

"That's why we blew it up," Carlotta said, smiling. "So there'd be no confusion." She hit the clicker a few times and magically, Ben's face and body came into focus. "Note the daffodil that Mr. Newsome is wearing in his shirt pocket."

Eva frowned. "What's that all about?"

"This is speculation on my part," Carlotta said, "but maybe it's some kind of signal to Bianca that he was successful in adding the poison to whatever it was he tainted."

Eva inhaled sharply and covered her mouth. "It was a soy shake. I remember. It was the morning of the marathon and I made my shake. I'd gone to grab my jacket and when I got back, I remember Ben encouraging me to finish it."

"You needed your strength," he said gently.

Eva took several steps away from him. "I heard the rumors about you and Bianca, but I never believed them." She looked at Carlotta. "Is Bianca in Atlanta?"

"The numbers on Mr. Canary's phone were traced back to a B. Thaler, female, in Norcross, Georgia."

Eva's faced flushed. "You brought her here? You've been supporting her all along by sabotaging me?"

"You're letting them sway you," Ben said, his voice cajoling. "I love you. We're going to be married."

"Did he tell you that diamond was real?" Carlotta asked, pointing to Eva's engagement ring, a nice cubic zirconia.

Eva took the ring off and threw it at him.

"Eva, obviously this isn't in the Atlanta PD jurisdiction," Carlotta said, "but a physician friend told me that if you'd had blood drawn after the poisoning, it would still be in the sample that was stored. The lab just needs to know what to look for."

Eva suddenly looked stronger as she crossed her arms. "My blood was drawn maybe an hour after I drank that shake. I remember because when I started feeling light-headed, I assumed they'd taken too much."

"Mr. Newsome," Carlotta said. "I assume you knew when you spiked Eva's drink that daffodil bulbs can be fatal if ingested."

"That's attempted murder," Jack interjected. "If I were you, Newsome, I'd run as fast as I could to a good attorney's office."

Jack's phone rang and he excused himself from the room. Carlotta wondered if the call was about her car. When he came back in, he looked somber and gestured for her to join him in the hallway.

"I have to go."

"Another body?"

He gave a curt nod. "And another charm. But this is getting more serious. The victim is Cheryl Meriwether—she's an assistant D.A."

Carlotta gasped. Every victim mattered, of course, but people who were targeted for crimes specifically because of the position they held in law enforcement received special consideration from their comrades.

"Go," she said, touching his arm. "Let me know if there's anything I can do."

"I will." He walked to the escalator, then turned around. "You had Rainie Stephens print a bogus statement to back up your story, didn't you?"

"It's not bogus anymore. I suspect Eva will run in the World Championships now."

He gestured toward Lindy's office. "You were pretty great in there."

She blushed and gave a dismissive wave. "You think I sound like Nancy Drew."

"No, I was thinking of the attorney with the long, dark hair on *Law & Order*."

"Which one?"

Jack grinned. "The hot one." Then he disappeared from view.

28

Wesley studied the photos of A.D.A. Cheryl Meriwether that dominated the front page of the morning's *AJC*. She was prettier in the pictures than he'd given her credit for—probably because she was smiling in them, and he'd never seen her smile the times he'd met with her. She had nice green eyes, too. But if he'd been asked, the only thing he would've remembered about her eyes was that she had two of them. Poor lady. He planned to attend her memorial service if Mouse didn't have him working all afternoon.

He felt a pang of compassion for the woman. She'd been shot in the back in her home and allegedly the charm in her mouth was also a gun. She lived in northwest Atlanta, in the suburbs. Meriwether was The Charmed Killer's most high-profile victim to date. With victims ranging from single young women to minorities to prostitutes to district attorneys, the city was officially in a panic. CNN was playing on the TV in the living room, airing press conferences from D.A. Kelvin Lucas who vowed to get justice for one of his most hardworking A.D.A's. The old toad even worked up a couple of crocodile tears.

The mayor had her say, as did the chief of police. Security systems were flying off shelves. Wes looked around and pulled on his chin. Considering all the things that he and Carlotta were into, a security system was probably a good idea.

He turned to the newspaper car ads and started reading. He'd given it a lot of thought and it only made sense to take his nearly ten thousand in winnings (minus a little here and there for essentials) and use it to buy Carlotta a new car, to replace the flambéd Monte Carlo. She was working so hard, and doing lots of nice things for him around the house—laundry and cleaning and unloading the dishwasher, which she normally hated.

Maybe he could pick up something small, with good gas mileage. Then he looked up and frowned. That made him think of Meg's Prius. Which made him think of Meg. They'd met in the hall yesterday and she'd made a comment about mafioso-looking Town Cars. He'd countered with a comment about older guys who dress like pussies, and they'd sidestepped each other.

He had the morning off from ASS because they were doing repairs in the building—thank God for shoddy state government construction. He'd slept in, jacked off in the shower (okay, okay, thinking about Meg's pink-and-green plaid bra), and eaten half an Oxy for breakfast. After Carlotta's grilling about the one lousy pill she'd found in the bathroom, he was trying to be more careful. Carlotta was usually good about respecting his privacy and he believed her when she said she was only cleaning, but if her suspicions were piqued, she might be tempted to start moving things in his room. That's why he stored all of his extra Oxy in a fake rock in Einstein's aquarium—she'd never go near it.

Although…his probation officer, E. Jones, had made a surprise home visit once, and had not only lifted out the snake like an expert, but had rummaged through all of his hiding places inside. Luckily the piece of shit handgun he'd hidden there had been removed by Coop when he'd come by to help Carlotta out by putting Einstein back in his aquarium. The python had gotten out once and had immediately made a beeline for Carlotta's bedroom. His sister hadn't been happy. Still, when E. went looking, the aquarium was clean.

Of course, that didn't mean she wouldn't come back and do it again.

He heard a few words on the TV that got his attention: a headless body had been found, its major identifying mark was one newly severed finger.

Even with the calming effect of the Oxy, Wesley's heart rate picked up as he walked into the living room to catch the story.

"A decapitated body has been found in Piedmont Park. Janitorial workers discovered the remains last night. The body appears to be that of a white male, medium build, age fifty to fifty-five. Police note that one of the man's left fingers was also severed. If you have any information about the identity of this man, please contact authorities. There's a secure, anonymous tip line you can use as well."

The anchor gave the number and while Wesley didn't write it down, he did memorize it. Chances were good, though, that the body didn't belong to the severed finger he'd seen in Mouse's car trunk…even though Piedmont Park was a favorite haunt of the big man's. He liked to cruise and check out young chicks in exercise gear.

Wes flipped through the newspaper for the story and found it on page six. Nobody cared much about dead dudes—people normally assumed they'd done something to deserve it. He scanned the article to see if it offered more details, but it didn't, only that officials were continuing the search for the head—and the missing finger.

The red phone in his pocket rang, startling him so badly he nearly knocked over his milk. Letting out a long breath, he flipped it open. "Yeah."

"You're not working this morning, right?" Mouse said.

"That was the plan."

"I'll pick you up in ten minutes in front of your house."

"Man, make it a block down, why don't you? I don't want my sister to get suspicious."

"Jesus, okay."

Wes disconnected the call and dragged himself to his room to grab his backpack and iPod. He decided to take some extra cash to roll up in his wallet, just because a man never knew when he'd need a bankroll on the fly. Plus, he just wanted to look at the money again.

He crouched down and opened his sock drawer, then moved aside the top layer to the vintage-style striped tube socks he liked to wear. He'd stuffed two red ones and two green ones with all the cash.

But all the socks were gone.

Panic squeezed his lungs and he fell back. Then he forced himself to calm down. He'd told Carlotta where he'd put it—she'd probably taken it out and done something "responsible" with it, like put it in an interest-bearing account. He'd call her later to see what she'd done with it. She was taking a vacation day to attend the A.D.A.'s memorial service, and was still sleeping right now.

He left the house on a bounce and whistle, trying not to worry about the money, trying not to worry about a lot of things. The Town Car was waiting for him one block up. He slid into the front seat and greeted Mouse with a "hey." They were spending a lot of time together and the guy wasn't too bad except that he had lousy taste in music and more gas than Alaska. But Wesley was immediately worried when he saw what was in a plastic bag in the floor-board by his own feet.

"Dude...is that a head?" Wesley jerked back.

"Yeah," Mouse said. "Special project today, I need you to pull out the teeth."

Wesley gaped. "What? I don't think so."

Mouse gave a little laugh. "You know, one of the reasons The Carver agreed to let you have this job is because of your expertise with dead people."

"I move bodies to the morgue, I don't disassemble them."

"I got you covered—chisel and hammer, pliers and gloves. Oh, and a safety mask 'cause it'll be kind of messy and a flying tooth could put your eye out."

Wes retched, then covered his mouth and pulled his feet back from the bag. "I don't think I have the stomach for it."

Mouse sighed. "Okay, Little Man, here's the deal—the low man on the totem pole gets the shit work. That would be you. Unfortunately, young people don't have the work ethic my generation had, so sometimes we have to store up a little collateral to get jobs done."

Wesley squinted through the haze of the Oxy, trying to follow what the man was saying. "Collateral? What do you have on me?"

"Your nice dress jacket soaked in that guy's blood right there."

Wesley blanched.

"Classy jacket, by the way. The monogram on the inside pocket is a nice touch."

"That's my sister's doing," he mumbled.

"Your sister has good taste. Anyway, just so you know, we wouldn't be turning the jacket over to the police—we'd be turning it over to this guy's friends, *capiche?*"

Wesley nodded miserably.

"So, I'm gonna give you a few minutes to think things over."

Wesley tried to swallow past the bile that had backed up in his throat. Jack had told him to call if he needed the cavalry, but Wesley hadn't yet turned in the phone to get the GPS chip installed.

And when it came right down to it, it wasn't life or death—it was just teeth. If he were a dentist, if wouldn't even be illegal.

"Okay," he managed to say. "I'll do it."

Mouse smiled. "Good decision."

29

Carlotta looked around at the crowd of somber faces at the memorial service for Cheryl Meriwether, and knew her own expression was equally tense. The Charmed Killer was slaying victims at a frightening pace, and his indiscriminate choice of target, M.O. and venue was frightening in its scope alone. Only his signature remained the same—always the charm, always in the mouth.

She stood in the back of the Cathedral of Christ the King with hundreds of other mourners, many of whom, like her, hadn't known Cheryl Meriwether personally, but had been so moved by the senselessness of her death that they'd felt compelled to attend.

There were lots of cops in attendance, some in uniform, most not. Jack was in her line of sight, standing on the left side of the church, surreptitiously scanning every single face in his vision. Maria was on the opposite side of the church, wearing a modest scarf over her hair, performing the same methodical exercise. Carlotta knew it wasn't unusual for killers to attend the services of their victims. It completed their compulsive circle.

In deference to his height, Coop stood in the back. She glanced in his direction a few times, but she didn't think he knew she was there. Behind his glasses, his eyes were sunken and dark-rimmed, lined with sadness. He appeared to be listening to the priest, but didn't participate when it was time for the audience to respond with affirmations. Coop struck her as a very spiritual man. Perhaps he wasn't Catholic. Or maybe he was experiencing a crisis of faith?

Peter hadn't attended, not that she'd expected him to. And he'd seemed surprised she was going. Carlotta bit down on the inside of her cheek when she realized she was playing right into Maria's profile of her, attending a memorial service simply because it was a case in which she felt invested.

She kept glancing toward the door looking for Wesley— he'd said he would attend if he didn't have a delivery to make. Apparently he'd met the Meriwether woman a few times during this last round with the D.A.'s office. Wesley had said the woman hadn't been anything special, but he'd used a tone of respect that said she hadn't been phony, either. Wesley appreciated people who didn't try too hard.

Carlotta tried not to let her mind wander too much during the service, tried not to think about secular things… material things. But never too far from her thoughts these days was what they were going to do with Wesley's recent windfall.

She'd love some new living room furniture, but she knew a TV would be high on Wesley's list ever since his beloved big-screen plasma TV had taken a bullet to the electronic brain during a drive-by shooting into their house. And she wanted him to be able to enjoy whatever they bought. He'd been so great lately about pitching in to take care of the household chores. She needed to remember to make more of an effort to thank him when she noticed that little things had been done.

"Amen," said the minister. "God be with you."

"And also with you," the mourners responded.

She filed out of the cathedral with the others into a muggy, overcast day, looking for familiar faces. She ran into Coop first and noticed little changes about him—his appearance seemed less polished than usual, but he had a ready smile for her.

"How's the library diorama coming along?" she asked.

"Slowly."

"You haven't called me or Wes lately for a pickup." She grinned. "Fess up—are you secretly working with Hannah?"

He laughed. "I'm working with a new guy—he's Abrams's nephew. He doesn't strike me as being very smart, but he's willing enough." Then he shrugged. "Besides, I don't like the idea of you working so close to the periphery of this case. It's just too dangerous."

"It's scary, not knowing when or where he's going to strike next," she agreed.

"Personally, I think he sees something he likes and he goes after it. If I had a wife or a daughter right now, I wouldn't want her outside."

Carlotta gave a little laugh. "That's not very practical."

"I know. I don't mean to be morose."

"How are things with you?" she asked.

"I can't complain," he said, but didn't make eye contact. "How about you? I saw in the paper this morning that you single-handedly found Eva McCoy's infamous charm brace-let and uncovered a conspiracy against her. Pretty impressive."

"Nobody does anything single-handedly," she said. "You were a great help. And the reporter might have exaggerated a tad."

"I know Rainie," he said. "She's honest."

"And cute," she said, wondering if Coop could be Rainie's source.

"Yeah, she's cute and bubbly," he agreed, then nodded to someone behind her. "Speaking of cute and bubbly."

She turned around to see Jack and Maria walk up.

The women greeted each other, then Maria smiled. "I'm surprised to see you here, Carlotta. Did you know the A.D.A?"

"Only through my brother," Carlotta said stiffly.

Jack shook hands with Coop, then looked at her and nodded toward the door. "A word?"

"Sure." She followed him, then realized that Maria was joining them as well. Outside the church, he stopped in the nearest patch of shade. "I just wanted to let you know that CSI was able to piece together the device that was on your car. That explosion was no accident."

She swallowed hard. "So what was it?"

Jack shook his head. "I don't know. But the more I think of those knuckleheads involved in that charm bracelet heist, this just doesn't fit. It's too sophisticated for them. I'll keep working every lead. Meanwhile, promise me you'll be careful."

She smiled and nodded down to her purse. "You'll be happy to know that I'm trying to get into the habit of having my hand on your baton."

He grinned, then wiped the smile away, probably for his partner's sake.

Maria stepped closer, between Carlotta and Jack. "You also need to know that the Georgia Bureau of Investigation is getting involved with The Charmed Killer case, so chances are good that they're going to want to question you again about your father as a person of interest."

Carlotta nodded. "Thanks for the heads-up."

"We'll talk." Jack waved, then he and Maria strode toward his car, purpose and teamwork in every step.

With Jack's warning in mind, she splurged for a taxi home rather than ride the train. When she checked her phone, she had several calls from Wesley wanting to know if she'd moved his money.

Carlotta frowned. Why would she move his money? She called him back, but he didn't answer. Imagining him peddling away, delivering some very important document across town, she left him a message asking if he was joking. Of course she hadn't moved his money.

On the way inside the town house, she suddenly felt magnanimous and not only stooped to pick a white dandelion flower to blow, but waved to Mrs. Winningham as well. "Hello!"

"Don't blow that in the direction of my yard," the woman called. "That's why you have so many weeds, you know!"

Carlotta laughed to herself and went into the house, pulling off her dress clothes and shoes as she walked to her bedroom. In the hall, though, she paused and looked to the closed door of her parents' room. So her father was still a "person of interest" in The Charmed Killer case. The GBI would probably be less gentle with her and Wesley than Jack had been.

She padded down the hall to the door and pushed it open, with the intention of examining her father's cigar box full of dried-up stogies.

But when she opened the door, she froze. Things were… different. Fresher…cleaner, maybe? Wesley had really gone on a domestic binge.

But then her gaze landed on a green scrubs outfit lying on the bed, torn and stained but neatly laundered and folded, and clearly imprinted with Northside Hospital.

She'd seen those scrubs before—Michael Lane had been wearing them in his infamous on-camera run from the law.

Her gaze flew to the unused door that led out onto the deck, the door that had been dead-bolted from the inside for so long…but no longer was.

Terror seized her as realization dawned. The scrubs belonged to Michael, who was somehow alive…and living in her parents' bedroom…doing extra chores around the house while they were gone…

Watching them at night when they slept.

Oh, God, and she thought she'd been imagining it.

She turned to run and slammed into a man's body—a man wearing a mask.

Carlotta didn't think, she only reacted with her hand that was already curled around the stun baton in her purse. She pulled it out, fumbling with the power switch as she fell back, trying to push herself away from the stranger, even as she pushed the electric end of the baton into his clavicle.

It was a direct hit. The man jerked, then fell to his knees, sprawled on the floor, his hands twitching. Only when she looked up to his face did she realize that she'd tasered Peter, who was wearing the dog mask from *Breakfast at Tiffany's*. Next to him lay the matching cat mask—presumably hers.

"Omigod, omigod, omigod," she said, dialing Jack on her phone, trusting him more than 911.

"Carlotta, what's up?"

"I just tasered Peter by mistake. Will he be okay?"

"Yeah," Jack said, although she could hear the laughter in his voice. "Give him about fifteen minutes and he'll be okay. How did that happen?"

"Well, I hate to be the one to break it to you, Jack, but

Michael Lane isn't dead. I came into my parents' room and found his clothes—the same ones he was wearing when he went over the bridge. He's been living here."

"That's beyond creepy. Was he with you last night when I was there?"

"I don't know. When I walked into the room, I freaked out and turned around and thought Peter was Michael so I zapped him."

"But you're sure Lane is gone?"

She put her hand to her head as Wesley's frantic voice mail message began suddenly to make sense. "Yeah. In fact, he has about ten thousand reasons to be gone."

"Look, I'm swamped with something at the moment, but I'll be over in an hour or so to look around. Meanwhile, I'll put out an APB on Lane and send a uniform over to keep you company."

She heard Maria's laughter in the background and—the tinkle of glass? Jack didn't sound as if he was in the car…maybe in a hotel room?

Peter groaned, a welcome sound to her ears. "He's coming around, Jack. Thanks."

She ended the call, then leaned over Peter as he opened his eyes and tried to focus. "What happened? Where am I?"

"I'm so sorry, Peter—I tasered you. I thought you were someone else. Can you forgive me?"

"Always," he whispered with a little smile. "I worry about you when I'm not around to take care of you." He squeezed her hand and wet his lips. "Why don't you move in with me? You can have your own room and I'll know you're safe. At least until The Charmed Killer is caught."

Carlotta sat back on her heels and looked around,

feeling desperate and vulnerable. How safe was this place when a psycho killer had been cohabitating with them and they hadn't even known? Not to mention the mystery SUV still stalking the street and the car explosion.

She had to get away from this madness.

"Okay," Carlotta said. "You win. I'll move in with you, Peter."

And the excitement isn't over yet!

*Where is Michael Lane? Who will be
The Charmed Killer's next victim?
And what's going to happen to Coop...and Wesley?*

Find out in:

*5 BODIES TO DIE FOR
by Stephanie Bond*

Available next month.

Here's a sneak peek...

"Going somewhere?" Jack asked, gesturing to the suitcases on Carlotta's bed.

She folded a pair of red lace panties and set them on top of the pile of clothes. "Peter invited me to stay with him for a while, and I accepted."

Jack picked up the red panties between thumb and finger to study them. "You're moving in with Ashford?"

"No," she corrected, still folding underwear. "I'm staying with Peter until things settle down around here."

"Until I catch The Charmed Killer?"

She nodded.

Jack pursed his mouth. "I understand, and I think it's a good idea."

She gave a little laugh. "I thought you might since you said I should marry Peter."

"That's not why I think it's a good idea." He brought the panties to his face.

Carlotta snatched them away. "Then why?"

He shrugged, unfazed. "Because I'm sure that palace of his is a fortress and you'll be safe there. Which means I can investigate The Charmed Killer without worrying about your pretty ass being in harm's way. I'm sure Ashford will keep you busy with polo matches and charity auctions at the club."

She frowned. "Does this mean I won't be seeing you?"

"You'll miss me, huh?" Then he was suddenly serious. "I'm liaising with the GBI and your name keeps popping up in the investigation. We're going to have to get you cleared, Carlotta, although this situation with Lane is a big step forward."

"You think Michael is The Charmed Killer?"

"We'll have to double-check the timeline, but right now, he's the best suspect we have."

"But Shawna Whitt was murdered before he escaped from the hospital."

"We don't know exactly when Lane escaped, and we still don't know if the Whitt woman was murdered. Since she was cremated, we may never know."

"But the charm in her mouth—"

"Could've been placed there postmortem. Maybe Lane broke into her place and scared her so badly she had a heart attack, then he placed the charm in her mouth. Or maybe he heard about the death and the charm after he escaped from the hospital and decided to adopt it as his signature. Who knows how a crazy man thinks?" Jack wet his lips. "All I know is that thinking about Lane being here in this house with you asleep makes me a little insane."

"But he didn't kill me, Jack. He had the chance, and he didn't kill me."

"I know," he said, then averted his gaze. She could tell he had his doubts about Michael being their man. Jack looked back. "Go to Ashford's and lay low. Forget the body moving business for a while."

"But Coop—"

"—could stand to take a break himself."

She blinked. "So you *do* think something's wrong with Coop."

"Nothing an AA meeting can't fix. Don't get caught up in Coop's problems, darlin', you got enough of your own. And keep that stun baton handy." He wiped his hand over his mouth, trying to smother a smile. "You got Ashford good, huh?"

"You don't have to take so much pleasure in his pain."

"You're moving in with the man, let me have a little fun at his expense."

"I'm not moving in with Peter...I'm staying at his house." Jack stepped closer and lifted her chin. "In his bed?"

Carlotta's chest tightened. "What do you care, Jack?"

He leaned his face close to hers. "Because it gives me that much more incentive to get The Charmed Killer off the streets."

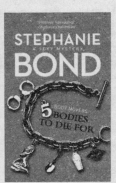
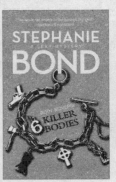

REQUEST YOUR
FREE BOOKS!

2 FREE NOVELS
FROM THE ROMANCE/SUSPENSE
COLLECTION PLUS 2 FREE GIFTS!

YES! Please send me 2 FREE novels from the Romance/Suspense Collection and my 2 FREE gifts (gifts are worth about $10). After receiving them, if I don't wish to receive any more books, I can return the shipping statement marked "cancel." If I don't cancel, I will receive 4 brand-new novels every month and be billed just $5.49 per book in the U.S. or $5.99 per book in Canada, plus 25¢ shipping and handling per book plus applicable taxes, if any*. That's a savings of at least 20% off the cover price! I understand that accepting the 2 free books and gifts places me under no obligation to buy anything. I can always return a shipment and cancel at any time. Even if I never buy another book from the Reader Service, the two free books and gifts are mine to keep forever.

185 MDN EF5Y 385 MDN EF6C

Name	(PLEASE PRINT)
Address	Apt. #
City	State/Prov.	Zip/Postal Code

Signature (if under 18, a parent or guardian must sign)

Mail to **The Reader Service:**
IN U.S.A.: P.O. Box 1867, Buffalo, NY 14240-1867
IN CANADA: P.O. Box 609, Fort Erie, Ontario L2A 5X3

Not valid to current subscribers to the Romance Collection,
the Suspense Collection or the Romance/Suspense Collection.

Want to try two free books from another line?
Call 1-800-873-8635 or visit www.morefreebooks.com.

* Terms and prices subject to change without notice. N.Y. residents add applicable sales tax. Canadian residents will be charged applicable provincial taxes and GST. Offer not valid in Quebec. This offer is limited to one order per household. All orders subject to approval. Credit or debit balances in a customer's account(s) may be offset by any other outstanding balance owed by or to the customer. Please allow 4 to 6 weeks for delivery. Offer available while quantities last.

Your Privacy: Harlequin is committed to protecting your privacy. Our Privacy Policy is available online at www.eHarlequin.com or upon request from the Reader Service. From time to time we make our lists of customers available to reputable third parties who may have a product or service of interest to you. If you would prefer we not share your name and address, please check here. ☐

BOB08R

Seduction by the Book

by STEPHANIE BOND

When four Southern wallflowers decide to get together
and form a book club, they never dream where their
literary wanderings are going to lead them. Because in
this club, the members are reading classic erotic volumes,
learning how to seduce the man of their dreams....
Atlanta's male population won't stand a chance!

Encounters—
1 blazing book, 4 sizzling stories

*Available only from Harlequin Blaze
in October 2009, wherever Harlequin books are sold.*

---

red-hot reads

STEPHANIE
BOND

32659 BODY MOVERS:		
3 MEN AND A BODY	___ $6.99 U.S.	___ $6.99 CAN.
32606 BODY MOVERS: 2 BODIES		
FOR THE PRICE OF 1	___ $6.99 U.S.	___ $6.99 CAN.
32482 BODY MOVERS	___ $6.99 U.S.	___ $8.50 CAN.

(limited quantities available)

TOTAL AMOUNT	$ _____
POSTAGE & HANDLING	$ _____
($1.00 FOR 1 BOOK, 50¢ for each additional)	
APPLICABLE TAXES*	$ _____
TOTAL PAYABLE	$ _____

(check or money order—please do not send cash)

To order, complete this form and send it, along with a check or money order for the total above, payable to MIRA Books, to: **In the U.S.:** 3010 Walden Avenue, P.O. Box 9077, Buffalo, NY 14269-9077; **In Canada:** P.O. Box 636, Fort Erie, Ontario, L2A 5X3.

Name: _____
Address: _____ City: _____
State/Prov.: _____ Zip/Postal Code: _____
Account Number (if applicable): _____

075 CSAS

*New York residents remit applicable sales taxes.
*Canadian residents remit applicable GST and provincial taxes.

MIRA®

www.MIRABooks.com

MSB0409BL